In Memory of Ellie Donoghue, Lorraine Colgan and Harry Donald

Requiescat in Pace

Photography by Fran Benison

Cover Design by Rory Dunn

Thanks to Peter Benison for editing and assistance in
publication of this book.

CHAPTER ONE

Relaxing on the bench gazing over at Fife he was smiling. He had forgotten how green it was. Even though it was November it was unexpectedly sunny and warm. Dudhope Park is littered with people lying on the grass enjoying the unexpected sunshine. Children are running about without a care in the world, their laughter filling the air. A football is being kicked between groups of boys; maybe he was watching some future professional football player in the making? Not a chance, they were too fat. He guessed they were about 10 years old and seriously over -weight. He turned to his right, the tennis courts are occupied, and the skateboard park is packed with youths watching two youths go through a complicated routine. Shouts of derision are being drowned out by encouragement. The four dissenters make their way from the display. The sun was starting to burn into his eyes, but he refused to complain, for all its faults and failures he was glad to be back in Dundee.

When he had arrived at Glasgow airport, he was looking forward to seeing his wife, but when he switched on his mobile there was a text message from her. No doubt, she is running late. How wrong he was. She was not coming. The message was brief, 'Can't come too busy. Explain later'. He refused to rise to the bait, she would have expected him to call her then berate her. He sent his reply; 'Might be back today or tomorrow Barbara Streisand on plane, going to her concert in Glasgow.' Now that would send her into a fit of rage. Jean was a huge fan of 'Miss Streisand' as she liked to call her, but she refused to pay the exorbitant ticket price. He switched off the mobile, and then made his way to the shuttle bus that would take him to Queen Street station. When he departed the shuttle bus at Queen Street he had time to go for a bacon roll, he was practically salivating at the thought of the taste.

The pleasant thought was quickly eradicated, he walked no more than 10 metres when he had a sharp reminder that he was back in Scotland. His ears barely made out the Big Issue seller or sales person as he and his colleagues were encouraged to address them. He looked at the poor wretched creature before his eyes, early twenties, scrawny and no life in her eyes. 'No thanks,' he replied to her barely audible voice. She looked the same age as his daughter; he shivered at the thought; if his daughter had experimented with drugs she might have ended up like the vision of misery before him. Suddenly he lost his appetite; no bacon roll for him, instead he went into the booking office to buy his ticket.

On the train he located a seat in the sparsely occupied carriage. He took the dog -eared notebook from his jacket and placed it on the empty seat beside him. He replaced the notebook with his jacket on the empty seat; he needed peace and quiet to study his notes. Though he had left the job, it had not left him. His two colleagues 'the two Daves' declined to take their annual leave back in the city that they had served well. Too many memories; most of them jarring. They opted to go to Cape Town; they had business interests there and as well as holiday apartments in a luxury beach resort. The last ten months had been a whirlwind of activity for him since he had retired early from the force. The two Daves had painted a picture of paradise about Dubai and their working environment, they had not exaggerated. His apartment was luxurious as promised and his working conditions exceeded their description. They all lived in the same apartment block Armada Towers; it was a mixture of apartments and offices. It had everything, a roof top café, health clubs and an array of shops that sold luxury goods. He lived on the 22nd floor; they lived on the 30th floor.

He thought that this luxury living and lifestyle would eventually make way for homesickness, but it never arrived, much to his surprise. They suggested to him that he takes a drive around Dubai to get the feel of the place, they noticed the concern that he was displaying; 'do you want one of us to chauffeur you about for the first couple of days?' His face lost the furrowed brow. 'That could wait till tomorrow, tonight we're going to the Jumeirah Beach Hotel for dinner, then early tomorrow morning Dave will come to your apartment at 6am, take you to your car in the underground garage and give you the guided tour, how does that sound?' He couldn't argue with that suggestion. They noticed he was looking tired, and suggested he went for a nap, they would call him in six hours' time, he would be ready. He asked them where they were going, they replied in unison; golf. They didn't offer him, they told him to drink plenty of water then go straight to bed; an eventful night was planned. They didn't hang about to explain. He was left listening to his conscience and the air conditioning. Had he done the right thing by taking early retirement? He didn't want to brood over his hasty decision, he was sure he had made the correct decision, he was part of the old guard, he had had his time, his record was exemplary, a sense of pride came over him, he left on his own terms, with a good financial package and with warm words from the Chief Constable. No, he was right, he had done the right thing, even Jean agreed, which was most unusual.

He went into the kitchen to withdraw the bottled water from the fridge. The fridge also contained an abundance of fruit, the water is Highland Spring. He gave a wry

7

smile, bottled water the biggest confidence trick played on the Scottish people. He remembered lambasting Joe Feeney about buying *water*, 'what's the matter with water out of the tap, or am I mad?' Feeney didn't lift up his head from his laptop. 'You're mad,' then took a swig of the water to annoy him.

Joe Feeney and Raymond Andrews, two indelible blots on his career. He took the water and went to his balcony; the heat hit him like a furnace, .Jumeirah beach was only five minutes away from the luxury apartment block, he cast his eyes away from the beach, a myriad of cranes were dotted around the landscape, he had never seen activity like this. Examining the landscape, he was familiar with some of it; Feeney had reams of brochures from his property investment club. Dubai was the next big thing.

He recalled how exasperated he had become when he screamed at him to concentrate on the matter in hand, the murders? Never in his wildest dreams did he think he would be living and working here. He had to let this wave of introspection run its course then move on. He was starting to use Feeney's phrases now. It must be the jet lag that is causing his mind to jump from subject to subject. The flight from Glasgow aboard the Emirates jet was spellbinding; this was the first time that he had flown Executive Class, and it was an eye opener. Dave had winked at him, 'change from Ryanair?' 'I don't want to rush my assessment, I'll be in a better position when we arrive in Dubai,' he replied with his face expressionless. What a flight that was, even Jean couldn't find fault. He found himself stifling a yawn, time for beddy-byes, his mind was slowing down he was grateful for that, one more slug of the water then he would retire to the bedroom. The phone rang. He opened his eyes trying to locate his senses, he quickly rubbed his eyes, he remembered he was in his new apartment; surely he had not slept for six hours? He quickly turned to the clock. He had. The phone rang again, he reached over for it. 'Hello?'

'Hope you enjoyed your kip, we'll be down in about twenty.

'Okay, what will I wear?'

'Try one of the light weight suits in your wardrobe, the yellow one will make you stand out, got to go,' he heard women's voices and laughter in the back ground.

'Enjoy the *golf*?'

'That's our caddies.'

'Of course it is, is Santa Claus there as well?'

'See you in fifteen; I have someone here who wants to meet you; she's from Dundee.'

'Really? 'What's her name?'

He heard him laugh then place the phone down. He put the phone down and looked around the spacious room, he felt more tired than before. He moved out of the large bed he caught sight of his large stomach, that'll have to go he thought. Yellow suit, he said, he opened the large wardrobe with dread. The rail contained at least a dozen suits, he counted them; there were twenty suits in all black and grey. On both sides of the rail were dockets each containing shirts; white shirts. He looked through the drawers, they contained every item of clothing that he needed from socks to ties. Below the drawers were six pairs of shoes; black.

They had thought of everything. The tiredness went and a sense of excitement lifted his spirits he was glad he had friends like them, they were his only friends in Dundee and now in Dubai. He just hoped against hope that they were less cavalier in Dubai than they were in Dundee. Real friends, but unconventional detectives. Some of the stunts they pulled still made him queasy when he thought about *certain incidents*, but the end justified the means was their mantra. He forced his mind to overtake the incidents he was thinking about. Time for that shower he was longing for. The power of the water hitting his body felt good. He was overcome with excitement, nervousness and some concern about the dinner at the Jumeriah Beach Hotel, they had been laughing when they said he would thoroughly enjoy himself. He came out of the shower more relaxed, observing all those suits standing to attention caused him some concern, Jean always bought his clothes for him how hard could it be to pick a suit, there were only two colours?

He went for the dark grey suit, white shirt and black shoes. Reluctantly he glanced at the full length mirror; he was looking good he had never said or thought that for years. His thirst had built up again, it must be the air conditioning, he picked up the wet towel then went to the kitchen, he placed the towel into the laundry basket then shut the utility room door. He took the bottled water and took a long drink, he felt better, much, much better. They knocked on the door and came into the lounge. 'You should always keep your door locked…you're looking well, how did you sleep?'

'I slept like a baby, thanks for the suits; I can't thank you two enough.'

There was a look between them that Eddings missed.

'I'll make myself a drink, Dave take him onto the balcony and explain the skyline to him.' Eddings was taking to the balcony expecting the various hotels and buildings to have a name placed on them. Dave turned to him.

'Look this is a different world over here, you have to shed some of your detective skills but retain others. You got out of the detective squad in Dundee at the right time, you've did your stint, you have to close the door on your life in Dundee…firmly.'

Eddings forced a smile. 'I know that, here it'll be more low-key? More relaxed?

'I'll explain more tomorrow when I take you out for the early morning tour of Dubai, but tonight is relaxation

time, and you have someone who is very, very, keen to meet you. So how do you feel? 'I'm fine, what time did you say we are going to this hotel at? Dave knocked on the balcony window and indicated to him to join them on the balcony. 'As soon as he finishes his drink, I would assume.'
'Enjoying your little chit-chat boys or would you rather be going?' He finished his whisky. 'Time to depart, I think.'
They looked at Eddings; who was displaying signs of

apprehension or nervousness.

***

It had been a long day but it had gone like a dream, he had secured the contract against all the odds. His excitement was contained, however he was sorely tempted to call his wife on the phone and tell her the good news, but he wanted to see her face rather than imagine it when he told her. His borrowed BMW had passed Inveraldie on the A90, the twinkling lights of Dundee came into full view. Not long now he thought, I'll be there in ten maybe fifteen minutes. This had been a life changing day, no-one had known about him tendering his price, his few friends, his real friends would be delighted to hear the good news. The others, who used to be his friends, would hope future problems would hunt in packs to bring him down to their level. At the Forfar Road roundabout he took a right then at the Downfield roundabout he realized that he was driving towards his old house. He had moved to Victoria Street in Broughty Ferry. The old rambling building looked better from the outside than the inside, but nothing could inhibit them from buying this old house. They weren't thinking of moving they were content to live across from Fairmuir Park, but his solicitor told him of the 'wee gem in the 'ferry.' It wasn't on the market yet, the owner would prefer to get it sold at a good price quickly; he was moving to Australia, he was the only child of his widowed mother. He would prefer to sell it to a family; he didn't want property developers dividing it up into flats. That seemed to be the *de rigueur* when these *large* houses came up for sale in affluent areas of Broughty Ferry. That would be his legacy to his dear departed mother.

After ignoring his solicitor for a week regarding the property, the solicitor called him and told him to meet him there, just to have a look, what did he have to lose? His wife who had given birth to their only daughter three months ago insisted she accompany him. Their home across from Fairmuir Park had four large double bedrooms, adequate for their two sons and new daughter.

The solicitor was waiting outside the property, the weather had turned gloomy, dark clouds were gathering in the sky a torrential downpour was ready to be delivered from the brooding sky. It was not the best day to show clients around the house, but he had the ability to turn a negative into a positive. They drew up beside his black BMW.

'Nice day, he laughed, and how is the little angel?'

'Screams like a banshee at night and eats like a horse during the day.'

'Ignore him Pat, she is like an angel.'

Her eyes moved towards the house. 'It's beautiful, really beautiful.'

Richard was struggling with the fold up buggy. 'How can you say that, you've not seen the inside?'

'I agree with you Diane, you recognize beauty when you see it, shall we go in?'

'Can someone please help me with this buggy? He said exasperated.

'Leave it in the van, I'll carry her around, lead the way Pat, he can catch us up.' Richard gave up trying to fold the expensive buggy; he threw it unceremoniously into the rear of the van, it landed amongst the various plumbing materials. He looked at the contents of the van, Diane was right he had to organize the plumbing materials.

He locked the van and observed how quiet it was here, no cars passing or pedestrians in sight. He looked at the house with a more critical eye, some parts of the roof needed renewing, the down pipe was cracked and the rain water was gushing out.

The windows would need overhauled, he wrote this down in his note book. He opened the wrought iron gate wide, the grating noise from the dry hinges sounded ominous.

Pat was disingenuous, he had left the impressive gates opened wide enough for them to squeeze by. He put the notebook in his back pocket of his jeans, took a deep breath then walked past the overgrown garden up to the door of this money pit. The door was slightly ajar; he pushed it wide open and the noise from the door was the first cousin of the gate. His minimum optimism had disappeared when he placed his note book in his back pocket. 'In here, Ritchie,' she called out. Her voice had no trace of disappointment. He walked along the hall, the old fashioned wallpaper defiantly challenging him to say something pejorative, his eyes fell to the floor tiles looked unkempt but the high skirting boards looked in pristine condition.

'Ritchie, what's keeping you?' Pat stepped from the parlour room into the hallway.

Ritchie was keen to see what all the fuss was about, his head had overruled his heart; walk away you can't afford the house never mind the refurbishment.

'Now is this not a lounge or parlour or not? Her arm was arcing into a sweeping motion inviting his pessimistic eyes to disagree with her. 'It's not bad...'

'Not bad are you kidding me? It's majestic, this room is history and our family could make this a living history,

we have to buy this Ritchie.'
He was looking at Pat. 'Diane I don't think we can afford this, our house in Fairmuir is mortgaged up to the hilt and I'm trying to build the business.'
'I can go back to teaching, even three days a week.'
'I don't know Diane, and the house will need a lot of money to bring it up to scratch.'
Pat coughed to grab their attention. 'This is a life changing decision moment Richard, the Gods don't smile on mere mortals often, you can afford it, and you can do the house up room by room, you have the rest of your lives to finish it. This house was tailor-made for your family Richard.'
'Thanks Pat, for adding the pressure that I don't need,' His eyes looking at the cornice. 'You have an eye for beauty,' Pat replied then smiled at Diane.
'Cut the charm offensive Pat what's the rest of the house like?
'Let's go and see,' they moved into the rooms on the lower floor. The kitchen and bathroom were in an appalling state. Diane was close to tears; her eyes were fixed firmly on Pat.
 'How did the old woman manage to live in these conditions?'
'She has been in a nursing home for the last ten years she wanted her son to live here; but he had the wanderlust gene in him. He was living a lie; for the last five years her mental capabilities were failing.'
 Diane had tears in her eyes. 'Oh Pat, how awful.'
 'It gets worse Diane, I'm afraid. She went blind, he pretended he lived here, if she knew he was travelling the world as a mining engineer it would have killed her. He used to write to her from South America or where he was at that moment, a nurse used to read her his letters, he always included some story about the house or garden, he always mentioned that her favourite robin always returned every year. The nurse loved reading

those letters even though she sometimes ended up sobbing.'

Diane left the room they could hear her trying to suppress her tears.

'You have the opportunity to make a lot of people happy not just your family but old Mrs. O'Neill and her son. This house is perfect for you Ritchie.' 'Pat I'm scared to ask...how much does the son want for it? He dreaded hearing the figure then telling Diane, it couldn't be theirs.

'He was hoping in the region of £400,000, but he'll take less, for a quick sale, probably £370,000.'

Richard is shaking his head. 'Just impossible Pat, impossible.'

Diane returned to the room with the baby gurgling away with contentment.

'Even the little mite loves the house...'

'What's the decision then?' Her eyes were ignoring her heart.

'You can afford it Diane, don't worry about selling your house, the entry date on this house, your new house is flexible, some figures just need rounded up, give me a minute I'll call the owner.' He left the room even though he was downstairs his voice travelled upstairs and could be heard quite clearly. His call ended and his footsteps could be heard echoing around the house

'It's a done deal, as you might have heard I told him that his mum couldn't have picked a better family.'

Her smile dropped to the floor. 'The price, what is the price we are paying for the house?'

'£370,000 Diane, you should really feel blessed, it's like Mrs. O'Neill has included you in her will, so to speak.'

Richard is looking decidedly under whelmed, the opposite of Diane, who has disappeared to explore her new house.

'The figures...in my head don't add up, I can't increase my mortgage.'

'Who told you that, has the Bank given you a limit?
'No, not exactly Pat, we want to be able to live as well,'
replied Ritchie.
'The Bank will release funds once they are made aware
of your new contracts, but it's up to you both, this is a
life changing moment, I've written down some figures,
that'll surprise you.'

***

'Are you sure this is the correct address?' Now he was
agitated.
'Are you taking cold feet…if you are, it's off. What is it
going to be?'
'Top floor flat…I'm ready are you?' He was good at
turning a question on his inquisitor. 'Leave the talking to
me, grab the bag out of the back and have a good look
up the street, anything that looks different just return and
we'll drive away.'
He removed himself from the Dundee City Council's
van. No one would bat an eyelid; they were two council
painters going about their business in a leisurely fashion.
He continued reading the tabloid or so it seemed to the
indifferent public who were walking by. The backdoor
of the van was opened and two paint strewn sport's bags
were removed. His colleague closed the van door and
then walked into the tenement close. The stench of urine
filled the entrance to the close which had an assortment
of fast food wrappers that the wind had blown to the rear
of the close. There were six flats in the building; they
had the key to the flat that was unoccupied on the top
floor. His older more grizzled colleague came into the
close, he took one of the bags and they made their way
up to the flat. The flat had been in a sorry state, the
previous occupant who had died from a drug overdose;
had seemingly been allergic to cleaning. The stairs
leading up to the flat had not seen a brush for a period of
time, the smell was becoming overpowering, their pace
quickened. At the flat the grizzled character took the

key from his pocket and placed it in the newly- fitted lock and turned it. The door was pushed opened; the council's cleansing department had done a fine job, the air was filled with the reassuring scent of disinfectant. He closed the door behind him. The flat had been stripped of its Spartan contents. He took the bag from him and walked over to the part of the room where no one from across the street could see into the flat, even though the ragged curtains were still in place.

He pulled the zip open and took out the ski mask and handed the sawn -off shot gun to his nervous colleague. He indicated to his younger colleague to hand him the hand gun. They were whispering now. He took out the scanner and connected his headset to it and switched it on, a babble of staccato of information came out. A smile broke through.

'Here's to a good day.'

His colleague had moved across the room; he was at the window peering out into the street, he pulled the overall sleeve above his wrist.

'They should be here in ten minutes. The last three occasions they were at the flat they stayed for ten minutes; maximum.'

He replayed every little movement in his head. His fear was now suspended. Outside a comic opera was taking place, a woman dressed in a shocking pink shell suit was walking her dog, she was on her mobile. She stopped at the van and encouraged her canine friend to empty its bladder. The dog didn't need any encouragement. An old woman on the other side was obviously giving her a lesson on doggy etiquette, the pink blancmange responded with inappropriate sign language. She pulled the small but powerful dog away.

His face decanted the mirth and became serious; they had arrived. He motioned for him to look for himself; 'that's our boys.' The car slowly came to a halt fifty metres on the opposite side of the street. There were three occupants in the 4x4; two emerged, the driver stayed put. They walked towards the close; one of them patted his stomach. He took off the headset and returned it to the holdall. They placed their ski masks on. Their gloved hands held on to their weapons, they moved silently but quickly to the door. Their ears were pressed almost to the door; they heard the unison pattern of footsteps ascending the stairs. Then silence. They came to a halt, and then move towards the door of the flat *they* were in. He moved away from the peep-hole, he held up his finger to indicate no movement from his colleague, who nodded. They listened to the short rap on the door opposite. They heard the door open almost immediately, then the welcome sound of it closing. Simultaneously he opened their door and walked two paces and kicked open the door before it could be locked.

The occupants were mortified when they burst in. There were four people in the flat. 'Phones…give me them now!' He shouted in an East European accent. They looked at the gun with silencer fitted. They were stunned into silence.

'Phones now!'

He repeated his request. 'Here's oors…we dinna want any trouble.' He slid the phone along the filthy floor.

'You're making a big mistake mate, you don't know who you are dealing with,' the scouser was either super cool or dense. He stepped forward to give him his phone. 'Stop! Do not come any closer.' He continued to walk towards him oblivious to the gun pointing at his head. He took another step forward then reeled back. His face crumbled; the mobile hit the floor before the deceased. They heard the loading of the shotgun.

'Here take the money…' he threw the plastic bag at his feet, it made a pleasant noise. He picked it up still aiming the shotgun at him. 'Drugs, give them to us.' The one who had patted his stomach let the heavy brown package fall to his feet and kicked it towards him, his face etched with hate. It was picked up in the same manner and placed in the holdall. 'Keys of flat,' he barked. He delivered them in the same manner. 'Turn against wall, now,' they moved towards them with their weapons aimed at them.

They were petrified and moved like it was a race to the wall, the scouser moved more slowly. They heard him talk in his native language to his accomplice; he spoke quickly in an aggressive tone.

'I don't want to die,' the sobbing accomplice replied. They heard the door being closed and the multi-levered lock been activated.

On the landing they took their ski masks off and stuffed them into one of the holdalls. The money and drugs were placed in the other holdall. He looked at his watch, less than two minutes. He gave him the paint strewn baseball cap; they both pulled them down to obscure their faces. They made their way down the stairs past the obscenities and graffiti that adorned the close walls. He looked through the smashed rectangle window in the close entrance door. He saw the 4x4 driver stare intently at the close entrance. He pulled the two large empty paint tins and two brushes from the holdall, he gave a tin and paint brush to him then they walked out from the close in a nonchalant manner.

He handed the paint and brush to him and his colleague placed them into the rear of the van. The van was started up, his colleague joined him in the front then he drove off. The driver of the 4x4 just kept observing them and continued to eat his crisps

'Went like a dream, in and out in five minutes; who's a clever boy then?'
'Did you have to use the gun?'
'No, but it concentrated their drug addled minds, didn't it...we have done society a favour.'
'I'm not criticising, you just took me unawares that's all,

19

and for all I care you could have done away with the rest of them.'

'Now that would have been daft, if our boy is correct, the drug squad will be there in five minutes, they won't find a big consignment of drugs or money, but what they'll find is a known drug dealer dead and another dealer from Liverpool in the flat, along with the two numpties. And the big fat guy outside in the 4x4, they have some explaining to do.'

'I know the scouser might not say anything, but the two junkies will, they'll tell the drug squad that it was two Polish guys that shot and robbed them.'

'Even if the driver said he saw two painters come out of the close, the police will check that out, but there has painters been in and out of the close all week, calculating how much paint their going to need to paint the close.'

'You had planned it well, you were good at keeping cool under pressure, how did I do?'

'The SAS couldn't have planned and executed that any better.'

'I asked how I did.'

'You did well, how hard is it to stay quiet and point a shotgun?'

He looked at him, he couldn't hide the hurt. 'I thought I did alright

'I'm only kidding, you done brilliant; you followed orders, to the letter, well done.'

'Thanks. What happens now?'

'We park the van in Hospital Street beside the rest of the council vans, the council premises across the road are being refurbished, and the car park is being extended.'

'I wasn't meaning that, I was talking about the money and the smack.'

'Patience, you must be patient. Everything has been worked out, bank accounts etc.'

'What about the smack?'

'It's been sold. When we leave the van in Hospital Street, you walk home. I have parked my car in Smith Street I have an appointment with a man with an interest in the heroin, we might not get the market value, but it's still a good price.'

'Once this makes the news, he'll know you were involved, are you not taking a chance?'

'This person I would trust with my life, anyway there will be a shortage of heroin in Dundee now, the price will be reacting to market forces…he knows he's getting a good deal, and so do we.'

He still had concerns. 'You've not mentioned me, by name, have you?'

'Well…what do you think?'

'I shouldn't have said that, I'm sorry.'

'No worries. Enjoy your night out tonight, remember don't offer too much of an opinion when people talk about the murder, people will talk and you'll hear loads of stories and conspiracy theories.'

Now he was laughing. 'Oh I know that, I'm looking forward to the smoker it will be interesting to hear what the consensus is.'

'Where did you say the smoker is taking place?'

'The Gleens, upstairs, there's a small lounge, probably holds about fifty. Then we'll head down to the Strath Bar, Frews, and then John Barleycorn's. That'll be as far as we go on the Hilltown, beyond that is the murder mile; no one will want to walk down the Hilltown. We'll get taxis from John Barleycorns into the town then hit a club. Have you got plans for the night?'

'Of course I have. I have got a plan to do nothing apart from watch some telly, and maybe have a can of beer.'

'You certainly know how to play it cool.'

'Perth prison is full of drug dealers and junkies, I'm not cool, I'm cautious,' the van was at the Coldside roundabout. 'Time to take your overalls off, take one of the bags, I'll turn into Milton Street you can get out

21

there, don't worry enjoy yourself tonight.'

'I'm fine, you enjoy your quiet night in.' The van turned into Milton Street, he stuffed the overalls into the bag, and then placed the earphones from his IPod on.

***

'Do you see him?'

'Affirmative.'

'Go! Go! Go!'

The cars came from opposite directions at high speed; they came to a halt on either side of the 4x4.The occupants from the car at the rear of the 4x4 rushed towards it, while they were doing this the four occupants from the silver car went into two directions, one rushed and smashed the windscreen with a baseball bat. Simultaneously the rear windscreen was being smashed into smithereens.

Chaotic shouts came from them, 'get out the fucking car! Get out now!' The driver's senses were being tested, he pressed the send button on his mobile, and then dropped it to the floor, the door was pulled open he was dragged out of the car and made to lie spread - eagled on the cobbled road. His hands were forced behind his back and he was handcuffed, when this was completed two of them stood over their neutered quarry. The other two ran across the street and galloped up the close to the top floor flat, they heard the door being crashed open by the hand- held battering ram. They kept the same momentum striding up the stairs, adrenalin pumping through them. They reached the top floor just as the door was dispatched from its hinges. Orders were being barked at the people in the flat then silence came far too suddenly.

The blood was seeping far and wide because of the sloping floor, no resistance was being offered from the

passive targets. The scouser was just blowing smoke rings, he was not showing any emotion he had no time to brief the others what to say. Exactly four minutes ago his friend was murdered and they were robbed of heroin, the others were relieved of the money. He had quickly come to the conclusion he was lucky, his friend was not; he warned him to stop being gobby. What could the police charge him with visiting a former inmate of Perth Prison? He had no drugs, they had no money, and no one had any firearms. He would be walking free. He could have kissed the Polish rip-off merchants.
'What the fuck are you smiling at?' The drug squad officer yelled. He blew a smoke ring in his direction. 'No comment, I want a lawyer.' He turned to the petrified junkies. 'No comment, I want a lawyer, say it!' The two junkies stared at each other puzzled. 'That's what you say to the bizzies, no comment, I want a lawyer.'

He walked out of the flat totally dejected and spoke into the mobile. 'Premises secured, one dead… I'm on my way down copy.' He went down much slower than he went up. He couldn't understand any of this. He was on the second floor; he heard the expletives, then the reply in unison: 'No comment, we…'

***

The van was parked in Hospital Street, other council vans were there, some were leaving and some were arriving. When he was parked he swept the van with his eyes, his smiling face said it all. The empty bashed Coke can was on the floor on the passenger's side. He stuffed it with a plastic bank coin bag which contained £100 and the key to the van. His friend was on a temporary contract with the council, he was due to leave next week, he needed a van to transfer various pieces of furniture as he was moving into his new flat in Bellfield Avenue. He subtly suggested that it needed decorated

23

throughout. His friend told him there was a colour chart in the passenger glove compartment, all he had to do was pick the colours and the paint would be in the back of the van, when he took the van, take the paint up to Bellfield Avenue then continue on to his old place and take the furniture to Bellfield Avenue. He was as good as his word. He texted him and told him that the van was in Hospital Street and there was money in the Coke can. He insisted he didn't want any payment, he had helped his younger brother when he had been remanded in Perth Prison, some low level dealer had tried to convince him to get his girlfriend to smuggle drugs in the prison while she was visiting him. That's when he came to Gordon Graham.

First of all Gordon had to establish why he was remanded in Perth Prison, it wasn't for a library book being returned late was it? He had been walking home on the Dens Road when he was attacked by four neds, unfortunately they discovered too late that he was an amateur boxer that would be stepping up to professional status; and he didn't drink. The Neds approached them and asked him to hand over his mobile phone and his wallet, and his girlfriend to hand over her purse, they would be taken to a cash point machine where they would give them the maximum amount of money the cash machine would allow, if they didn't he would be battered and she would be raped, what was it going to be? He gave his answer. He knocked two of them out in an instant, the other two tried to run away, because of their alcohol and drug cocktails, they weren't going to break any speed limits. He caught one and dispensed summary justice, he advised the other to return or his friend would be pummeled. The friend obviously didn't hear as he continued running up Dens Road screaming for help. When he stopped running, he was met with the same punishment.

While this was going on his girlfriend called the police.

The police turned up in record time, they were taken to Bell Street to be interviewed, after their statements were taken, the police interviewed the Neds. The other two Neds who were in Ninewells Hospital were able to give statements even though their speech was impaired because of their swollen lips and missing teeth. It was now six am, three hours after the menacing confrontation on Dens Road. Their parents were at Bell Street, they couldn't understand why they were still being held, they had given their statements. Why were they not allowed to take them home? They would now find out. He was being charged with serious assault; he would be detained in Bell Street till Monday, and then taken from the cells to appear at the Sheriff Court. He appeared at the Sheriff Court his application for bail was declined, his next appearance would be in two weeks' time. Shock and disgust filled the public gallery; the world had taken leave of its senses.

Gordon then came to the fore, he advised the brother to change solicitor; Patrick Connelly was the man to defend his brother. He took his advice. Patrick Connelly had two choices; he would defend and embarrass the new Procurator Fiscal who insisted the boxer be charged; whose premise was 'he should have called the police and no incident violent or otherwise would have taken place. Instead this soon to be professional boxer took the Law into his own hands literally and near killed four human beings. There was only one correct way to proceed. He had to be charged and hopefully sent to prison; Dundee was becoming more violent. A line had to be drawn in the sand.'

Or he would send a friend of a friend to 'advise' the four young scamps to have a review of their statements, then go to the police and withdraw the allegations. Their bravado and counting of their future compensation claims startled to look forlorn; when they found out on the evening news that Patrick Connelly was defending the boxer. They were all unified in their thoughts; unwanted visitors would be planning home visits to them. Pat would chart a course of the former rather than the latter.

This was in contrast to the Chief Constable's annual report, violent crime was coming down. The public were mystified at this assessment; they had seen violent and aggressive behaviour become more prevalent. The Chief Constable was awarded a five figure bonus. It was never established if there was a connection. The normally placid Dundee public crystallised their view after The Sun published a montage of the four victims' criminal history: drug dealing, house breaking, serious assault and rape. Businessmen and businesswoman contacted Pat, they would pay for the boxer's legal bill, and they all repeated the same message, 'tell him well done.' Pat had their conviction sheets sent to him through the post; Pat in turn faxed them from the council chambers where an office was empty because of refurbishment to The Sun. When the case came to Court, Pat toyed with the 'victims' 'it must have been a terrible experience…were you and your cerebral friends out on stroll maybe taking in the beautiful architecture that is omnipresent in Dundee, even at three am…you must be keen students.' And so it went on and on. The Procurator Fiscal objected on a regular basis, Pat had made his point. 'They were out to assault maybe murder an innocent passerby, was that not the case?' One by one they entered the witness box; it was tantamount to placing their own head in the noose. Not guilty was the unanimous verdict. The Sheriff left the Procurator Fiscal with what could not be called a ringing endorsement, 'Why this case came to Court is a mystery to me, vanity on someone's part?' He just stared at the Sheriff and gathered his papers. Pat was his usual courteous self. He thanked the jury, 'it's good to see Dundee still has common sense inhabitants, and then he looked momentarily at the Procurator Fiscal, then again…'

The jury laughed with him, until the Sheriff rebuked Pat. 'Enough… Mr Connelly.' The four Neds were now in their own exclusion zone, they couldn't venture far from their flats, not in daylight hours anyway.

***

Gordon Graham examined the text message; just a series of question marks. He knew what it meant, the police were puzzled. The police didn't have any intelligence, which in turn would mean they would have to examine every crackpot theory on social media. They would be taking statements for weeks. Great news!

Gordon would give the soon to be laid off painter a job, he would feign he had hurt his arm, would he decorate his flat if he did get paid off? He examined Hospital Street, joiners carrying trestles, painters carrying paste tables, tins of paint and sports holdalls the same as his. He moved from the van, walked up to the top of Hospital Street then took a right turn into Clepington Road, some of the tradesmen were coming from the Direct Labour building, they were going into The Glens, he walked past it and made his way to Smith Street where his Fiat Uno was parked. At the pedestrian crossing while he was waiting on the green man to appear, three police cars with their lights flashing and sirens wailing went through the red light, I wonder where they're going he thought mischievously, he looked at the holdall like he was seeing an old friend for the first time in years. He wouldn't succumb to excited thoughts of how much money was in the holdall. That would be an afterthought. The green man invited him to cross the road. He strode across the road to the short distance to Smith Street; he was showing no signs of nerves or agitation. At his car he opened the boot and threw in the holdall, disrobed himself of the painter's overalls and threw them alongside the holdall. He

27

closed the boot and was opening the door at the passenger's side as the lock was temperamental on the driver's side, when a voice ran out, a female's voice.

'Oi! Mate are you a painter? '

He looked around trying to locate the voice; he heard the same question again.

'Up here…' He looked upwards, he saw a young woman lean out of the window. I've just bought this flat, its needing done up, could you give me a price?'

'Give me your number, I'm busy at the moment, but my mate will give you a quote, he'll phone you tonight.'

'Hold on,' she disappeared momentarily then returned with a business card, she threw it down to him, he picked it up. 'I'll phone him now.'

***

'Are you not curious who this young lady is that wants to meet you?'

'Young lady?' He replied.

'Youngish; late forties, young to us.' The Daves were laughing out loud.

Eddings tried to suppress his embarrassment.

'And who is this youngish woman then, and why does she want to meet *me*?' 'That's what we want to know, but she certainly knows a lot about you, are you sure you've not came across her, maybe ships in the night?' 'Highly unlikely, does she have a name then?'

'Morag,' they both replied in unison. It would be a pointless exercise saying he doesn't know of any Morag. His face lit up.

'Oh, Morag, yeah, I know Morag really well, but I've not seen her for, let me think, at least 15 years, has she still got blonde hair?'

The Daves were disappointed that he knew her, the taxi journey to the Jumeriah Hotel would be less fun now, they couldn't extract the urine from him anymore, he would become coy.

'So who is she then, Dave asked.

'It's a long story, then he smiled broadly, long but very interesting. But that's for another time. Who else will be here tonight?'

'Never mind that, who is this Morag?'

Eddings turned to look out of the window, trying to conceal his mischievous smile. 'Now she is a woman who had it all, money, looks and loads of luck, then she suffered a run of bad luck, but if she is over here, she must have built up her fortune again. It'll be good to see her again…did you say who will be here tonight?'

The two Daves are walking in their minds towards the hook that has mystery for bait. 'She is divorced I do know that.' Dave replied.

'I didn't know that, I never heard her say that, and I was hanging onto every word she said, are you sure?'

'Well she never said that she was divorced, but she wasn't wearing a ring…'

'I wouldn't be surprised, not with her track record,' Eddings added.

'So she has been married and divorced?'

'At least four times when I knew her, and that was at least 15 years ago, who did you say was going to be at this party tonight?'

'Do we know her previous husbands then?'

'I wouldn't thought so, we or rather she moved in more refined circles, no vodka and coke for her.'

***

The four drug squad officers were drinking in the bar at the West Port. They ignored the normal lager that they consumed in vast quantities after a successful raid. The barmaid knew that today's raid had been less successful. They were all on vodka and lemonade. She wouldn't be asking any questions, they would tell her of their own volition; once they had drunk themselves into a stupor. The only thing she would offer was a plate of bacon rolls. Tuesday night the bar was dead, save for a couple of students. Then again it was only 6pm. The drug squad had been in for 4 hours, their hushed tones were raised now. Over and over she heard one say 'the information had been compromised,' then the three pairs of eyes were returned to him, he was saying what they were thinking.

The afternoon had been a brainstorming session, names were being bandied about, some raised eyebrows others raised objections. Their personal informers were above reproach, they had delivered time after time; all at a price, unofficially of course. Tenner bags of heroin were the popular currency and help from them in seeing that certain individuals were 'sorted out.' It wouldn't be from them personally, but in the blurred world of the Law and Justice, justice had more than one set of clothes. They went to see the head of the drug squad: Joe Feeney. When one of them started to explain how things had went wrong, Feeney interjected, 'your information was second class, now the fucking Poles are ahead in this game, we have scousers and weegies all over this city dealing, now we have fucking Poles, how embarrassing is that? Get the fuck out of here and come back with a strategy…fucking Poles, I ask you.'

Feeney was hated but respected, he managed to suppress the bungled raid from being printed in the Evening Chronicle; the journalist would be given an exclusive insight into the 'new kids on the block.' Feeney told the journalist that they had built up an impressive layer of informants in the Polish community; however, if the story said that it was members of the Polish community that murdered a fellow dealer, the politicians would be screaming from the roof tops that it was blanket racism.

He knew that the Poles who carried out the murder lived in the Angus area under the guise of fruit pickers and fish packers that commuted up to Peterhead. They were still building a case against the perpetrators, if they made arrests; they had the means and money to access the finest solicitors. But once we have all the information you'll be the first to know, you will even be invited to accompany the officers who will raid the houses that they live in.' The journalist finished his coffee and thanked Feeney then left. Feeney returned to his desk, kicked off his shoes and placed his size nines on his desk; the one that the retired Chief Constable offered him when he left, not because he was his friend, but because the incoming Chief Constable was someone he hated; he didn't elaborate. Feeney didn't probe. He was doing well in his career; he was aware that some of his underlings saw him to be of illegitimate parentage, he took comfort from this and he acted accordingly. He didn't go on the celebratory drinks after there had been a successful raid. Only when the dealer or dealers were sentenced to jail terms did he go out with them to celebrate. This showed he was not premature in assuming the dealer would automatically go to prison. Only when he heard the turn of the key in the cell door would he raise a glass; that's why his squad respected him. He drunk moderately and spaced his drinks. He bought rounds of drinks for his squad, usually double vodkas accompanied by lagers.

Padlocks came off their tongues more quickly, illicit information about informants were whispered in his ear when he was at the bar. Carping about senior officers but never once did he hear any officer was on 'the take.' That's the way he wanted his world to operate. Now his world had been invaded, and his future earnings was under severe pressure; pressure that had to be alleviated. The calamitous raid by the drug squad concerned him not because the Poles had got away with drugs, money, and literally murder, but *his* dealers would have heard about the murderous Poles and their deadly deed. For some years *de facto* dealers had been allowed to operate in Dundee, as long as they paid him his tariff, not directly but through a third party. His contacts told him that consignments of heroin and cocaine were being driven up to Dundee from Liverpool; they gave him the registration of the vehicles that would be used. Result; dealers arrested and heroin off the street; kudos from politicians, press and the Chief Constable. Unbeknown to all and sundry, *his* dealers were exchanging their deadly wares with the minimum of fuss while other dealers were being busted and their 'goods' confiscated. The Poles had shaken the kaleidoscope, just like his world. His dealers would be becoming nervous and might relocate to other towns and cities where their products were in high demand. In Feeney's perverse financial strategy, he had invested £300,000 along with other individuals in a private rehabilitation clinic to wean heroin addicts off their life curtailing drug abuse. The government was paying a King's ransom, no question asked. Since politicians opened the clinic over five years ago, only one of thousands of addicts was now not dependent on drugs. No government official ever asked how many addicts were now free from drugs. They were receiving taxpayers' money for dispensing needles and methadone to drug abusers, as well as receiving taxpayers' money- social security benefits- that the drug abusers spent on heroin from *his* dealers.

The Poles could be the catalyst that may stop the flow of his income. They had to be caught and dispensed with; but not before they told him where the well that they were drawing the information from. He had no idea. If another drug raid was compromised, *his* dealers would leave.

***

Entering the hotel Eddings couldn't help but be impressed by the opulent grand entrance; calling it a lobby would have being doing it an injustice. He felt his elbow being tugged. 'She's coming over for you.'

Eddings couldn't pick her out from the mass of swirling blondes that were moving in every direction. Then she emerged, a smile as wide as the Tay moving in to capture her prey.

'I am so glad you managed to come, come with me I want you to meet someone.' The two Daves didn't have time to react. They were gone.

'Morag gets what Morag wants, who the fuck is she?'

'I hope you're not jealous…surely not!'

'Me jealous…too right I am, what does she see in *him*?'

'You need a beer son, to cool your ardour,' he looked over to the left; the beautiful people have arrived.

Eddings was perturbed. 'Sorry do I know you from somewhere?'

'No you don't, I need your help.'

'Why then did you say to my friends that you knew me?'

'I wanted to talk to you on your own as a matter of urgency,' she slipped him a business card which he placed into his wallet.

'So how can I help?'

'This is not the place or time to discuss anything; call me tomorrow after dinner, but not before nine pm.'

'Okay,' he replied.

'Just enjoy yourself tonight, but don't get smashed like your two friends, they start to talk about activities when they were detectives in Dundee, some of the audience that were being engrossed are not pleasant people, but I'll explain everything tomorrow. I will walk away now, go and see your friends.'

He turned round and made his way over to his friends, who had a lager waiting for him.

'Back already, Mr Eddings?'

'A brief encounter, she's looking really well, she was very complimentary about you two, gentlemen she kept on calling you two; gentlemen, I told her are you sure we're talking about the same men.'

'That's us; she's a good judge of character, that's

obvious.'

Eddings had to eke out information about Morag. She was a mystery to him as well as the two Daves. 'Where did you two meet Morag then?'

'At the opening of a block of flats, they always have a party, any excuse for a party…'

'A block of flats! You mean…a luxury contemporary lifestyle in a luxury condominium development.'

'Sorry that's what I should have said.'

Eddings laughed he had to tread carefully. 'I didn't have time to ask her how long she's been living over here or why she chose to leave Dundee.'

'She's pitching luxury flats and villas, she's the top sales executive in Dubai, her company built our luxury condos, and she has made millions in the three years she has been here.

She's not a shark she just believes in her work.'

'You said her company; do you mean she owns the company then?'

'You two can talk shop I'm going to see someone I need to see, enjoy.'

'Okay, mind your time, and behave!'

Eddings was keen to keep the conversation on track. 'What was I saying again?'

'About Morag and her company, she used to own it but she was bought out on her terms, she insisted that the new owners' employ her as the senior executive in charge of sales, as a term of their conditions when they bought her company, they won't allow her to set up another development company or buy any or part of an existing property company…she's that good.'

'She'll have a wide circle of friends then, I mean here in Dubai.'

'Put it this way, you'll never see her standing on her own, others seek her out, she doesn't have to try and make friends. When she told me and Dave that she knew you, we didn't probe too much, Dave, believe it or not thought you must have been lovers, but he didn't describe it like that…as you can imagine!'

'He's as rough as sandpaper sometimes, but he's wrong, I just knew her from a family gathering, her cousin stays in the same development as me, sorry to disappoint you and Dave for that matter.' That was enough information; he would drop Morag from the conversation. 'Morag obviously likes you, more than us anyway that's for sure, but in saying that any new development that is having a party, she always leaves invitations for us, she always said us Dundonians have to stick together, and I think she really means it.'

'Do you ever feel homesick then,' Eddings asked skillfully changing the subject from Morag.' You've got to be kidding me!'

'Then that's a no then, what about Christmas, the City Square with the big fake tree and all the decorations…'

'This is us working now, and I include you, look all around you, look!' He insisted Eddings has at least a 180 degree vista. 'Now ask me again, do I miss drug dealers, murders and general lack of respect for the Law, that's Dundee I'm describing, or this. A job where I haven't had to raise my voice in anger, imagine getting paid for this.'

'I can see what you mean, polite society versus chaos and criminality, there's no contest really is there?'

'Your words my friend not mine and you don't have any spotty youth telling you how to do your job.'

Eddings couldn't suppress his laughter. 'Yeah, I got told about that, it was covered up wasn't it, then Dave over there was invited to apply for early redundancy , he was delighted with the hush -money, sorry enhanced redundancy package, then he insisted you get offered the same package or he would go to the newspapers. They blinked, he held out his hand for the pen and the rest is history as they say.'

'That's what I miss gossip turning into fact then

hilarity. You were nearly right, but there was much, much more that Dave had on them, not just one person...I'll tell you later, the real story not canteen gossip from Mr Mars, a man I just couldn't stand, the first words he always said; 'have you heard about so and so.' Dave told him if you concentrated less spreading gossip and less on eating pies you might have people stop laughing at you.'

'He wasn't popular he was always envious of people moving house or buying a new car and everyone was always getting more overtime than him, he was quite paranoid about overtime. But he doesn't have to worry about that anymore, since he had that heart attack...'

'I was sad to hear about his heart attack...sad it wasn't fatal. But he got his just desserts one winters' night he was left in some mess, broken leg, and broken arm, now I wonder who would do that?

'There were loads of stories who was behind that; we needed proof before we could visit the suspect.'

'It wasn't who everyone thought it was, we even heard that when we were at some party, we heard a whisper that was surprising, but it has some substance about it. We even heard the reason, and if the reason is true, he got off lightly, don't ask who the alleged attacker is, I'm saying that not to be mysterious but to protect you.'

'Well it's quite plain that the jungle drums are working well over in Dubai... look our friend is returning.'

They watch him move towards them, he stops and speaks to an elderly Arab gentleman. He motions them over. Eddings waits for Dave to move.

'Who's that wee guy he's talking to?'

'Your boss, a perfect time to meet him don't you think?'

They walk through the throng of invited guests with much difficulty.

Omar Madni was keen to meet Eddings, the Daves told him that he would be leaving Dundee and setting up as a private investigator; his field would be industrial espionage. Eddings, because of his array of contacts he made over the decades was much respected; his talents would be wasted that was why he would be concentrating on the commercial sector. Omar Madni asked if he would be a useful addition to his counter-surveillance team; yes was the chorus. Madni had been fortunate; his car had been blown up at 9am, the time when he would have been in mid-traffic in down town Dubai. He had been up all night with stomach pains, his private doctor told him to stay in bed, he was advised that it could have been a viral complaint, the doctor knew it would have been another case of gluttony; he was prone to over eating, but the doctor would omit to tell him this. He told him he would be over at 8.45am. The doctor went through the same charade as before then came to the same conclusion; a viral complaint. His prescription was the same as before, 'retire to bed and drink plenty of water and fast for the day. ' Reluctantly he agreed with the doctor's diagnosis, he wouldn't stay in bed that would be tantamount to house arrest, he would loll around the villa probably move to the swimming pool before the temperature became unbearable, perhaps he would have a little snack. Then they heard the unmistakable sound of an explosion. His hearing became dulled, the doctor pulled him to the floor; he had seen and heard this situation before on the West Bank. Once the dust and debris of the car had settled Omar called the Daves and told them of the assassination attempt. They drove out to his villa on the outskirts of Dubai and spoke to him and his head of security. Omar wanted to speak to them alone, he asked the head of security to trawl the cafes and building sites for informants; he was sure he knew the reason for the assassination attempt. The security consultant looked relieved. They watched him leave by the entrance that led to the pool. Omar trusted the Daves with security of his luxury apartment block; the wealthy residents were pleased that they and their team were on call 24/7. Omar asked for their opinion.

'Your security details have been compromised, the American has to go.' The other Dave nodded in agreement. Omar protested; 'but he comes from the marines, from their intelligence corps, are you sure this is wise?'

Dave produced a folder from his briefcase. 'See for yourself Omar.'

He took the folder and sat on the massive sofa. The folder contained photographs.

He rubbed his chin repeatedly saying, 'this is most worrying.'

He placed the photographs back in the folder and put them on the table.

You are correct he must be relieved of his duties, but first I will call him back and ask him to explain...'

'Not a wise move. Omar, keep these photographs here in your safe, his new employer will be aware that the attempt on your life has failed, he trusts us.'

'...however, if he sees the photographs he will know that we have been keeping him under surveillance,' Dave interjected.

'Then how do you suggest I relieve him from my employment without compromising your positions?'

'Relieve us from your employment as well, unofficially of course, but tell him that we will be allowed to stay in the apartment till our contract is up which is in three months' time. That way we will see if he moves to his new employer, he might ask us along as well. Meantime call this security company they're good they'll take over all the operations till we find out the reason behind this attempt on your life. When we leave, call Scott in and tell him that we have been released from our contracts, unfortunately so has he because security has been breached, then we'll play it from there.'

Omar was glad for this succinct overview from his

Scottish friends, they may be over indulgent in their alcohol intake but they were good, very good.

'Now is as good time as ever to tell Scott the bad news, I won't detain you any longer, I'll still be attending the party tonight.'

'Not a wise move Omar, lay low for a few days at least, people will be nervous if you turn up, release a statement saying your scheduled appointments business and social have been cancelled till further notice.'

'He's right Omar, just go through the motions, and listen to what Mr Kennoway says, he's thorough and the consummate professional, he's expensive but he's worth it, we'll get going now, we'll be in touch.'

'Thanks gentlemen, your contract will be sorted out; I think you'll be pleased with your salary adjustment, when you are leaving send Scott in please.'

Dave pointed to the folder. 'It might be better for us to take the folder.'

Omar agreed he had seen the photographs with his own eyes; he had been betrayed. He handed him the folder. They left the compound, the smouldering wreck of the car was still there, but it was covered with a tarpaulin sheet.

'Do you want to drive?' He was laughing. 'Scared that Guy Fawkes has left another sparkler in our car, don't be a big baby, get in and start the car.'

'I'm just winding you up, but just in case there is a bomb, do you want to say anything to me?'

'Sure, you're still due me a $100, or have you forgotten...again?

They get in the car. 'Well are you ready...here goes.' He turned the key and the car purred into life.

'Oh what a disappointment, not even a wee bang.'

'I hope that Omar doesn't ever realise that Kennoway works for our security company.'

'Who's going to tell him? Certainly not me, relax...another day another hundred grand.'

The upstairs lounge of The Gleens was nearly filled to capacity; the groom to be had picked this lounge because he had been there previously at a leaving party for one of the older colleagues.

It had everything, an upstairs toilet, Sky television and most importantly a bar which you didn't have to battle to reach. The party was in full swing, older more crusty colleagues could be seen shaking their heads in disapproval at the exotic dancer who was gyrating up against the groom. Lenny was watching them more than the well- proportioned young woman. Time to make an approach to the four older men.

'See they young lads nowadays…no shame have they?'
'Aye, in our day you got a ten second look at her arse then she was gone, but now, anything goes.'
'Lighten up Eddie, go with the flow is that right Lenny? I hope you have come over to ask us if we want a drink.' The four of them downed their pints in a synchronized fashion and held out the empty glasses for Lenny to replenish.

'He's not slow is he, I came over to ask what you thought of the entertainment, and I get conned into buying four dinosaurs drinks.'

'The entertainment is fine Lenny, now go and get us our drinks like a nice boy.'

Lenny did as was suggested and returned with the drinks, the exotic dancer was now completely naked.

'The barmaid said would you all mind and close your mouths because you are causing a draught,' he handed them their drinks from the tray. They didn't thank him for the drinks, they were staring at the dancer; and then she was gone.

'Pity that, I was enjoying that, I wonder where she has gone,' remarked the junior of the four.

'She works down in the bar; she does this before her

shift starts… so how was work today then?'
'She actually works in the bar!'
The other three look at him with disdain. 'Ernie, when are you going to learn, he's taking the piss.'
Lenny clinks his glass with Ernie. 'I'm not longer wet behind the ears old timer, I think you old gays, sorry, guys should be looking for a big green field to graze in.'
They all laughed. 'After today's fiasco Lenny, you might be right…'
It was like a light had been switched on. 'Something went seriously wrong, they arrogant pricks… it couldn't happen to a better bunch.'
The others were bursting to add their two pennies worth. 'I'm lost lads, what are you talking about?'
They all looked at each other and smiled then downed their lagers. 'The old guys are thirsty Lenny, do the honours.'
'If I wasn't a nosey bastard I would tell you lot to go…'
'C'mon Lenny have respect for four aged detectives, go and get us the drinks there's a good lad, when you come back we'll tell you about the fiasco.'
'I hope it's worth it, I'm not a fucking barmaid you know!'

***

Diane had cleared the overgrown rear garden over a six month period; she turned round after pulling out the overgrown rosebush at the rear fence. Her back ached but the pain vanished as she stared at the house, *her* house. She sensed the house was silently approving of her energy -sapping endeavors, and then a sudden moment of sadness engulfed her, her thoughts turned to her mother who had recently died. Trying to rid herself of these troublesome thoughts she threw the trowel on to the newly trimmed lawn, and made her way to the bench under the large kitchen window. Bending for her bottle

41

of water, her back ached again.

Her eyes stretched beyond the long expansive lawn down to the fence. The house -warming party had turned out to be less successful than she and Ritchie had hoped. Of the twenty or so friends that they knew from childhood only four had turned up. No telephone calls saying that they had other plans or any other excuse; they just didn't turn up. The two couples that did turn up were aware that they would be the only ones who would turn up. The reason that the others didn't turn up was because of jealousy. They were now the ones who were in the most expensive house, the others didn't take kindly to being knocked off the top of the tree. Ritchie took it as a personal snub, they weren't having the party to show off; it was just a facsimile house- warming party that they had thrown when they bought their first flat on Strathmartine Road. The two couples were pleased for Ritchie and Diane, they had worked hard over twenty years to land in this house; it wasn't an overnight success. Ritchie dredged his mind of the many favours that he had done for his friends or former friends as he would now call them. Burst pipes in the middle of the night he repaired, flooded kitchen caused by blocked drains. He stopped counting, it was making him depressed. And he never took a penny because they were his friends. Bastards. Ritchie and Diane's family had deduced why their friends failed to come; jealousy. Diane had great difficulty in accepting her own disturbing theory, 'jealous of us mortgaged up to the hilt, surely not?'

Ritchie asked the two couples to help him dispense the food and drink, he asked Diane to come into the kitchen also. The two women told Diane that the consensus was that they were acting the big I am. They knew they weren't.

'Forget them, we're here.' Ritchie piped up. 'I won't forgive nor will I forgive them, inverted snobs, that's the kindest thing I could say. Forget them, get the drinks down and the music turned up, we've got a life to live.'

She sipped the water, her thoughts returned to her dead mother, 'you would have liked sitting here mum,' .blossom from the tree landed in her open palm. The negative thoughts floated away, a comforting warm feeling replaced them. She gently closed her hand then closed her eyes.

***

The detectives left The Gleens to allow the young police officers' to enjoy the rest of the night. The barmaid informed them that the taxi they had ordered was at the front of the pub. They were heading to the Westport; that was their fiefdom, they could relax in the area from the Perth Road to the Westport, anywhere else and they were inviting trouble. They were a tight team, but that had not always been the case, one of the original team was suspected of sharing information with certain individuals who had evaded justice on occasions when it looked certain that they would be convicted and sent to prison for financing drug dealing in Dundee. They put up the investment and were guaranteed a thirty- per cent minimum return. The person who took their investment passed it on to the dealers, he took a fifty- percent cut of the gross profits, then passed on thirty- per cent to the original investor. These three individuals to all intents and purposes were solid citizens who paid their taxes. They all owned thriving businesses, and lived in the more salubrious areas of Dundee.

In four years they had accumulated millions, but like any other canny investors they placed modest sums at first with old-established investment companies in Dundee, from an acorn an impressive oak tree grew. Their affluent neighbours respected them who were financial advisors, currency traders, accountants and tax advisors, over summer drinks at the barbeques that were prolific.

And they would be dispensed with advice; they would act all wide-eyed when they heard various strategies for maximum return on their investments. Then they would say that they had an endowment policy maturing in the next couple of months and they were looking for a safe haven for the maturing policy. Another washing machine for their blood stained money. In their own unregulated minds, their hands were scrupulously clean; they tried hard to convince themselves that they were not involved in the drug trade. That was until they were told that there would be a moratorium on their investment, an investigation was ongoing. That was the cryptic message, instead of keeping their heads down and going about their daily business, the three of them met on the golf course at six am to discuss their next move. One of them said he was out, he had a bad feeling, he had accumulated more money than he could ever spend. The other two didn't try to dissuade him from his original thought. They would take up his investment option; more money for them. Two months went by; there was no call for investment from them. Another hastily arranged game of golf, this time panic was eating into their mind set. They were now losing money; no further investment meant no return, were they being sidelined? Was it a coincidence that their friend took a rapid exit from their investment strategy? He handed over their money, they didn't know the recipient who took their money, had their friend continued to invest, shutting them out from the vast profits?

***

Jim McAveety was from a long-line of policemen; his father had served the people of Dundee with honour and trust. His son had been a total disappointment to him. He was not suited to the disciplines of a professional police force. But in Jim's curious and far from cogent mind, he was a future Chief Constable. He was more cunning than intelligent, because he was a keen student of Sudoku he thought he would be more of use as a forensic accountant unravelling money trails that would lead to a Mr Big, rather than pounding the beat in crime-ridden areas of Dundee. He didn't keep this hubris thought to himself, his colleagues encouraged him to approach the head of the drug squad; Joe Feeney. When his same colleagues started calling him by the sobriquet 'supermac' another layer was added to his voluminous ego.

Joe Feeney was mortified when he came into his office and heard this indecent proposal. McAveety left his office convinced he had impressed Feeney, he was correct on his assumption; he had left an impression; but not a positive impression. Feeney had known his father, at first he had fallen out with him, which was not an unusual occurrence. But Feeney was in his debt, and had been for over ten years, Feeney had been charged and caught on CCTV viciously assaulting a well-known drug dealer, surprisingly the dealer reported him to the police; big mistake, he would now be exposing himself to the searchlight of the Law. McAveety's father had been walking up to the Perth Road from Seafield Road when he came across Feeney kneeling on top of the dealer punching him relentlessly, he pulled him off.

When Feeney was charged with serious assault the CCTV was shown in Court, the dealer was seen to be placing his right hand into his left hand inside pocket of his expensive suit. The dealer said he was reaching for his mobile phone, the solicitor begged to differ he said 'Mr Feeney feared for his life that he was reaching for a firearm, and thus reacted in a professional way to pre-empt this dangerous situation as there were members of the public in the vicinity. Sergeant McAveety had earlier told the Court that he had heard you say you were going to blow Feeney's head off, are you calling him a liar?'

'Too right I am, Feeney broke my jaw' replied the dealer.

'Do you know officer Feeney?'

'Yes.'

'Has he arrested you in the past for drug dealing?'

'Yes.'

'I put it to you that you threatened officer Feeney because he had brought your murderous trade to a premature end, and you shouted threats including you were going to blow his head off because he was instrumental in you being sent to prison.' Verdict? Not Guilty. Pat Connelly thanked the jury. Sergeant McAveety had perjured himself for Feeney. He owed him, but unbeknown to Sergeant McAveety if he was aware of his son's appointment with Feeney he would have told him ignore his request, 'he's not cut out for the police, never mind the drug squad.' However, McAveety had retired, Feeney mistakenly assumed he knew or encouraged him to enquire about stepping-up to the drug squad. This was the silent favour being called in, he had to acquiesce. Damage limitation would be his watchword. He called in his most trusted colleague whom he had appointed as the most senior detective that planned and coordinated the intelligence that led to successful confiscation of money and drugs. He was instructed to baby sit 'supermac.' Feeney read his face he didn't agree with this addition to his well- trained squad. McAveety had a mouth that couldn't react to his brain; he would undoubtedly compromise intelligence. It was not a state secret he loved to flash his warrant card; if he was in the drug squad he would be unbearable. Feeney listened smiling and nodding his head at this accurate assessment. 'I have no other choice.' There was no further debate; it would be a pointless exercise asking why he hadn't a choice. He left Feeney's office demoralised. Feeney on the other hand, was becoming slightly more optimistic, if *he* was under suspicion about passing intelligence onto to suspected drug dealers, supermac would be the fall-guy.

Jim McAveety opened the letter he was expecting; his application to join the drug squad had been successful. Astonishment was the emotion amongst his uniformed colleagues, quickly followed by bitterness. McAveety became insufferable, the office of Chief Constable was far in the distance but he could still see it even though it was out of focus. The future was now in his hands, he didn't need to ask his father to smooth the way, he had done it all on his own. The increase in salary would be a Godsend; his recent divorce had financially crippled him. He would move out of his flat in Constitution Road, a more affluent area would be beckoning him. No more arguments with the students who rented the flat above him and insisted playing their music at deafening levels. He had to reluctantly call his father after he was detained in Bell Street after he was arrested for assaulting one of the students. His father called someone who was on the periphery of criminality, who kicked the student's door down, pulled out the student, and left his blood on the walls of the close. The following morning the student accompanied by friends went down to Bell Street and withdrew the allegations. McAveety couldn't leave this fortunate outcome alone; he went to the students flat the following week at four am in a state of severe intoxication. He reminded the student, who was boss, anymore noise and his *friend* would return, he had an older woman on his arm, she was swaying not with the music, but with the copious amounts of alcohol she had consumed at the North End Club. 'The Gasman' had been lucky again.

***

'I am so pleased to meet you Mr Kennoway; I hope your accommodation is to your liking, you have come highly recommended.'

Eddings did not look perturbed at this moniker; he was working in a surreal environment. 'The apartment is beautiful; I hope I can help you if you are experiencing any difficulties.'

The Daves had briefed Madni well. Kennoway would not discuss specifics, he understood why Eddings was calling himself Mr Kennoway, his company First Rate Solutions, came with an enviable record according to the Daves. He had no reason to doubt them. Mr Kennoway had worked in the background, special forces in Iraq and the first Gulf War. He was expensive but professional, unlike the myriad of security personnel companies that were operating out of expensive offices in downtown Dubai. The Daves had no prick of conscience by conjuring up an alias for Eddings; Madni would have asked their advice which company could bring a solution to his recent problems. They told him that they had to leave for Scotland, a former colleague who had been in the Special Forces, and his forte was intelligence, he had just retired early from the police in Dundee, he had formed a company five years previously that had specialised in freeing hostages in Iraq from their Islamic captors. He had run the company from his house which had banks of computers; his men kept him up to date. The company First Rate Solutions was looking to expand into the UAE. They were going on annual leave they could run this problem past him, he might be interested. Madni told them he would appreciate this.

Feeney had called them in Dubai he was concerned that Eddings had mental health issues, he was worried that he would end up losing his pension, could they find him a position in Dubai?'

That was the reason they were heading for Scotland, Eddings was from the old-school, he had helped many colleagues over the years, now it was their turn to help him from his mental turmoil. Madni's problem would be the solution to Eddings problem. They had absolute faith in their persuasive skills; Eddings would be the owner of First Rate Solutions, the money from the contract, £100,000 per month excluding; expenses, would be split equally. When they were sure he was coming over to work in Dubai, they would tell him his real salary, rather than the inaccurate salary package they told him in his house in Fairfield Grove, Dundee. They were all experienced detectives, they would find out who was trying to murder Omar Madni and why. Eddings would be wined and dined, and when Madni greeted him by his new name Kennoway; they would study his reaction, if he floundered they would step in and come to his assistance, but there would be no need for this Plan B. The only thing that had slightly altered this plan was this woman Morag, had she something to do with the attempt on Madni's life?

***

Ritchie was looking forward to the weekend; he had decided to finish at 8pm rather than 4.30pm.An old cottage was being renovated in Fairmuir Street. Parking was one of the hazards in the street as well as cars being broken into. The CCTV that the North End Club had in situ were not a deterrent to the feral youths, the CCTV were a challenge that they didn't take seriously. The cars were a means to an end. Sat-Navs were the latest must have motoring accessory; which in turn could buy the heroin that their scrawny drug-addled body demanded. Ritchie knew that his newly- acquired van resplendent with expensive tools would be an easy target; they would strip the van of the tools and materials like ravenous piranhas.

The owner of the cottage offered his garage which backed on to Fairmuir Street as a safe haven for his van and its valuable cargo. Ritchie was grateful for this generous offer. He told the owner that he would work till 8pm, he would be finished on Friday evening, if he came to the cottage on Saturday morning he would test the heating system, and when he was satisfied he could pay him there and then. The owner agreed to this request. Ritchie looked at his watch it was nearly 9pm, he had been running the boiler for the last hour; he went through every room checking the pipes and radiators for leaks and air locks. Everything was in working order, he was feeling quite pleased with himself; all he had to do tomorrow was walk the owner through the controls of the boilers. The boiler was now on timer, it would kick in at 8am, he would meet the owner at 9am, check there were no leaks and receive the cheque then hand over the keys. He called Diane, he would be home in 15minutes; he was leaving now. He made sure the cottage was locked up then he left. His mood changed; some moron had parked their expensive car directly in front of the garage. Taking deep- breaths he assumed it was someone from the North End Club, maybe they had a valid excuse; he called the club giving the registration of the car. He waited 5 minutes and called the club again. Ten minutes later, still the owner of the car failed to arrive. He called the club again this time with the caveat, if the person doesn't turn up in the next minute he would call the police, oh and there was young lads 'admiring' the sat-nav system.' He heard the door of the club been opened by someone in a hurry. At last thought Ritchie.

'What's the fucking problem pal?' the portly man shouted at Ritchie.

All bets were off. Ritchie let rip. 'Some fucking moron parked in front of the garage I can't get my van out…any idea of the moron's name?'

'Who the fuck do you think you're talking too?' He was now six feet away from Ritchie who was leaning against the cottage's garden wall.

'A fucking moron, I guess, just move the car!'

'You don't know me do you? I'm supermac and that might give you a clue what type of character I am, and I ain't a fucking moron.'

' Supermac...after the burger?, That makes sense, do me a favour *supermac* move your car, oh and look at that you're parked on double -lines as well, I suspect you wear glasses.'

'Who the fuck do you...'

'...a moron called supermac, if you don't want to move the car, I'll call the police, what's it going to be?' He walked up to Ritchie who he smelt the alcohol emanating from him.

'I am the police,' he proudly showed him his warrant card. Ritchie was visibly unperturbed.

'Are you attending the secret policeman's ball then...'

'Are you trying to be funny?'

'No I'm trying to get home, are you going to move the car or are you going to stand there like a dick...your warrant card implies you are a detective, if that's true, your pissed, should I call you to arrest yourself' ?

A female voice rang out from the door of the club, 'what's happening Jim?'

He turned round and shouted, 'I'll be back in a minute, order the drinks up,' he turned back to Ritchie, 'That's my chick...'

' Chick? More like a well-fed hen, you must change your optician Jim; I noticed she didn't call you supermac, problems in the bedroom department?'

Jim walked away reluctantly there wasn't any chance of intimidating him, he got into the car and moved it six feet away from the garage.   Ritchie opened the garage door and entered the van and reversed out into the street; Jim watched him as he left his van and closed the up and over garage door and lock it. He made sure Ritchie saw him write down the registration of the van. Ritchie got out of the van again and walked towards the Audi, he nonchalantly knocked on the window he retracted the window. Ritchie popped his head into the window, 'evening sir, have you been drinking…here's my business card, you haven't got your glasses and your pissed, that'll save you writing the name from the van in your wee note book, evening all.' He walked away, Jim couldn't muster a reply, but revenge was mustering in his mind. 'I'll get you, don't worry about that.' Ritchie drove off, shaking his head, who would have believed that encounter that just happened. There would be more meetings with this plumber he lived in Broughty Ferry, just five minutes away from his new flat in a divided sandstone house. But the next time, he would be in the ascendancy, he would not be getting away with the comments he had directed at him; a police officer that was keeping the streets of Dundee clean from the vermin that ran wild in this street. Imagine if he did call the police; would he have been able to talk his way out of this predicament? He would have said he was working undercover there was a suspected dealer in the club; the subtle handshake was less potent nowadays.

***

The intercom was being buzzed in a manic fashion; he wasn't distressed it was Lenny. He turned down the music then threw the remote on to the sofa that was covered with dust sheets. From the capacious lounge to the hall was twenty metres, why he kept on counting he didn't know. He lifted the intercom handset.

'C'mon up Lenny,' then he pressed the button that released the newly installed security door. Gordon had gone round all his neighbours and invited them to his house-warming party. There were eight flats in the close; at the party some of the neighbours had met each other for the first time. Times had changed; everyone used to go out of their way to meet one another, not anymore, today's lifestyle had brought technological advantages that their parents would have classed as fanciful, now the populace went to their place of work in their cars, if they lived close to their workplace they would hurriedly make their way avoiding eye-contact this was the eyes-down society, everyone was a potential attacker or victim. Houses and flats were personal fortresses; curtains were drawn at night. Everyone had imposed house-arrest on themselves. That was Gordon's theory he had seen at first hand the fear that had gripped Dundee, but that was when he was a police officer. His life was bobbing along quietly and happily against a sunny horizon.

Then Joe Feeney sunk his ship, how he managed to turn the tables on him was subject to much speculation and conjecture; it didn't matter anymore, he was forced to take early retirement against his better judgement, which wasn't worth anything. He had concerns about the sudden departure of Valentine Eddings from the detective division, he now felt deeply ashamed he had swallowed all the lies and innuendo that was being circulated by emails and text messages, in a nutshell, he was alleged to have been protecting Raymond Andrews the missing MSP who was wanted for questioning into the spate of murders of junkies and policemen. He had known Eddings for over twenty- years; and he had betrayed him not deliberately but by stealth, moreover, he passed all the information that Valentine Eddings had told him in complete confidence.

Then like a school sneak he had slithered up to Feeney's office with Valentine Eddings' theory why Raymond Andrews was being set-up. Feeney was horrified, and asked him if he thought Eddings had mental health issues, to his undying shame, he replied yes, without any doubt. The following week Feeney took him for an informal chat with the soon to be retired Chief Constable. He repeated to him what he told Feeney, however Feeney fashioned the question that *he* had concerns that Eddings was having a nervous - breakdown. In the febrile atmosphere in the Chief Constable's office he didn't attempt to correct this imperfect version of events that Feeney had told the Chief Constable. He ignored his instinct to clarify what actually was said because Feeney convinced the Chief Constable to offer Eddings a generous financial package, and he felt he played a part in achieving this.

A short time later the two Daves turn up from Dubai and sell it to Eddings. Eddings asked him what should he do, he replied 'grab it with two hands and don't stop till you reach Dubai, you lucky bastard, wish it was me.'

Feeney was then promoted to head- honcho of the drug squad, he was going to reconfigure the drug squad, it had got too flabby and complacent and he wanted to replace quantity with quality. The bean-counters were delighted with this; the projected savings were to be in excess of seven figures; Feeney spoke their language, after that Feeney's requests went through without a quibble, state of the art surveillance equipment to 'miscellaneous expenses'; they were approved as long as Joe Feeney's signature was appended to the request. Then the clear-out began in earnest, only twenty- per- cent of the original drug squad were left intact. Gordon was recruited, he would be Feeney's eyes and ears, that should have raised the first red flag, but instead of acknowledging it he waved it high in the air. Feeney bled every minutia of information about Eddings, he told him everything about how Eddings was not convinced that he (Feeney) was who he was saying he was, he didn't elaborate. He had been due to meet one of his informant's in the car park across from the Snug bar, they had both been members of the same fitness club that straddled the car park. He went for his usual Saturday morning work-out, and then he would see the informant briefly in the car-park. When he had finished his brief conversation with the informant, he opened the boot and threw in his sports bag, then all hell was let loose, seemingly from nowhere, four of his colleagues ran towards them, he was annoyed they had compromised his informant, he would now clam up; how he wished that was the case. In the confusion he was thrown to the ground and handcuffed, his sports bag was searched in front of him as he lay prostrate on the ground. They took out the kilo of uncut heroin; he was asked to explain, he told his colleague it was part of a sting operation, Joe Feeney had authorised it the paperwork was all in order, Joe Feeney had signed the paperwork to allow the confiscated and tagged smack out for this sting operation. He was taking down to Bell Street and detained for three hours. He was relaxed. Once Feeney was traced to his Lodge on Loch Tay he would back- up what he was saying.

Feeney was contacted; he denied all knowledge of what he had said, the signature was not his, it was proved to be a forgery that was classed as professional. He was charged. He was not relaxed. Before the trial he was advised by his solicitor to change his defence strategy; no mention of Feeney; and you'll walk. Mention conspiracy you go to jail. Pat Connelly never spoke a truer word. Verdict. The bastard verdict. Not Proven.

Lenny ambled up the stairs to GG's top floor flat; GG had advised him taking the stairs three at a time caused noise, created tension and drew attention.

The door was left open he walked in and closed the door. The long rectangular hall had been repainted, the colour was more calming, GG said the colour was autumn gold, Lenny disagreed with this he called it beige, but kept this to himself, GG was becoming more like his old -self, if he wanted to call the colour autumn gold, so be it. The lounge on the other hand was still the sickly toffee colour apart from the ceiling and cornice which were brilliant white. He moved the dust sheet from the sofa and cast his eyes around the room.

'It's coming on GG, you'll soon be sitting in a smart flat, once the walls are done, what will you do next?'

'The bathroom suite and I'm going to add a separate shower, there is plenty of room, after that the kitchen.' He moved into the kitchen, and brought a mug of coffee through for Lenny.

'That's the home decoration discussion completed how did it go at The Gleens?'

Lenny was displaying his trade-mark broad smile. 'They know absolutely nothing.'

'But what did they actually say?'

'They are split, some think that it was rival dealers from Liverpool who have followed them before, the other two think it was an inside job, but they didn't elaborate when the other two detectives challenged them and asked then to back up the theory...they were quite annoyed.'

'Was it Morrison and Welsh that were annoyed?'

Lenny brought the mug down from his lips, 'yes, how did you know that?'

'I'll tell you later, but that's good news, anything else they said that made you uncomfortable?'

'Just that if it happens again it's the same Polish gang that were operating in Merseyside, remember there was a piece on Channel Four news about gangland figures being executed in Manchester, the reporter said something along the lines that police sources told him it was East European organized gangs that had at first operated in conjunction with the Merseyside gangs, then there was a dispute, more than likely about money, that ended in bloodshed.'

Gordon was returning his smile. 'The perfect storm for us, what are the plods saying?'

'It's the same gang that was operating in Liverpool and Manchester.'

'Perfect...don't offer an opinion unless asked, then

agree with them. On to more relevant subjects, the money is here, are you still happy for me to invest it for you, no second thoughts that I might get greedy?'

'I'm happy, if I'm not touching it, I can't be connected to it, can I?'I don't know who you are dealing with and I don't want to know, I've managed to save up ten grand, that's taken me four years, since I joined the police, and with me doing plumbing work on my days off, no one will be suspicious.'

GG was not smiling. 'Hope you are still thinking about a flat and not a house?'

'Relax, I'm talking about a two- bed roomed flat in the Strathmartine Road area, in about four months' time, Linda has a policy maturing, I won't be flashing the cash, no fancy car...nothing.'

'Stay in the flat for about five years then and only then move into a house, nice but nothing to raise suspicions...'

'GG, I'm not a thicko, I'm making more money from plumbing jobs than my take home salary; everybody knows that, it's not as if I'm the only one moonlighting.'

'You are now a very rich man, money alters people's way of thinking, they get lazy, but you won't and I won't.

When you sell your flat, I will release some liquid capital to you; that should ease you and Linda into your new house.'

Lenny finished his coffee. 'Liquid capital? You're even talking like a financial advisor, but unlike them I trust you.'

He takes the mug form him and refills it, Lenny has moved from the sofa to the window. 'Nice view from here, your location is perfect, what about the students at the weekends?'

'Here's your coffee...I'm lucky no students live here, it's mostly professional types, I had a house warming before the flat was to be decorated. Anyway, if someone in the close decides to sell, I'll buy it and place my choice of tenants in.'

Lenny turned around quickly alarmed. 'Will that not arouse suspicions, where did he get the money, that sort of thing?

'I'll own the flat but it won't be me that buys it or owns it.'

'Oh right,' he said slowly, puzzlement emerges from his face.

'Covering my tracks that's all, nothing for you to worry about, you've not asked me about the money or how much I sold the smack for, aren't you curious?'

'Not really, as I told you, I trust you...'

'...£80,000 in cash and the smack was sold for £100,000, better than plumbing eh?'

'Doesn't seem real does it?'

Gordon moves from the lounge to the bedroom, and returns with a plastic Tesco bag, he hands it to Lenny. He pulls the washed socks and underwear out; various denominations of notes are in the bag.

'It's real alright; the bag doesn't seem that heavy does it?'

Gordon takes the bag from him, 'there's another one in the bedroom, the bags will be gone by tonight,' He returns the bag to the bedroom. GG is smiling.

'Seeing the money instead of talking about it makes your senses more focused, I thought you should see the money before it goes to work for you and me.'

'Are you not nervous of burglars or the police raiding your flat?'

'I just wanted you to see it; I don't normally keep the money...'

'...normally? You've did this before then?'

'You're the plod, you've worked it out, it's best you don't know anything, it could make you nervous, when people get nervous, mistakes follow.'

'Your totally correct it's best I don't know, I'm just in a

bit of a shock that's all, it's a wee bit like the Sopranos, hard to believe what a world I've entered.'

'You've done the citizens of Dundee a favour, and you've been paid a fair sum for your time.'

'How did you know I would be willing to moonlight to this job… robbing the dealers?'

' Judgement… you have social mobility about you, no one had anything bad to say about you, you've not been off on the sick since you joined the police, upstairs have you marked out for higher duties. Do you recall last year when you found the wallet in the cubicle in the nightclub, stuffed with £50 notes, you told one of the senior detectives that was at the bar, you wanted him to witness you counting it out in front of the bouncer and you got their signatures all agreeing the sum in the wallet and the other contents, credit cards and business cards?'

'Yeah, the bouncer took the business card and knew who the guy was, I told him to call his mobile, which he did. He thanked me and tried to make me take two £50 notes; I told him there was no need, and walked away.'

'You didn't realise who the guy was at the time.
The wallet being left wasn't an accident, you, were being set- up; twice. First you didn't keep the wallet, the second you refused the reward. This was all captured on the club's CCTV, careful editing would show you receiving money from the grateful member of the public, they would have used that to blackmail you, if you didn't play ball, but you passed the stern tests, your colleague however, failed that was why he was let go when Joe Feeney re- organised or in his words streamlined the division. He had been under suspicion of passing on information, our suspicions were confirmed. It was me; who passed the intended blackmail operation on to Joe Feeney; it was equivalent to me resigning. Now is the time for you to accept Feeney's invitation to join the drug squad.'

***

He finished the email it was meant to brief, but it evolved into an epic missive by his standards. Jean replied after five minutes, ending why don't we talk like this at home. That was exactly what he had been thinking, he could have been honest, 'you interrupt me while I'm talking, you can't when I'm emailing can you?' But he contained these thoughts rather than express them. He looked at the clock 10pm, time to call Morag. Her business card was beside the laptop, he picked it up and started to turn it back and forth, he was having second thoughts. He picked up and the phone and punched the numbers in a careful manner. Three rings and its answered.

'Hello?'

He introduced himself, once the niceties were exchanged her tone changed.

'Don't make long term plans or financial commitments here, Dubai is changing and not for the better.'

'I've not been here long enough to make any plans,' he was laughing.

'I'm leaving to go back to Dundee in four weeks' time, you should be doing the same, you have come to Dubai at a dangerous time.'

'Dangerous…how?'

'Look, it's better if you come over to the villa; I don't feel comfortable talking over the phone.'

'Do you mean come over to your villa…now?'

'It's only a twenty- minute taxi ride away, do you have a pen handy, here's the address, just hand it to the taxi driver, don't tell your friends where you're going, it's important that they don't know, okay?'

'Okay, it's a wee bit mysterious this clandestine night-time meeting,' he wrote her address down carefully, his writing was not the best.

'See you soon, bye.'

He googled the address, it was on the periphery of
Dubai, it meant nothing to him. There was a short series
of raps on the door. He closed the laptop, went to the
spy hole; it was the Daves. They were dressed in casual
clothes. He opened the door they were met with a fit of
laughter.

'C'mon in, where are you two nice boys off to then, to
a gay, happy place?'

'Ignore him he doesn't recognise style.'

'We're going out on to the tiles, fancy joining us?' He
was looking at his watch impatiently.

'No, I'm not used to this hectic social life yet, but
thanks for the offer.'

'Right, we're off see you later,' they made their way to
the door.

'You didn't try too hard to change my mind did you?'

'Life's too short, enjoy your cocoa.' Then they were
gone

Lenny left GG's flat in an excited frame of mind.
Seeing the money had changed his perspective now. Joe
Feeney had been invited to Alyth golf course, that slime
ball Mars would be passing him all the gossip, he had
been trying to weasel his way into Feeney's cadre of
friends. Feeney only tolerated him because he might
have something to offer. Mars couldn't keep his mouth
shut; he had told a number of plods that he and 'Joe'
were playing golf at the weekend. Lenny would be the
gooseberry who would be welcomed by Feeney but not
by Mars. He would bump into them at the car park, his
tee-off time was booked for 9.30am, and their tee-off
was booked for 9.10am. Feeney would invite him to
join them, or he hoped he would. If he did he would let
Mars dish the dirt on some unsuspecting plod, he wasn't
brave enough to sully any of Feeney's detectives'
character. GG had explained to him that when he was
accepted into the squad it wasn't the same as being

accepted by Feeney's acolytes. He would be tested to the limit. He would be under surveillance for six months; today would be the last time he would be in GG's flat in Bellfield Avenue. GG would contact him; Lenny would not attempt to contact GG. He had to think for himself, explore every situation, and never get complacent. That was GG's downfall, he trusted Feeney far too much, insofar; he was fawning. Lenny would be given a map to avoid those pitfalls. Universally respected by his fellow plods and detectives, his resistance to the calling of Feeney was well-known, some of the plods fell out with him, they couldn't understand why he would resist better conditions, salary and female constables throwing themselves at him. He was playing the long-game. When he did heed the calling, no surprise would surface. When he was established his former colleagues would be able to keep him up to speed what was happening on the streets of Dundee, instead of 'studies have shown criminal activity was down etc.' Many of the plods would be marking his card, maybe Lenny would vouch for them when they wanted to leap onto the ladder. The consensus was 'Lenny would see us all right.'

Lenny would wait for the optimum time before he reaped the bountiful harvest of real intelligence. One person he would have no doubt would be livid about him joining the drug squad would be fat boy Mars. Feeney's head would be filled with information that would be malevolent. He wouldn't dismiss Mars as a fantasist, but he was borderline. Even lunatics were useful. Saturday on Alyth golf course would be a seminal moment, when he was invited to join Feeney and Mars he would feign resistance. He would ask Mars if it was okay with him, he just wanted to see the excess skin on his chin, turn red as it normally did when he felt under duress.

Mars had an enormous appetite for golf, food and gossip. His appetite would be curtailed because he was there;

Feeney would draw him in by flattery, that's what he did with Gordon Graham.

***

The red-brick built church in Broughty Ferry was the unlikely meeting place for the two atheists; Wednesday morning 10am, the church was empty. This would be the only time they would meet face-to- face. The first protagonist had seated himself at the rear of the church on the right -hand side; he had parked his car in Douglas Terrace. This would be a renewing their vows meeting or it would be a decree nisi; he was indifferent, this partnership had been fruitful but it had had its moments when a dissolving of the fragile partnership became ineluctable. He was pondering what he really wanted. The door opened and cold air rushed in, he turned round he was here. He knelt beside the pew and blessed himself then shuffled along the pew and sat next to his business partner. 'I didn't know you're a catholic.'
He looked at him, 'I'm not, I always wanted to do that, see if I felt anything, I didn't.'
Ok, why the unscheduled meet today??'
'You have to shut down the brothel in Blackness Avenue, some neighbours have reported seeing oriental woman coming and going, it's going under surveillance from Sunday, they don't think it's a brothel they think it's a cannabis farm.'
He was ingesting this. He watched him take out a cigarette, and tap it against the pew then lit it. No wonder the public has lost respect for the police.
'Ok, will do that by today. We'll suspend business, for at least a month we've bought a house in the west end which is more ideal, not far from Magdalene Green, it's secluded, it's well back from the pavement and is surrounded by a high wall. The workmen should be finished in the next couple of weeks; I'll ask the foreman if his men would consider working through the night and weekend that means it would be finished in a week.

Contacting the clients wouldn't pose any insurmountable problems.'

'That's good to hear,' he was blowing smoke rings high into the cold air.

'Are you not worried about someone coming in seeing you smoking? Normally you're paranoid about your movements and being incognito, don't you think your chancing it a bit?'

'Not really, no one will come in here this early, religion is dying out now, people are watching day-time television, that's the new God, and B&Q is their church.'

'Is there anything else on your mind, or something I should be aware of?'

'No that's it all. Any interesting developments in your field?'

'Just the usual initiatives, from a new think- tank from the Scottish Government on drug abuse.'

He finished the cigarette and dropped it to the floor; he extinguished it with his foot.

'Oh and what initiatives are those?'

'Initiatives that will increase our cash flow from the Scottish Government, our request for more funding has been agreed, the money for another four social workers will add more to our profits, we'll employ four newly qualified social workers that'll at a stroke add £40,000 to our profits, the additional funding is for experienced social workers who have worked with drug abusers.'

'Is that not taking an unnecessary chance, what if it shows up on the audit from the Charity Commission?'

'Leave it to me…have you not seen who the independent directors are?'

'That's what I mean; will they not pick up on newly-qualified social workers instead of experienced social workers?'

'Not in the slightest, have you seen their expenses? That's why they are unpaid; they know they are onto a good thing. They like meeting the political big hitters at

Holyrood, not forgetting the overseas trips, four in the last year, one in New York, two in Basle and one in Jamaica.'

'When do you propose to take the charity into the private -sector?'

'Next year, I'll be resigning from the Social Work department due to a work related illness, with a generous pay off. Fortunately for me once I regain fitness I'll be head-hunted by the independent directors.'

'You're lucky you can stay in the shadows, I'm in the firing line everyday…'

'…You're getting well compensated.

' I can't argue with that,' he looked at his watch. 'Got someplace to go have you?'

'I've always got someplace to go…I'll leave first, you stay here and say a wee prayer then leave.'

He moves from the pew then drops to his knees and blesses himself, and winks at him then leaves.

Staring at the altar he wonders why people believe in God any God for that matter; religion was just a means to control the people, make them fearful, and if they behave they'll go to heaven when they die, and meet all their past generations. How can sane and intelligent people believe that? He felt the cold air once more on his neck, don't say he has forgotten something; had he left his lighter a cheap plastic one at that? He turned around it wasn't him it was the priest, he instantly went on to his knees, he didn't want to engage him in a conversation theologian or otherwise. Ho hoped he didn't smell the cigarette smoke. Or notice the crushed cigarette butt. He knelt down as if to pray.

The opportunity came and he took it. The priest shot him twice in the head. Feeney had met the same fate; he was sprawled in the vestibule of the church. The killer offered a prayer of thanks and left.

***

Jim McAveety had completed the course successfully. He was the oldest and he felt it. He was back in Dundee he felt empowered, he was of the opinion that the drug squad like to display a mystique and aura about their day-to-day work. The intelligence meetings before raids were exactly what the public saw on their television screens on a nightly basis, from various police series British and American. He *knew* who the big players are in Dundee; he didn't need any seminar or covert intelligence to enlighten him. He was under whelmed. Two months on the street studying junkies from the Hilltown wander into the town centre, meet other junkies at the front of the Wellgate Centre then wander to a low-level dealer in Lochee wasn't exactly the French Connection. His colleagues didn't impress him either, from the outside all the plods respected these hi-tech detectives, however, he was on the inside now, he saw with his own disbelieving eyes the wasted man -hours, the' intelligence led' raids that could have been done in the same day as the target they had under surveillance. Why did they watch this junkie go through his same bland and boring routine everyday including Sundays for six weeks? Why not follow him to the low-level dealer; someone could keep an eye on him where he would lead to someone a rung up the drugs ladder. The money men behind the drugs didn't live in the sprawling and crime infested schemes; they lived in the more prosperous areas; his father told him that over 10 years ago, nothing had changed.

He kept these thoughts to himself. Then everything changed; Joe Feeney had been lured to a church and shot by an informant, that was the rumour going about the office, as for this Social Worker guy, it seemed he was in the wrong place at the wrong time, he popped in to pray for his ill mother, he must have come across the murderer during or after his deadly deed. Was there a link to the murder of the Liverpool dealer by the Poles?

For the first time in his adult life he learned to keep his mouth closed and his ears open, especially in the room where everyone was encouraged to let off steam and say what's troubling him or her. He would just repeat the least inoffensive query of his colleague. This clear- the - air meeting was the brainchild of Joe Feeney; everyone agreed it was a benefit to the squad and individual. It certainly benefited Joe Feeney he would uncover who was probing too much and who was thinking that results was mediocre. He would shift the more enquiring minds onto back-office work; and less probing minds into the field. His theory was simple; Feeney was meeting his top informant, the informant had been followed on a previous occasion.

Feeney would have been identified as his handler; both now had to go. The informant called Feeney on the pretence of passing information, perhaps about the Poles. The clandestine meeting was arranged for the church, and bang, bang, goodbye Joe. The informant would now be probably dead, and the Social Worker just unlucky.

*** .

The bright lights of Dubai were now a distant memory, another five minutes and he would be at her villa. Where he would go from her villa would be up to him, if he was feeling invigorated he would meet up with the Daves, if he wasn't, he would return to his apartment. News was managed in Dubai rather than reported. The assassination attempt on Mr. Madni was reported as an electrical problem that had ignited the fuel tank. Just as he had been told it would be reported. The taxi stopped at the villa. He paid the taxi-driver and ambled up to the gates. He pressed the video-com button, the gates eased open, he walked up the narrow path which was lit by sunken lights. The villa wasn't as grand as he imagined it would be, she was waiting at the door, her body language was sending out more relaxing signals.

'Just go straight in.' He followed her instruction, he felt the cool air from the air conditioning, the lounge was smaller than he anticipated, he sat down without an invitation.

'What's on your mind?'

'Murder...what would you like to drink, beer or spirits?'

'By murder do you mean the attempt on Mr. Madni?'

She ignored the question. 'Beer or spirits?'

'Could I just have water please?'

She returned from the open-plan kitchen with the bottle of water, he opened it and took a long drink. She was drinking a generous measure of white wine. How much would that cost in the Ferry?

'No, the murder that took place yesterday in Dundee.'

'In Dundee...yesterday...but, but, we're in Dubai, I'm lost you'll have to explain more to me Morag.'

She placed her drink down on the tiled floor, and returned to the kitchen, she went to the laptop which was open; she brought it over to him.

'See for yourself.'

He studied the report from the Evening Chronicle website. The banner headline screamed out; Drugs Chief shot dead in Church. He found it hard to comprehend as he skimmed the report, he read it a second time more slowly, the gunning down of Feeney was a planned hit, nothing would change his instant assessment. Feeney must have been on the verge of breaking a drug smuggling operation.

'It's hard to take in, I worked with Joe Feeney, is he related to you?'

'No, no, but I know of him, I knew he was going to be murdered three weeks ago, Feeney was someone high up in the drug squad, 'he was going to be taking care of,' that was the exact words he said.'

'Wait a minute Morag, you're jumping all over the

place, start at the beginning.'

He lifted the wine glass from the floor and gulped down the full contents; she went to the kitchen and retrieved the bottle. She poured herself a generous measure and placed the bottle on the floor.

'Okay, I'll have to stand up and walk and talk at the same time. I was at a function in one of the new hotels, celebrating another apartment of condominiums being sold out in record time. There was a large crowd of ex-pats and celebrities in attendance.

Everyone was euphoric the bonus money on top of the commission had made even the junior members of the sales team £50,000, remember this is tax free. Later in the evening one of the young Arabic sales team, told me there is a group of policemen from Dundee over in the corner, some detective was having a stag-night, he was pissed, he was becoming louder and louder, they didn't try to hide that they were policemen. The hotel security was called to advise them to calm down. This they did, most of the group moved out from the hotel to go to some other place. The soon to be groom stayed with two other men, I went to the ladies, he was standing near bye, he was on his mobile obviously talking louder than he realised. He was repeatedly shouting, 'Feeney has to go, he's went too far, he's set up my mate, he'll go to jail, no doubt. That means I'm next to be lifted, he's got to be taken care of.'

Eddings listened with some scepticism, he had interviewed hundreds of witnesses over the years, they were positive they saw something or other, however, when he walked them through their statement, they invariably changed it. Definite turned into a maybe.

'Why didn't you speak to the Daves?'

'You've a lot to learn the only thing Dundee has in common with Dubai is they both have capital D's. I wouldn't trust any policeman from Dundee.'

'Then why tell me?' He was clearly offended at this

69

sweeping statement.

'They painted you as incorruptible; you can't get a more ringing endorsement.'

He wanted to keep her talking. 'This detective on the phone do you know his name?'

'He has two names; he paid a deposit on a condominium with a credit card Trevor Perkins.'

'Doesn't ring a bell…'

'…his friends were calling him Welshy.'

'I know him, Paul Welsh.' Now he was thinking.

'And he paid for all the hotel rooms with this card, I found this out from one of the closers on the sales team, her sister work's at the hotel, they were there for a week.'

He was worried; Paul Welsh was friendly with the Daves.

***

Michael Jameson looked round the bar, it was heaving, and every table was awash with drinks. Tuesday in Fibbers Magees was quiz night, and it was very competitive. But he wasn't here to be tested on general knowledge. He was here to meet his friend who used to be his adversary. He should have been here over an hour ago, normally he was paranoid about time keeping, but tonight he was in charge of the cue ball. He had re-located to Dubai against his will; he had reluctantly accepted his solicitor's advice. His days of operating freely in Dundee were coming to an end. At a charity event, his solicitor was advised to discard certain clients; his name was mentioned. A new broom had been given maximum powers to drive out the money-changers from the sink estates of Dundee; the new broom was Joe Feeney. Jameson thought he would be immune from the draconian powers that the police were using on a regular basis. At first he told his solicitor he wouldn't be going as far as Arbroath never mind abroad, when the solicitor suggested Dubai, he reacted not with anger but laughter. His solicitor then unearthed the secret that was buried deep within him. If he did not quit Dundee word would be leaked to journalists and dealers alike that he was a CI.

A criminal informant, his file would be sent to another solicitor who was suspected of being connected to organised crime in Dundee. He had never owned a passport, now he would be going down to the Post Office to apply for one.

This was a blow but some other news came the week before he was due to take up residency in Dubai, his loan-sharking business was coming to an end. .

Every aspect of the loan-sharking would be operating as normal, except for the money would be diverted to some other businessman. No compensation package would be offered; his life would be spared only on the condition that he never entered Dundee again. The caveat to this; he would be allowed to be buried at Balgay cemetery beside his wife; it could be arranged if he wished to meet his wife in the afterlife. He was still a multi-millionaire but giving up a business that generated £700,000 per annum was hard to take. He was fifty-three but looked much, much older. He had his hired thugs if someone didn't pay the exorbitant interest on a weekly basis, but the people who were strong-arming him out of Dundee were people he would doff his cap to. There were no ifs or buts, he had to hand over his customers' names and addresses to his solicitor then someone would come and collect the expansive file. His solicitor would make sure the income from the shop leases in the city centre and Broughty Ferry would be transferred to his account in Dubai. That would be the last transaction between him and Michael Jameson. Another recommended solicitor would be taking on Michael Jameson as a client, at a higher cost, naturally.

Tonight would be the start of the fight back to regain

what was rightly his and his father's before him. He sipped the cold, cold Guinness, but it never cooled his burning desire for revenge, but it evoked memories of his last pint in Dundee in the Waterfront Bar, he had arranged to buy the bar and turn it into a live music venue, then the call came from his now former solicitor about leaving Dundee. Why he tortured himself of what might have been, he didn't know. The woman who ran the Waterfront was a first class entrepreneur; she had turned his dream into a financial reality. Up and coming bands were desperate to be booked, and A&R people from major record companies were represented in the Waterfront frequently. The older clientele were catered for with well-established combos playing music that appealed to them.

Simple Minds had been playing at the Caird Hall concert hall, after the concert they popped into the Waterfront to see a young group in action, that was the plan but they were coerced to play on the small stage, they gave an hour's impromptu performance, word spread like wild fire, that Simple Minds were playing in the Waterfront, the doors of the bar were closed immediately. They stayed there till closing time, after people had their photographs' taken with them they were left to enjoy their beer. Michael Jameson was envious, they were his favourite band, if he had bought the Waterfront he would have been there that night…that was the real reason he wanted to have a cold Guinness on that Tuesday afternoon, he wanted to sip his Guinness and imagine his heroes playing feet away from. But that was then this was now, he felt the tap on his shoulder. Paul Welsh was grinning.

'Did you not think I was coming Mike?'
He looked at his watch. 'I wasn't too worried…you're here now what do want to drink?'

'A lager, I have tried the Guinness, it doesn't taste the same.' He ordered him a lager.

'So what's this news that will cheer me up?'

'How would you like to go back to Dundee, and I don't mean in a pine-box?'

Jameson looked at him keeping his emotions in check.

'For a holiday…no thanks I value my life, I'm enjoying life here.'

'I'm talking going home and reclaiming your former business.'

He lifted his Guinness and sipped it more slowly.

'And how is this going to work out, do I have to pay a fee to you and that guarantee's my safety, in other words protection money, no thanks, I would be murdered anyway.'

'No, no, Mike, things have changed in the three years since you left Dundee, I can't explain, you just have to trust me. I have never let you down in the past have I?'

'I'll agree with that, you've helped me, I won't take that away from you, I trust you …up to a point.'

'Why don't you look convinced?'

'You've taken me aback, tell me how I'm going to go back to Dundee, and live and as a bonus, I get my money lending business back, there must be a tariff to pay?'

'Oh there is…a £100,000, but it's worth it if you can go back to Dundee and regain your loan-sharking business.'

'I give you a hundred grand and I'm allowed to walk about Dundee and get back my *money lending* business, this is *guaranteed?*'

'Nothing in life is guaranteed, but you have to trust me on this Mike.'

'Okay, okay, I give you a hundred grand, you take care of the problem, what happens if the problem arises again, I'm not prepared to dole out thousands of pounds every time the problem pops up, I'm not daft you know.'

'You've got it all wrong…the problem will be finished, it won't trouble you again, I promise…'

'…but can't guarantee, you can't blame me for being

sceptical, the people you're talking about are top dogs.'

'This should put your sceptical mind at rest and this is much as I can tell you, so no more questions okay?'

'Okay.'

'You pay me £100,000 you come back to Dundee six months after the deed is done, this will allay any suspicions, because you can imagine the chaos this removal of your problem will bring. Once you are back in Dundee you start earning again from your loan-sharking business, you pay me ten percent of your annual turnover, that's it.'

'I'll go for that…when do you need the money and who do I give it to?'

'Contact your solicitor; tell him that you have been looking at buying another apartment from an ex-pat and tell him to make out a Bankers Draft to Trevor Perkins for £100,000, here is the bank account number, rip it up after the money has been deposited, and things will start to move. Don't contact me, I'll contact you.'

'Does the apartment exist, just in case I come under suspicion?'

'Mike, you're not that important, I don't mean that disrespectfully, the apartment exists all right, everything is taken care of. I have to go, I'll be in touch.'

He leaves; he has barely touched his lager. The quiz ends; and music is blaring out from the jukebox. 'Don't you forget about me,' He smiled.

***

The murders of a senior officer and the head of a social work department, continued to dominate the news media. Conjecture had morphed into fact as far as the public were concerned. There were many outlandish theories and some more cerebral. In the pubs, sheriff courts and solicitors' offices the theory was that Joe Feeney had been set-up, he was meant to meet an informer, instead he met his killer, the killer met the innocent social worker who sometimes went to church; wrong place, wrong time.

Feeney had made enemies in the drug trade because of his impressive record in breaking -up drug cartels that were trying to make Dundee the hub for drugs distribution for the east of Scotland. He had become too successful and was becoming a cult figure for the news media. However, there were no leads, plenty of theories but no firm evidence, no eye- witnesses, nothing. Speculation was mounting who would be filling Feeney's size nines. Office politics were at their worst, runners and riders were putting themselves forward. Laughingly; Jim McAveety put himself forward, without any encouragement from his more experienced colleagues. Their laughter filled the office, McAveety didn't take this as a form of ridicule, he took this as a ringing endorsement. Senior management was keen to fill this void, a rapid interview process was initiated, the final question to the applicant was the more pertinent; 'apart from yourself, who do you think the ideal candidate would be?'
Paul Welsh was the unanimous reply, except from Jim McAveety, he suggested Feeney's deputy, who was universally disliked. The interviewing committee came to a unanimous decision; Paul Welsh would be offered the job, after the obligatory interview. That would be in six days' time when he arrived home from Dubai.
  Paul Welsh was respected he had come through the ranks, he refused to be fast-tracked, he wanted to spend another two years on the beat, before he accepted the invitation to join the drugs squad. He would use the two years to cultivate and propagate the users and abusers of Class A drugs. His notebook was nearly full with the criminal informants he had accrued, at a monetary disadvantage to himself, slipping an odd tenner to a strung out junkie. Or his favoured policy of searching

low-level drug dealers and saying to his colleague that the suspect was clean, when he had a small supply of ten pound bags, which he kept as a supply for his informants. The low-level dealer didn't question the results of the search; Welsh had saved them from a weekend in the cells and a Court appearance on the Monday, which could lead to a remand in Perth prison. Welsh had also built up an impressive if disturbing portfolio of constables who were friendly with career criminals in and around Dundee.

Useful ammunition when strong-arm tactics would have to be used. He had gained respect when he joined the drug-squad and had challenged Feeney's decisions frequently. Feeney didn't take these criticisms lightly, what made it doubly awkward for him was that he had chosen Welsh personally and he would dilute the barbed comments from Welsh by saying, 'he respected his concerns but he was the boss, end of.' Welsh was just voicing the concerns of the majority of the squad; but they were not prepared to come out and say anything; he was. Primarily, 'why were intelligence led raids ended prematurely, when if they were left another week they would have some of the really big players in Dundee?'

Feeney was remarkably cool under hostile questioning from Welsh. 'Intelligence… if we wait we would compromise future, much larger drug deals, and put informers in danger.' No one could argue with this response. Welsh wasn't buying it, something just wasn't right, he would keep his concerns to himself from now on, his colleagues had not only changed their tunes they had thrown away their instruments. Instead of confrontation he would adopt a more conciliatory and pragmatic approach when Feeney does his monthly assessments of the previous months raids. No longer would he be the voice in the wilderness. Then the following year his mind was finally made up. After his friend and colleague was stitched up in Mains Street in the car park, he went into surveillance mode, watching Feeney at every opportunity, he had to be involved in the drug trade. No way would his friend GG be involved in drugs, Feeney said he was unaware of the meeting in the car park with a well-known dealer.

He kept these concerns from the rest of the drug squad, when GG was mentioned he would say, 'how stupid he was, but who knows what else he was up to, he had no sympathy for him.' This was music to Feeney's well-tuned ears.

Welsh became more subservient to Feeney's eleventh-hour amendments to agreed plans and raids. His nocturnal habits were an eye-opener for Welsh. He met some people he had met at forums on drug abuse, etc. Why was he meeting the same person on a regular basis? On the surface the head of Social Work had an enviable and respected position in the destruction of families because of drug abuse. He had openly called for more resources to open more clinics, he understood that the NHS budget was under severe pressure, however in Holland there were independent clinics who were making remarkable progress in slowing down dependency on heroin, and it was less expensive than NHS treatment clinics. Political self- publicists from the main parties concurred with this far-reaching but sensible suggestion. Thus an independent clinic was opened in a quiet leafy street in the west end of Dundee. Hundreds of thousands of public money was poured into the clinic in the shape of grants. Welsh had read in the Evening Chronicle about this innovative clinic. If it helped families it must be a good thing, however, he was concerned when he saw Feeney meet the catalyst for the clinic, in curious places.

***

The walk from Bellfield Avenue to Dundee Airport would take less than twenty minutes; he had arranged a helicopter flight over Dundee at four pm. He was posing as a consultant from a company that would be advising SEPA on their much vaunted and far-reaching flood prevention policy. The flight path he would give the pilot would be west to east then north to south. The digital lightweight camera would be fitted to the underside of the helicopter, the resultant images would be transferred simultaneously to his laptop. The flight was uneventful, the pilot accepted the subtle hint that the client was not one for conversation; he sat in the rear seat opened up his laptop and placed on his headphones. Thirty minutes later the helicopter was hovering above the airport, the pilot watched him remove the headphones and close the laptop, once landed he offered to release the camera from the underside of the helicopter, this offer was politely declined. The consultant thanked him and left, no tip was offered.

GG walked from the airport in an ebullient mood, the camera was light-weight, compact and very expensive. He had removed it from its rightful owner; Tayside Police. When he was suspended after the sting in Main Street, he went to Bell Street against the advice of Patrick Connelly to remove his personal belongings; that was not the real reason, he wanted to gauge the feelings of his colleagues, not hear second or third -hand gossip how the land lay. Much to his disgust blank stares and contemptuous comments were numerous, he was left in no doubt, they unanimously thought he was corrupt, just like Eddings, who took the coward's way out and resigned, thus keeping his pension. He had to keep his emotions under control this was mob rule, they were all probably descendants of the morons who hanged witches hundreds of years earlier in Dundee. He asked them if anyone had anything to say, but they all turned their backs on him in unison. His emotions were tearing at his moral safety net. 'Ian, I would watch Phil if I was you, he's been spreading gossip about your gambling or was it your cocaine habit? Thanks for all your support lads, oh before I go, I know all your secrets.' He walked away with his heat filled head held slightly elevated. The long corridor seemed the length of an unending runway, but he kept the same steady pace, no hurried footsteps were heard behind him, not a whimper of a raised voice.

The deadness of his eyes flickered with signs of life if not optimism, he swung the black dustbin liner over his shoulder, he stopped and turned round, no one had come through the swing-doors, he continued along the corridor, he was near to Feeney's office, the door was ajar, he couldn't resist, he pushed the door open, the office was empty, on the chair was various boxes which contained hi-tech surveillance equipment, he removed one box, it contained a camera, he slipped it into the black bag, closed the door, and walked triumphantly along the corridor. He felt good, the fight back had begun, but many battles lay ahead. In his car he felt revulsion, why did he steal that camera?

***

The silver Mercedes glided along Strathern Road, he felt pleased with himself, he was sure others would be equally as pleased. The rusty gate had been given a coat of black paint as had the railings, they looked luxuriant. The trees that had partly obscured the railings had been lopped. He alighted from the car still casting a critical eye over the garden. The house now had kerb- appeal. The weather beaten eaves and down pipes had been given more than a lick of paint. He made his way to the door, the path had been freed from weeds, he was impressed, he pressed the polished brass button, he pressed it again, maybe they hadn't had it repaired yet? The thought was just out of his mind when the door was opened by Diane.

'Oh Pat, come in.' He walked in; the hall had been transformed.

'Very nice Diane… very nice.'

She chaperoned him into the reception lounge, she was pleased with his appraisal, she took him upstairs two bedrooms and the upper hall had still to be decorated. He told her that they had done a magnificent job; he saw the disappointment on her face.

C'mon Diane, these things take time, you have the rest of your life to do up the house, how about making me a nice cup of tea?' They went down into the newly-refurbished kitchen.

'Keeping the best to last Diane…it's beautiful, it really is.' Her mood lightened.

She told him of their disappointment of their friends shunning their house-warming party; apparently they thought they were showing off. Pat told her that was the point of a house -warming party, the friends were jealous, simple as that, and their infantile behaviour proved they weren't real friends. She and Ritchie had nothing to beat themselves up about; Diane was reassured by Pat's assessment. She felt better about herself now, she wished her mum was still here to see this house, she would have been so proud.

'That was a fine cup of tea Diane; you must have Irish blood in you.'

'Probably, somewhere down the line,' the doorbell rang out.

'That'll be Ritchie, he always tests the bell before coming in, he's paranoid about that bell, probably because it was me who fixed it…but that's another story.'

He shouted along the hall, 'is the bell still working?' She boomed back, 'yes.'

'Does he do this every night?'

'Yep… every night.'

Ritchie came into the kitchen and was surprised to see the welcome visitor.

'Pat! How's things…do you want a cup of tea?' He

looked tired.

No thanks, I just had one, Diane was telling me about the bell ritual…everything's fine, I have some good news for you and Diane.'

The tiredness left his face. 'What's the good news?'

Diane rose from the farmhouse table and switched the kettle on.

'How would you feel about having a new partner in your plumbing business?'

'I like owning my own company Pat, and we're grateful for all you've done for us.'

'I agree with Ritchie Pat, work is coming in thick and fast, Ritchie is thinking of taking on other plumbers, we like making our own decisions.'

'You will still be able to, the partner will be a silent partner, he will not interfere in any way, shape or form, I apologise for using clichés, but I have known him for many years, and he will tender for lucrative maintenance contracts, he's a wily old bugger. This is his proposal, he will clear your debts on the new vans, he will fund new vans and equipment, and he will pay you a £200,000 as a goodwill gesture. The profits will be split 50-50. I'd bite his hand off.'

Diane was open-mouthed and Ritchie looked as if he was going to be sick.

'What's the catch Pat?'

'The beauty is there is none, he sees you as a prodigy, he sees you as he was when he was young, he likes young people who are willing to take a chance,' Pat looks around the house.

'Pat I don't know what to say, we can clear our mortgage…'

'…exactly! That's what I said your reaction would be.'

Diane chipped in. 'Everything is above board Pat; he's not dodgy is he?'

'My dear Diane, do you think I would propose

something that's illegal; I thought you knew me better than that?'

'I didn't mean to question your integrity; this is like a bolt out of the blue.'

'I can understand your question, but you underestimate your intelligence and business nous, you pay your debts first and foremost, and that's the foundation of business. Now if you accept this offer, you move up another rung on the ladder, you can get in tradesmen to finish your upstairs, how long would that take to complete...three weeks?'

'Pat what is your advice?'

'Take it, clear your mortgage with the goodwill gesture then your salary is yours to enjoy or invest.'

'Invest?'

'I would advise you to start a property company, you two are naturals, but you both have to agree.'

'Property... us?' They both stare at each other.

'I'll guide you through everything, I'm your friend as well as solicitor...I hope!'

Ritchie was flushed with excitement. 'Of course you are; when do you want me to come to your office to sign the paperwork?'

'No need it's here,' he pulled out the documents from his jacket. 'What are you thinking Diane?'

'I think this house has brought us luck, it sounds daft I know...could you guide us through the clauses of the contract Pat?'

'Of course, it's straight-forward, it was I that penned the terms and conditions, bring your chair over here, you too Ritchie.' Pat the consummate professional went through the two page contract line by line. Any fears that they harboured were vanquished, Lady Luck had indeed smiled on them. Ritchie signed on the bottom line.

'Great Ritchie, now I am instructed by your partner to ask you to recruit another six plumbers and two apprentices. Pat pulled out another document.

'I like the jacket Pat, how many pockets does it have?' Diane asked.

'This jacket is thirty -years old, it has seen me through the best of times and the worst of times, I'm glad to say this is the former rather than the latter. This is a tender for the maintenance contract for the schools and social housing in Dundee.

Append your signature here Ritchie, as you can see you have quoted your figure, which I think has an excellent chance of being accepted.'

'Are you sure Pat, the figure seems a wee bit on the high-side…and everyone knows that Lamberts have the council contracts sewn up…'

Pat took the signed document and returned it to his inside pocket. 'To quote Mr Zimmerman, times are a changing. Leave it with me.'

'Who is Mr Zimmerman, is he in charge of contracts at the council?

'Oh Diane, oh to be young again, no Mr Zimmerman is also known as Bob Dylan the singer.' Ritchie was laughing.

'I don't know why you're laughing; you didn't know he was Bob Dylan, did you?'

She is annoyed.

'Of course I know who he is…'

'Children, children, concentrate on the matters on hand, are we not going to celebrate this union?'

'Diane, do we still have a bottle of champagne somewhere?

'A whisky would be fine, keep the champagne until the house is finished.'

Diane moved from the kitchen to the reception room to retrieve the whisky from the drinks cabinet.

'It's all been a bit of a shock Pat, business has been building up, more word of mouth than any advertising, but this business partner…he won't try to force me out will he?'

'Not at all, he sees your company as a fledgling, in five years' time; your company will be the dominant plumbing and heating company in Dundee. Keep this partnership silent, as far as the world is concerned, you're the sole trader.'

***

Eddings returned to his apartment after the meeting with Morag. He refrained from writing anything down just in case the Daves accidentally came across his notes. His wife said his head had room for another brain; he would store the information there. The problem he was wrestling with was the conversation she had overheard was one way, Welsh was talking into his mobile, but she could have mistaken certain snippets of the conversation, on the other hand she could be 100 per cent correct. It would have been the perfect hit, set up in Dubai executed in Dundee; literally. His built- in partner, his instinct, was telling him in no uncertain terms that Morag was correct. The tension was making its way from his stomach to his head. He loosened his tie and kicked off his shoes and pulled his socks off, he felt better when the coolness of the tiles touched his feet. Into the kitchen he took a bottle of water from the fridge, he went to the balcony and closed the double- doors behind him. The twinkling of Dubai was pleasing to the eye, but heavy on the heart. Even on a cold winter's rainy day, the view from the Law (hill) was more uplifting, he liked to sit on the seat where a small brass type plate was screwed on to the bench it said, it was 'the best view in the world.' It was where a squadron leader who had served in the Falklands conflict liked to come and view Dundee and over the Tay to Fife. He didn't know 'Jock' but he felt he knew him, he often wondered who he was. The noise from the highway was never ending he wouldn't be driving here, it was just too dangerous, the roads were modern but the driving was manic. When he was going home for Christmas he would find out all he could about Feeney and Welsh, he wondered if GG knew anything. GG, he took some ribbing for his name, Gordon Graham, his father was called Gordon and his grandfather Graham.

He passed the baton of ridicule on to his son. GG actually liked his names Christian and surname. He always said he stood out from the crowd because he was unique, he certainly was and he is a good friend. However, when he was in Dubai he learned GG was arrested for drug dealing, he tried to contact him but he wouldn't return his calls or reply to his emails.

.According to the Daves, he had money problems, and tried to muddy the waters by bringing Feeney into the case. He may have been found not proven, but that was not tantamount to not guilty.

Now he was over in Dubai, he thought he was away from the drugs and murders that were common in Dundee, most of the murders were drug related, dealers were being swept off the streets and put behind bars, but no sooner were they jailed when another Burberry attired army of dealers would be selling their wares, prison was not something that inhibited them, they just treated the threat as an occupational hazard.

A generation of dealers was being born to their drug-addicted parents, the cycle looked impregnable. Soon there would be more social-workers than police officers. Feeney was being buried next week; there had been no developments in the case.

The Daves were shocked as he was about the death of Feeney, but the circumstances were more disturbing; assassinated in a place of worship; and an innocent member of the public shot dead as well. They agreed with the Press reports that Feeney was on the verge of cracking a drugs deal. Eddings just agreed with them, he wanted to ask if there was a connection with the dealer;

being gunned down in the bleak tenement flat, it had not been raised in the Press, the Daves didn't raise it with him either. Morag had been hitting the bottle at nights because of the stress caused by Welsh's mobile phone conversation. He had arranged to go out with her tomorrow night to the Dubliner's bar in the area of Le Meridien, it was popular with the ex-pat community, whether they were flying in or out of Dubai, they made their way to the Dubliner's, because of the close proximity to the airport a mere five minutes away. Morag had been there before and had felt comfortable in its surrounding, a lot of her sales closers liked to celebrate there. She had said that she would pick him up in a taxi about ten pm, she saw the look on his face, she explained Dubliner's was open till three am, officially, it was known to still have customers when it officially opened at ten am. Eddings was not a big drinker but this bar appealed to him, some of the clientele may get careless and allow things to slip out of their inebriated mouths. He was thinking more about the attempt on Mr Madni, rather than Joe Feeney. Morag may see him as someone to sound off about, she had been reticent about her life and business dealings when she had lived in Dundee, he had never came across her before, and he had never heard of her name. He had been here just over a week and he had knew of one assassination attempt on his employer, and one successful assassination on his former colleague in Dundee. Where would he be in a year's time, in Dubai or Dundee? He was nonplussed, that was okay saying that now when he was on the balcony of a luxury apartment observing the sky-line of Dubai.

Tomorrow he was playing golf with the Daves, tee-off time was at ten am, the sun would be burning, he had not played golf for years, but he would give them a run for their money. This job was just as they had said, mundane interspersed with games of golf, night time was when they worked even when they were out socialising, their job was building up intelligence reports on Mr Madni's business rivals. Morag had promised to give a running commentary on a number of ex-pats who were now ensconced in Dubai, not because they wanted to but because they had to leave Scotland. Some of them were not without sin and were unfortunately from Dundee, respected businessmen at home.

But they were different when they shed their skins as charitable Rotarians. The *real work* took place when they were socialising. He was interested in the Daves now.

***

Her phone rang, she reluctantly opened one eye, she reached over for the mobile, the name of the caller was displayed; it was 'supermac.' It was ten a.m. she had been nightshift; she had been in her bed for less than an hour. She finished her shift at six am, came home showered, threw on her track suit and went for her daily run. When she returned to her flat she would shower have breakfast, then watch some TV recordings. Her flat to Magdalene Green was five miles; she covered this in forty-minutes. Since she started running and giving up the pies, burgers and kebabs she had shed two stone, her weight was a respectable nine stone, not bad for her height of five- foot ten. She was dreading the surprise party for her fortieth birthday, a week on Thursday having had failed to get the sergeants position. She was assured that she would be successful, that was the only reason she had slept with him. The successful candidate had followed the same route. Now she felt like a fool, an old fool at that, she had given up her successful career as a nurse to pursue a career in the police force, thinking it would be a breeze, she was well-educated, and had been encouraged from her fellow- nurses, unbeknown to her they were in an indecent hurry to see the back of her voluminous derriere. However, she thought that they were saying she was selling herself short, she could go far in the police force; the further the better as far as her many detractors were concerned. She may have been short on basic morality but she wasn't short on ambition, and had chartered a course to marry a doctor then she would be set up in life. She enjoyed holidays in far-away destinations, two weeks in Mauritius, hill-walking in Peru, and weekends in New York accompanied by doctors who varied in age. All in vain; the fourth finger was still naked. The pursuit of a Hollywood lifestyle came with a heavy price tag, she was thousands of pounds in debt, she had to downsize from a divided mansion in Broughty Ferry to a flat in a tenement which was occupied by students, that was one of the reasons she worked overtime on Friday and Saturday nights, the other reason was she couldn't afford to go out anymore. She started her keep-fit regime to convince her more affluent friends that she was abstaining from the booze and burgers.

'Hello,' she said, she couldn't disguise the sheer exhaustion in her voice.

'It's supermac, I've rolls and bacon here... do you want me to pop up?'

'I've been nightshift...what beat have you been on... Kirkton?'

He was laughing, 'Jane...you must keep up, I'm in the drugs squad now, three months now, I thought you knew.'

She bolted out of her bed, 'I can't sleep, I'll see you when you come up, bring up milk, I've none left.'

'Okay, I'll be up in ten, bye.' She was elated, supermac in the drug squad how fucked up is that? Time for asset management.

'Sauce on your bacon supermac?'

'Please...so what happened to the lovely flat in the 'Ferry then?

'Promise, you'll keep this between us and I'm only telling you because we're friends… remember my sister went to live in Spain a couple of years ago?'

'Yeah she's a doctor…'

'No, no she's a nurse, anyway they have been hit by the property slump in Puerto Banus, without going into too much details, they had the house, the cars, maids, but didn't have the money to sustain it.

She would have to give up her job and lifestyle in Spain and come back to a crummy flat in Dundee. So I sold my lovely flat gave her the money and I bought this, it suits my needs.'

'God…what a thing to do, I'm humbled at hearing that, not a lot people would do that Jane.'

'She has always been good to me… I was going to say keep this under your hat, but you don't wear one anymore do you?'

He was struggling to answer as his mouth was packed with the contents of the roll.

'Oh, you mean I'm no longer a plod. I'm enjoying it, I felt I wasn't being appreciated, I'm a lot happier now I can tell you.'

She cut her bacon roll in half and offered it to him, he didn't need any enticement. He couldn't keep his mouth shut, either from shoveling copious amounts of food and gossiping.

'Well I'm glad someone is happy.'

'I can understand how pissed off you didn't get the job, keep this to yourself she was sleeping with him, that's the reason she got the job, and he's not happy anymore.'

'How's that?'

'Someone told his wife of the unusual tasks that she had to perform while they had a one-on-one interview, he's been chucked out, the marriage is over… kaput!'

'I didn't know that! Was he shagging any of the other candidates?'

'I don't know, but I heard a couple of them are raising

sexual harassment charges against him, he's being suspended on full pay. The word is he'll resign. Did he try anything on with you Jane?'

'I couldn't say at the time but now I can say, he made it very clear what he wanted, but I told him to fuck off, just like the other police officer who tried it on…'

'…That was just a misunderstanding.

'Supermac, who are you kidding! You put your hands on my tits when we were parked up on the Law what was there to misunderstand?' She took great pleasure seeing his discomfort.

***

'It's a pity Val couldn't make it tonight, he would have enjoyed this evening.'

'I think he is having difficulty adjusting to the real Dubai, not the tourist version.'

'That's to be expected, he may have been a hard-bitten detective, but this place operates on another set of hidden rules. Anyway, he will have someone else on his mind.'

'Morag?

'How did you guess David…you weren't a detective by any chance were you?'

'The fucking best, you weren't so bad yourself. Look at this place, heaven on earth, and we are getting paid for this.'

'Mr Madni doesn't approve of this place, but he understands this is where secrets are let go, without too much persuasion.'

'This is where the old world meets the future, who would suspect that the three supermodels over there are hookers?'

'Discretion from the hotel and discretion from the customers…and the world still turns without any difficulty, drink up; you've been nursing that lager for a while now.'

'On you go, just an upset stomach, I want to be fine for

the golf tomorrow,' he lifted the glass and gulped till the glass was empty. The other Dave went to the bar then went to the restroom.

He sat and smiled at the ladies of the night who were pleased to see their protectors keeping a discreet eye on them. They weren't doing this as a chivalrous act; they were being paid by the ladies management company. The Hotel management was fully aware of the love contracts that would be exchanged during the evening, the customers were wealthy individuals, and some didn't have to pay for these optional extras. These executives who had concluded contracts couldn't believe their luck that they got involved with a party of young people who were celebrating someone's birthday party, and as luck would have it, the executive would take a shine to one of the young women, the karma would be reciprocated. They would be flying back to the United States or Europe the following day. After the night of love, he would feel invigorated, first of all by concluding the multi-million dollar/euro contract, then secondly the unbelievable night at the hotel. No money had been exchanged; he believed it was his charm that enticed the young lady to spend the night with him. Who said mirrors don't lie?

He couldn't help compare the difference with the prostitutes that stood huddled in the bus shelter on the Arbroath Road, willing to satisfy every carnal desire for twenty quid, just to keep at bay the terrors of the withdrawal symptoms when their emaciated bodies were screaming for heroin.

'Penny for your thoughts amigo?' He placed the lager beside him.

'Just thinking about the golf tomorrow, why is this place more busy tonight than normal?'

'The new golf complex and marina is opening in two days' time, this will be the architects and project managers getting together.'

'And how do you know that?'

'Because the guy at the next urinal next to me told me, and I learnt that someone has been arrested for the car bomb.'

'Already? Madni won't wear it, it's too soon.'

'I knew I should have told you later, you worry too much, but we're still going to get paid and Val's stock is going to rise is it?'

'Has Madni been told?'

'He's unavailable till tomorrow, I'll tell him tomorrow, you play golf with Val, I'll explain to Madni, who it was, why he did it, and I can have him deported, all without a fuss.'

'He'll want to meet Val and personally thank him, will Val play ball?'

'David, David, ye have little faith, of course! I'll brief Val, he won't rock the boat, this is a brand new world for him and I can't see him upping sticks and moving back to Dundee can you?'

'But what if he suspects we've being using him, he might...you know.'

'He won't...and what is this nonsense about us using him? He was having a nervous breakdown; they were thinking about getting rid of them, he was suspected of taking bribes from the MSP Raymond Andrews who if you have forgotten is suspected of killing a number of people, including police officers. We're looking after his welfare and ours'

'Okay, I know all that, I just think he'll think what we're doing is unethical, he is, more ethical than us, you do know that?'

'He'll be fine, he is enjoying life over here, his emails to Jean are brief; you would think he's running out of ink. His daughter in Australia is a different matter, they chatter non-stop. He even invited her over to Dubai next year, but first he would have to ask the Daves.

Every keystroke he does on his laptop is replicated on

my laptop, so if ever he's getting uncomfortable I'll know, surveillance has moved on since the Instamatic camera you know.'

He was laughing now. 'You're right, we're not taking advantage, he's getting well-paid, he's enjoying himself, he's met Morag and we saved him from getting the bullet in Dundee, I feel better now.'

***

The workmen had packed their tools and had gone home. The drawing room had been returned to its former glory, the lounge at the rear of the property had been completely gutted, this was contemporary, expensive Japanese wall coverings, sumptuous deep piled carpet, and four large leather sofas completed the look. Original Warhol paintings hung on one wall, Jack Vettriano paintings competed for envious eyes. The hidden sound system could fill the room with any music genre; a television screen could appear from the floor at the touch of an obedient button. The building originally housed eight bedrooms this had been reduced to six; the two original bedrooms were now multi-functional. He had waited and waited; now it was his. The house was in a perfect secluded affluent area in the west end; it sat there evoking privacy and solitude. It was surrounded by four fifteen foot stone walls, large mature trees stood proudly like sentries as back up for the stone walls. The property was not overlooked by adjacent properties. The house was two hundred metres from the iron gates where the gravel drive began. CCTV were discreetly positioned on the narrow lane outside of the property, the other cameras covered every conceivable angle of the property. At the rear of the property the enclosed garden, had an envious secret, beyond the large bush was a discreet gap in the foliage where someone in a hurry could make their way to the next property which was owned by someone familiar to the club members.

Pat Connelly had brought his dream to reality and at a great expense. The house had been turned into a club for professional people who had shared interests. Gambling and activity of a sexual nature. It was called the Thirty Club, only thirty members were allowed, there was a waiting list of more than double the membership. The members' were allowed a maximum of two guests. The membership fee was thirty thousand pounds per annum. For this hefty fee, the member would have unlimited access to the gambling suite, roulette, blackjack and one arm bandits that paid out tokens that were worth one thousand pounds each. Every drink and meal that their palate desired would be met, and an impressive amount of drugs were on hand, drugs would be taken discreetly. Women of various ages were available for entertainment for the men and women members. The female members had their choice of men or youths. The Club was open on the first Friday of each month. No cars would arrive at the property, if members were from outwith Dundee they would be advised to park their cars at a city car park and take a taxi to the Perth Road and walk the short distance to the Club. Members were given a pre-arranged time to arrive at the Club. All phones would be left on the table in the vestibule of the hall. If their phones rang, they were left to go automatically to voicemail if it was an important message the member would be alerted.

This would be an oasis in a cultural desert for like-minded individuals. Pat was aware couples travelled hundreds of miles to hotels and country houses in England to enjoy themselves and the company of others. The cost of the refurbishment would be paid back within six months of the Club opening. Wealthy individuals who enjoyed a gamble, too enthusiastically were targeted.

This would be Woodstock with dinner-jackets and evening gowns. Pat would never be present when the

Club was open, the company from Glasgow would oversee the running of the Club. Because it was an illegal gambling Club running costs were not as high as a bone-fide establishment, and no taxes needed to be paid so the odds and prize money were more tempting and generous.

The former owners had died and the surviving family members wanted the house sold as quickly as possible, Pat was able to assist by relieving them of this potential money-pit. In a short space of time Pat was able to locate a buyer who liked a project, namely a house which had fallen into disrepair. However, the house was slightly over-priced and with the property market in a decline, he would advise them to accept the offer which was twenty thousand pounds under the asking price. Twenty thousand pounds would turn the kitchen into a place where a Michelin star chef would be proud to work. The gaming tables and the bedrooms would be equally busy; the guests would be treated like royalty as were the members. Some of them would be flying into Dundee airport from as far away as Jersey. The membership list had been vetted as thoroughly as humanely as possible. Credit history, family-background and sexual peccadilloes, anything that suggested violence or financial impropriety would result in the potential member being declined membership without any explanation. Four days later the Club would be welcoming the members and guests for the first time.

The genetics of the gambling rooms were a testament to modern science; the lightweight gambling tables could be turned over to resemble an old fashioned dining table in the unlikely event of a surprise visit from the police or tax officials. The plumbing had been installed by Ritchie, and he had his friend install the rudimentary electrics. A specialist company from London had installed the gaming equipment, as far as they were lead to believe the Club was a bona-fide establishment, the certificate and licence were on display. The shop fitting company had been subject to a lengthy investigation by the immigration service for employing illegal immigrants, the company were cavalier to issue or request paperwork. Pat had researched and spoken to the Greek owner, he didn't speak Greek, but Pat spoke his language. When the bill was presented the owner requested cash as he was experiencing difficulty with the Inland Revenue, Pat understood completely. The money was handed over by someone who said he was Pat, but was twenty years younger. This was a security measure in the unlikely event the Greek had to identify Pat sometime in the future.

***

Another exhausting night shift; and another dreaded day awaiting the postman to deliver financially perennial bills. Sleep didn't come any easier as she thought it would in the first floor flat. She couldn't help comparing her previous flat to her incumbent abode. The comparison was startling. Outside of her window was the depressing sight and sound of seagulls ripping open the stack of black bags that lay outside the Indian restaurant. Even the seagulls in Broughty Ferry had better manners. The profit from her flat had to go to her numerous creditors, what was left she used as a deposit on this flat. Her mortgage was still £95,000. Her income didn't match her lifestyle; at least the payments on her BMW would end next year. To her colleagues she was a high-flyer in the making; they were shocked as she was when she didn't achieve the rank of sergeant. Her already precarious financial position was dealt another sickening blow when she was overlooked for the sergeant's grade; she was depending on the increase in salary to pay for a loan she had taken on to pay for the new kitchen.

She was now desperate, measures that would have been thought fanciful and dangerous now crept into her head.

McAveety might facilitate her aims. He was an inspiration to her; if he could manage to be recruited into the drug squad, surely, she would be at least considered?

The drug squad under Feeney fostered misogyny; he was very open he didn't trust women police officers, period. None of the officers raised any objections, they were like-minded. Feeney only gave way when word filtered down from a higher power, that they had to recruit at least one or preferably two females to the frontline, not stuck in an office doing back office work, they had to be seen on the television participating in raids. Photographs in the newspapers would show female drug squad officers arresting dealers. Feeney's alibi was that there was no vacancy; Jim McAveety filled the last one, if they wanted to recruit a female whose budget would it be taken from? Feeney was now dead, his untimely death had created a vacancy, she was sure she could apply her feminine charm to McAveety, he would be the unwitting cheerleader for bringing a female into the drug squad, and this would alleviate any perceived charges of misogyny. Her low self-esteem was slowly fading; optimism was winning the race over the pessimistic shadow that had hung over her since she moved into this flat. When she joined the drug squad not if, her sights would be set higher than ever before, she was well-educated with real- life experience behind her, this would impress the leading voice for policing in Dundee. Her voice was higher and more vocal than others, where were the female officers in the drug squad, why aren't there senior officers of the female gender in the drug squad? These questions landed on Feeney's desk in an increasing and regular timescale. He had been summoned at one point for ignoring a request for answers, Feeney pointed out 'he was too busy arresting dealers than indulging in a war of genders.'

His impressive record in arresting dealers had saved him from a reprimand from the Police Committee Board.

McAveety had told her that Paul Welsh would be Feeney's replacement; this was the feeling amongst the men. Unusually, the selection committee had reached the same conclusion; he was the outstanding candidate. Even though he was on holiday in Dubai he was keeping in touch and was helping in the investigation of the murder of Joe Feeney. This was causing tension amongst the murder squad detectives, they wanted to investigate this themselves, they saw Paul Welsh as an impediment to their investigation, namely because he used to be one of them, but he jumped ship for the glory not the gory. Welsh on the other hand had long complained of their lack of patience; sometimes they had made up their minds who had committed the dastardly deed, even before the crime scene had been fully and forensically examined. Gut instinct and sometimes prejudice overrode preliminary scientific evidence. That was the reason why he decided to join the drug squad, it had been a Herculean task to open closed minds. He spoke to his counterpart in the CID, he congratulated Welsh on his new appointment, Welsh told him that was premature, and he was here to assist the murder squad in solving the crime. One favour would be asked, and it would be conceded, if it wasn't he would just have to lift the phone and go above him, he wanted Feeney's office sealed till he came back, there was sensitive information that was party to Feeney and himself. He didn't want informants' names being sold to the higher echelons of the drug trade, he didn't mention this to his counterpart, he just spoke in general terms. At first this suggestion was received unenthusiastically, then Welsh suggested if there was a problem in getting agreement, he could go higher, then added poignantly if his request for the office to be sealed was declined.

Old suspicions about less-pristine characters in his squad would undoubtedly be brought in from comfortable shadows. Once the landscape had been etched before him, his voice became more receptive, he himself added a caveat to this unusual but reasonable request, if Welsh was going to examine documents etc., he would have to be accompanied at all times. Welsh felt the warm glowing feeling rise from his stomach to his heart. He skillfully switched the conversation around to more leisurely pursuits, he knew he was a keen golfer, so he told him about the wonderful golf courses he had played on, the conversation ended more friendly than it had begun, in a gladiatorial fashion.

An urge to ask who the prime suspect was defeated he was told that they had someone in mind near the end of the conversation, but he would tell him the theory when he arrived back in Dundee. He would not rebuke him for jumping to conclusions, he would be less critical and would keep his concerns to himself, this would make the investigation less problematic, in his case anyway.

***

'So what's so important that you got me out of my bed,' Lenny was clearly irritated.

'Ah, what a shame are you tired son, are you hungry?' He rubbed his face energetically he was still cranky due to having only two hours sleep.

'I'm sorry for being crabbit...we had a busy nightshift, there were fights all over the place, and the Hilltown is still the worst...'

'...are you telling me something new...do you want something to eat, yes or no?'

The smell and sound of the bacon frying defeated any insipid resistance.

'Two rolls and bacon and a mug of tea, please, so what's the problem?'

'Problem, what problem is this Lenny,' he went into the kitchen.

'GG I can't be bothered, you either tell me or you

don't.'

He could hear his big throaty laughter; that means there is no problem, he was relieved, he decided to go through and assist him, GG heard him rise from the chair.

'Don't bother, sit on your arse, I'll be through in a couple of minutes I'm buttering the rolls, the Sunday papers are in the bag at the side of the sofa.'

Lenny did as he was instructed, but was disappointed that the newspapers were broadsheets, the Sunday Times and Scotland on Sunday.

'I'm alright, I can wait,' he walked over to the bay window and examined the silent street; last night it would have been filled with the impoverished throng of students on the lash.

'Here we are,' GG put the tray on the table, 'help yourself son.'

Lenny sipped the steaming hot tea, 'that's good I needed that, again I'll ask what's up?'

'Enjoy your rolls Lenny it can wait.'

'It can wait! Now you are taking the piss, I was only in my bed for two hours, what is it,' he threw the half-eaten bacon roll onto the plate.

'Calm down, I'm only kidding, you're night-shift next week right?'

He retrieved the roll from the plate, nodding his head in response to the question.

GG left the table and went to his bedroom, he returned with a grey folder.

'Have a look at that, and tell me what you see?' He went to the kitchen to refill his cup.

'Houses that are not very well insulated, money being wasted, am I right?'

'Correct, but look at the photographs again, more closely.'

Lenny was trying to figure out the puzzle, GG obviously knew the answer.

'You're not thinking of going into the loft insulation

business are you because of the government grants?'

'No, no. Concentrate. Where in Dundee are the houses that are losing the most heat?'

He looked at the photographs again, 'here in the west end and a place in Fife.'

'I'll put you out of your misery…they're cannabis farms.'

'Are you sure…in the west end, what about that place in Fife?'

'The place in Fife is a nursery, not for kids, Lenny plants…'

'I'm not that thick, I worked that out for myself, and they have perfect cover okay, but in the west end?'

'I've checked them out, remember the addresses are houses, rented houses, I've been watching four houses randomly the tenants are Chinese nationals, the tenants say they are at the university, they're using forged paperwork. Over in Fife the family business has kept the same name but it was sold last year to a company, it's a front, simple as that. Next week we are going to pick up some plants and I have a buyer, how do you feel about that then?'

'I'm in, what's the plan?'

'Simple, we don't bash in the door, we open the door ourselves take the plants, fill the hired van with them and I hand the van over to my friend…alone.'

'Where did you get the keys for the houses?'

'Lenny the less you know the more it benefits you.'

'Okay, okay, how much are we talking about here?'

'Plants or money?' He took his mug and walked into the kitchen to refill it.

'Money…the money.'

'In Dundee…I'm guessing about a £100-150000, mind that's between us not each.'

'I'm not complaining, how many days are we talking about to enter and take all the plants?'

'One morning, we have to do it all in one go, and I'm

talking about the place in Fife as well, that'll be our last stop. We leave the van at a pre-arranged place, they take the van and the money is delivered to me, the best plans are always simple Lenny, then you go back to your bed.' Lenny face had lit up two fold, the simplicity of the plan, and the detail that GG had spent formulating the plan. Tiredness vanished, he felt more alive than ever, Sunday was always the most mundane of days, today was the exception to the rule. I take it the Triads are behind the cannabis farms and the Fife nursery?' GG smiled. 'I think you could be right, or it could be someone from Dundee…'

***

August had been a total washout, it rained and rained and rained some more. September started in much the same vein, however the second week the sun gave a much appreciated if unexpected return. Paul Welsh had been on the telephone the previous evening for more than an hour. The agreed procedure about searching Feeney's office had been altered; Welsh would be a passive observer with no input or suggestions how the office should be searched. Welsh probed and probed, why had things changed so dramatically? The senior officer was unyielding, the conversation was now turning into an informal interview, Feeney's lifestyle was brought into question. Who were his friends in the force and outside of the force? Welsh told him if he wanted to interview him or his men on the record he didn't have a problem with that. But the reply made him uncomfortable, 'your officers don't interest us but you do.'

If this was the juicy worm for him to explode into indignation it wasn't working. Welsh turned inquisitor sublimely, he went on to say that he heard that some of the underemployed officers from the serious crime squad were alleged to have been seen betting large amounts of money at Perth racecourse, could be innocent or could be more sinister. Welsh knew that his inquisitor was a regular at Perth racecourse. He thought he had a kindred spirit in GG, he thought that was his moniker because he liked a flutter on the horses, he was bitterly disappointed to learn that was his first and last names; Gordon Graham.

'What type of Father calls his son a name like that,' was his more polite reaction. Welsh was told Feeney's office had been sealed as he had requested, however, his inquisitor's senior officer had told him, 'any further requests from the drug squad whoever is in charge had to go through him, if it was up to him he would have told Welsh to mind his own business.'

Welsh unsuccessfully tried to make a joke about the internecine war between the murder squad detectives and the drug squad. No laughter was heard from the other side. Tomorrow at nine am Welsh would be a guest as files, folders and computer equipment would be removed from Feeney's office. Welsh knew that their relationship had dropped to a more chilly temperature; his inquisitor had been leant on. The conversation was ended in a more cordial manner. Welsh's mind was racing, tomorrow would be a seismic time in his life, not because it was his birthday but because of the search of Feeney's office. No leads on the murder, no suspects, nothing. He reached for his coffee from the marble fireplace, it had lay untouched, the phone conversation had went on longer than he had envisaged , but he was none the wiser. He returned to the old but comfortable sofa, he sat on the dustsheet and looked around the room, some of the cornice was missing but the ceiling rose was intact. The large bay windows projected his eyes to the view over to Dundee. Even with the ugly scaffolding obscuring part of the vista Dundee was looking magnificent, but like other post- industrial cities, the underbelly told another violent story. Someone was probably staring out of one of the multis looking over to Wormit and wishing they were there. That's what he had done when he was a youth, time had granted his wish. Dreams were there to be chased...and caught.

Police and criminals danced together on the dance floor but at the end of the evening they sometimes went home together and formed a lasting relationship, to others it was a brief encounter to be forgotten about. He took the cold coffee into the near empty kitchen, only a microwave and a Belfast sink stood in the depressing vastness. The ping of the microwave took his mind off the cost of the refurbishment, his wife a French teacher contributed the lion's share of her salary, and it was her who chose and negotiated with the builder. He was like God, no one saw him but the builder knew he could present himself at any time.

The owner of the small building firm assumed his wife would be a soft touch, and it would be an easy task to blind her with building science about the complex nature of the refurbishment. Unbeknown to him, she had introduced herself to her neighbour who was retired builder himself, he walked in and around the detached property with his dog-eared pocket sized notebook, jotting down what needed to be replaced and what could be saved, and in brackets he jotted down the cost of the materials and an estimate of labour costs. Sarah was able to remove 'complex' from the builder's vocabulary and replace with the more acceptable 'straightforward.'

Then as a caveat to the conversation 'that's what my dad said he's the building inspector with the trade and standards at Edinburgh City Council.'

Amazingly on the Monday the estimate for the project had come down ten thousand pounds. Apparently the builder had been able to source some materials below cost price. Another month and the builder would be out of their hair. Walking from the kitchen into the lounge he walked around the room wondering who was the first person to live in this house; and was it built at the time of the first Tay Bridge? Did they see with their own eyes the collapse of the Tay Bridge; and the train career into the depths of the unforgiving Tay? He would have loved to have stood in their shoes and to have stared at the landscape of Dundee, which would have had a myriad of chimneys spewing out pollution form the Jute Mills. They would have never thought in another future century, the scourge of opiates would have invaded the bodies of the young.

Society had progressed undoubtedly, but paradoxically it had regressed into a living hell. He now had the opportunity to improve the lives of the citizens of Dundee, there would be a change in his mission statement how the police would now police Dundee, for too long it had soft-soaped and showered the criminal elements that operated in Dundee, tomorrow would be the dawn of a new day and a positive one at that. He had Feeney's USB from his computer and laptop tight in his hand.

***

The rain was lashing down on the mourners at Balgay cemetery, the Press was there in numbers aiming their telephoto lenses and clicking furiously at the mourners from a discreet distance. More discreet were the Police Complaints Investigation; they were photographing and videoing from four different angles. Welsh was irked by their presence, did they have the same theory as him? There were no unscrupulous businessmen amongst the mourners, family, friends and colleagues only in attendance. While his façade showed extreme sorrow, his mind was focused; he was studying particular mourners looking for a defect that would betray their innermost feelings. The reverend had giving his well-thought out sermon which hit every nerve of Feeney's family, the howls of anguish and the rapid clicking of

105

cameras competed with audible human sorrow. Slowly the mourners at the rear of the throng made their way from the graveside, collars were being turned up, umbrellas; were unsuccessfully trying to be opened in spite of the gale. Women were having their skirts whipped open; some thought this was the perfect occasion to display their autumn fashion sense, no doubt influenced by the expected television crews. The Bonar Hall was the place chosen by the family for the wake, Welsh declined, he had another pressing engagement.

The PCI in the background added another weight to his already heavy burden. Everybody seemed to be watching each other, no one could really speak, the outlandish theories had been emptied from the reservoir of malicious gossip, and fear was within the drug squad now. This self-imposed purdah at the moment suited Welsh, however, he would have to bring a sense of the reckless again to the surface, a night-out would have to be arranged, everyone would be encouraged to speak freely, and no repercussions would follow. He made his way back to his car which would return him to Bell Street, where he would be told officially that he was Feeney's replacement. He slowed down, he thought he heard a voice from one of the mourners that he recognised, he wanted to turn round but he knew he couldn't, if he slowed his pace anymore he would have caused a log-jam as the mourners were moving quickly to find refuge in their cars. He gave into his resistance, pulling his collar of his overcoat more tightly he discreetly aimed his eyes in the direction of the voice, he wasn't there, maybe it was the wind that distorted the nasal pitched voice.

He had looked at every mourner approaching and departing from the graveside, he was thorough in his observation, but his ears were winning the battle over his eyes. He did hear *him*, he was positive, he was discounting the evidence of his eyes; a first for him. Tonight he would take the trip over to Wormit rather than the weekend, Feeney's notebook needed to be examined again, this time laterally.

Tonight's jogging would be postponed with his fellow runner, a QC, who was covertly bi-sexual, but always up- to -date with police and criminal gossip. Welsh had literally run into him when he was making his way down on the steps from the Perth Road to the Digital Media Park. They used to see each other in the west end , they didn't know what each of them did for a living until they saw each other at the High Court in Dundee, the QC was defending, Welsh was the prosecutions' most important witness. The QC tried various legitimate if amoral tactics to cast doubt on the probity of his evidence. Welsh had been there and seen that movie before.

After the trial, the QC came up and congratulated him on his evidence and the way he had deflected flawed points of Law to the presiding Lordship, the QC was rebuked for straying out of legitimate cross-examination. Welsh's' hostility was diminished by the frank and concise congratulations and apology; it was all in the game. Rumours circulated in the legal world that he had married late into his forties, it was a marriage of convenience, for both parties. His wife was content with the lifestyle that her husband's career brought; status and money. He was ecstatic he had acquired the final piece of the jigsaw; a wife, this would bring stability and scotch the rumours that he batted for the other side, he was convinced this kept him from reaching a higher station in the legal world. Welsh had heard this assessment in the courts and bars in Dundee. He was open-minded, and could not have cared less; he remembers the searing gossip used to be aimed at Roman Catholics in the nineteen-seventies, so his father, a policeman at the time told him. Catholics would be allowed to join the police but in miniscule numbers, and they would always stay as constables, times had moved on for them, now gays were the victims of discrimination. Did he trust the QC? Not a millimeter.

He was a member of a flying club and had invited Welsh to a flight over Dundee; he accepted this unusual but kind offer. When they were up in the air, the QC asked him if he could speak to him off-the- record. Welsh acquiesced to this request, he was working on a case that was slowly grinding to a halt, and he was hoping the QC would supply the answer why raids were being compromised. It was nothing to do with his surveillance team; it was of a personal nature. A career criminal and one of the toughest in Dundee, was trying to blackmail him with rent-boys. He told him of his marriage, he didn't indulge in the company of rent-boys. He gave the criminal's name to Welsh. Welsh told him not to worry he would look into it discreetly. Welsh was not sure if he was being recorded. The criminal, who drank in a city-centre bar from twelve to four then always took a taxi home. The taxi arrived promptly at four, he said his goodbye's to his fawning cronies and into the taxi, he was mortified when he discovered the taxi-driver was Welsh, who told him to lay- off the QC or *his* house would be raided and his computer taken away and examined, child pornography would be found. The criminal laughed.

'My solicitor would have you up in court, before you could say, 'Dundee's police are corrupt, so it might work with the young lads but it doesn't work with me, but anyway thanks for the free taxi ride that saves me twelve pound.'

'Monty, Monty, you don't really understand what I'm saying so I'll explain it once, then you can go to your solicitor and he'll explain it to you again.

When you get home check your emails, one will be confirmation of your credit card details, and then check your online bank statements your debit card shows that you have been paying for child porn direct to your computer. Now how would that look, when its emblazoned over the Evening Chronicle think of what your lovely third wife would have to say, and not forgetting your lovely children, think of the abuse they would have to endure at their school, and their friends would stop coming over to your big house for sleepovers.'

Diffidence had edged out confidence.

'Tell your friend, everything's cool...'

'No, everything's not cool, you try anything like that again, and you'll disappear, your friend protecting you is no longer here, I'm your new best friend now. You realise that there will be an administration fee for this news Monty, and because of the vagaries of our relationship and the eroding power of inflation, your unsolicited payments to me have to be adjusted...'

'What the fuck does that mean in English?'

'What did you pay Feeney?'

'Ten grand a month, no more no less.'

'That's just a tad parsimonious.'

'What the fuck does that mean?'

'Twenty grand a month is the new figure, and if there is any slight deviation or limp excuses, you will disappear; now do you understand me and more importantly do you believe me?'

'I understand, and I believe, why wouldn't I? You killed Feeney and his friend in that chapel.'

'I'm glad you have thought about that, you will be killed in Martini time.'

'What does that mean...Martini time?'

'It means anytime, anywhere, but it won't be clean and quick like Feeney, your death will be slow and lingering and I will take enormous pleasure in watching you beg for a bullet in the head. I know everything about you Monty; you're not a model citizen.' He glanced in the mirror and watched him move slightly in the back seat. There was no response. He had struck a nerve and the nerve made him release information. He assumed he had murdered Feeney and the Head of a Social Work Department, But Monty had said *his friend*. He would look into this with vigour.

'This is your stop Monty, nice house. In your youth you used to break into houses like this, funny how someone's life can change or end, dramatically.'

***

The QC met him at seven pm at Magdalene Green, he told Welsh that the criminal had contacted him and said he wouldn't hear from him again. But one thing hovered in his mind; the criminal didn't say what he wanted from him. Welsh told him to remove all theories from his mind, it didn't matter. They ran up as far as the technology park in silence, then retraced their steps and then ran to the City Quay and back to Magdalene Green, the QC apologised for being less communicative than normal, he just felt relieved. Welsh patted him on the back and left with silence between them and jogged the short-distance to his house. Monty had really surprised him, for him to know Feeney was unlikely, but for Feeney to be on his pay-roll, that was in the epicentre of fantasy. Monty had become complacent, being protected by Feeney had made him think he had become invincible. He went to the same garage, Indian restaurant and small corner shop as Welsh.

Welsh was friendly with one of the owners, who was copying credit card details and selling them on to a third -party who used them to commit fraud on the Internet. Welsh had found this out, he advised him to get rid of the cloned credit card reader, but first he asked for Monty and other criminals' credit cards and debit cards details. Monty was part of the cartel of the drug trade in

Dundee, free-market policies on competition were not in place. Prices would rise and fall just like any other commodity. Feeney would have been the cartel's early warning system, who was under surveillance? When and where would the next high profile raid? Going by Monty's face the cartel would be extremely worried now that they were operating under a new regime that was headed by Welsh.

Tonight he would study the notebook more closely; there were clues in the notebook about the identities of CI's. He hadn't managed to break the code, how would he able to separate who the CI's were from the dealers? He couldn't go to anyone else, word would spread that he had Feeney's notebook, and he was in no doubt that his future in the drug squad would be curtailed if he was fortunate, the other more likely scenario would be an unfortunate accident which would see him retired prematurely from life

. The QC was the spark he needed. A drug dealer was trying to blackmail him for a reason unbeknown to him and the QC, he knew Feeney was corrupt, if Monty could attempt to blackmail a QC, Feeney must have approved of it, why? He was killing two rats with one stone, Monty's fear turned into paranoia, because he had told him about his credit card being used to purchase vile child pornography, had Feeney tipped off Monty that he had suspected he had rumbled him? Monty assumed he had killed Feeney and *his friend.* He didn't try to dissuade him. The QC had not been frank, he had something that he needed to hide, Monty knew his secret; rent boys.

***

This was her first night; she had the body language of a school-girl on her first date.
Dundee Contemporary Art Centre on a Saturday night was bustling with students and the more refined citizens

111

of Dundee. McAveety walked in, she hoped he wouldn't see her, she had declined his invitation to join him her at the DCA. Things were looking up for McAveety she thought to herself, the woman who had her arm interlocked with his was in her early fifties, the downside of him going for a younger model was that she wouldn't have a free bus-pass. The price of love. She needn't have concerned herself, he and his companion made straight for the bar, they were loud, the patrons at the bar parted like the Red Sea to allow them access to the bar.

Her wine glass remained untouched she was normally a continental beer drinker, but she had to revert to type. The nervous looking stranger approached the table and smiled. He was in his forties, and of middle-eastern appearance. She had her ears open to his conversation and one eye on McAveety and company, who had been served and was looking for a table, her fear was realised; she had been spotted, they were making their way over to her table. Before they arrived she thought quickly of an exit policy.

'It's quite hot in here isn't it?' The gentleman in him agreed.

'We can go someplace less humid if you like?' She stood up immediately.

'That would be nice, are you hungry?'

'If you wish to eat now, I'm ravenous.' She walked from the table, McAveety was three metres away.

'Don't leave...have you met Anne before, and who is this?' His jealous eyes stared at her companion.
'Got to go, I'll speak to you later, nice to have met you Anne, no doubt we'll meet again. Anne was indifferent she was glad they now had a table.

'Oh, alright, mind and enjoy yourself.'
Jane explained before she was asked. 'That was an old friend of mine, an ex-colleague, he was released from his contract, to let him take time off to come to terms with

his illness; he's an alcoholic, so sad really, but as his sponsor I don't like to cast judgement.'

'I totally understand.'

'Would you like to go to the new casino?'

His eyes flashed with excitement.

'Yes I would like that very much, but I thought you said you were hungry?'

'That's okay, I can eat later, I can order dinner and have it sent to the apartment in the casino, where we can relax.' He smiled at that, there wouldn't be much relaxing tonight. He had paid nine hundred pounds plus vat for the services of the escort girl. He had been overseeing advances in the treatment of certain cancers in the research facilities at the Smith Kline building at Dundee University. His time in Dundee had come to an exhausting but fruitful end. Or so he had hoped.

***

The private clinic for the treatment of individuals who were dependent on drugs or alcohol had managed to convince the Charity Commission that this was a positive move. If they treated any of the thousands of individuals who were now dependent on heroin, they would need to build a large extension to cope with the mountainous waiting-list. The NHS in Tayside was bursting at the seams, the NHS could no longer treat drug dependency; independent facilities would have to be considered. In other words the addict on benefit would be treated the same as an erstwhile rock star; in a private clinic.

Feeney didn't own paper shares, he had owned a third of the clinic as had the social worker, fortunately for the remaining living partner he now was the sole owner. He had been advised to have a board of directors who had hands- on approach and an input into the Company. They were hand-picked by the social worker, they had the correct public image, they were relaxed when being interviewed and treated the television camera as a confidential friend. But their biggest asset was they could understand or read a balance sheet, all the social worker needed was their signatures on accounts. Changing from the private clinic to a charity gave it a more tax advantageous position. There would be a professional media campaign raising awareness of the charity and raising funds from wealthy individuals and public subscriptions; mainly street collections. It also helped that in senior management it was beneficial for the NHS to out -source their clients on the waiting list to the clinic that was now operating under the charity umbrella. It was more cost-effective to out-source drug - dependents than treat them within the NHS. He was more likely to accrue a healthy financial bonus. The clinic was in a win-win situation.

An avalanche of money came in from the NHS but when the accounts were published the clinic would make a small operating profit on paper. However, the reality of the situation was completely different; it had made millions in its first year as a charity. It had masked this by inflating 'costs and services' and staff costs and pensions. The employees' pension contributions from the charity didn't match the figures on the balance sheet. Not one of the young employees' challenged this black and white discrepancy.

The social worker had chosen his young but arithmetically challenged staff with the precision of a surgeon; they had too much goodness in their hearts. One person was now the sole beneficiary because of the untimely deaths of Feeney and the social worker, their shares would now pour into his overseas Bank account. All this person had to do was make sure he picked someone who would be the new Chief Executive Officer, he or she had to have impressive academic qualifications and had to be educated up to degree level, had experience in the charity and private sector with excellent references. One other quality they had to possess; gullibility

***

He was drifting in and out of his slumber, the loud sharp raps on the door made him bolt upright. He rose slowly from the sofa; he had only been snoozing for thirty minutes. The raps continued on the heavy door. He reached for the water that lay at the side of the sofa; he took generous amounts of the water, which made his senses become clearer, still the noise on the door continued. He walked to the door and looked at the security monitor; it was the Daves. He opened the door, they walked brusquely passed him.

'Come in lads…'

'Shut the door…this is important.' Eddings recognised the steeliness in his voice, he closed the door and joined at the table, his friend went into the kitchen and brought through two beers and placed them on the table. Eddings took a quick swig from the bottle of water.

'Congratulations, Valentine, that's not just congratulations from the both of us but also from Mr Madni,' they raised their beers in his honour.

'How…what have I done?'

'You have identified the assassin who failed to murder Mr Madni, and here is the dossier you will personally hand to him in about forty-five minutes time, take a seat and I'll quickly give you a rundown of its contents.' He went on to explain that the failed assassination plot was committed by a Palestinian who had been paid by a rival of Mr Madni. 'The Palestinian had organised the Indian workers' on two of his projects to withdraw their labour. The UAE government does not allow trade unions. Mr Madni had had a temporary financial funding problem, the strike on the two luxury hotels had exacerbated his liquidity, and rumours were gathering pace amongst

115

other financial institutions that his bank was going to be calling in his loans, an amount in excess of one billion US dollars. Suppliers were refusing to deliver building materials, and workers had been told that their wages would be delayed; that was when our Palestinian friend arrived at the hotels with others. He spread panic and consternation and was heard to have told a small group of workers' that Mr Madni would not be troubling them anymore. If the assassination plot had been successful, a consortium of business rivals would have stepped in and taken over his business empire, at a much reduced cost leaving the banks with a heavy loss. However, in light of your experience as a detective, you have detained the Palestinian and you await Mr Madni's instructions in what to do with him. That's when we voice our opinion; we recommend that he is deported, no fuss, no publicity and Mr Madni continues to expand his businesses, mainly construction and leisure. Have you got all that Val?'

Eddings was looking unsure of himself, he didn't know how to answer he had many questions to ask.

'Yes, I hear what you're saying but I don't understand, what's going on? '

'Absolutely nothing to worry about, it's just politics Arab style.'

'Who's this Palestinian and did he attempt to kill Madni?'

'You're learning fast, the person who attempted to assassinate Mr Madni is talking to you now…it was us.'

Eddings leapt from the sofa. 'What!'

'Take it easy, no one is going to get hurt, we're just going to be wealthy, and that includes you.'

'He's correct in what he's saying, it was us, or me who organised the plot, everyone benefit's, Dave, myself, you and Mr Madni.'

Eddings was calm now, nothing would be clear if he raised the temperature of the discussion it would end up in a heated argument. 'Could someone explain what is happening here?'

'Madni was going to get rid of us…'

'…kill you!'

'No, no, the American advised him that we were leaking his movements to his rivals, and he told Madni that he suspected we were involved in industrial espionage against him, leaking information to his business rivals. We have been exemplary employees for the last five years, and we have been paid well, this has been our garden of Eden, our American friend wanted us out so he can bring in an ex-army colleague to re-evaluate his security, which would have been more expensive. So we decided to show Mr Madni our true worth to him. The driver was in cahoots with our American friend, so he became collateral damage. As you can imagine Mr Madni was alarmed at the attempt on his life, so we suggested an expert who worked alone and was experienced in industrial espionage. You. So now Mr Madni really appreciates our personal security skills, and our American friend is no longer with us ditto the driver.'

'What about this Palestinian guy who doesn't have a name?'

'We told a wee white lie, he had nothing to do with the assassination attempt as I have told you, but he tried to organise strikes and he was working for Mr Madni's business rivals, he was going to be deported anyway, so we just brought him into the assassination plot.'

Eddings is laughing. 'I just can't believe what I'm hearing; you have used me and the Palestinian as pawns…'

The Daves looked at each another and raised their bottles to one another.

'I can't argue with that Val, but you're out of Dundee and over here getting well-paid, and meeting interesting people…like Morag.'

'Here he comes now, perfect.' He walks from the house, carrying an armful of books; they watch him disappear from view from the cul-de-sac towards the Perth Road. He starts the van's engine with a smile on his face. 'Another day another hundred grand,' the van inches towards the detached villa then does a u turn so the van's door is close to the garage door.

'Are you sure no one else is in the property?'

'Now, now, I used to be a detective, remember? I've watched our friend for the last three weeks, he is a full-time student at the university, and he has the perfect cover.'

'Okay…normally they have someone who stays in the property all day, known as the gardener, that's what I was meaning…any dogs?'

'Four bull- terriers.' Lenny looks alarmed.

'I'm only kidding, follow me.' They leave the van and GG takes the key out of his overall pocket, he place's it into the garage lock, then pulls the up and over door open.

Lenny pushes up the rear door of the Luton van. They surreptitiously walk into the garage, which is empty, apart from one bicycle which has a flat tyre.

'I hope that's not his getaway vehicle!' Lenny laughed at this the tension subsides. GG opens the connecting door to the garage. 'Whoa! Do you feel the heat? God it's like a furnace,' they walk to the source of the heat.

GG stops Lenny; he then pulls out a pistol from his overall pocket. Lenny looks horrified. He beckons Lenny forward and whispers in his ear, 'just insurance.'

He turns the handle slowly and edges the door open, the intense heat rushes out, he finally pushes the door wide open his eyes grow wider. 'Jackpot!'

Lenny moves inside the large room and is amazed at the volume of plants, which are intertwined with electrical wires and water hoses.

'Do you think we'll get them all in the van?'

'We have to, start taking them onto the van, I'll have a look about, c'mon what are you waiting on, they won't eat you.'

'The electric wires don't look safe, could you shut off the power, and I'll be able to move quicker.'

'They have by-passed the meter, even if I shut-off the power, the wires will still be live, just take your time and try not to touch them, I'm away to see if there are any other plants in other rooms.'

Lenny overcomes his fear by thinking about the money; he goes about his task with gusto. GG searches the other rooms they're devoid of plants, the front of the house looks non-descript, nothing would suggest that this was a cannabis farm. The windows were not covered with curtains and there was no silver insulation material unlike the back of the house; which had blackout curtains fitted and were lined with insulation, the heat from the lamps would not escape from that room. He wandered into the bedroom where the student slept. It would be more productive if he came across personal effects. In the sturdy free-standing wardrobe were an assortment of clothes, jackets, shirts and heavy jumpers. On the top shelf were different sizes of boxes, he took one down at a time and looked through the contents, paperwork in mandarin, he repeated the procedure, the other boxes contained paperwork, all in mandarin. He placed the last box exactly as he found it, he opened the old -fashioned drawers; his eyes were envious. An array of mobile phones still intact in their boxes stared back at him, he counted them; seven in total. One for every day of the week? He rubbed his hand along the underside of the chest of drawers; he felt something, something made of paper. He took out the heavy drawer and crouched down to see what his fingers had touched, it was a small white envelope that usually was sent with flowers, he stepped back his instinct called on him to remove the envelope and examine the contents. He moved forward examining it like an unexploded bomb that could be booby-trapped

Fingers were placed carefully into the envelope, removing the contents; a plastic blank card with an electronic strip and a ten pound note. He placed them into his pocket. Excitement aborted the search, he had found what he was looking for, but didn't know why the card and money were significant. Looking around the room, everything looked as he had entered it. Joyful noise could be heard coming from downstairs; he made his way carefully down the creaking stairs. Lenny had removed more plants than he had imagined, he was puzzled at his productivity , the puzzlement didn't last long, in came Lenny dragging a trundling trolley behind him, similar to the one's which are used in warehouses.

'Seek and ye shall find,' commented Lenny as he was loading the plants onto the trolley.

'Where did you find that?'

Lenny nodded over to the cupboard in the far corner of the room.

'Makes the job a lot more easier...grab some of the plants and we'll out of here a lot sooner.'

'How many plants are there?'

Lenny stopped loading the trolley. 'Exactly five hundred, but I suppose you knew that...c'mon load this up.'

'The information that was given to me was up to four hundred...today has been quite fortunate, more money Lenny, more money.'

'He stopped suddenly. How much more?'

'I wouldn't like to say...but we're talking thousands rather than hundreds, keep loading, and less talking.'

They are in the van, pleasure is radiating from them.

'We'll are you happy now Lenny?'

'It went a lot quicker and less stressful than I thought it

would go, how soon do we visit the next place?'

'As soon as we pick up the next van.'

'Which is where?'

'You'll see, just five minutes away, c'mon let's make it interesting, where do you think we're going?'

'We'll give me a minute and I'll work out the route,' he took a long drink of his water.

'Five minutes away, you say, we're heading up the Perth Road…Ninewells car- park?'

'Nope, try again.'

'I can't think, is it a car -park?'

'You're right about that it is a car-park.' The van deviates from the Perth Road moving towards Riverside Drive.'

'Tesco's?' GG nods his head in agreement.

'Will your friend be there and do we hand over the van?'

'No…we leave the van and pick up another van, then repeat it one more time, the last van will be bigger because of the place in Fife, we leave that van over in Tayport, that's where a car is waiting for us. Three hours and we'll be done.'

'When do you expect to get the money?'

'A week's time, no more than a week…and don't worry, I can trust him, he came up with the money the last time…no problem.'

'Stop talking for a minute I see the van, over there to the left of the store, do you see it?'

'I see it Lenny, I see it,' he parked the van next to the stationary van. They left the van, Lenny moves towards the van. 'Keep on walking towards the store; we're going for a coffee.' 'Is that really necessary?'

'A coffee and a bacon roll will boost your energy levels.' He can see Lenny is not in total agreement with this instruction not suggestion, but when he sits down and bites into the roll, his opposition recedes. 'They are still clueless about Feeney being bumped off, loads of mad, mad theories.'

'But that's their problem we have to concentrate today on our removal business, are you finished with that roll or are you admiring it?' Lenny takes this as a rebuke, and finishes his roll. They walk out of the store; Lenny stops. 'Our van is gone!'

GG stops and places his reassuring hand on his shoulders and smiles. 'Professionals'

CHAPTER TWO

The area of the Overgate Centre was cordoned off; policemen were being verbally abused by irate shoppers who wished to spend -a -penny. Inside the cubicle they refused to respond to the officers' request to come out. Eventually, he spoke then passed a business card out from below the cubicle. The Vice-Squad officer handed it to his commanding officer; the officer took it reluctantly and cursed under his breath. He instructed the officer to call the number, the call was answered immediately. The officer identified himself and told him of the predicament his client was in, the phone was passed under the cubicle to the client, then passed back to the officer, he was told his client would not be coming out of the cubicle until he arrived. Twenty minutes later he arrived, he asked who was in charge, the commanding officer anticipated this was the start of the legal semantics. The solicitor spoke to him and asked why his client was being harassed, he requested that his client would be released into his custody, any request for his client to be formally interviewed would be considered. He wanted the cordon removed and the policemen deployed somewhere where their presence would be appreciated by the taxpayers. He was further advised that a formal complaint would be raised against the person in charge of this operation.

The commanding officer knew he was being systematically undermined, but he insisted, 'his client and his friend would be interviewed at Bell Street, if he was far from happy about this he can add this to his complaint, now tell your client to come out or I will have the cubicle door removed, you have five seconds.' The solicitor knew he wasn't grandstanding, he told his client to come out...they were all going to Bell Street. The commanding officer told his officer to remove the blue and white tape that cordoned off the entrance to the toilets. Seconds later the public rushed in some with screaming toddlers who were desperate to empty their bladders. The solicitor walked out with his client and his friend, the public in the toilet took not a blind bit of notice; they had more pressing matters on their minds.

The commanding officer took the lead once they were outside in the car-park, he watched the solicitor place his client and his friend in the back of his spacious car, he walked over to the grim-faced solicitor. 'Sorry to disturb your Saturday, but I have to be seen to be backing my men...I didn't know anything of this operation, that's what worries me, do you think you can extricate him out of this?'

'Who made the complaint...was it a member of the public?'

'Not as far as I'm aware, no member of the public made a complaint; it was an intelligence led operation.'

'Good, you'd better get back to your men; this will be a short and not so sweet interview.'

At Bell Street the solicitor asked for a room so he can speak to his client alone. This request was granted. He spoke to the client and his *friend* he told them he had heard enough. He went out of the room and asked to speak to the officer who lead the operation, and advised that the commanding officer be present also. The three of them went into a room. He spoke to the officer and asked him had there being a complaint from a member of the public? The officer told him no complaint had been made.

'Was there a surveillance camera in the cubicle?'

'No,' the officer replied.

'Then why was my client being harassed in a public toilet then?'

'Because he was behaving in a libidinous manner with a youth.

Who was known to frequent public conveniences looking for clients, what other reason would two males one a male prostitute be in a cubicle together?'

'There could be a plethora of legitimate reasons…have you any evidence that my client was committing an illegal act?'

'No…but I…'

He stood up and placed the notebook back in his case.

'I have heard enough, please release my client and his friend, there has been no complaint; and no offence has been committed.'

'I don't agree with that, I will be charging him with gross indecency.'

'I request both of them be released, I would think very carefully of what you have said, you can charge him if you wish, but the Procurator Fiscals office will not proceed. It could be argued that you have a vendetta against my client, which could lead to you being sued in the civil court; defending civil actions are very expensive to defend. That's an ex-gratia piece of advice. Now if you don't mind I request the release of my client and his companion…please.'

The officer looked at his commanding officer for support, his face reflected non-committal.

'Give me a minute, I wish to speak to my commanding officer, we'll be back in a minute.'

'Okay,' he looks at his watch, showing restrained impatience. They leave the interview room and go into the corridor. He slumps against the wall.

'I've made an arse of it, haven't I?'

'Why didn't you fucking tell me? Why didn't you crash in the door when they were at it, instead of shouting at them through a locked door?'

'I know, I know…they'll have to walk now won't they…when I saw that card with Patrick Connelly's name on it my heart sank. I'll release them, I have no other choice, I can't even fucking caution them.'

***

The flight was on time, the four guests should be through customs by six pm. They had all been selected after a thorough background check by the security consultant who had a contact in GCHQ. They had similar personal tastes and personal wealth. An MPV waited on them exiting from the airport, the driver tried to guess who the four passengers were, they had been given the car's registration, they didn't know that on the small plane from London City Airport there were other compatible individuals who craved excitement in their mundane lives. They were wealthy, some were married others were not. One partner in the marriage could have been unaware that their better half had a different secretive side to their nature. They were all professionals, wealthy and had their own companies, mostly in the financial sector.

Twenty individuals would be meeting for the first time at the Club. Four of them would come face- to- face when they completed the short walk from the airport to the waiting car. The driver had successfully picked out two of them; the men. He was instructed not to initiate any conversation, if the guests spoke to him he would reply, but not in a verbose manner. The two men obviously liked what they saw; the two women were in their early thirties, tall and slender, wearing fashionable apparel. The women entered the vehicle first, their perfume subtlety replacing the beeswax aroma that filled the vehicle. The women were first to introduce themselves, soon they were all laughing and joking, anyone would have thought they had been friends for years. They never went beyond asking the driver how far the Club was.

The car drove down the narrow lane and came to a halt outside the newly-installed gate. Each of them followed the instructions literally. They placed their card in the unobtrusive slot, the blinking green light became steady, the gate silently opened slightly, then closed after five seconds. The other three waited patiently and repeated the same procedure. This was a deliberate policy; anyone who flaunted the instructions would have had their membership rescinded after their weekend at the Club. No reason would be given. No correspondence would be entered into. They walked up the tree-lined path that straddled the driveway that ran at right angles adjacent to the wide cobbled path.

  The house came into view it looked like any other stone built house that looked over Magdalene Green, inside however was a totally different scene that would separate it from the other houses. The subtle CCTV equipment which were located in various trees and in the nooks of the tall stone wall; monitored every step. When they reached the door they repeated the procedure that they did at the gate. One card in one person in. They may have not been virtuous in their personal lives but they were virtuous in their patience. They heard the chatter and laughing of the other members that emanated from a room at the end of the hall, beyond the staircase. A waiter in full uniform smiled as he invited them to take their pre-ordered drinks from the tray. These four didn't do diffidence; they were on this earth for a good time, not a long time. Drinks in their hands, they strode along the long hall eager to meet their fellow members. They wondered where they would end up in the house and who with. The hostess met them as they came through the heavy mahogany door. Her smile was welcoming and natural. She effortlessly guided them to meet other members then she left them to interact. Ten minutes later she climbed the colossus of a staircase and inspected all the bedrooms. Their small cases were placed on the high backed chairs that were in every room. She returned to the ground floor and went into the room which was directly opposite the staircase. This room was the gaming room; the room had been modelled on the gentleman's club in Mayfair. She went round each of the croupiers and spoke to them this would be a defining moment in their lives, each of the croupiers had been sub-contracted from another gambling operation in the Home Counties; they had flown into Edinburgh Airport and had been driven to the house in Dundee. They would be only here for tonight's gambling then flown home from Edinburgh. They were all consummate professionals; no mixing with guests, no personal meetings with them for any reason or the mortal sin; romantic liaisons. Any incentives offered from members had to be reported immediately. When the member was at home they would be informed that their membership was now at an end.

Once satisfied she made her way to the discreet bathrooms. Everything was in order, in the small soap dish were cocaine and a nasal implement, she glanced at herself in the mirror she suited her hair up with the blonde highlights shining through.

This was her last chance mixing with the real beautiful people; if the takings from the gambling didn't meet the expectation she would be out on her well -rounded derriere.

Failure drove her to be successful, she had failed at almost everything else that she had attempted in her adult life, but it wasn't for trying, oh she longed to get away from her hum-drum life. However, fate had given her a second chance of achieving her dreams. She didn't apply for the job, she had been on a job interview but at the time she hadn't realise that;, she thought she was street-wise and savvy, in this world that she was operating she was just a naïve school girl. She thought she was in control of events, now her face flushed with embarrassment; events were in charge of her.

Luck had been an unused substitute in this game.

She had been identified, nurtured then snared, not enticed. She had been a willing victim walking into this world with all her wits about her, she could have turned around and declined, but that was not an option, she could climb higher in this world than in her parallel monotonous job. For that's what her career was just another job, some perks like other professions, but not as glamorous as the public thought. She was just an ordinary police officer with the same everyday worries in addition to her perilous financial predicament. She promised herself, she would do *anything* to escape from her financial prison.

***

Patrick Connelly took the client back to his house, the young man was not offered the same invitation; he was left in the Bell Street car park. Pat only offered him one salutary piece of advice; remove yourself from Dundee immediately. The journey from Bell Street was short and uneventful, the client had been previously walking on thin ice, for some unknown reason he chose to ignore this. Why? He had moved from the west of Scotland to the more sedate if not boring City of Dundee. His wife and children were reluctant to follow him through to 'Scumdee' as his daughter called it. Though he had never lived in Dundee, he robustly put up a good defence; the west of Scotland was hardly a place where individuals could walk in the streets or city centre, without the fear or violence, rape, murder, or the festering sore of sectarianism. Dundee seemed poetically idyllic.

However, in Dundee, his old demons resurfaced, he went kerb crawling, the seamier the pick-up, the more sexually gratified he felt. He was an accomplished academic with more letters after him than junk mail. In Pat's house he seemed to go to pieces; he was having great difficulty being coherent. After a whisky he became more lucid, he was being blackmailed, by a criminal called Monty. Monty had used young men as bait and he took it. He was on the Legal Aid board, it

129

was on his instruction if payments were agreed to or modified. Fictitious payments were being honoured on his say so. Now they were becoming bolder and frequent, eyebrows were being raised at three solicitors' practices in Dundee. He arranged a hastily meeting with Monty, and told him the game was up; no more payments would be authorised, this bank had run out of cash. Blackmailing didn't make him fearful anymore; if Monty wanted to expose him to the Sunday papers go ahead, anymore inflated invoices and he would personally go to the police himself, and he would mention Monty as the blackmailer. Monty's reaction was swift; he beat him black and blue. Still the victim failed to concede to Monty; he was secretly hoping he would be beaten to death, his life was in turmoil; he just didn't care anymore. Pat told him to take gardening leave for at least three months, go somewhere that you have always wanted to go to, and enjoy and think about life, when he came back life would be back to normal; Monty would see the error of his ways. But he added a caveat; the secret life was over, pipe and slippers and fireside chats would be in vogue, did he concur with this?' He agreed emphatically.

'But what about Monty, will he give up so easily?'

'Without difficulty...now what would you like to drink, Bernard?'

Pat poured him his drink, he joined him, he never condemned him outright, he just pointed out that the life he was leading would lead to the break-up of his marriage and his children would disown him. Pat listened to Bernard chastening himself. Pat topped up his drink and listened to the heartache. Two hours later, Bernard was leaving in a taxi from Pat's house. Pat closed the door with a triumphant smile; he thought he knew everything that went on in Dundee.

The more illegal the more his ears were finely tuned.

The three solicitors' practices strong-arming Bernard seemed illogical. However, he heard it with his own ears, he subtly managed to elicit information that Bernard had told no-one else about the solicitors inflated bills, probably for fictitious clients. And the bona-fide clients' invoices would follow the same path. He never asked how long this had been going on for, but he would find out. He used to have a barrow-load of respect for Monty, that was until he found out that he was a criminal informant, that was in vogue in Dundee at the moment, the more handier with their fists, the more likelier they were loose with their tongues in Bell Street, unscientific, but true all the same. If he was blackmailing Bernard, how many others is he blackmailing? He went up to his bedroom on the top floor of the house, he was smiling, he could be lucky, it was a clear day, he went to the wardrobe and felt the top shelf, after what seemed an eternity his fingers located them. He walked to the large bay-window and placed the binoculars sharply to his eyes, he focused them over to Fife, to Wormit, near the top of the hill. The scaffolding was being dismantled, yes, he's there. He watched him fumbling into his overalls. The speaker -phone dialling tone filled the room he didn't wait for the introductory hello.

'You'll do yourself an injury running about with that wheelbarrow.

'Who is this?'

'It's Patrick; I see you're enjoying your Saturday afternoon.

'Pat…what's with the Glasgow accent, how are you… are you looking at me?'

'I am that, and it's an impressive sight, I hope you're not renovating that impressive house on hard- pressed council payers' time,' he laughed.

He sat in the wheelbarrow and waved.

'Something up Pat?'

'On a scale of one to ten…its maximum, what time are

you going to be finished today?'

'Let's see, it depends how interesting the tale is, is it interesting?'

'Unbelievable, I'm still coming to terms with this I've heard some stories in my lifetime, but this one is so outrageous it must be true, that's why I'm calling you, could you drop by as soon as?'

He watched him unseat himself from the wheelbarrow and stand upright then give him the thumbs up. 'No problem Pat, I'll see you about say...six...is that okay?'

'That's perfect, I promise, you'll find it interesting, see you at six.'

Pat observes him wave goodbye.

Paul Welsh would hardly believe that his nemesis, Monty was at the eye of this storm. Welsh arrived at Pat's house, ten minutes late. He guided him into the drawing -room.

'I know I've said it before Pat, but you can't hide money, where's the lovely Mrs Connelly?'

'She and her well-to do friends are at The Rep, I'm not complaining, sometimes being on my own helps me think, I can sit and look at that view all day, now what can I offer you to drink?'

'A beer Pat, I left the car, took the bus over, it's only a short walk, to your house.'

He returns with his beer, they both settle down at the table set beside the window.

'I see what you mean about the view...now what's on your mind?'

Pat told him the sordid tale of his colleague who is on the periphery of legal circles, he didn't want to name him to avoid embarrassment, he told him that Monty had set him up with a rent-boy, this was no chance encounter.

Unfortunately, his colleague took a more romantic view...and the rest was history.

Welsh drunk the beer from the bottle and placed it on the

circular table He was clearly angry.

'Tell your friend not to worry, he won't hear from Monty any more, you have my word on that, I will be killing two birds with one stone...'

'...two birds with one stone?'

'I mean... I have wanted to sort him out myself, this will be the perfect opportunity, is your colleague shaken up?'

'He's alright now, I advised him to change his lifestyle, this time I think he will, well let's hope so.'

'Did he pay-up to Monty?'

Pat nodded. 'Through a third -party, so to speak, but I'm glad you will help. Paul, he was suicidal.'

'Why do they anal activist's take such chances...Saturday afternoon in the toilets in the Overgate, how risky is that...or is that part of it, the more public the more of a thrill they get?'

'I really don't know...another beer?'

'Yeah, that would be fine, don't worry about Monty, I'll see him next week, probably Tuesday, that's when he goes to the Counting House. I won't mention the incident, but he'll know who I am talking about.' Pat left the table, in a more relaxed frame of mind he had emancipated his friend from Monty, he could concentrate on the three solicitors' practices...something was seriously wrong there, had there been a new partner that had joined the practice? He returned with the cold beer. Welsh was standing at the window gazing across the Tay to Wormit

. 'I can't see my house from here Pat?'

***

'We're ahead of schedule Lenny, the nursery is on the next left, it's about a mile and a bit from the main road, I don't think we'll have any problem...why the long face?'

'What about members of the public, it's a lovely day,

some might be here.'

'No, no, no, this place is a commercial nursery; they grow plants for the garden centres and supermarkets, why do you think we are driving a bigger van with a Dutch name emblazoned across it?'

'Sorry, I'm just nervous, my mind is less worried now, how many staff is there?'

'Where we are going there shouldn't be anyone, the poly-tunnel is beyond the nursery, it's guarded at night but not during the day. If there is someone there, unlucky for them, they either cooperate or they stay quiet for good, I'm not fussed.'

They drive past the entrance of the nursery and follow the sign that directs commercial vehicles; they continue up the bumpy narrow road then take a right on to the dirt track.

'There it is Lenny, a nice pile of money waiting on us.'

He reverses the lorry on to the meadow, then continues towards the entrance to the closed poly-tunnel. No one is about; they both unzip the flap to the poly tunnel. Heat blasts them in the face, generators are running, water pipes are in a more orderly fashion than the house in the west end.

'You bring them to the front of the poly-tunnel and I'll place them onto the lift then pack them into the lorry, that's the quickest way to do it Lenny.'

They agree that this is the best and expedient method, an hour and half later they have completed the job.

'Easy money, easy money.' Lenny's stomach is gurgling with the amount of water that he has consumed.

'Ten minutes down the road and our job is done, now that wasn't so tough a morning was it?'

Lenny laughs. 'Now that's it's over, I can say it was easy, but I wasn't thinking that at the time, but I'm glad that it went without a hitch, you weren't worried were you?'

'Worried about what? I did my homework, fail to

prepare, prepare to fail is the old but true maxim, and I've got another wee surprise for you... don't ask.'

He drove in silence, smirking intermediately, Lenny was feeling nauseous, he tried to quell this by consuming even more water.

'There we are Lenny ship ahoy!'

In the lay-by is a Corsa, it's a hired car, they pull up behind it and leave the lorry, with the keys still in the ignition.

'Are you not going to turn off the engine?'

'Global warming is a myth,' he strolls towards the Corsa and feels under the arch for the magnetic box, he brings it out and takes the key from it, he clicks it, the doors and indicators respond.

'Homeward bound son, oh ... and feel under your seat.' The car moves off, Lenny pulls out a holdall and opens it, it's filled with banknotes.

'How much is in here,' he whispers, his voice barely audible. 'Exactly £200,000.'

***

The theatre diners had left their tables much to the delight of the regular patrons of The Social, the bar that lay at a juxtaposition to The Rep; which was playing to capacity audiences. Different strata's of society gathered to pay homage to nostalgia. The play Balgay Hill was met with universal approval, the play was set in Dundee in the nineteen eighties, the time when the enigmatic Billy McKenzie was in his pomp, then he descended into his nadir. He enjoyed the glamour chase seeking stardom, after he achieved it he was bored, but once he had reached the summit, it was far from glamorous. Everyone claimed to have a story about Billy McKenzie, Monty's was the most revealing, Monty was at the same school as Billy McKenzie, he tried to pick a fight with Billy, Monty's ended his story by saying Billy could turn from an effeminate Lionel Blair type into a Mike Tyson, unfortunately for Monty, Mike Tyson turned up when he tried to head butt him. Rumour had it that was why he turned up at The Rep; he wanted to see if this incident would be included in the performance. That was the only time he had been defeated in his violent life. He had waited on McKenzie after school; the pupils were impatient for a rematch at four pm. Monty had friends that would make sure that the rematch would end in his favour. The baying crowd waited in Graham Street, Monty had built himself into a frenzy state, he welcomed the crowd, McKenzie just strolled out from the school gates, and he was not alone.

Monty saw that behind him there were at least a dozen other pupils, that were not academically stars, but they were devoid of fear; they were the Kirkton crowd. One of them stopped McKenzie, and then walked over to Monty; they spoke for at least a minute while the bloodthirsty mob grew impatient for violence. Monty turned away and moved back to his six acolytes. One of them threw his denim jacket at him and they turned on their heel to a chorus of cat calls. Billy McKenzie, took a right turn and made his way home, the Kirkton boys took a left. The crowd groaned with disappointment.

Monty never forgot this encounter with the Kirkton boys; individually he could beat every one of them to pulp with one hand, but if he did this to one, he would be like a rabbit being ripped apart by a pack of ravenous wolves. They were loyal to one another. Nearly thirty years on Monty was the top dog in the city, he had beaten four of them since that hazy summer afternoon, not with his fists but with his wares. They had contracted HIV; they were junkies. He took great pleasure in hearing of their slow, painful and lingering deaths. Two of them were left, and much to his disgust they had beat the challenge of poverty and lack of educational qualifications. Both were now professionals, they had the trappings of a genteel middle-class

136

existence, one lived in the west end, the other in Broughty Ferry, they were also members of the sailing club. Nothing gave them more pleasure reminiscing about their childhoods in Kirkton. They were well-read now, and they traced their enthusiasm for reading to one teacher at St Michaels; Mr Lonie. He took one of them aside and told him that 'you were in this class not because your thick, it was because of your behaviour.' The other kept this information from his friend, who had been told the same; word for word. They both had a natural ability for writing essays and using words that were not in everyday usage. But like any other fourteen year olds they chose to discard this gift. They were the only ones who started work after leaving school, one a bricklayer the other worked in the Coca-Cola factory sardonically twenty- metres away from St Michaels. Bored watching thousands of bottles being filled up and whizzing past him, a thought came to him, life was the assembly line and it was whizzing past him. How Mr Lonie's words came back shouting at him as he tried to conjure up happiness in his uneventful life.

'At least I'm better off than most of my mates,' he heard himself talk out loud, no one could hear him above the din of machinery and the rattle of the bottles. It takes a lot for a youth to admit he set out on this journey of failure, he had made his bed, and he must undoubtedly lie in it. He lived for the weekend, even though he was sixteen he was tall for his age, he would go to the Copper Beech and the Claverhouse bars in Kirkton. However, once Monday morning came the melancholy engulfed him once more, he had been putting a brave face on his miserable existence, and he was hurting badly. Some of his pals were smoking hash, he declined, he didn't see the point of it. Now his moral compass was going askew, he might try it, what had he got to lose?

The alarm went off at 5 am he threw the blankets off;

the ice cold air that engulfed the room woke him up than any shrill alarm clock. He still felt seedy from the night at the Claverhouse, his friends seemed happy, they had no jobs, no prospects, but they were happier in spirit and had more money than him, how come? Sitting on the edge of his bed, he looked at the metal-framed window; moonlight was streaming into the room, through the frosted windows on the inside. He stumbled across and scraped the frost from the window, the street was white with snow, the wind was blowing the snow off the neighbours' hedge, he better wrap up well. His mind went into an unexpected elevation. The smile grew wider and wider, his music centre was sitting proudly, it had cost him over £200, that's what you're working for! How many of your mates have been struck dumb at being able to tape LP's while you can shout and sing along at the same time. Standing in a proud stack were his tapes next to the music centre; his mum had commented, 'you could have bought a car for less.'

She was right, 'but I'm only sixteen, which makes me illegal to drive mum.'
'And when did they lower the age from eighteen to sixteen to drink in pubs?'

His mum was right, she was always right. He started to shiver; he grabbed his Levi's from the back of the chair. He pulled them on, he was still unsteady on his feet.

Last night was a good night. He looked around for his shirt it was on the 'horizontal wardrobe,' as his dad called it; the carpet. He grabbed it and opened the drawer and pulled out socks, he crept out on tip-toes to the bathroom. The icy blast made him nostalgic for his warm bed; the cold water in the sink revived him as he quickly splashed the water about his face. He could still smell the Denim aftershave, it didn't work as advertised on television he came home alone. He quickly dried himself then descended the stairs into the kitchen, the temperature was warmer; it was marginally above freezing point. He took the matches and lit the temperamental old fashioned oven, the heat was welcoming he would wait till the back of his legs were warm, then and only then would he switch the kettle on. It was five fifteen, he wasn't hungry, but he would need a cup of tea to warm himself up, before he faced the bitter and lonely trek over Caird Park golf course and the steep climb up Graham Street to the Coke factory, the thought of it was killing him, he had wanted to be a bricklayer like his mate with the Council, but his dad told him 'he had no chance, because they only employed sons of Freemasons,' everyone knew his dad was not a Freemason. How he wished his dad was a Freemason.

His legs had warmed up nicely, he had to walk across the kitchen in a curious manner, his jeans were so hot when they touched his legs they burnt him. He switched on the kettle, the back of his jeans were cooling down, he went into the larder and took out the tea caddy and the nearly empty milk bottle, he was feeling better now. He made the tea and pondered his future as he sipped the boiling tea he still had five minutes to spare, he crept into the hall trying not to disturb his parents and took the jacket off the peg it had Kestrel emblazoned across the back, he lifted his boots also from Kestrel, he had been giving the jacket and boots from one of the older men that drank in the Claverhouse. He took the boots and jacket into the warmth of the kitchen, his breath showing up in the freezing hallway, and placed the jacket across the open oven door to capture some heat. How he wished he worked at Kestrel, they were the aristocrats of the Dundee workforce, great wages and great working conditions, he hinted to the man that gave him the jacket and boots that he was willing to do anything to get a job in the Kestrel. He was told he was too young, when he was eighteen in fourteen months' time he would get him a job; guaranteed. The only condition was he kept his job in the Coke factory meantime. The shop steward was worried if he gave up the job he might succumb to the allure of drugs that were now becoming prevalent in Kirkton. That's what kept him going, the thought of Kestrel, and double the money that he was presently earning. The shop steward when he met him always asked him if he was still working, he told him that he'd something about him; he would go far in life. Oh how he wished he was right. But he was far from being convinced.

How many times in the prevailing years had he churned over those prophetic words? He had lost count, the shop steward was true to his word, he met him in the Claverhouse when he was celebrating his eighteenth birthday, an anti-climax; he had been a regular for 2 years, he came over to him bought him a drink and told him he was starting at Kestrel when he worked out his notice at the Coke factory. He was dumbstruck and feigned he needed the toilet as he had just downed a full pint of Tartan Special, he went into the deserted toilet, straight into the cubicle, and burst out crying, tears of frustration and utter relief. He heard someone come into the toilet, he grabbed the toilet paper and wiped the tears running down his face, he could taste some of the salty tears that found their way to his mouth.

'Are you alright in there?' his friend shouted.
'I'm fine…I just downed that pint too quick that's all.'

That was over thirty years ago, and going back to that moment he could trace his path to riches. Now he was in The Social enjoying a meal with his wife, he was looking all around him he felt comfortable with the middle- classes, it was some friends from his schooldays that couldn't come to terms with his standing in life now. They talked the talk but didn't put their hiking boots on to walk the walk. His dad told him, 'not to worry, they were jealous and he was proud, now get me a half pint and a nip.'

Would Balgay Hill (the play at The Rep) be the sandpaper that rubbed the misery of the Coke factory from his thirst of nostalgia from the nineteen seventies and eighties? His wife was at the bar, he was in a reflective mood he thanked Danny the shop steward silently for being true to his word, he progressed, after six-months labouring which he loved, he got him started as an apprentice welder he took to it like a duck to water, 'thanks Danny,' he whispered, his eyes were becoming misty.

'Fancy meeting you here Ronnie or is it Ronald now, are you going to see the play then?'

He did not try to disguise his contempt for him.

'Are you on leave from Perth prison then arsehole, or is it anal retentive now?

Are you going to see Balgay Hill?, That'll bring back memories, I wonder if they'll show Billy McKenzie knocking the shit out of you, what do you think…arsehole?'

'Millionaire or not you're still a Kirkton gadgie…enjoy your night you never know how many you have left do you?'

'I see you still need your male fiends Monty, still scared eh?'

'Your wife's coming over, we'll probably meet again,' he raised his glass to him and walked over to the other side of the bar.

She looked ill at ease. 'Who was that?'

'Someone who is scared of the past, I was at the same school as him, he's not changed.'

'You don't seem to like him; surely he doesn't bear a grudge from your school days?'

'He's alright; I was just noising him up that's all.'

***

He struggled on the wonky step-ladders, but he refused to toss them into the skip that lay adjacent to the driveway on his completed refurbished home. Eventually, he placed the angel at the pinnacle of the Christmas tree. Gingerly, he reversed down the step-ladders, keen to view his handiwork from the opposite end of the lounge. He switched off the table lamps; the flickering tree lights were mesmerizing. However, the flickering lights over in Dundee were running them close. It was Friday, his wife was in Dundee on her Christmas night out, he was on holiday for the next three weeks but he was on call if needed.

Drug busts were being reported in the newspapers more often, his face was being recognised out on the streets of Dundee, due to his prolific appearances on the television news after each successful drug raid. Some of the detectives in the Serious Crimes squad were building- up antipathy towards Welsh; he was becoming a media star. Welsh had been reluctant to go in front of the cameras, but was encouraged to do this and speak from a memorised script. Buzz words and clichés were being spouted, much to the delight of his superiors, they met regularly with civil servants from the Scottish Government, they were impressed by the way he was making arrests.

And warning the dealers that there was no hiding place, the public lapped this up, Welsh was making Dundee safer. He agreed with this perception, he was making Dundee safer, not because he had more wherewithal than his reclusive predecessor, but because he was in league with them, that was the unvarnished truth. He had been able to establish a link between Feeney and the social worker, Monty guided him in that direction with his comment in the taxi. Monty had been paying him money every month as requested.

A consignment of heroin would be coming up on Saturday from Liverpool, he gave the registration to him as he requested, this car would be intercepted south of Perth at the Broxden roundabout, a car travelling a half

a mile behind the drugs consignment would be carrying
the largest ever load of heroin. It was worth five million.
Welsh would make sure this car would be able to
complete the journey to Dundee without any
interruptions. This was his first test; Monty couldn't
contain himself, as he would be the sole distributor.
Even Welsh demanding a hefty fee was met with a
smile. This would be the best Christmas ever.

Monty had to spend the weekend in London, under the
guise of having been on a theatre-break. He and his wife
had tickets for Oliver! They were staying in a hotel in
Mayfair, convenient for Harrods, Regents Street and the
west end. While he was in London he made contact with
the suppliers, he told them that he needed stooges to
drive the car which would be stopped and searched at the
Broxden roundabout, he was told that if the car behind
was stopped that would be the death of him and his
wife…they would spare his dog, they weren't
completely callous.

They had one but important caveat; the two hundred
thousand pounds that would be paid to Monty's 'inside
man' would be paid after the heroin was in Monty's
tenure. He agreed but knew Welsh wouldn't accept this,
so he paid him the two hundred thousand pounds out of
his contingency account. He wasn't doing this because
he had complete faith in Welsh, he didn't. He would
rather lose two hundred thousand than lose his life.
Monty passed the registration of the BMW onto Welsh;
four kilos of uncut heroin would be secreted in the spare
tyre. He had to convince the Liverpool dealers it was in
their future interest to lose four kilos of top grade heroin.
After a day of brainstorming the dealers succumbed to
pragmatism. One of them was convinced that they had a
police informer amongst them, use him, if he doesn't get
stopped, he's the informer. If he does he goes to jail, if
he gets a light sentence; he's out of their hair, they can
deal with him in the jail or when he leaves prison,' time

143

is on their side.

Welsh is sitting in total darkness save for the twinkling Christmas lights, he feels the tension build up, is Monty going to deliver or will he procrastinate? He removes the glass of Drambuie from the laptop and places it on the floor at the side of the high-backed chair. While waiting on the Internet connection, he glanced at his watch, five- thirty pm, thirty minutes before he arrives. The electronic map is still static, doubts come into view, he stops himself getting into a debate with his mind, there will be no any or what ifs…patience would see him through the next ten minutes, he lets his left arm drop down hunting for his glass, he brings it close to his lips but doesn't sip, his eyes are gazing at the static scene.

The 'what ifs' are bubbling under the surface, he rejects the temptation to look at his watch; the screen displays the time, he knows this. Movement comes, his silent hope comes to fruition, and he's on his way. He watches his progression, he's now on the Coupar Angus road, he's really shifting, then he stops, momentarily at the cross roads, is this because of tea time traffic? Two minutes pass by, then movement occurs, soon he is on Riverside Drive, the pigeon is coming home.

He finishes the drink and moves from the chair, he walks to the hall and turns the key in the sturdy lock, all in complete darkness; his eyes have acclimatised to the eerie unsettling darkness. He moves to the rear of the house and repeats the safe formula, then climbs upstairs; the view from the window is expansive and informative. Monty has crossed the Tay Bridge, and takes the right hand turn, his speed is within the legal limit now, he should be coming into vision soon, very soon.

The laptop is placed on the floor in the upstairs hall; he can watch his progress on the laptop and out of the bedroom window. He is in the shadows but sees his four -by -four come into view. He stops twenty metres from his driveway, and emerges with a holdall, he walks onto the drive and tosses it into the skip, he walks back to his car and drives off. The modified satnav has worked perfectly. He moves away from the window, and rushes downstairs, and out of the back- door he grabs empty plaster bags and walks to the skip, he throws the bags in while scouring the vicinity, he retrieves the holdall and retraces his steps to the rear of the house once inside he closes the door with utter liberation. He moves into the lounge and frantically pulls the zip back. The money is there not in neat bundles but a cornucopia of bank notes some old, some new. He takes the holdall and places it in the meter cupboard. He moves up stairs and watches the return journey being enacted on the laptop, he's coming off the Tay Bridge; he takes out the new mobile, and waited on the registration number coming to his mobile. His work is complete, or nearly complete, he shuts down the laptop. The mobile indicates it has received a message; he opens the message, black BMW with registration leaving Liverpool midnight. He dials the Crimestoppers number and with a Liverpudlian accent relays the laconic message stating it's on its way to Aberdeen.

The unsettling feeling in his stomach has evaporated; the much spoken about Christmas spirit has entered his house. He returns downstairs with the laptop, and secretes it in the meter cupboard, he takes out the holdall then looks round the house one more time; this is a lucky house he thinks to himself, maybe this was because the holdall was influencing his well-being. He locks up the back door then moves into the hall way, every step echoing off the walls. He walks to his car, he is unable to resist looking at the twinkling Christmas tree, there is no room in his heart for melancholy. The boot responds to the electronic key, he throws the holdall in with abandon. The air is filled with the unmistakable pungent aroma of the Tay, the tide is out. In the car he takes out the mobile and removes the sim card, he places it on the passenger seat parallel to the mobile. When he emerges from Newport he stops the car, he takes the sim card and mobile and puts them in his pocket.

He moves to the wall high above the Tay and lights his cigar, no one is about, this spot is where people come to use their mobiles, Newport is notorious for poor signal strength. No need for any charade, he flicks the sim card into the Tay, like a croupier would flick a gambler requesting a card for Blackjack. The cigar follows suit, into the Tay. He continues the short journey to Dundee, on the Tay Bridge he watches the traffic zoom past him, nothing is behind him, he lowers the passenger window, and guides the car near to the safety barriers, he tossed the mobile into the Tay, and closed the window. The two hundred thousand pounds would be in the Isle of Man bank account on Monday morning. His solicitor would be able to disguise this money from the sale of his house; for a modest five per cent administration fee. Then from the Isle of Man some of it would continue on to Dublin, he could imagine an outraged Pat Connelly, incandescent, for using another solicitor.

CHAPTER THREE

GG had the bankers' lamp on examining the ten pound note, he turned it over and over, he felt there was something significant about the note, but he couldn't see it, it was his gut feeling that was making him anxious. He threw the note down on the desk, he was feeling frustrated, he picked up the card with the electronic strip, this was connected to the note, but how? It was three am, the note had invaded his sleep pattern, it was irritating him, and it was keeping him from much needed sleep. Exasperated; he rose from his bed, and sat in the lounge, only moonlight penetrating the darkness. He moved from the chair over to the window, the street was empty; some lights were on in the tenements opposite. He could see one female studying various papers intently, the light on her desk was coming from a green banker's lamp, he had one on his desk, but had never used it, but it was worth a try. He went to the kitchen and switched on the kettle, he had a plan of action of some sorts, he took the notepad and pen from the kitchen drawer and placed them on the desk, and switched on the bankers' lamp, the click of the kettle made him scurry into the kitchen, he poured the water onto the coffee, and added milk. He moved back to the desk, and took out the note and card. He wrote down the numbers from the note, were they the pin number for the card?

There would be a plethora of combinations; he would only have three chances; then the ATM would withhold the card. He wrote the numbers down; no light bulb went on in his head. Two hours later and four cups of coffee consumed, he felt more frustrated and helpless than before he rose from his bed. He had been sitting at the desk for over two hours, this solitary exercise was only broken by visits to top up his cup and empty his bladder. Usually the stress was broken by going out for a walk, but this didn't appeal to him, some drunken stragglers could try to pick an argument with him, he didn't have the capacity to ignore morons. But another thought came to him, he would have to go to an ATM in the early hours of the morning, he couldn't take the risk of someone behind him at the ATM spot the white card with electronic strip being inserted a number of times into the machine. Now he was feeling gloomier.

He opened the desk drawers looking for inspiration; he didn't know what he was searching for. Various office supplies still in sealed packets were in abundance, he looked underneath them, he picked out a ruler what for he didn't know, he placed it beside the note. He closed that drawer and rumbled through road maps of Britain, he took them out and placed them back, as he was doing this one of them fell to the floor, and a small magnifying glass showed itself; was this his initial step out of the depths of frustration, he thought so. He tore the small glass from the map, and examined the note under the light from the lamp; he adjusted the light to make it more intensive.

Concentrating on the serial number, he observed the numbers and letters through the magnifying glass.

Disappointment engulfed him; he had built himself up to an optimistic frenzy. Refusing to believe his own eyes, he rubbed them and looked again, this time his eyes responded to his heart, he saw the small indentation under four of the numbers and an additional one under the letter t. T for Tuesday or Thursday? The numbers would be entered from right to left, if the machine didn't respond, he would enter the numbers left to right, today was Tuesday, the opportune time to see if his theory matched reality. He quickly wrote the sequence of numbers down on the notepad and ripped the page out; he was feeling optimistic, even the rain hitting his window couldn't dampen his impatience to venture out into the freezing rain.

The nearest ATM machine was only about ten minutes

from his flat, he went to the cupboard and took out a short jacket and a baseball cap, he opened the door, he was finding it hard not to run down the stairs, instead he walked in an orderly and quiet fashion down the stairs. Into the street he was headwind into the rain, he was perversely pleased that it was now chucking it down; it might have made any malcontents take a taxi home.

Walking down the Perth Road, he was surprised to see students oblivious to the inclement weather; and they're meant to have the brains, he chuckled to himself. He approached the ATM in a pessimistic mood and entered the numbers, wrong PIN number, he inserted the card again and reversed the sequence of numbers, his heart was leaping, his eyes steady on the screen, different options came up on the screen he touched the display balance, it came up five hundred pounds, he wasn't expecting a large sum to appear. He selected withdraw cash, he entered five hundred pounds, the machine responded, he placed the money in his wallet and made his way up the Perth Road. Elation emanated through every pore, he felt more fulfilled by the five hundred pounds from the ATM than the thousands of pounds in the holdall. He felt for the page in his pocket, he didn't need it, the numbers were embedded in his brain, he would keep this mathematical conundrum from Lenny. Next Tuesday he would go to an ATM in Perth, he had to go and see and old friend who had fallen on hard times, he would give him one hundred pounds of the five hundred, after they had a day out on the beer, he would give him the money as he was boarding the train, yes that's what he would do. His friend was practically a non-drinker, now he was teetering on alcoholism, his wife had a brief fling with the satellite installation engineer who had installed the satellite dish, and unbeknown to him she had been seeing other men, including a colleague of theirs. He turned to him for advice, he was blunt, 'end the marriage, things will never be the same; you won't be able to erase the memories of her adultery 'He took the advice, moved out, and started divorce proceedings.

***

The air-conditioned departure lounge was filled with the ex-pats' returning home for their six week annual Christmas break. Eddings wished he could be amongst them, but he was here to see Morag off. Her constant chatter about Dundee was making him feel homesick. He couldn't see himself returning to Dubai when he would follow in Morag's footsteps, they had arranged to meet up in Dundee, when he was home, he would desist from telling his wife about Morag, she wouldn't believe their relationship was platonic, so why open himself to imaginary Shakespearian plots; Jean would cast herself as Iago and make him out to be a willing Othello.

The Daves' circumvented the Law when they were detectives in Dundee, but blowing up people so they could get rid of an American security consultant, was just…criminal. He could barely think this, he omitted Morag from this information, but if he told her about the driver being hurt in a car bomb, she wouldn't have been surprised, her cogent thinking was thus, they were friendly with Welsh, she heard him say that 'he has to go,' then Feeney gets murdered in a church. Was this a coincidence or conspiracy? He always rebuked anyone who subscribed to conspiracies, that was until a murder trial, was switched to Edinburgh from Dundee, because a Dundee jury would be prejudicial to the accused who lived in Dundee, the QC who was to conduct the case for the Crown and he was replaced by a more quietly spoken, demure QC, who was competent, but would be no match for the aggressive defence counsel, and a judge who had doubts about the science behind DNA.

Result; a majority of eight to six verdict from the jury in

the defences favour. That repugnant smell still hung over the city. The conspiracy theory was thus, the accused was from one of Dundee's old- moneyed family, family relatives were in prominent positions in the legal hierarchy, for example they agreed to every defence motion, some evidence was withheld from the jury because again it would prejudice the accused.

Eddings was a late subscriber to the conspiracy theorists, but he didn't openly say so. Who would have believed a heretic like him would be part of a conspiracy in Dubai, which could have resulted in serious injuries to the driver? The Daves told him there would have been a loud bang and black smoke would have engulfed the car, but there was never any chance of the driver being seriously hurt, frightened, yes, but hurt, no chance. The loud explosion was caused by a small can of barbeque lighting fluid being attached to the exhaust system, when this heated up the can would explode thus setting off black smoke similar to black smoke in theatre productions. While he was relieved, he was still unsettled that they would actually carry out this 'prank' as they called it. Notwithstanding he was the superhero who solved the 'assassination attempt.' He needed to get out of Dubai soon, who knows when 'pranks' assimilate into the real thing, he wouldn't voice any concerns, he would play the homesick card. Sparingly.

***

The slamming of the heavy door was met with relief. That was the last of the members gone, the Club roulette wheel had brought in more than expected but the blackjack table had underperformed, that would have to be looked into, but overall the opening weekend had been an unqualified success. She hoped that she had performed well as the hostess. This was easy money, the members were people she felt comfortable in their company. She didn't recognise any of them. Some had clipped accents, some a trace of a foreign language. This

151

was the bubble that she craved to live in, the fight back to enter their world had started, money was tumbling in to her bereft bank account, her salary had many claims to it, the bank took over her finances, mortgage, council tax, etc., were ring- fenced, any money left over was placed in her everyday living account, which was meagre.

The staff started from the top of the house, removing sheets from the beds and throwing them onto the landing, another person concentrated on the cleaning of the en-suites, this procedure was carried out with vigour, they did the same job in one of the five star hotels in London. Downstairs, she hovered about the rooms that had been cleaned, checking and double checking that everything was in perfect condition. One hour later, everyone was gone except for her, she waited in the lounge, glancing at her watch, he should be here soon, she speculated what her commission would be. Four figures which could vary up or down, depending on the money generated by the Club. The money would be going to pay off part of her horrendous credit card bill that she failed to alert the bank about. This was at another bank. Silence was unsettling for her, the Club had an impressive opening weekend, and the Club would revert back to a house for another month, she hoped she would be retained. The front door's lock had been activated; she straightened her belt on her jeans. He came in smiling; it was her date from the casino.

'Hello and how are you?'

'I'm fine thank you, and yourself?'

'Very happy, very happy…thanks to you. The members were most pleased; they are looking forward to the next time.

'This is for you,' he handed her a white envelope. She masked her disappointment, the envelope was on the small side, she took it and placed it in her shoulder bag.

'Thank you very much, I enjoyed the weekend, it was

controlled chaos, but there were no problems.'

'That's good to hear…I'll see you to the door, you have your card for the gate?'

'Yes.'

'Could I have it please?'

***

The Counting House was busy; it was Monday Club time once again. His eyes were on the door that led onto Reform Street; smokers were coming in and going out much to his annoyance. Normally, he would have left much earlier, but he stayed later than normal as part of his ploy. Sky sports news was on the big screen televisions, he looked round the crowded bar, some of the early morning drinkers were looking weather-beaten, he laughed at the term, his mum used to say that to him when he was a kid when his dad came rolling home from the pub, he wasn't allowed to say drunk, it was weather- beaten. Over at the dining area were students and office workers, then the thought that always arose no matter where he was piped up again in his head. Fifteen years ago when he was making a name for himself, he suggested to his now deceased business partner, that they buy the former bank and turn it into a pub, his business partner laughed at him in front of guests from Glasgow, and apologised on his behalf, 'he's still learning' he chortled, all eyes were on him, incessant laughter rained on him from all sides, except from the elderly gentleman. He had done his research, the bank could be bought for a song, if he went through an intermediary, even though there would be a transaction fee to cover various expenses, the future pub would be a license to print money, even though he was printing money at the time without a license. When the bank was turned into a thriving bar, seven days and nights a week, he wasn't the only one who felt angry, the elderly gentleman was known as the banker, he sourced the finance for projects such as his suggestion, he contacted his business partner, who invited him through to see how organized crime works.

They stayed in the Hilton in Glasgow, for the weekend, a boxing match was on their itinerary, it would be a weekend to remember. It certainly was. They were wined, dined and supplied with beautiful women, on the Sunday evening in their suite a discussion was taking place about expansion of the drug trade not just in Dundee and its hinterland, but all the way up to the oil rich capital Aberdeen and beyond, it was untapped markets. He was agog at the research and business expansion that was aired. That was the first time he had heard of the Yardies that were causing havoc in London, they were using Uzi machine guns on the streets against indigenous dealers and police with relish. Things had got so bad that Scotland Yard were in the process of forming a Yardies specialised unit, they had been given a subliminal nod from the Home Office to operate a shoot- to- kill policy, with a reassuring caveat; no officer would ever face criminal charges. There would be no stop! Drop your weapon! Police Officers. It was bang, bang, stop, drop your weapon, police officers, and there would always be passing members of the public who heard the officer telling the armed suspect to stop. The Yardies were not stupid; they decided to relocate where the police were unarmed and less Gung -Ho; Scotland.

They had to protect their fiefdoms; their informant in Scotland Yard told them Aberdeen would be the hub of their empire.
The police wouldn't intervene unless bodies were strewn across Union Street. The informant would tell the 'Glasgow Boys' when the Yardies were ensconced in Aberdeen, and more important, where they were staying…the rest was up to the 'Glasgow Boys.' The Yardies were followed from Aberdeen train station to affluent areas in Westhill, Cults and Milltimber. With synchronized military planning, raids took place on a

Saturday night, the 'Glasgow Boys' dressed as policeman went to the various addresses and executed them, and left as they came without noise and fuss. The bodies were removed and burnt in the public incinerator, the Aberdeen public was unaware of the state-sponsored slaughter that took place within their communities, and the rule of law had been temporarily suspended. The 'Glasgow Boys' implemented the Yardies expansion plan, with the exception; Dundee would be the hub for the north- east market.

Monty sucked on his cigarette, the banker ended his speech. He looked at Monty and asked; 'do you think you can handle that son?'

A malevolent silence descended on the room, Monty was the focal point of their stares. He stubbed out his cigarette.

'I can handle that, me and Sammy will…'

'…No this is about you; not Sammy, he won't be around anymore.'

Sam looked pleased; he had been told that he was going on a journey, where he would appreciate the heat. Sam felt exalted; he was going to Spain, to sort out logistics. He leaned forward from the couch and held out his hand to Monty, who responded immediately then stopped. One of them stepped from behind the couch and wrapped a silk tie around Sam's neck pulled him down on to the couch; Sam was struggling; his hands clawing in vain at his garrote, his eyes pleading for help from Monty.

Monty was transfixed at the death scene taking place in front of him, he smelt the excrement coming from Sam, his face was purple now, his eyes rolled back, his executioner removed the tie and folded it and placed it in his trouser pocket.

'Another drink Monty?'

His mouth was dry, he couldn't take his eyes of Sam, his eyes bulging, he had the look of a man in the process of ejaculating. He sent his tongue round his mouth hunting for salvia.

'I'll have whisky…please.' The banker nodded to the executioner who brought him the drink. Monty thought this was his last drink. 'You're numero uno now Monty, don't feel bad about your pal, he was an informant, he got greedy, he set up a separate business with Joe Feeney, he got greedy as well, he goes sometime next week. If he gets tipped off, you follow him into hell. No one apart from the four of us in this room is aware of Joe Feeney will be dead next week, you understand that son?'

The whisky glass was increasing in temperature, he was mortified.

'Yes,' he said slowly. 'I remember you from years ago suggesting buying that bank building in Dundee, others laughed at you, I didn't, I did what you suggested and bought bank buildings in Glasgow and Edinburgh, I sold them seven years ago, we knew that the smoking ban was being proposed, the information we had at the time was it was going to be defeated. I went with instinct, and won the argument, we made millions Monty, all because of you. You're smart, it's a pity your chum didn't see that. You've done well, the police know who you are but have no proof of anything to do with drugs, don't get greedy, the money is rolling in, we have the market sewn up; no interlopers would dare mount a challenge. Drink up, there's a taxi ordered for you, it'll take you straight to your house, the driver has been told to keep the conversation to a minimum.'

He had never felt fear like that; he was petrified that he would be shot any place between Glasgow and Dundee, and his bullet- ridden body dumped. He was in no doubt that the taxi journey was made to make him think long and hard about Sam's betrayal. It worked…up to a point.

156

The bar was filling up with off-shore workers having a last drink before they made their way to the train station for their stint offshore; they were easy to spot big holdalls and big long faces, quaffing big drinks. He ordered another pint, he eyes looking for *him*, and then *he* came in through the door just like any other offshore worker, carrying a holdall. He turned his back, he was alongside him now, it was fast approaching six o clock; he asked the barmaid to turn over to the STV news. Seeing is believing; it was headline news, police had stopped a car near the Broxden roundabout near Perth, a substantial amount of drugs was recovered from the vehicle, the occupants, believed to be from Liverpool will appear in court tomorrow.' It was all on the screen in glorious sub-titles. The occupants driving the drug consignment following the intercepted car had seen the police intervention; their heroin was being cut and distributed as he sipped his lager. The 'offshore worker' had seen enough he edged the holdall near to Monty, downed his pint and nonchalantly strolled out of the bar. Monty's stock would have risen in the eyes of the banker, he had financed the sale from the Liverpool suppliers, he always insisted it was the Liverpool suppliers who drove up to Dundee, less chance of his men being caught and informing. Monty showed no nerves as he walked from the bar to the door where his taxi would be waiting for him. If he and Welsh didn't get too greedy they both would live long -fulfilled lives, he had made up his mind when Welsh compromised him in the taxi about the child pornography, he would kill him if the opportunity arose; this would be his Christmas wish. The banker was coming to Dundee next week, he would explain that this patsy drugs operation was a one-off, he hoped he would agree.

***

Walking up the Perth Road, the biting wind couldn't

157

cool their expectations, passing the swaying Christmas tree added to their excitement. The doubts had been blown from her mind like the snow from the tree; never apologise and never explain. Her best friend for more than twenty -years had at last came out what she had been harbouring; alcohol had loosened her thoughts and added viciousness to her diatribe. They had been enjoying a girls Christmas night out, she was not keen to go, but Ritchie told her to go, he wanted her to see what her friends were really like for herself. Ritchie had seen that movie before, he was invited to a friend's fortieth birthday party in the summer, he was looking forward to it, near the end of the night, one of his long-time friends passed a comment about his business expanding rapidly, 'where did you get the capital?' The laughter died down, this was not a spontaneous or jocular remark.

'From the banks, you should know that, are you not having difficulty paying the small mortgage on your flat, because you wife went mad with credit cards?'
A perfect but visceral response the small circle of friends hadn't heard of his difficulty. 'That's rubbish! Who told you that?'

'I can't tell you, I met him in the bank last week, I wouldn't worry about, you know how jealous and envious people get, especially when it's friends who start doing well…are you still living on Strathmartine Road then?'

There would be no inquisition on how his plumbing business was doing; as it was well-known he had secured lucrative maintenance contracts for council buildings.

'I'm not happy with what you said Ritchie, I'm not struggling, remember I had a BMW years before you.'

'I know that, but unlike you, I put money into paying off my mortgage, I think It's nearly paid- off, did you say that your still in Strathmartine Road, I remember you said our house in Fairmuir was a money-pit, you were right, the money we made off that house allowed us to move into the 'Ferry, then from there we released equity, and purchased more vans, the rest is history. It's all about risk, you either have the balls or you don't. Your BMW, how old did you say it is?'

He felt the hatred, he had reversed the roles, he had told everyone a plausible explanation with ease and confidence, his jealous and spiteful friend was made to look angry and nervous, and more to the point, his suggested financial well-being was holed beneath the water-line due to his wife's spendthrift ways, whether this was true or not he couldn't have cared less. His friend had been spreading stories about him that suggested his house was going to be re-possessed and his company was going bust. He was glad he had the perfect opportunity to set the record straight.

Diane would face the same canards, not one of her friends showed any warmth; they just wanted to quiz her about her house, and lifestyle. Her night started out in cordial fashion, about two hours and several bars later, the catty comments came out. 'Lovely shoes Diane…how much!'
Diane played them at their own game. 'I'd rather not say,' she was looking shy.

'You usually boast about how everything costs, how much?'

'I beg your pardon! Explain what you just said there…what have I boasted about?'

'Your big house in the Ferry…amongst other things.'

'You asked me about the house and how much it cost, I told you, that's not boasting, and I remember you said you and Norrie were thinking about selling your flat you were expecting to make big money, that's what you said, big money, but you said Norrie said wait till next year and you would make even more, so is this what this is really about, you can't sell your flat because the markets flat, you're just picking a fight is that not the real reason?'

'No it's not, we've decided to stay where we are, and at least we can go on holiday and switch on our heating!'

Diane struggled to contain her laughter. 'My dear,' she said in a very patronizing voice, 'I'll explain, not just for you but for the rest of my so- called friends. My shoes were bought in New York, I bought them from a little store on fifth avenue, the shop is called Donna Koran, did I not tell you me and Ritchie went over there *New York* last week, and the only reason we went there was because I knew a bitch like yourself would ask about my shoes. And I can afford my heating, thanks for your concerns.

Now I'd like to ask you something I was told, the real reason that you can't move is that you and your two-faced husband borrowed money against the future value of your flat, and bought a BMW for you and him…doesn't seem a wise move now doesn't it …dear?'

Her friend burst out crying. Diane stood up. 'Thanks for the wonderful night out, I wouldn't like to tell you the price of the shoes because there would be mass suicide at this table. Merry Christmas.

She left the table with pleas not to go she had pricked their collective conscience. She felt exhilarated as she made her way through the throng of humanity. Her thoughts turned to her mother; she would have liked that, she could hear her voice above the loud music. Well-done Di that was a long time coming! Half way to the exit the song playing on the juke box struck a chord with her.

Even though she had heard it many times before, it was Frankie Miller singing Caledonia, it was like the first time she had heard the lyric, '…lost friends that needed losing and found new ones along the way.' She had kept quiet about the incident when Ritchie asked her how the night-out had gone, she said it was boring.

It was dark now nearly five pm, she wanted to say that

160

the Christmas tree on the Perth Road was the highlight of her night out, walking past the tree with six wines inside her lifted the hurt she had felt. 'Why do friends enjoy seeing strangers get on in life, but hate friends that get on?' Things needed to be said on the night-out, she had absolutely no regrets. Even when her friend called her on her mobile and apologised she was still in an unforgiving mood, she told her 'that she knew she was spreading wicked lies about her and Ritchie, didn't she know everyone was laughing at her and Norrie up at the club? Their friendship was finished, she would acknowledge if she saw her in the town or in pubs, but please for the avoidance of embarrassment don't bring up the night-out and don't apologise. Goodbye.'

She was shaken out of replaying the incidents over and over in her head, as Ritchie pulled her arm.

'Why did I listen to you and leave the car parked in the Overgate?'

'Stop moaning you always said you liked a stroll up to Pat's office, another ten minutes and we'll be there, aren't you excited?'

'A slight correction, I enjoy a stroll in the summer not a hike in an arctic gale, is the snow getting thicker?

'It is and it's lovely, look at the tree it looks like its dancing.'

'Probably it is dancing to keep warm, oh no, look who has pulled up?'

They get out the car, and block their path. 'Car broken down?'

'No, haven't you heard, our car has been repossessed, and we've no bus money,' she pulls Ritchie beyond them, 'keep walking, see you later Norrie.'

Ritchie is mystified. 'What was that all about?' She tells him about the remarks about her shoes at the night-out. He is laughing. He tells her about his sarcastic remarks to Norrie when he was being baited at the fortieth birthday party. They both congratulate each

161

other for at last standing up for themselves.

'Just wait till they find out that we have bought a tenement block in Scott Street, now I am excited, jealous bastards! Did you tell her that the shoes cost fifteen quid from Primark?'

'Ritchie! There is no need for swearing; no I didn't tell her… it's us against the world and our friends.'

'Former friends, as long as we've got each other, that's all that matters.'

'Are they still there?'

He turns around and they are still there parked directly beside the Christmas tree.

'Yes and it looks as though Miss Perfect is crying her eyes out, I feel a lot better now.'

'Who would have thought we would own a block of flats, life is curious, isn't it?'

'Well, here we are, I have never really noticed how imposing Pat's office is.'

Ritchie is looking nervous, Diane squeezes his hand and pulls him up onto the first step, they both match step for step then enter the lobby of the reception area. The receptionist has been briefed she has been expecting them. She removes herself from the desk and walks towards them.

'Just go up he's being expecting you both, would you like coffee brought up?'

'Yes please, it's getting wild out there now,' replied Ritchie.

'Did you walk up from the town?' she said incredulous.

'Long story…' They went to the lift.

'Are you nervous?'

'Excited, but not nervous, I hope the paperwork is not confusing, that's when I always worry.'

'Don't be daft Diane, Pat will walk us through it, he explained it quite clearly at the house, you didn't seem worried then…cold feet?'

'Yes, cold feet and cold all over.' The lift door opens at

fourth floor; Pat is there to greet them.

'The snow makes it more Christmassy, and Santa Connelly has brought you a nice present, you know the way.' They take their coats off and take a seat on the sofa in his office.

'Everything has been completed; I only need your signatures, would you like me to run through things again?'

Diane keeps quiet. 'That would be a good idea Pat,' said Ritchie.

'Fine no problem. The tenement block is in Scott Street, there are eight two bed roomed flats, double glazed with central heating, the fabric of the building is weathered that means it could do with being stone-cleaned. The roof is wind and water tight, but again it could be doing with being replaced, and the flats are let out through an agency; they charge fifteen per cent commission. The flats are let at five hundred pounds a month, which gives you a gross figure of four thousand pound a month. After loans, commission and interest payments are deducted you are left with the princely sum of six hundred pound which will be subjected to tax which leaves you with three hundred and sixty pounds net. That's the official story. The reality will be much different I am pleased to say.

'A new property management company will take over letting the flats out; this company will be owned by you both. The maintenance contract for the central heating will revert from the incumbent company to your company. The building will be stone-cleaned, re-roofed and the close painted next year, grants will be made available, up to fifty-per cent of the cost, the companies doing the work will be owned by you both. Any questions?'

'That's fine, that's just how you explained it last week, but I am a wee bit concerned about you putting yourself in a tricky situation , with your client, matching him up

with us the buyers' as we are also your clients…this
conflict of interest, you won't get into bother will you?'

'The Law is made of a very flexible material, respect it
and it's very pliable, the other client has temporarily
moved to another practice, so that removes the conflict
of interest.'

Diane coughed. 'Pat could I ask you a question?'

Before she opens her mouth, there is a knock at the
door, it's the temporary secretary with the coffee, she
comes in and places the tray on the low table, and leaves
with not a word spoken but is smiling.

'You were saying Diane?'

'Why is the owner of the flats selling so cheap?'

'That's not quite accurate, he purchased the block of
flats at the top end of the market, when the prices were
unsustainable and the interest payments were temptingly
low. Four years on, the interest rates have nearly
doubled, the rental market in Dundee is saturated thus
keeping rents down, or even lower than the peak four
years ago. He had no choice, he was been pressurized
by the bank, as you can imagine, he either sells at a
lower price and stills make a profit.

Or the bank comes in and takes the property back and
his house. It's an ill-wind that brings you some fortune,
no-one is buying, the usual suspects in property
development are treading water, believe me. They may
have their personalised number plates, and large houses
in Broughty Ferry, but it's all a sham, a facade. Behind
the scenes they are trying to off-load plots of land,
blocks of new build flats from the west end to the
disaster at the City Quay. The old families from
Broughty Ferry are picking up rich pickings. Always
remember cash is king, as long as you have twenty-five
per cent as a deposit, the banks' will love you, anything
less when the market turns difficult they turn nasty, and
they show no mercy or patience. Does that ease your

mind Diane?'

'I knew things were bad, but I didn't realise how bad.'

'Bad for impatient speculators, but good for you both and myself, now would you like to sign four pages of legal documents?'

'Sure, I like the pen Pat it looks very old,' he signs the paperwork and hands the pen to Diane, she takes her time with her signature, then lets out a sigh of relief, and hands the pen back to Pat.

'That pen was used to sign the nineteen sixteen proclamation for Irish Independence, you both should feel privileged. '

'Where did you get it Pat?'

'A long, long story, I will tell you one day, it's a story of triumph, disaster and betrayal.'

***

He takes the empty glass in both hands and holds it in front of his face, turning it slowly with his thumbs. What he is looking for is unclear. He can hardly see out of the window but he feels at ease with himself, the snow flurries have been replaced by a steady rainfall, the vista over to Dundee has been erased by the grey darkness and the rain. The darkness in the lounge is a welcome friend, the laptop is open, but Feeney's USB refuses to divulge any secrets. He is no computer expert; the screen is emitting mystery, and a white screen with large letters username and password. He has tried various combinations, some more cerebral than others, the same depressing message comes up; username and password not recognised. He lifted the cup of coffee which was now lukewarm, he pulled the screen down, that could wait, the USB might just hold trivial information, on the other hand, it may betray other corrupt detectives, bizarrely which he didn't count himself in that camp.

He could take it to his friend in the IT department, the same one who had placed the tracking device in the satnav used by Monty, but he was concerned that would alert other detectives who were less than scrupulous. He had to play the waiting game, Monty's words about Feeney and his *friend* still bounced around his head, when he had spoken to detectives about progress they were making, they never mentioned anything apart from 'the poor bastard who walked in at the wrong time,' plenty theories but no evidence. That pleased him. His mobile rang it made him jump, he looked at the caller's name McAveety; he sighed and let it run to answer machine. He played the message on speaker phone,

'Boss you'd better get over here it's a blood bath, four of the main dealers have been tortured and executed, one of them is Monty, I'm in the industrial estate on the Old Glamis Road, I took a call about an hour ago, advising me that there were drugs there.
If you haven't eaten, good; see you soon.' He took the USB out and shut down the laptop, a feeling of hopelessness came onto him like an anvil. Pointless rushing about, he took the laptop and placed it in the meter cupboard.

He took the USB and wedged it into the gap into the skirting board. He called McAveety, told him he was on his way, he asked him to go over again what the scene was like, then suddenly McAveety added something, 'they must have been picked up in a vehicle their cars aren't here.' He told him he was on his way over, he drove over the Tay Bridge but didn't directly go to the industrial estate; he had to retrieve the satnav system from Monty's four- by- four. On the Coupar Angus road he formulated a plan, if no one was there he would smash the window and take the satnav himself, if the car wasn't there …that could open a can of worms, if the detectives found the car and satnav, they would soon know it had a police tracking device, then they would find out it wasn't an official operation, problems could hunt him in packs, would his IT friend tell them that he was ordered to do and he thought it was a legitimate operation? He prayed that the sat nav was in the four - by -four, his mobile rang.

McAveety observed the murder squad detectives with intense scrutiny; they had cordoned off the industrial unit which used to be a machine shop, lathes were still in place, the company had went into administration the previous day.

The four victims were naked sitting with their hands tied behind their chairs   Pools of blood lay on the oil-stained concrete floor at each chair. Their heads all uniformly slumped forward exposing the brutal gash in their heads. McAveety smiled but changed it to a wry smile as one of the detectives turned to him and asked 'what was so funny?'

He replied meekly he 'was shocked at the violence used,' then he was told brusquely 'to vacate the crime scene.'

The switch went off in his head. he had had enough; he wasn't in uniform now.

'If you wanted him to move, you would have to do it yourself or get help from one of your boyfriends; I'm staying put till my boss gets here, ok?'

The detective backed down, McAveety was no longer a joke figure, and no-one had heard anyone speak to this detective before like that. Two portable drills were lying behind one body, the knees had been attacked with the drills, no other body had been drilled. Monty was the one who had been tortured, McAveety observed the four corpses; he was staring at the most violent and vicious drug dealers that had become untouchable in Dundee, but that was until tonight. They had been lured here, with the promise of riches or drugs, something had gone wrong. Whoever had done this deserved a medal in his eyes, the successors to their thrones would be able to match their achievements, and it wouldn't be too long before their shoes would be filled. The forensic team was happy now no-one was allowed to enter the area marked out; countless photographs had been taken after the video was completed. The drills were tagged and bagged, their interest turned to the engineering wire that bound their hands. He pulled out his phone he felt it vibrating, it was Welsh, it was a brief call, telling him to watch everyone especially the detectives, he was surprised at this, but obeyed this order.

Two of the detectives were in the corner away from the bodies they were so close together whispering and nodding and shaking their heads. The other one seemed to be going over the executions in his head, standing behind each one taking a stance with an imaginary gun, one he pistol whipped and smiled, he stepped back and spoke into his mobile, smiling. He called the other two over, and acted out the death scene. One of them was rubbing his chin, he was pointing at each corpse, he indicated the order in which they were executed, he others agreed with him, then they went into a huddle their backs turned to him. They went into a deep conversation and went in different directions.
Then they came back into another huddle. He felt a hand on his shoulder.

'Who is no longer with us?'

'Have a look for yourself, how many times have you seen these guys in the same room together?' The detectives turned and acknowledged Welsh. He had no problem identifying them, he strolled back to McAveety 'Brutal, just brutal, someone made sure there were no witnesses.'

***

The Chief Constable was incandescent with rage, he hadn't been long in his job, and he had been surprised as others that he was selected. He thought because he had come through the ranks, constable, sergeant and inspector he had reached the glass ceiling. The rank and file was not letting off any rockets in celebration; he was old school, not a slavish disciple of 'modern police methods for the twenty -first century problems.' His mantra was less complicated, harass criminals wherever they operated, known drug dealers, go to their homes in early morning. Disseminate malicious stories to low - level dealers that that their boss was an informant, thus paranoia accompanied them when they woke up and even went to bed. He didn't see eye-to eye with Feeney, who dismissed him and any uniformed officer with disdain. He regretted Feeney didn't see him rise to become Chief Constable, he would have looked forward to giving him a verbal ear bashing, his methods were out and his would be implemented. Feeney's successor was more attuned to his thinking; he had a new strategy and wanted Welsh to zealously follow his diktat. Events had overtaken his strategy; the four dealers executed with impunity changed his world.

The Daily Record had run a front page story which said that the executions were in retaliation for Feeney being murdered. The implication being that a police officer or officers had taken the Law into his own or their hands. This would be a major distraction, from the real investigation.

Whoever had murdered Feeney the head of the drug squad; and whoever had murdered four citizens of Dundee who had convictions for drug offences would face justice. That was the statement he gave to The Courier, he had no time for tabloid speculation. Welsh would be coming in to see him separately; he didn't want him and detectives from the murder squad scoring points off each other. The murder squad detectives called the members of the drug squad 'glamour boys' this was a pejorative rather than a term of endearment.

The way he looked at it, Welsh was likely to name the person or persons who he thought had carried out the murders, it was obvious that the murders were drug related, Welsh was aware of offering incentives to

169

informants, his record could stand up to scrutiny. The detectives investigating the murders would have to liaise with their enemies; the drug squad. He would lay it on the line to both squads any animosity should be left at the door; any personal vendettas that carried on would be dealt with. Welsh would be told that he was the real investigating officer because of his contacts. Forensics drew a blank this would not be solved in a half an hour CIS type of television programme. Someone had to talk; was it inconceivable that the four dealers were executed by one man? He firmly believed that Feeney and the social worker were murdered by one person.

***

Lenny arrived at GG's flat, it was just after nine pm, he was going on duty at ten. He came through with his coffee. 'Thanks, so what do you want?'

'We have reasons to be thankful on one hand and other reasons to be annoyed with the carry-on at Old Glamis Road.'

'It was more than a carry-on! It was an execution…you didn't have anything to do with it did you?'

He scoffed, and sat down. 'Why would I…why would I kill the golden goose? No more golden eggs for us Lenny, thank God we got our money just in time.'

'Are saying one of dealers told you about the cannabis farms?'

'Yes, and one the dealers who ran the cannabis was murdered; I think it's the Triads not happy with their customer service. I think they guessed who had ripped them off and decided to go for a job-lot rather than the dealer that they suspected.'

'No one else knew about the cannabis farms and the nursery in Fife, that makes sense and it keeps us out of the picture which is good. Did you see the story in the Record about it? They are saying it could be a revenge killing, because of what happened to Feeney; that suits us.'

'I'm not so sure…I hope my friend didn't mention me before he was killed, if the Triads know I was behind the harvesting of their plants, I don't want any customer service manager giving me a personal visit.'

'No, no, if they had extracted your name from the dealer, you'd be …well…dead, do you want to tell me which dealer it was then?'

'I don't think it would help, but he helped us; and the money is cleansed now and making more money, at least we were left a legacy. What are the uniformed boys saying about it?'

'They're just as bad as the tabloids. A rogue cop with a conscience, a distraught parent who has lost a child because of heroin, a wealthy parent or sibling who lost a son, daughter, brother or sister, hired a hit man. Or some supplier didn't get paid, or the favourite the Poles lured them all there with the promise of money and ripped- off the drugs and killed them. That's the latest, up to now.'

'That's good, confusing fantasy, the more outlandish the better, no mention of Triads, you've got to admire their methods, and they're letting any potential rip-off merchants know that they don't hang about if they're not satisfied.'

'A bit extreme I suppose, but it cuts out any dialogue, saves paperwork. I'm tired tonight, I'll get going. The intercom buzzes.

***

The flight was enjoyable, the other passengers in first-class were sleeping, he had tried to lose himself in a book but his mind kept deviating from the story, which was losing his attention, finally, he cast it aside. Closing his eyes he felt more relaxed, calmness came over him, Dubai was not what he had expected, give me the Hilltown over the soulless shopping malls and streets with no names.

When he was settled back in Dundee, he would call

171

them and tell them that homesickness had become unbearable, but thanks anyway for the opportunity. That was the path he would take. Morag had sent him a text asking him to meet her, nothing to worry about. He had never planned Dubai to be long -term, he was prepared to live and work over there to help erase his failure to solve the murders in Dundee of the two youths, two policemen and a solicitor, the prime suspect was Raymond Andrews who had disappeared and had never been seen.

Since then Dundee had erupted into violence, Joe Feeney assassinated in a chapel, along with an innocent early- morning worshiper, then four dealers found in an industrial unit executed, the 'untouchables' as they were called.

He couldn't muster any sympathy for them, he was aware of every broken bone they had inflicted on their clients and of their other activities, what goes around comes back around. The Daves…now they really shocked him, but they didn't seem to think they had done anything wrong, at least his shock at their methods proved to him he still had a moral compass. Jean would be indifferent when he told her that he wouldn't be returning to Dubai, he would just tell her that the stifling heat was unbearable. His bank balance was heavier and he was now three stones lighter, he put this down to drinking water, walking more and eating less. Jean probably wouldn't notice, it had been his birthday, he didn't receive any email wishing him happy birthday, she just mentioned that when he was coming home on leave she would order the decking for the lower garden, and when he could get stuck into that. Love was still in the air.

He replied in a more erratic fashion, he wrote that he was involved in a theatre- class and he had played the lead actor in The Taming of the Shrew, he looked forward to resuming this when he arrived in Dundee, could she contact The Rep to enquire if they required experienced actors that had performed in the Middle East? The next day he received e-mails from his daughter, asking if everything was okay, he replied telling her that he was just having fun with her mother, don't tell her, tell her that you think that it's a good thing...keep it going. He finally came round to asking himself, what would he be doing now for the remaining years of his life? Golf?, he rejected, suicide by walking, keeping the weight off would be a challenge, but he didn't fancy joining a gym, there were more criminals there than in Perth prison, he might convert the double garage into a gym, if Jean approved.

***

McAveety had become insistent with his texts, she didn't need him anymore, her career would not benefit by joining the drug squad, and she didn't have to use him anymore. Out of good manners she arranged to go out with him for a drink and that's all it would be, the gas man would not be servicing her tonight or any other night for that matter. She would be using him for information; she had no idea what she would do with this information. Sitting on the bench overlooking the Tay, the view from Perth Road over to Fife was breathtaking, the short -distance was worlds away from Dundee. Tayport and Newport were oases of tranquility, Dundee...well was Dundee. Apparently crime was down. Really?

***

The cold was gnawing at her unprotected knees, but she felt good times lay -ahead, her weekend as a hostess was met with universal approval, four thousand for a weekend's work couldn't be turned down, she thought she would have been paid up to a maximum two grand. There was no guarantee that she would be required again, this was explained to her when she was handed

173

the envelope, it was designed to keep her on her toes. Her uncle had been involved in criminal activities including card schools in the late nineteen eighties then he left Dundee in a hurry, her mother and father didn't expand on the reason, when she asked.

'Enjoying the view then?'

'Do you enjoy creeping up on people then?'

'That's why I'm in the drug squad, have you been waiting long?'

'No, but I'm hungry, I was just thinking how Newport must seem so quiet compared to Dundee, I fancy living over there one day.' She stood up and wrapped her scarf more tightly around her.

'Newport? Are you kidding, they call the police when it's windy. It's too dull. Now where do you want to go to eat? I heard they serve good meals at the new casino, do you fancy going there then for a change?'

'I can't be arsed, I just wanted to go to the pubs about here, you pick the restaurant Chinese or Indian, I'm not fussed.'

'We'll go for a drink first in O'Malley's then we'll go for an Indian, the whole works, Nan bread etc.'

They walk from the bench then stop and stare at the tree. McAveety is impatient.

'I thought you were cold, it's only a Christmas tree, and c'mon I'm freezing.'

'Just give me a minute, doesn't it make you feel better, the way it sways with the lights all bobbing about?'

'No, and no again. I'm surprised it's not been vandalised, it's a waste of money if you ask me, how long are you going to stare at it?'

'You can either wait with me or go to the pub; does it really do nothing for you Jim?'

'Absolutely nothing, are we going?'

***

'Come in take a seat, tea or coffee?'

'I'm fine Chief Constable.'

'Forget being formal, okay?'

Welsh was taken aback at this. 'Fine with me, I was just giving you your place.'

'These murders won't force me to resign unlike my predecessor because of the Raymond Andrews killings from last year, we have to solve them, and I include myself. I have shaken the murder squad detectives up; everything takes second place to Feeney and the dealers. I want cooperation between your squad and them. That story in the Daily Record hasn't helped, it's just added to my in- tray. Some people actually believe the story, and that's what will make this job harder. What are your thoughts at this early stage?'

'First of all concerning the dealers, a transaction of some kind has went wrong, the killer or killers have sent out a message like writing in the sky, meddle with us at your peril. As for Joe Feeney, I think that's more complicated, I can understand he was meeting someone then he was killed, the same with the social worker, was he an innocent bystander as he has being portrayed?'

'That's interesting, you're the first to disagree with that, and do you have another explanation?'

'No, I just think accepting this theory is too easy, it's the old saying repeat a lie often enough and it turns into fact. I'm not privy to any information the murder squad have, but I'd be very surprised if they swallowed that one without checking if Feeney and that social worker have met before or did they know each other socially, that's all.'

'The murder squad think the social worker was just at the wrong place at the wrong time, I agree with their assessment, unless you have other concrete evidence.'

'I don't have any evidence, and I can imagine the pressure they feel they're under, act in haste repent at leisure, I just think they should sit down have a breather and don't be swayed by newspaper stories probably written by spotty teenagers.'

'That's really interesting, I'll mention that, what about the executions, any hope of solving that?'

'I hope so, but I would think someone has been brought in, sub-contracted if you like, and carried out the killings.

And they were all tied up so the killers needed certain questions asked, why was Monty's knees drilled with power drills and others weren't?'

'That's what the murder squad told me, some of them have ripped- off suppliers and didn't pay or did a scam of some kind, Monty must have been the target of their suspicions, at least you both are thinking along the same lines on that one, that's a good start.'

'His house has been searched you won't be surprised to learn that there was nothing incriminating him. But we always live in hope. The forensic accountants might throw up something; he might have got careless; you can't live in a house like that without a substantial income.'

'With the greatest of respect, you don't get to be a multi-millionaire and operate openly in Dundee without fear. On the surface he was a successful business man, but we all know where he got the money to legitimise his businesses, proving it is the hardest part.'

'Well we will just have to wait and see; we won't have to worry about him anymore.

At least for a short while, someone will be getting measured for his suit as we speak, let's hope it's not someone who's smarter than Monty.'

'I've seen the intelligence file on him, he doesn't come across as a master criminal, yet he strolled about like one, plenty of expensive cars, big house, a villa in Sardinia, and yet no one could prove that his money was not legally earned, why is that?'

'Believe it or not, Monty was not the number one criminal in Dundee; there are plenty of legitimate businessmen, who have financed drug- deals in Dundee, they use pawns like Monty who take some of the risk, they only risk their capital. Monty in turn uses someone else who will go down to Manchester or Liverpool for the heroin, they make money as well, but they are taking the bigger risk. If they pick up the drugs on a regular basis without any problems, they move up the ladder the risk is placed on another young novice mule. It's a Ponzi scheme.'

'Have you tried to get an informant inside the organization?'

Welsh laughed. 'It's not a large organization, Monty had three people who worked directly under him, the less people there are the less chance of mistakes, and the three others got paid very well, they went about their lives in a nondescript fashion, they live in modest houses, drive modest cars and have unspectacular jobs. I can't see them giving up their other source of income. On the other hand, they might be smart and say we've made our money, time to stop; Monty's demise could be the incentive for them to retire. That is a strong possibility. They are probably hovering near millionaire status.'

'With all this information, you already have someone on the inside?'

'No, I wish that was the case, I'll cut a long- story short, I managed to turn a mid- level dealer to give me information, using methods that would be called unlawful, I won't go into the methods, he told me after nearly a year how the soliciting, payment and collection of drugs operated. Each individual had one task and one task only, the methods they used were ingenious, but importantly so simple.'

'Monty's methods were that ingenious, that you were the only one to turn one of his gang?'

'Yes, it wasn't easy, he wouldn't tell me of all of their ingenious methods, so I had two choices either I agree to his demands or he clams up. His demands were put to me by his solicitor; either I lose some evidence, so his trial is abandoned, or we go to court where certain allegations will be put to me when I'm under oath. I told the solicitor that I will see his client in court.

'He put certain allegations to me saying I offered him immunity from prosecution, and I wanted him to inform on other dealers etc. The judge intervened and told the jury to disregard these allegations but the solicitor had made his point, these allegations would stick in their minds. He was found not guilty by a majority.'

'I remember that case, that was about three years ago. He was lucky then to walk free.'

'His luck came to an end when he was released from the dock. About six weeks later, he was found hanged in his garage. His wife blamed the pressure of the trial which is a reasonable explanation, if he was found guilty, he would have got five to seven years, he would have been out in three to four years.'

'It does seem unusual looking back, do you have another explanation?'

'He was silenced by others unknown to us but known to him.'

'Is that the consensus, or is that just your opinion?'

'That's just my opinion, our job in the drug squad is not all glamour, some of the reptiles we discover under stones are not pleasant sights. No matter what other people say about the drug squad '

'Like every other police force petty jealousies can be an impediment to cooperation, if there is no cooperation the only winner is the criminal fraternity.'

'You won't have any opposition from me it's certain persons that are reluctant to share information…'

'…that's what your colleagues in the murder squad said about the drug squad.'

'I'm not surprised at that, Joe Feeney made his feelings well-known, he thought the selection process was curious, that's all he said. But everyone knew what he meant. He followed through with that sentiment, he streamlined the drug squad, he believed in less is more. You can argue against his methods but everyone in the squad was right behind him, he got the latest laptops and new offices for his team, that's what started the resentment, no I'm telling a lie, he got us a new coffee percolator, you would think we were all driving in swanky BMW's! Anyway someone put in an official complaint about resources being wasted; the coffee percolator. The complainer was told he had paid for it out of his own pocket. The complainer came back and asked who would be paying for the annual safety check? That's what you're up against, so if that's all, I'll get moving, I've got work to do.'

Welsh's anger never subsided, his mind told him in the early hours of the morning that he would be found guilty, however, the worm of niggling doubt was burrowing deep into his mind. He caught himself shouting out loud while he was shaving on the morning of the jury returning, the jury had been sent to a hotel overnight, a bad sign, there must be conflicting views. Over in Pat Connelly's house he was singing along with the radio as he showered, they lived near to each other in the west end, but their demeanours were in conflict. Pat would have a full and hearty breakfast, Welsh would struggle to finish a small bowl of muesli, his stomach was turning over in tandem with his turbulent mind, outright depression hung over him.

Trying to rid himself of this he decided to walk to the Sheriff Court even that annoyed him, why hadn't he been tried at the High Court than the curtailed sentencing powers of the Sheriff Court? He lashed out at a plastic bag full of rubbish on the pavement. From the comfort and safety of his car Pat observed this unruly behaviour, it might add to his annoyance if he stopped and offered him a ride to the Sheriff Court, he chose the more sensible and prudent path and abandoned this thought of being polite. At the top of Roseangle he was held up by traffic, he watched Welsh loosen his overcoat; he was obviously in some discomfort.

The traffic moved slowly forward. He turned onto the Perth Road the traffic was reduced to a crawl; a burst water main outside The Queen's hotel was causing huge tail backs. He was near the hotel and the water had flooded the pavement, traffic was being controlled by a man with a stop/ go board, he was being harassed by late commuters. He looked at the hotel with a wry but satisfying smile; this was the place where his client would be taken out for breakfast once the jury returned with their not guilty majority verdict. It would be one in the eye for the Crown.

The jury had lunch for the last ten days in the Nosey Parkers restaurant, they had talked openly and loudly about the case, one member of the jury was discovered to have a penchant for cocaine at the weekend, he didn't disclose this to other jury members, but Pat Connolly was able to eke this out, each member of the jury was followed home and their details would be revealed from the voters roll, from there a credit check was compiled through a credit agency, these findings threw up interesting facets of their lives. The cocaine user was at a party, where the alcohol and cocaine made him more talkative, he spoke about the trial and the evidence. On the Sunday evening he was out running along Riverside Drive, a fellow runner caught up with him, and told him that he could go to jail for discussing the case, even if he went to the police the trial would have to be abandoned after a defence motion. He was told to take this small device and place it under the table when the jury had lunch, and remove it when they had finished, he had to sow doubts in the jury's minds.

He was told that the cop giving evidence was corrupt, he was not threatened with any physical violence, he told him to use his skill as a psychologist to sway them, not all of them, but enough to have a majority. He would be well-rewarded. The device was thrust into his hand. A car came up alongside them and the runner jumped in. He was shaken by the encounter, but as he ran along Riverside his fear disappeared. He would use this passive suggestion as an experiment, he would supplant negative and positive thoughts into his fellow members of the jury, he could write a paper on this but omit that it was a real criminal trial, and if the trial had a positive outcome, he would be well-rewarded. He didn't for a second entertain the thought of going to the police, if the police were made aware that he had discussed the case from day one they would surely know about his cocaine use. He had eight days to convince, cajole or browbeat the rest of the jury. After two days three of the jury said over lunch, 'that the police were out to get this guy.' That would be three he didn't have to persuade, others were saying 'why would the trial last two weeks, they had other things to do.'

His stride grew longer and quicker, this could be money for nothing. The lunches were recorded every day and analysed each evening. The psychologist didn't have to exercise overt mind -mapping. Two other jury members were becoming sceptical of the evidence displayed in court, which made six including him. He had still another five days to invite the others who didn't voice concerns one way or another; he just needed another three, which would make a majority of nine to six. He was listening more and talking less, some of these jury members fancied themselves as lawyers, they were picking holes in the prosecution case, and acting out why the prosecution were suggesting things than actually saying 'this is what happened, instead of I suggest this is what happened.' He just nodded in agreement His work was being done for him, as the days went on the jury became less restrained, camps were being set up in their minds, past cases were being brought up which resulted in miscarriages of justice, they wanted to be definitely clear and be convinced that the defendant was guilty. Someone suggested that it couldn't be too large of a majority in the defendant's favour as that would raise suspicion.

Why don't they tell the court officials that they needed to spend a night sleeping on it? This went down with all of them, they enjoyed each other's company, and some had romantic plans to bring into play.

Pat Connelly couldn't have wished for better, he listened to the tapes each night making copious notes, he was an amateur psychologist himself after four days of tapes, he was firmly in the camp of a not- guilty verdict, the jury had becoming less talkative of the case and more prone to talk about personal matters, including divorce and job satisfaction.

***

Ronnie followed the removal van from Robson Avenue to their new house on Blackness Avenue, a five bed roomed detached villa he was in old money country. The contract had been secured, no more offshore work for him, his office would be in the garage, originally he was going to work from a room in the house, but was advised he would feel hemmed in, even when he finished his work for the day. His wife was reluctant to leave their house in Robson Avenue, but when she viewed the house on Blackness Avenue, her resistance waned. He had chosen well, and it was near to her work in Ninewells Hospital, she didn't need to take the car, she could walk or Ronnie would drop her off. At fifty years of age he was now mortgage free, money would be flowing into his bank account instead of stopping for a weekend break.

All he required to run his business was a computer, telephone and fax machine. His manager on the platform was reliable and kept him informed of the progress, he had four welders on the rig, he could have employed more welders and gained other contracts, but he deferred from this, he wanted to keep his company a specialised company, his welders were the best paid, earning ninety-thousand a year, they had the best holiday entitlements in the off-shore industry, every other welder was aware of this, he had e-mails popping into his inbox every day. He had planned to retire and sell his profitable company which would be expanded in the last year, to gain the maximum price.

He was a keen fisherman; he would go to Norway and Canada to fish; him and his friend from Kirkton. The thought of boredom didn't concern him, his mind searched out knowledge, he would enroll in the university to study local history, and brush up on his education that he opted out of when he was younger. He had self-educated himself, but didn't have the certificates to tell the world that he was well-read. No one on the course would know who he was; he would be just passing time. The removal van stopped at the house, he would be there in person to supervise every move. The last removal into their house in Robson Avenue had some problems, the professional remover had connected up the washing machine, to the untutored eye this would have been a simple task, connecting up two hoses, one red the other blue. Three days later a puddle of water appeared in the lounge; one hose had not been connected properly. The manager of the company came out and said the wooden floor would be replaced; and apologised profusely, he didn't come back, and he ignored phone-calls, emails and faxes. He didn't ignore the civil summons to appear at the Sheriff Court, that's when Monty arrived at the house to advise him this course of action was not wise. Ronnie showed fear on his face and took him into the garage so they could talk. When Monty turned round to close the garage door, a baseball bat struck him on the collar bone, fracturing it. Monty had decided to come alone; an unwise decision. Ronnie told him the terms that he would settle to avoid going to the Sheriff Court a thousand pounds for the floor, and four thousand pounds for being disturbed on a Tuesday night. The money was delivered the following morning; it was placed in the blue wastepaper bin at the side of the house. The following day he received a letter from the Sheriff Clerk informing him that the case had been settled to his satisfaction, was this information correct? Ronnie faxed back; the information was incorrect the civil action would still be going ahead. At the court the Sheriff advised them both to come to an amicable agreement before court proceedings began, Ronnie agreed, so did the manger from the removal company, everything was settled in Ronnie's favour, for some unknown reason the manager seemed disturbed by the eye- contact from Ronnie. Monty was in the public benches replete with his arm in a sling. When Ronnie was leaving the court, he asked him if he wanted to go for a game of golf at the weekend. Monty didn't reply, his facial expression more than conveyed his answer.

That was the reason why he didn't completely trust the removal company. In any event the removal went without any problem, Ronnie tipped them generously and asked for the business card from the owner of the small firm, he might be able to generate some business for him. The owner didn't have any, Ronnie advised him to get them printed as soon as possible. Later that evening the owner dropped by with the business cards, Ronnie took him in and gave him a drink, he had a contract for him, twice a week he needed welding supplies to be taken from Dundee to Dyce, he showed him the contract that the company he was using at the moment, they were becoming unreliable and they had increased their charges. The owner told him he could do it for thirty percent less, and he had a new pick up arriving next week. Ronnie told him to put it all in writing; he gave him the terms and conditions of the original contract. Ronnie had just discovered that the original company was a subsidiary of the removal company that he had taken to Court. The increased costs were a consequence of the court case; they were trying to recoup the money that they had left in the blue wastepaper bin. Ronnie would not renew the contract even if they had halved their costs. Monty had told people who enquired about his collar bone that he had fell while hill-climbing, no-one offered any alternative explanation. Ronnie didn't expect Monty to forgive and forget, but in turn, he warned him that if he had as much as an enquiry about his health over the telephone, he would have cause for regret. Monty couldn't resist his reputation becoming weak within the criminal fraternity; he would have to exact revenge on Ronnie himself. He would suffer more than a fractured collar-bone. He planned to beat him within one inch of his life, something that would make him regret using the baseball bat, he had another choice of weapon; a power drill.

***

The Eastern cemetery always gave him a sense of perspective, everyone no matter who they were in the station of life ended up in places like this. Rich, poor, important or not, all have one thing in common, they enter life with a scream and depart their life with regret. The infant mortality rate was startling four children dying from the one family before they reached the age of ten; and this was from a merchant who was wealthy. How many children survived from poor families? His hands thrust deep in his overcoat pockets, the autumn leaves being scattered on to the graves, only the fresh snow impeding the leaves on their journey. November had been unseasonably warm, however, December made up for it, it was bone-chillingly cold. The noise from the top part of the cemetery suggested that ground was being broken by a small mechanical digger, the ground was frozen solid. He wasn't here for a local history tour; he was here to meet Michael Jameson.

 Jameson had a morbid fascination with death, he often spoke about an afterlife, Welsh never engaged him in that discussion, Jameson took it the wrong way when he had replied, 'you'll soon find out soon enough.' He didn't mean that to sound like a threat, but he could understand why Jameson thought it was when he found out the place where they would meet. Soothing words brought him back to the subject of the meeting. Feeney was no more, and in a short while he would regain his loan-shark business. Jameson had been back in Dundee for two weeks, he was living in a new build flat on the Arbroath Road. He liked to take long walks in Baxter Park, with a caveat; only in daylight hours. His appearance had changed his hair was now closely cropped he could be easily mistaken for a Polish construction worker. Boredom never entered his flat, he was ecstatic just to be back, cold wind, days that poured with rain, he welcomed the lot. His days would be filled with a walk to the paper shop, rolls and The Courier were purchased, then he would fry some bacon , make tea then settle down to breakfast. This simple routine gave him enormous pleasure.

   After a shower he would walk into town to visit the library, he had no fear of meeting Feeney did he? After an hour of browsing he would walk up the Victoria Road on his way home, he didn't take his home town for granted anymore, his exile in Dubai had created a thirst for knowledge about Dundee, the first steps to quench this thirst had been initiated, he was going on a walking tour of the ancient Howff cemetery with a local historian.
   Welsh had been as good as his word. Feeney had been removed and his business was back with him; the

rightful owner. He had wondered how he would manage to or persuade the owner of his loan-sharking business to hand over all the paperwork and monies due to him. The answer came in The Evening Chronicle; the four dealers who had been executed; one of them ran his loan-sharking business; that bastard Monty.

He wasn't dressed for the weather, sweatshirt and jeans with trainers; he wasn't a slavish follower of the sartorially elegant. He looked across the street at Ross's bar, he would venture into there that evening, he felt safe enough to risk a visit, the thought of a cold Guinness annulled any sense of fear; two pints would suffice then back to his secure top floor lair. Dubai had many selling points to the average Dundonian, sun, sand and leisure facilities, but you soon tire of them. Your day had to be filled with meaning, thank God for The Dubliner, without this he would have gone into a mental breakdown. But that was a part of his life that he wouldn't re-visit, it may have been boring but it had kept him alive; unlike Feeney and Monty.

The Eastern came into view, no more thinking about death and the inconvenience that brings, life would be lived for every fulfilling minute, Welsh would be at the gravestone of a sea captain, he had much to thank Welsh for, but he wouldn't over praise him, that would lead to the thorny subject of money, and how he could really thank him. There would be more facial expressions than warm words, he didn't anticipate a long meeting, Welsh was not a fan of the cold. He turned into the cemetery, even the graves didn't hold any fear over him anymore, he moved up the steep path and saw him studying the engravings on the head stones, the sound of his feet on some parts of the snow covered path alerted him, he looked at him, smiled, and then continued to study the head stone.

'A wee bit cold the day, don't you think?'
He held up his hand to silence him.

'Just give me a minute, I'm fascinated by this,' he finished reading and muttered something inaudible, and then turned his attention to Jameson.

'Let's walk, I see you're not feeling the cold, are you settling in the flat okay?'

'Yes, its fine nice and warm, neighbours keep to themselves, but it's only temporary, so what's on your mind?'

'You'll have read or heard about Monty and his crew up in Old Glamis Road…I had nothing to do with it, but it benefits you and me. The second thing I wanted to ask you is everything back to normal with your business?'

'As you said, the only thing that would change would be the growth of the profits, that's true, Monty must have had better contacts than me, money is coming in right left and centre, that's what recessions do, an ill economic wind sometimes is welcomed. Banks are not lending …'

'…I know all that, I've another business proposition for you, at first you'll think I'm ripping you off but hear me out, the tenement block in Scott Street, you're going to sell it, and it won't be on the open market, you're going to make big money in a property slump, there will be no debate.'

Jameson took him tightly by the arm and stopped him.

'Why are you doing this to me? I kept to my side of the bargain, I paid you the money, and as an act of good business practice, your percentage of the turnover is in your account in the Isle of Man.'

He removed his arm. 'Keep walking, you've not been listening, if you placed the block of flats on the open market in this slump do you think you would get the market value?'

'No, anybody could tell you that, but I do not want to sell…'

'I'll ignore the second part of your answer, if you were guaranteed that the block of eight flats would generate a quarter of a million pounds over the market value, would you sell?'

'Too right!'

'Good then what are you getting upset about, do you feel better now?'

'Yes, did you say you have a buyer lined up?'

'There's nothing the matter with your hearing...when the deal goes through I would appreciate say, ten percent of the gross profit, which comes to twenty five grand, I trust you're happy with that?'

'Sure, but that depends on achieving that figure above market value.'

'I said a quarter of a million pounds, so that's what it'll be.'

'Who is the buyer, someone local?'

'Yes, a company that is cash rich, they want to get in to the property market, buying traditional tenements, not new -builds, and in locations where students rent.'

'Who is the solicitor representing the company?'

'Pat Connelly... why the long face?'

'He'll come up with a fault of some kind, he'll cut into the quarter of a million, he has a reputation, I know he done conveyancing years ago, he only does criminal defence work now.'

'He does both, he likes to keep his hand in, big property deals like this he loves, there won't be any bother, trust me.'

'Okay, okay, I suppose stories get puffed up, I don't want to go to his office, can he come to the flat?'

'I've got a better idea, come over to my house tomorrow night in Wormit, you and him will thrash out the deal, it'll go smoothly, that'll give you time to maybe think what you're going to do with the money, he might have an investment strategy for you.'

'I don't think this is the time to invest, I don't have a car yet, could you pick me up?'

'No that wouldn't be wise, get a taxi over to the Wormit

Arms, I'll see you there at seven.'

'Will you be in the pub or outside in the car park?'

'In the car park, my house is just minutes away.'

'This Connelly, how did he know about Scott Street?'

'He didn't, I mentioned it, he was acting on behalf of a company that has surplus funds, if they don't use the money it will disappear in taxes, so it's better for them to take on debt to invest.'

'I can understand that, but he won't try to shaft me will he?'

'Not at all, it's in his interest to wrap this up as quickly as possible; he's not doing this as an act of kindness.'

'Okay, is there anything else I should bring with me, passport, and driving licence?'

'All you need to do is bring a pen, for your signature, everything will be straightforward.'

'Okay, I understand, Connelly will send all the paperwork to my solicitor and then my cheque will follow, how soon?'

'I don't know the procedure, but I'm sure Connelly will explain everything to you, I'll see you tomorrow, I'll have a wander about here for a while,' he walked away from him.

Jameson made his way to the Arbroath Road, the bitter cold was piercing his sweat shirt, he had plenty time to ruminate the machinations of the deal, the proceeds from the sale of Scott Street would partly fund a residence on Jersey, he would go to the library then surf the Internet for properties in Jersey, whenever he found one he would call his financial advisor there and arrange finance. Things were looking brighter for him. In the summer there were regular flights to Jersey from Dundee, he had business acquaintances over there they were surprised he was moving to Dubai, but he just told them an opportunity had arisen. Feeney and Monty were the impediments that kept him from returning to Dundee, now they were gone he would gradually resurface in

Dundee, he would be diversifying some of his business interests, he would broach this with Connelly tomorrow night.

History was repeating itself, he acquired Scott Street in the 1980's the property market was in the doldrums, the landlord had ran up significant debts at The Chevalier casino, popular with a cross section of society, especially on a Tuesday night, Asian shopkeepers, Chinese owners of restaurants as well as taxi drivers who lived on the outskirts of Dundee, sometimes they would tout for business at the end of the night. Jameson had a female friend who worked as a croupier, a creepy taxi driver had tried it on with her, Jameson was able to convince the taxi driver that he should desist from this practice, when his broken arm healed he paid his debt but didn't return to the casino.

The croupier told Jameson that a landlord had run up considerable debts and was being leant on to settle his accounts, he was at the end of his tether, he was drunk that night and needed a shoulder to lean on, he said he had property but couldn't sell because the market was dead. Jameson became his white knight, he went to his office and told him that he was interested in Scott Street, Jameson gave him a fair price, he could have offered him significantly less, but he wanted the landlord to become his friend, he had friends who were in the property business and some of them were seeking an exit. Jameson met them and took their assets off of them again at a fair price, they had another reason to sell to Jameson; he was white. Asian landlords were trying to squeeze the price down; Jameson was giving them a premium.

Nearly thirty years on he was being offered a premium, he didn't feel any pressure, Scott Street had served him well over the decades, he had borrowed money against it to fund other property ventures, he would be sad to see it go, the proceeds from its sale would alleviate some of the crocodile tears.

Connelly could alter his plans dramatically; instead of a slow sell-off of assets he might be able to entice someone to purchase his assets as a job- lot. Shop leases, factoring agreements, and plots of land, that would still leave him with his money-lending business, he wouldn't be keen to dispose of this burgeoning cash generating asset. He was aware of upstanding members of the business community who were financing projects that he would not for a second entertain; drugs.

The businessmen tried to ignore where the money would end up, in their defence they said they had loaned money to a certain individual because the Banks declined, and one had seen their business plan, and had seen merit in it, so he loaned the money, at above the interest rate norm. New builds did spring up as the business plan forecast, but a large share of the money lent purchased drugs from Liverpool. It was inevitable that some of their family members were scourged by drugs, which was when they had seen the error of their lending policy. Jameson might have been unscrupulous in many of his business practices' but he had a conscience. Violence would be used if someone threatened him with violence, and if the perpetrator was too much to deal with, he either paid up or sought help from the police on a one- to -one basis, no official complaint would be made, no statement would be given, everything would be spelt out in a quiet location, if the problem was dealt with, he and the officer would come to an amicable arrangement. Welsh had more humanity than Feeney, he had never hidden his hatred for him, he wasn't here to be loved he was here to make money. The exile had ended when Feeney's life ended, Welsh was much more approachable than Feeney, he was out to make money as quickly as possible, and 'the war on drugs was the most expensive failure ever.' He knew it and so did Welsh.

***

Lenny was trying not to be too, angry; GG may have been a diligent detective but his timekeeping was woeful. That however was not the real source of his anger; he had been informed that his application to join the drug squad had been rejected, based on his inexperience. He would have accepted this reason if he hadn't have learnt that someone more inexperienced than him had been accepted. As soon as he was made aware who it was he hit the road and went for a long run in the freezing drizzle. In the shower his anger subsided, he had reasoned it was not that he was the inferior candidate, it was plainly based on political correctness, and the successful candidate was of the female gender. If Feeney was still alive this wouldn't have happened. GG had been his inside information but that had ended, he was prematurely retiring, Lenny would have fitted comfortably into his shoes. The Plans of mice and men.

This could be the end of the profitable partnership with GG, without real information it would be a pointless and dangerous exercise. The wind was sending the rain hard into his face, there was no shelter except for the tree which was shorn of its leaves, GG advised him that coming to Bellfield Avenue was too much of a risk. He could've chosen someplace that gave him more protection from the relentless rain, Dudhope Park was deserted, and not even a crisp packet was floating in the wind. He saw him climb the steps that emerged from the car-park; he was dressed for the weather.

As the figure came closer he was overcome with anxiety, he was smiling.

'Surprised Lenny?'

'Where's GG?' He instantly regretted the question.

'Do you really want to know?'

'What do you mean, of course I want to know, he was meant to meet me here, and   who are you?'

193

'That's of no concern of you, GG won't be contacting you again, and I'm your contact and your saviour.'
He hands him a piece of paper. 'Read it.'
He holds it loosely in his hand; the wind is blowing it furiously.
'You better not lose it,' he tightens his grip on the paper.
'Where's GG?'
'Do you really want to know?
Lenny shrugs his shoulders.
'What do you see in front of you?'
'The west end...'
'...beyond that?'
'The Tay...'
'Well done, he's in there, or he was in there, he's probably in the North Sea now, or at least some of him will be, but his heart is still in Dundee.'
'You...you mean he's dead,' he said quietly.
'Is easy to see you're a police officer, pity there weren't other police officers like you Dundee's crime rate would be zero.'
'Why?'
'Are you taking the piss now,' he said angrily.
'No, no, why did you kill him?'
'Cannabis plants, the prick that bought them tried to sell them back to us, he didn't know we have more than one supplier, quite a stupid move. That's what happens when you try to rip off the Triads, he gave GG's name, we didn't have to try too hard with him to give us the names, GG went down fighting, but there is only a certain amount of resistance any man can repel, they got your name out of him after three hours, you don't want to know what they did to extract your name do you?'
Lenny is cold not just from the winter weather but the thought of the pain that GG suffered to protect him. What was required of him? He slowly released his frozen fingers that were wrapped tightly around the note.

'Have you studied it enough? For fucks sake it's only one name! Give me back the paper,' he gives him it back and watches as he rips it into tiny pieces and casts them to the vagaries of the wind, they both watch as the tiny pieces fly into different directions.

'What do you want me to do?'

'Kill him.'

Now he's laughing. 'You're kidding?'

'I don't think you have a choice, if he lives you die, and you should think yourself lucky, the Chinese believe that a good deed wipes out a bad deed.'

'And you really expect me to do this, then everything goes back to normal, you must think I'm mad?'

'Oh no, they don't think your mad, if they did, you would be enjoying the same watery grave as your pal, they want you to work for them, but only after you take care of our friend.'

'How can you expect me to believe you, they'll just kill me after I have killed…'

'…they won't they're an honourable organization, they do a lot for charity, that doesn't get reported.'

Lenny couldn't contain his mirth. 'You actually said that with a straight face, you could have been describing the Rotarians, have you forgotten you've just told me that they tortured and murdered GG?'

'Only because you and GG stole from them, they have a low -tolerance when it comes to theft.'

Lenny was incredulous; he really believed what he was telling him.

'If I agree to do this what plans do they have for me?'

'Plans that are beneficial to your wealth and your health, how much of the population benefits from both?'

Lenny feels more relaxed, he has a curious empathy for the messenger.

'Why do I have to kill him…what did he do?'

He pulled the baseball cap down further, the wind had changed direction, his face was being battered by the rain, but he wouldn't shift direction.

'You're straying into dangerous territory, once you have removed him, ask me again, and I'll tell you, but it's best to be blessed with ignorance.'

There was malevolent hardness in his Liverpool accent.

'How do you want me to do it?'

He pulled out a small plastic bag from his raincoat. 'It's loaded, do it when he gets out his car on Tuesday night, you'll be under the cover of darkness, plenty of trees in the street, just get up close, two shots in the back of the head, you'll have a motorbike to remove yourself, then you start your nightshift, just leave the bike at GG's.'

'Ah no, I don't want GG to take the rap for this, I can't do this, I can't do it, I'm sorry.'

'There's no backing out now, I've told you enough, GG is not here is he? He is your alibi, have you thought about that?' He hadn't.

'You know how to ride a motorbike?'

'Yes.'

'Good, the bike will be parked at GGs flat, he was regular as clockwork, arrived home at six, after you have completed the task go up to his flat and change into the clothes there, leave the gun in the fridge. Do you understand all that?'

'Yeah, but I feel as though I'm desecrating his grave and his memory.'

'You're not, he'd be proud of you, he thought a lot of you, I'm going now, see you on Tuesday.'

'Are you coming, I mean are you going to be there?'

'We'll be there every step of the way.'

'Okay,' he didn't know if he felt threatened or reassured. 'What's to stop me pulling out the gun and shooting you?'

'I touch my cap or GGs cap, and your head would be removed.'

'I don't understand?

'Okay… do you see the Bell Street multi-story car

park?'

He nods but is clearly confused.

'Good, now watch for flashing lights from a car when I touch your head, are you ready?

'Yes,' he replied nervously.

He ruffled his hair like Oliver and Hardy doing a comedy routine. All eyes were on the top of the car park. A car flashed its lights three times and the driver's door opened, it was left ajar, no one stepped out of the car.

'Did you see the light show?'

'Yes I did, but what's the story with the door, why has that been left open?'

'A simple explanation; if I touch my cap, and I walk away, a bullet knocks a hole in your head; you don't want me to touch my cap, do you?'

'Fuck no! I believe you, what have I got myself mixed up in,' he gulped.

He mockingly laughed and walked away, before turning round.

'See you on Tuesday Lenny.'

Lenny pleaded with him, 'don't touch that cap,' and then ran in the direction of the tennis courts. His mind was overcome with grief and foreboding, he didn't expect to live if he carried out the order, 'but what else can I do,' he shouted out repeatedly into the howling wind. The elderly woman walking her dog; heard his anguished cry, she turned round, he looked embarrassed and smiled. At the tennis courts he stopped running he tried to gulp as much air as his lungs could take. His car was parked on the road that led up to the Dundee Law. Inside the car, he took some kitchen paper from the glove compartment and wiped the rain and sweat from his face and brow. How he wished GG was here, he would tell him not advise him what to do.

Fucking unbelievable! He would have to carry out the assassination, and then hope he was good as his word. What else could he do? He started the engine and thought for a second, then moved off, he'd go home and have a shower. Then think, was there some way out of this murderous conundrum? He couldn't go to the police and explain about ripping -off drug dealers, and then casually mention that they happened to shoot one of them dead. He was at a dead end; his head could not accept any more questions. Today was Sunday, the start of his nightshift, in a few days he would be pumping bullets into his head, and GG would be framed for the murder, his stomach felt queasy. Even in death GG would be helping him out, he would be interviewed along with the other constables and detectives; he would just be in shock like the rest of them. He looked at his speedometer he was doing fifty, and he didn't have his wipers on. He pulled into the side of the road, turned the engine off and opened the window, the cold air and some rain hit his face. He closed the window, started the engine, indicated, and activated the wipers. More deep breaths, he felt calmness return, he moved off.

***

Sitting on the train going to Edinburgh, brought back all the regret and frustration, the root cause of his sleepless nights; Raymond Andrews. Morag interrupted his self-flagellation.

'You've went quiet, something bothering you?'

'The truth being yes, but I don't want to discuss it; if I do you won't get me to stop.'

'Oh right,' she was hurt at the answer.

'I don't mean I don't want to talk to you about it, I don't want to talk to anyone, it was just something I was working on, my last case before I retired, that's all.'

'Okay, change of subject, are you sure you don't want to go back to Dubai?'

The furrowed brow became less prominent. 'I have absolutely no doubt, the security business is different from police work, I appreciated what the two Daves did for me, they saved my sanity, and I would have gone into my shell in Dundee. Dubai was an experience, but it was not for me, I got paid well, lost weight, took up golf again and got a tan, so it wasn't all that bad.'

'I fell out of love with Dubai, there were too many dubious characters becoming involved in the property business, and what convinced me to follow my instinct was a police officer, Paul Welsh, using a credit card with another name.

'And him becoming the senior officer of the drugs squad because his senior officer gets a bullet in a church.'

'I know, I know, I've been delving into certain matters, I still have some friends on the force, information has been coming to me thick and fast, I have to filter it, I believe someone is giving me misinformation, I'll tell you about it later, now why the daytrip to Edinburgh?'

'I don't want to be seen with you in Dundee or the 'Ferry, and I like Edinburgh, we'll have lunch and visit the National Galleries, you said you like art didn't you?'

'Lunch I like, but art…?'

'…of course you like art you're not a philistine, I'm a good judge of character, the National Galleries is quiet and the perfect place to talk, I feel comfortable surrounded by art.'

'Could you give me an indication, what the subject will be about?'

'Okay, but don't press me till after we have lunch, you promise?'

'I promise.' he said wearily.'

'Our friend Paul Welsh, his money exceeds his lifestyle.'

'Have you not got it the other way round, his lifestyle exceeds his salary?'

'I know what I said, I made no mistake.'

***

Dundee was looking idyllic from the summit of the

Law, outside the temperature had plummeted to minus three. He was on a journey with nostalgia, good times outweighed the bad. Now he was all alone, he had allowed the probationary officer to go home four hours early from duty; on the explicit understanding that he would be picked up outside his flat in Stobswell at five - thirty am, and then they could sign off together. There was no resistance from the probationary officer. He activated his number again; dead just like its owner. Fife looked a million miles away, the nursery where they relieved the poly-tunnel of its lucrative plants, seemed to be taunting him, the light shining from the poly-tunnel was brighter than ever before, it was back in business, he placed his binoculars on the dashboard.

His appetite was completely diminished, his mind was focused on Tuesday, if he had any doubts about the organization he was involved with, then this morning proved that they had him encapsulated. After one slice of toast that he couldn't finish, he had a warm shower, then went to bed, any tiredness that hung over him was eradicated by the money spread on his bed. He counted the notes; twenty-thousand pounds.

He placed the money in the small suitcase, which concerned him, but not as much as how they had entered the flat without activating the alarm. So much for the reassuring warm words of the engineer who had installed the alarm; that were now hollow. Perhaps he had forgotten to set the alarm, maybe so, but how did they get in? The door was multi-locked. They were experts in everything, locks and alarms would cause them no moments of angst. He remembered when he came in this morning he had reset the alarm before it went off, he had twenty seconds to do this. The money must have been meant to reassure him, that they were men of honour, he had doubts about that. Where was the rest of the money that GG had or invested, the Triads must have the account number? He remembered being told, 'they had big plans for him,' hmmn, was the twenty grand part of the proceeds from the dealers and cannabis rip-offs? The money would have to remain dormant in his wardrobe, until after Tuesday, and if they were true to their word, they would tell him the best method of making it grow and be invisible to the outside world.

GG never knew that they were onto him, if they were he kept that to himself, he was shielding him. Then a memory floated then landed on him, the night he was over at GG's flat, the intercom buzzed, GG went into the hall and came back quickly, he said it was someone who had left their key, they needed buzzed in, he didn't seem worried then. It didn't matter they were onto GG and had killed him. They were now onto him, he just hoped that when he did the job on Tuesday that would be his reprieve from death, he didn't want to see his short life on earth come to an end after being tortured, sliced up and cast into the Tay. He wouldn't be able to look at the proud river with the same affection; it must be the secret acropolis of Dundee.

***

'I see everyone seems to know you Morag, from the concierge to the waiter, so you are not a stranger to The Scotsman hotel?'
'I'm known to most hotel staff in Edinburgh, I enjoy autumn and winter in Edinburgh, when I came home on holiday from Dubai, I met many influential people in the financial world, I scratch your back, that sort of thing.'
They walked past the four marble pillars towards the North Bridge Brassiere, he felt more relaxed, the wooden paneled walls were comforting. The waiter guided them to the table.
'Are you not going to take that Bison off of your back?'
She didn't look up from the menu. He felt his face rise in temperature.

'Oh… right,' he stood up slowly looking at other diners, no one was paying him the slightest bit of attention, the same waiter came over and relieved him of his heavy overcoat.

'Are you going to look at the menu or do you wish me to choose for you,' her eyes lifted from the folded menu. 'I can manage thank you very much, now let's see…ah, the rump of Perthshire lamb, with potato…I'm not sure about the aubergine caviar…'

'My congratulations on your choice, I thought you were a pie and chips man…the aubergine caviar is delicious.'

'I trust you, so I'll go for it, then I'll have pie and chips, if that's okay?'

'You're kidding, tell me you are?' she leant forward and whispered.'

'We'll see; are we having a drink?'

She smiles at the waiter; he comes over on this latent command, takes the order and returns with the drinks.

'So when did you first come here then?'

'The first Hogmanay it opened I stayed in a suite, expensive, but worth the experience, it rained on New Year's day, and in my heart it was thunder and lightning, but that was the fag end of my marriage, I don't wish to discuss, if you don't mind.'

'Sure, I understand, sometimes it's better to break a marriage rather than just shuffle along…so what happened then?'

'God! What a cheek you've got…I paid out plenty on my therapy; I just can't believe you have asked, when I explicitly asked you to refrain from asking or probing.' She raised the glass to her lips and tried to suppress her smile.

'Was he having an affair then, and who was he having it with?'

'If I told you you'd be in shock for the rest of your life, but I won't tell you, how is your marriage?'

'Too exciting, if I told you, you would just feel

envious, so who was the other woman?

'Who said it was a woman?'

CHAPTER FOUR

The car park was an eerie, cheerless place, and the multi-coloured Christmas lights could only act as a contrast to the shadowy car park. He could understand the apprehension when Jameson stepped out of the taxi, if he was in fear for his life, this dark, cold and exposed place would ignite his imagination.

Connelly was already in his house, his mood as always was ebullient, and he was at his charming best. He had arrived early, he had said that he had unexpected good news that may have been of interest to Michael Jameson; he didn't elaborate or hint the good tidings that he had brought. If this was designed to alter his mood, he had succeeded. He told him that he would go and pick him up from the Wormit Arms, in case he was early. He needed time to think before Jameson arrived; an extra ten minutes sitting in the car might trigger something. Twenty minutes had elapsed; Jameson had not contacted him to tell him that he was running late and why he was running late. Connelly's good tidings were wiped from his thoughts. The car park was flooded with light, he lifted his arm up to shield his eyes. He opened his eyes slightly, he saw the sign on the car roof; Jameson had arrived. The taxi still had its lights on full beam. Jameson's silhouette was walking towards him, he switched on his lights, then on to full beam, the driver threw up his arms more in alarm than surprise, he started gesticulating then showed his limited lexicon of rude sign language. Jameson entered the rear of his car.

'Where have you been?'

'Don't even go there, the explorer, sorry taxi driver thought Tayport was Wormit, but I'm here, has Connelly arrived yet?'

Welsh was listening and watching the taxi-driver work himself into a near cardiac apoplexy, he took his seatbelt off, and was shouting, he walked to Welsh's car and yanked open the door.

'What's the fucking story with the lights pal?'

Welsh looked at him. 'That's not a wise move, go back to your car and toddle off back to Dundee, that's if you can find your way out of a deserted car park.'

He placed his stocky arms on the roof of the car.

'Do you want to show me the way out, or do you want to stay in your car and look like a prick?'

Welsh silently loosened the seat belt, the taxi driver didn't move, he head-butted him in the gargantuan stomach, he staggered back from the car, Welsh quickly moved from his seat, the taxi-driver was in obvious distress, Welsh grabbed him by the ears and pulled him towards the taxi and flung him against it, no words were spoken. The taxi-driver didn't look back; he got into his car, and commenced a U-turn, then gave him an uncomplimentary wave with one finger.

'Taxi -drivers don't you just love them!'

'New York taxi drivers are meant to be the rudest in the world, Dundee has taken over that mantle.'

The car stops outside the house. 'Very impressive, and they say crime doesn't pay.'

Welsh gave him a withering look.

'I hope you don't mean what I think you mean?'

'No, no…I meant you stopping crime because you're a detective, nothing sinister, no offence meant.'

'Well, I am offended, remember you'd still been in Dubai humping camels, so cut the crap, you understand?'

He nodded apologetically, he had never seen Welsh look or sound so angry.

'Right out of the car, watch what you say to Connelly, he's not as forgiving as me, no smart comments, okay?'

'Okay, I've learnt my lesson, point taken.'

The walk up the driveway to the front door, Welsh opens it and Jameson sheepishly follows him in. Welsh introduces them to one another, they all move to the table beside the bay window, Welsh closes the heavy curtains. Pat goes through the contract line by line, Jameson signs all the forms. The bargain has been concluded. Pat insists they celebrate with a drink, Welsh does not join in the celebrations.

'Do you have a plan for the money Michael?'

'I have nothing on my radar, do you have any suggestions?'

Connelly momentarily changed his gaze from Jameson to Welsh then back to Jameson.

'There will be an opportunity in Dundee very soon, people pass by it every day, someone writes to The Courier about an asset to the City, but time marches on and the asset becomes less lovable, do you know what I'm talking about, Michael?'

'I am afraid I don't.'

'The Silvery Tay Hotel.'

'Mr Connelly, many developers have tried to buy the building and have submitted plans for flats, and even turn it back to its original splendour, all have failed.'

'But that was then, things have changed, Historic Scotland will be changing, some people are due to retire, the people who will replace them, are more attuned to my thinking.'

'Right,' he said slowly. He continued trying hard to hide his obvious interest. 'Are you looking for investors?'

'Better than that, do you wish to own The Silvery Tay Hotel?'

'It depends on the price and if I'm allowed to turn it into flats, I can take a risk.'

'The property market is dead, but in two or three years, well it will be back to the boom times, especially with the Waterfront right on The Silvery Tay Hotel's doorstep. And not forgetting the new train station; when the Waterfront comes on stream, I'm talking millions, but let's not get ahead of ourselves, let's stick to The

Silvery Tay Hotel, do not ask about any investment in the Waterfront, do I make myself clear?

Jameson is taken aback at this. 'Crystal clear.'

'Good. My information regarding The Silvery Tay Hotel is that other developers will be submitting plans, mostly for apartments, because of the economic climate, they will have great difficulty in securing funding from the banks, the days of companies in particular construction companies going bust leaving creditors in their wake then starting over again but with a new name are over. Historic Scotland will be insisting that the plans are accompanied by secure funding that is already in place; that eliminates ninety percent of your competitors, you will have the funding with a substantial contingency fund, the company that will refurbish The Silvery Tay Hotel will have experience, the company specialises in Victorian and historical hotels.'

'Okay, but what about the cost of buying and converting the hotel?'

'That is where you have to show a remarkable amount of trust in me, I have the plans and the finance in hand now, I need a down payment from you of two million, then when the work commences on the hotel another three million, when everything is completed you will have a minimum profit of five million. You will not be a director or shareholder on any documents that pertain to the company.'

'I can understand that, but I'd like to have a look at the plans…'

'…I'm sorry that is out of the question, the company concerned have invested too much time, money and effort in drawing up the plans, they can't take a risk of them leaking out to their competitors, I am sure you understand.'

'Let's be clear here, you want me to invest five million pounds without my name being on any documents, and I am not allowed to see any of the plans, how do I know this is not a scam?'

'I can totally understand what you're saying, but I did mention having trust in me, and you have a premium on your block of flats in Scott Street.'

'I know, but five million being handed over,' he starts to rub his chin slowly while his mind is in turmoil.'

'But I won't press you, think of the minimum five million clear profit and I stress minimum tax free.'

'You didn't say that the profit would be tax free, and it's all legitimate?'

'No signature on the documents, or directorship or being a major shareholder. Of course it's legal you are not investing are you?'

'What do you think Paul?'

'If I had the money, I wouldn't think twice, Pat has made you money on Scott Street hasn't he, what is there to think about?'

'You're right I'm in, what account do I put the money in, it'll take a few days to set up.'

Pat takes out a business card, and gives him a pen to copy the bank and account number.

***

Sitting outside, nerves shredded, different scenarios battling against each other, this was the worst feeling that she had encountered. The door opened, she studied his face; poker face. He swept his hand indicating she should come into his office. No smiles were exchanged. She waited till she was invited to take a seat. His desk had a folder which was opened, her eyes caught the name; her name. He closed the folder and leant on it with both elbows, he looked at her, studying her, was he trying to make her shift in her seat?

'Why do you want to be a member of the drugs squad?'

Her confidence returned, her answer was corroded with clichés, he intervened.

'That's all very well; I want to know why you want this

208

position, the real reason. This is your final chance, if I don't think you're telling me the truth, I'll stop you…continue.'

She had gone over every eventuality in her head, her answers were delivered by rote, he had seen through her, flashing of eyelashes didn't impress Paul Welsh.

'I'm in a difficult position here, if I truly say what is on my mind, I definitely won't get the job, everyone knows who your preferred candidate is.'

His face was an open window. He leant forward to intimidate her. He scowled.

'Well, well, you are in an awkward position, up to now you have failed miserably, you can only get better, or do you wish to cut your losses and leave?'

'Okay you asked for it, I want to be in the drug squad, because I believe it's been infiltrated by dealers, I sincerely believe that information is being passed to them concerning operational matters. I'm exempting you from my analysis, I think, no; I know I can find out who is passing information to dealers.'

He looked at her saying absolutely nothing. She had no information whatsoever to back up her serious allegations; she knew it would strike a chord with Welsh. He must welcome her into the drug squad now. He opened her file and seemed to be studying it.

'That's a serious allegation, but an allegation that I can't take lightly, now comes the difficult part, where's the proof?'

'I can't say…just yet. I can understand if you dismiss the allegation, but you asked why I wanted to be an officer in the drug squad, I told you.'

'Okay, I can understand protecting your source, how long have you had suspicions?'

'Two years.'

'That was in my predecessor's time, did you speak to him about it and if not why not?

She was shaking her head

. 'No…I didn't trust him.'

'Why was that…do you want a coffee?' She had him hooked.

'A coffee please with milk, no sugar.'

He picked up the phone and ordered the coffee.

'First of all, he didn't like women; that was obvious, and he hated smart women. If I told him what I just told you, he would have spread stories about me and made my life a complete misery, hoping that in the end the ridicule would get to me and I would resign. I wasn't prepared to take that chance, today I am.'

'You're either very brave or very stupid, only time will tell.'

The knock on the door reverberated around the voluminous room.

'Come' he barked out loudly. The coffee was brought in by a petite woman in her thirties, she planked the tray down in the middle of his desk; she smirked at her.

'I see she's happy at her work.'

He ignored this remark. 'The way I see it, we that is, the drug squad have done really well in jailing dealers, Feeney was probably murdered because he was throttling them out of business, or do you think he was murdered because of something else?'

'I'm not totally convinced that's all I'm prepared to say at the moment.'

'You're inferring a lot, but you're not saying much.'

'I know, but you asked me to state why I want to be in the drug squad, I've been honest, and I don't want to be the token women, I'd rather be in on merit.'

'I think your honesty has talked you into trouble.'

She put down the coffee on the saucer and stood up.

'Whoever said honesty is the best policy was an idiot…thanks for the interview.'

'I've not finished, you'll get a letter in the next fourteen days, you've been the most outstanding and frank interviewee, but keep this to yourself, if I hear that you have said that you've got the job, the letter will be delivered earlier but with bad news, do I make myself clear?'

Her hands were gripping the chair.

'I understand… you won't regret it.'

She turned and left his office.

Welsh grimaced, what does she know exactly? Better to have her in the tent than out of it. She must be getting information from someone in the drug squad, and that someone must be talking to her or is involved with her. If he can find out in the next couple of weeks who she is seeing, he would have a better idea whether the information is true or gossip. If the guy she is seeing is saying too much true or false, he can engineer a situation that would make him resign from the force never mind the drug squad. Tonight he would have an educated guess, going over his squad's character, he had to start there ask innocent questions that gave an incisive answer.

***

'Was it that boring?'

'Art, I'm afraid I don't think it's meant for me, I heard what you said in there, but I can't work myself into a lather…like you. It's getting chilly best to keep walking.'

'I don't work myself into a lather; its passion a fundamental difference. Where do you want to walk to then?'

'I'm not fussed, it's better than standing here on the steps of an art gallery.'

'It's not an art gallery, it's the National Galleries, don't you appreciate your heritage?'

'Sometimes,' he takes hold of her elbow and guides her down the steps.

'I can manage myself thank you, where are we going?'

'Down to Princes Street Gardens, we can walk and talk there, I forgot to thank you for the lunch, thank you.'

She was taken aback, no one of her friends had thanked her when she took them out to lunch it had become an acceptable ritual.

'No need to thank me, I'm glad you enjoyed the meal.'

'So what's on your mind, Morag?'

'Our detective friend is more interesting than I first thought. Since I've been back in Dundee, I have been able to check out certain property transactions, he has been busy buying and selling, the money has been transferred to Cyprus, Northern Cyprus to be exact, and we're talking about seven figure sums. I know he is well paid, but he couldn't have accumulated millions by legitimate means, and that's only in Dubai.'

'Seven figure sums! You said the money ends up in Cyprus…'

'Northern Cyprus, there is a significant difference.'

He stops walking. There is?' She keeps walking.

'Come on keep up, Northern Cyprus doesn't have an extradition treaty with the U.K. Now why would he place millions in banks there, and I mean plural banks?'

'Under assumed names I expect. If you are correct in what you heard you think he is linked or connected to the murder of Joe Feeney.'

'I'm convinced, he was in a position to take a natural advantage when Feeney was murdered and he did.'

'There won't be any argument from me with your assessment, and he had the perfect alibi, he was on his stag night, week on the drink, in Dubai.'

'And also using a legitimate credit card with another name on it that had a limit of forty thousand.'

'Yeah…clever Trevor, and he has been very clever, your contacts in Dubai, are they suspicious of your enquiries, about him.'

'No, we have to do a myriad of checks, there are plenty of fake bonds swirling about, and fraud or attempted fraud is an everyday occupational hazard. To let you understand, what Welsh is doing is not that unusual, he

212

has not been defrauding banks or finance houses, transferring money to Northern Cyprus is unusual, I don't know if the money stays there or goes on a journey, then does the money end up in the U.K. I can only guess.'

'Do you have the paperwork showing that the funds leave Dubai then go to Cyprus?'

'I have all the relevant documentation, in my bag; I'll give it to you to read on the train.'

'Well it's a great start, a true saying follow the money.'

'I wouldn't get too excited you could come to a dead end in Cyprus, I'm not being overly pessimistic, but that could happen, then what do you do? You're out of the force; things will be more difficult to check.'

'I wouldn't be too hard on yourself, don't build yourself up for a fall, it's a Scottish trait, we dance with pessimism and bury optimism'.

'Why do you think Welsh had Feeney murdered then?'

'We can't even think like that, you end up getting fixated, you end up missing warning signs and clues, we'll start with Trevor's business transactions in Dubai then the transfer of the money, that usually opens doors or a door at least. I can check the bank in Cyprus, what for I don't know. At night I can watch Welsh, he might meet interesting people.'

'You're more upbeat now, you're even walking faster, you must miss your job.'

He stopped. 'You're absolutely correct, I didn't think I did or would, but I miss real detective work, going out into the field, up into tenements where posties fear to enter, talking to the scumbags, letting them know we are on top of them, I miss that.'

'Then why did you leave?'

'That's for another day, I didn't entirely leave of my own accord, I didn't realise that at the time, but I came to that conclusion sitting on my balcony in Dubai, weird eh?'

She choked off her response; he looked crestfallen as if he was in disgrace.

'I shouldn't have asked, I apologise, the Daves' think the world of you, I know that.'

'You don't have to apologise, God I ask enough questions don't I, ah the two Daves what a team we were. But you can't look back, only forward, unfortunately.'

***

The closing of the door made a welcome sound, Jameson had left. Connelly and Welsh stood still, suspending conversation. The taxi could be heard pulling away. They smiled at one another, Welsh made his way to the table with a drink for Connelly.

'There are no doubts in his head. He's one of the few people that can listen, digest and come to a decision, I have a sneaking admiration for Michael Jameson, seemingly of low-intellect and devoid of friends, but he gets on with his life.'

'By and large, there are worse people than him in business.' replied Welsh.

'Don't underestimate him, he's shrewd and cunning, The Silvery Tay Hotel will be a worthwhile investment, everyone is a winner, the city, tourists, businesspeople and the investors, and that includes you.'

'Forgive me going into pessimistic mode again, there will not be a last minute challenge from the courts or another development company will emerge?'

'Do I really have to answer that?' He finished the drink and motioned for a refill.

'I know I shouldn't have asked that, it's just nervous energy, I'm just looking for reassurance,' he filled the glass with a more generous measure.

'Just leave the details to me, it wouldn't benefit you in any way, to know what the process will be, remember I'm a silent investor as well, our money is safe, don't have any doubts. Now are you reassured?'

'Yes,' his hands were thrust deep into his pockets and he was pacing the room.

'To take your mind off it…how is the investigation going into the murders?'

'Which one…the dealer being shot, Joe Feeney being assassinated or the four naked amigos?'

'If you don't want to talk about it, there's no problem.'

'No details, nothing, the longer it goes on the harder it will be to piece together the motives, the dealer being shot, in the flat, that was a sting of some kind, I've heard that the story about Polish gunmen, is looking shaky, now I'm just passing on what I've heard.

'According to someone who I don't know, reckons it was the scousers who did it, nothing to do with Polish gunmen.'

'Joe Feeney's death was curious, is there any linkage to the dealers being murdered?'

'Nothing I've heard of, have you heard something?'

'Nothing, I was just thinking the head of the drug squad is murdered then four of the most prominent dealers in Dundee are shot, I'm looking for a motive, usually in murders its very unusual for someone to kill someone without a motive.'

'That thought has come to me on a regular occurrence, but I can't see any connection…just now.'

He lifted himself up from the seat. 'Time to go home now, I've work to do.'

***

Princes Street Gardens was busy with people going to the rides that were ensconced for the upcoming annual Hogmanay street party. They had walked and talked for going on two hours; both were weary but comfortable with each other's company. Eddings suggested they should be making a move towards Waverley Station if they were going to catch the 15.30 train to Dundee; his curiosity was eating into his patience. They made the train with minutes to spare. He didn't need to ask for the documents, she majestically handed them over. He devoured the information, underlining certain parts of the information. He placed them back in the envelope.

'It's alright for me to keep hold of them for now, that's if you have no objection?'

'Keep them they're of more use to you than me, I thought you would be interested.'

'Interested! We are talking about a serving police officer, the head of the drug squad, laundering money, that's the minimum, millions of pounds, sloshing about in bank accounts in every tax haven imaginable, but one thing is remiss, there is no record of money being transferred to any U.K bank account, I can handle that just now, I just need to do more digging about Trevor.'

'There is someone behind him, who would give him so much money, why would someone place so much money in his accounts?'

'I don't think that's his money, he'll be getting a commission, for arguments sake say ten per cent, according to the information over a six month period twenty million went through his bank accounts; that's two million, and that's only in six months. How long has he been laundering money, what has he been doing with his commission, has that money been used for illegal activities?'

'Keep your voice down.'

'I didn't realise I was talking loudly,' he looked to see if passengers were staring at him, to his relief no one was, they were engrossed in reading magazines and newspapers, others were listening to their Ipod's.

'Does Welsh have a house that exceeds his salary?'

'I don't know about now, but he lived in the west end, nothing grandiose, his wife's a teacher. No he doesn't live beyond his means, but I'll find out that won't be too difficult.'

216

'Follow the money…I've never truly understood what that meant, I had an idea, but when you know the person and see his bank transactions, I fully understand now. How do you find out about the people who deposit the money in his accounts?'

'Speaking to a forensic accountant years ago, he showed me how money changes into property, high value motors and even antiques, however, some of the items have to change back into money quickly.'

On the twenty first floor of the Alexander multi-storey, he peered through the night time vision binoculars; the bedroom was losing the chill that filled it. The halogen heater was battling hard, trying to defeat the debilitating bitter cold night air. This was the side of the drug squad that he had dreamt of; surveillance. This was the third night and everything was forming a pattern; a monotonous, tedious pattern. He could observe the transient nocturnal residents go into tenement blocks on the Hilltown, then reappear hours sometimes minutes later' he was interested in the car that was stopping at different tenements. The passenger was in and out of the close, sometimes less than a minute. This was the drop-off, but they wouldn't be stopped and their car searched, the Number Plate Recognition Camera had identified the owner of the car, but he knew the owner wasn't driving; he was being detained at Her Majesty's Pleasure. But his business was still in motion. Long unfulfilled hours lay ahead. The object of his attention had not appeared anywhere, the intelligence they had received was looking ambiguous; he was meant to be carrying in his car, drugs, guns and money. He wasn't going to be dropping them off at any of the tenements; they were to be dropped off to be picked up later, at the mosque.

The Hal Al butchers were early starters, normally they would open up at four am; perfect cover to deliver the drugs, guns and money to the mosque. To fill the tedious early morning hours, he noted down the comings and goings from the tenements, just junkies buying and selling smack. The new legal high that weekend clubbers were taking was called Bubbles, a concoction of various dangers chemicals that gave a high similar to cocaine and ecstasy. Dundee was the birthplace of this new drug. Production was moving into commercial fields. The money that paid for the premises and ingredients allegedly came from the four executed dealers. There was no doubt in his mind that indeed was the case. Unfortunately for them all, one of them tried to go behind the other three's back and set up a distribution network, not only in Scotland but down to North West England as well; including Liverpool.

He had cut a deal with the dealers from Liverpool, and then he sold it to the other three. A meeting was called where monies would be handed over and the network of distribution would be carved up, each of the dealers would have a role to fulfil. A million pounds would be required to buy into the cartel.

Everything was in place. The dealers arrived within five minutes of each another. They had no fear for their lives or the money they had dealt with the Liverpool dealers for five years. There were no limit to Monty's avarice, he was prepared to do anything; even have his best man executed. He thought he was double crossing his fellow three dealers, which he did, but his Liverpool counterparts double crossed him. He didn't realise that until he deposited a bullet in the head of his third victim.

***

The welcome rap of the letterbox and the scattered thud brought the usual junk mail, she leapt out of bed, her heating had not come on due to her boiler giving up the ghost, she fell to her knees, scattering the special offers from the pizza parlours and Chinese restaurants, her eyes were aware of the colour of the envelope. She grabbed it and ran back to the warmth of her bed; she ripped it open, and then held it close to her chest. She was in; she would be going on the training course in January. Jim McAveety would be spending time at his own flat, she had no need for him, she had extracted every minute piece of information, she had written down the names and places of individuals that were of significance.

However, he teased her about someone who was known to the public for their charitable acts, coincidently when a camera was present. She didn't push him for the name, she couldn't guess with confidence whether the someone was male or female, even when McAveety was drunk and she topped up his alcohol level he always held back from revealing the name. His resistance surely couldn't last infinitely. December the eighteenth was penciled into her memory diary, the Club would be opening for the weekend, and different members would be arriving for the first time. Money from her hostess duties would pay for a new boiler, she was fed up paying repair bills for the combi-boiler.

She had seen an advertisement in the Evening Chronicle from a local plumbing company offering a special offer on gas boilers, with a three year guarantee. The price was noted, she scoured the Internet, the boiler was reliable and companies couldn't come close to the price. She phoned around various heating companies, they couldn't understand why the company could make a profit, she was told that the company was ready to go into administration, the three year guarantee would be worthless; food for thought. Unperturbed, she emailed the company outlining her concerns. The reply was succinct the company had sourced the boilers in bulk orders, thus making it cheaper for them. The boiler could be paid over a twelve month period; interest free. She decided to call into the company's showroom, and disclose the conversation with the heating company. The sales manager laughed, he told her that there had been a cosy arrangement between companies for too long they had agreed prices amongst themselves, this company refused to join the cartel, and no, they wouldn't be going bust. This was music to her ears, she would decide there and then to ask if there was a discount if she paid cash. The manager agreed to a discount of ten percent. The boiler would be fitted sometime next week; the company had been overwhelmed by the response.

The company had an immediate stockpile of five hundred boilers, which unbeknown to the Dundee public had come via a circuitous route. A heating company from Guilford had over extended itself in the credit crunch, construction had come to a painful grinding halt, it had to get money in or it would go bust. The bank was unsympathetic to the company's plight, even though it was explained that the company had a bulging future order book. The new hospital contract was worth millions, but that was not due to commence till late spring. The bank was unequivocal; the company was in breach of its banking covenant, if it didn't pay its due money to the bank, the bank would go to court and freeze its assets then put the company into administration.

The managing director was under the impression that the young bank manager didn't understand what he was saying; he said it again if the bank couldn't take a more relaxed attitude, and they would lose the contract for the hospital. The bank manager told him he understood the managing director completely. He hoped the managing director understood him. The bank would be sticking to its original decision. The managing director asked him what he could do, he had a warehouse full of gas boilers that were gathering dust, and he couldn't sell them, because of the collapse in the construction industry.

Later that day, the managing director received an

unexpected but welcome call, it was from Pat Connelly, he didn't give his real name he told him that he could relieve the financial pressure; he had a buyer for the boilers. The managing director sat bolt upright in his chair, he had been offered a fair price in the circumstances, an agreement was in place in a matter of hours.

Money was deposited in the company's account much to the delight of the bank manager; the boilers were on their way to Dundee the following day. The bank manager received confirmation of his holiday to Las Vegas, which puzzled him and his wife, any confusion was swept aside when he took a telephone call from Pat Connelly, telling him that Las Vegas was a wise choice for a holiday.

Ritchie grabbed the boilers and sent the cheque after he received the information from Pat about the difficulties that the Guilford Company was experiencing. Pat guided Ritchie through a business plan; the company would be making a net profit of four hundred per boiler fitted. However, the customers would be made aware of the competitive breakdown policy that their company could offer. The managing director of the Guilford heating company was able to work through the financial morass due to the telephone call from the agent who knew a company from Dundee who was cash rich and were looking for a block purchase of boilers. In essence there were no losers only winners; the bank, heating company, Ritchie's plumbing company and of course the Dundee public. Pat was the oil that moved static mind sets. If in the unlikely event that the boilers were not taken up by the public, they could be used for the apartments that would be included in the refurbishment of The Silvery Tay Hotel. The company would be successful in the tendering process, the company would attract criticism; it was becoming too prominent in winning tenders. Pat had the answer; he would set up another company.

***

The noise from the demolition of the shop front was causing problems with neighbours. The shop had to be completed in the next week; the sign that lay in the basement was a testament to its history. It would be offered to the McManus galleries; the shiny plastic new sign lay proudly beside it, Property Management in garish colours. Diane looked anxious as she picked her way through the building materials, this would be her office, her company. Amateur landlords were not impressed by the low returns after the management fees were deducted from the rent. Her email box had plenty of enquiries; they had a management fee of nine percent against the twelve to fifteen percent that other property companies were charging. The new apartment block in the west end failed to attract a single serious enquiry, the bank were insisting on cutting the prices of the luxury flats, the developer couldn't see any way out, he was leveraged up to the neck. Diane arranged to meet the developer in person, she was not impressed. He wouldn't budge from his single-mindedness; he would not be renting out the apartments, he had to sell them. After an extensive overview of his property portfolio, this was just the tip of the ice-berg; he had to pay the bank six hundred thousand on the first day of February.

That would not have caused any consternation eighteen months ago, the property sector was booming, but now it was on life support; a housing association had enquired if he considered selling? To his well-financially endowed neighbours he had rejected this offer out of hand, but he was in early negotiations, word had leaked out, by the developers own mouth though he denied any suggestion that he wished to start an auction. The housing association backed out of their tentative enquiry, they were guided towards the City Quay, the

222

sellers of town houses were more receptive to the overtures of the housing association, and the other potential buyers followed them to the City Quay. Diane made her pitch for the apartments at the end of the frustrating negotiations; his appetite had been whetted. She concluded the price after ten minutes; he had the money to settle with the bank in February.

He had ignored the advice of his former solicitor; Patrick Connelly. He was rapidly expanding, Pat had told him to dispose of properties before starting more ambitious projects; Dundee didn't have the economy to fund expensive apartments that rivalled London for prices.

Where there is a loser there is a winner; Diane. He had talked it over with her and Ritchie, she needed something to call her own, both could have conversations across the dining table now, Diane had felt she was a deadweight on Ritchie's ambitions.

Pat arranged for her to work in his conveyance and rental sector of his practice ten hours a week. Like a duck to water, her eyes came alive, her brain absorbing a plethora of plus and minus points of the property rental market. Financing the property management company wouldn't cause a challenge.

***

The stars were illuminating the semi-dark but unblemished sky; he enjoyed a semblance of peace of mind in the stillness of the warm silent room .The moon cast its expansive light on to the mirror smooth Tay. Workmen were shot blasting the old rail bridge; he couldn't recall any refurbishment of the proud bridge in his twenty five years in the west end. The eerie lights under the high girders of the bridge made him shiver momentarily; the men must be freezing.

Money was being washed then invested, in legitimate profitable companies. No guilt hankered over him, Ritchie and Diane were being given a push towards social mobility, they unwittingly were working in an unseen laundry room. They deserved to join the burgeoning race to be middle-class. Pat was careful, money came from austere banking institutions, but the lion share came from a company that only lent money to fledgling businesses; a front company. The confidence that lay hidden in Diane burst through when he spoke about setting up the property management company.

They in their wisdom left all the turgid loans, tax and vat to Pat, who in turn passed them onto a friend in the small discreet office in Crichton Street; no brass ostentatious plaque sat proudly screwed to the wall. His office was on the second floor, well-established families from Broughty Ferry and the west end let him handle their tax returns. This was a one man operation, any additional help would be seconded from his elderly wife, and discretion was their invisible motto. Pat and Ernest had similar backgrounds; they came from impoverished backgrounds, went to university and made their money in impoverished Dundee. He always slipped into nostalgia in the early hours, sipping coffee, enjoying the view of the bridge and Fife. Memories that made him smile other memories that made him clench his fist, who's laughing now, a silent retort to his detractors from his youth. Spots of raucous rain hit the window, his thoughts returned to the concern of the workers on the Tay Bridge, clouds were speeding across the sky, and the trees were stirring in his garden. Ferocious wind was driving the rain against the sash windows, he picked up his watch from the table; two thirty, he still felt wide awake, pointless going back to bed. The noise from the wind was channeling down the chimney, the embers from the fire responding to the wind by turning bright red then fading.

Across in Wormit, he saw the lounge light of Welsh's house come on, he went to the cabinet and retrieved his binoculars, his eyes tried to adjust to the binoculars, he saw Welsh, he was talking into his mobile, his arms

were moving in different directions, he bent down and lifted a drink from the free standing bookshelf he was sitting on. Now he was pacing the room, someone at the other end of the conversation was annoying him.
The phone was thrown, probably onto his sofa; he was walking towards the bay window, his hands rubbing his temples, then his hands went to his pockets, obviously searching for something. He moved away from the bay window, then the light was extinguished. Pat didn't see the hall light come on, once more the house returned to darkness. I wonder what that is all about, he thought to himself. The wind was showing no sign of easing, tiredness had crept upon him. He tried to focus on other thoughts but his mind returned to Welsh.

He acted on his instinct gnawing at his stomach, he would take the car, and watch Welsh come off the Tay Bridge and follow him to where he was heading, he wouldn't take his car, he would take his wife's Fiat Punto, his car would be too conspicuous, curiosity swept away the tiredness. He sped down Riverside Drive, very few cars were about, his eyes stretched to the Tay Bridge he watched a lone car move at speed towards Dundee, he turned the car at the roundabout and parked nose front in the parking bay overlooking the choppy Tay. Shortly he saw a car head towards the west end, he looked into his side mirror it was Welsh. He eased the car out of the bay and onto Riverside Drive, Welsh was not in sight any more, the car was doing sixty now, the tail lights of Welsh's car came into view, he would hold back he didn't want to alarm Welsh, he was second guessing where he was heading, it wasn't his house in the west end, it looked as if he was heading for Perth, he now had doubts, he didn't wish to go any further than Perth, against his better judgement he dismissed his overt fears, if he felt uncomfortable again he would turn the car round and go home.

Welsh didn't continue onto the A90, he was moving in

225

the direction of Ninewells, he had eased his foot on the accelerator, he estimated he was driving at a more sedate forty mile an hour, he didn't turn into Ninewells Hospital, perhaps he had realised he had been followed? Nothing ventured; nothing gained. He followed him onto the Kingsway, then he turned off and was heading in the direction of Birkhill, a warm satisfying thought came to the fore, he was going to Coupar Angus, if he was correct he would wager it would be to Monty's house. He knew a quicker way to Monty's house where if he had called it correctly he would be able to observe Welsh from a perfect locale, but more importantly safely.

He drove cautiously along the old road that was just passable in places; Monty's house would be the beacon that attracted this curious moth. He waited, and then saw the dancing lights of the headlights; Welsh had been cautious driving through the heavy rain. Lights were proliferating in Monty's house, Welsh parked his car outside the monumental gates, and then walked up the path, he could hear the noise from his hurried footsteps on the gravel, a security light came on, he stopped running, the door opened and a female stood to the side to allow him in, he walked past her and she looked outside then closed the door. He had seen enough, he didn't try to understand, but he knew something malevolent was fermenting. He eased the hand brake off, the car silently gathered speed.

***

The headline of the Evening Chronicle didn't obfuscate its view on the executions of the four drug dealers. ''Dealers Buried Tomorrow''. Some of the families of the deceased took exception to the headline. The editor took the calls himself; he didn't shy away or apologise for the headline, he repeated the line 'Factually correct' was peppered throughout the tense conversation, Monty's family were the most vociferous. The editor repeated the mantra; the shrill voice was yelling in reply 'I know where you live' then ended the conversation.

The Evening Chronicle had at last started to reflect public opinion instead of its vain, tiresome and futile modus operandi to form political opinion. Falling circulation sales had altered the ship, a new captain was recruited. He was relatively young to be a newspaper editor; forty two. He was not the perfect candidate, he was an active trade unionist; the publisher was not a hotbed of left-wing rhetoric. Never the twain shall meet. However, they liked what they heard, even though it didn't correspond with their brand of Conservatism, he told them their views were outdated, and it was bad for business; start reflecting what people in the city were saying, the police, politicians and courts don't reflect what the people think. He gave the perfect example from the late nineteen seventies; 'where was the condemnation when Dundee councilors were jailed for corruption?' Everyone was aware that planning schedules could be altered in their favour if a stuffed envelope was offered, why didn't the Evening Chronicle echo the publics' thoughts?' If you didn't change the paper would die, the Internet was the challenge, the time may come when the Evening Chronicle would be given away free, to retain advertisers, the world was changing at whirlwind speed.'

He took the call in his office in Edinburgh, the job was his if he wanted it; he would be giving a free reign to edit the paper as he thought fit. He was invited through to Dundee, at the Apex hotel, he declined he wanted to come to the publisher's office; he wanted to meet his staff; he wanted to see who wanted him to succeed and who wanted them to fail, the salary details could wait. He spoke to the senior management and then spoke to the editorial staff on a one- on- one basis. They felt the

227

same as him, things had to change. His first day in charge he called a meeting with all his staff, he outlined the falling sales, the public were bored they had too much choice; the paper had to be brought back from a coma induced by boredom. They had to seek out stories, what was the public saying about politicians local and national. Were the police aiding victims of crime or ignoring them. The first week he was in the job, the story erupted about the dealers being lured and executed. His staff wondered, sometimes out loud, how the paper would cover the story; they did not have long to wait. Married to the headline was their past lives and their convictions they had accumulated over the years. Inside the paper a montage with a photograph of each dealer and their criminal lives recorded in print. The public were left in no doubt; Dundee would be a better place without them. Sources connected to the police gave a chapter and verse of their criminal activities. Any sympathy that the public had for the executed dealers melted away; after they had read about their drug dealing and people smuggling activities. The following day at the funeral of Monty in Balgay cemetery the photographer and reporter from the paper were viciously beaten by some of the mourners. No police were present as a spokesman said 'the mourners cold take exception to this.' The assaults were aired on the evening news the public were horrified that the thugs who had carried out the assaults didn't seem to care that the young photographer was of the fairer sex. Emails, text messages and irate phone calls deluged the office of the Evening Chronicle they all had a common theme why weren't the thugs arrested? There was a gathering storm. Who was running Dundee, drug dealers or the police? The paper's headline the following day mirrored the outraged public.

'No Response from Police. Why?'

Politicians from all parties knew which way the wind

was blowing and hitched their wagons to the public's outrage. The police gave a short statement to the paper. Investigations were continuing; they had no witnesses that had come forward.

Even though every punch was captured on film. Circulation had risen twenty per cent. An editorial meeting was hastily arranged, it would be difficult to keep the momentum going. A four page supplement reflecting the ire and helplessness cried out in print, heart and gut wrenching stories about how drugs had ended young hopeful lives. He had asked that senior management be at the editorial meeting, they turned up. He spoke with passion, the police seemed to be compliant with the moneymen of the drugs trade, that was not him speaking, that was the public, they had to get the dealers before the courts, the public were not prepared to report suspicious movements of alleged dealers, they needed prompted; cash was always a good persuader, will the management agree to set up a hotline and money? Approval was given, the budget would be generous.

Paul Anderson had come of age. He wanted to offer a minimum of five thousand pound to the public that lead to an arrest of a major dealer, and depending on how comprehensive the information was forthcoming the reward could rise to twenty thousand pounds. Complete anonymity would be guaranteed. This would make the dealers nervous, and the public more relaxed about informing. The paper outlined their method to the public, this was money well spent. Neighbourhoods were infested with drugs; addicts were doing reprehensible acts to fund their gluttonous habit. Information was coming in throughout the day and night, names were passed onto the police, some didn't raise any eyebrows but one did, maybe this was someone who shared the same name? This would not be the case.

***.

Patrick Connelly was in his office before the rest of his staff. His sleep had been broken by plots and subplots forming in his mind. Paul Welsh had been at the epicentre of his restless night. If it was Monty's wife that had answered the door, she must have met him before, he had just walked into her house; did he know her and Monty or just her? He felt nervous, if he was planning to do anything that could be considered illegal, he asked for advice, why hadn't he come to him and tell him about the contact with Monty's wife? Michael Jameson was coming into his office later that morning, about investment strategy, that was his reason, but he thought there would be an underlying reason for the appointment. Things were moving so quickly and silently, he was being left asking questions; that had never happened before. Daylight was still some hours away, yawns were being stifled; his brain was running smoothly, questions being answered as soon as he had thought of the question. The temptation of the soft leather sofa had won him over, the office was warm in contrast with the early morning snow that was falling lightly, he slipped out of his shoes and placed them neatly behind the sofa, he would leave the green bankers' light on, but he would dim it. He lay on the comfortable sofa, where his mind was more controllable; he beckoned sleep to come upon him. He dismissed the rumour that was circulating amongst the legal fraternity; that the Financial Services Authority was probing certain solicitors' practices; dirty money was alleged to be flowing in, and nice clean shiny banknotes leaving. That was the rumour, however, the real reason was that criminals' money were being invested not in run of the mill property deals, the money was being invested in solicitors practices, that was the information that he had passed on to the FSA anonymously.

He had seen some of the targeted solicitors at the

Sheriff Court, they had been enjoying the sleepless nights as much as him, but he reassured himself, he had only one night's difficult journey to the land of nod. They had over four weeks' of innuendo, scaremongering and sleepless nights. The senior partner of the practice who had knowingly brokered the deal with the criminals' solicitor in Glasgow, was not able to disguise the nervousness that displayed itself amongst his legal friends, they were starting to distance themselves from him. They were under the impression that the Special Branch was involved with the FSA. The swagger that he had included in his defence of suspects was being shorn at every court case, his eyes looked round the public benches; any person that was smartly dressed could be keeping him under public observation. His confidence was wilting while his waistline was expanding; his pallor became an unhealthy sickly white. Too much fine wine in fine restaurants made him more loud when he was taking various girlfriends out, boasting that one client of his was guilty of murder, when the jury found him not guilty, he had 'friends' that had lost vital evidence. One of the 'friends' was undoubtedly Feeney. The irrepressible boastings in restaurants had contributed to stories surfacing amongst the throng of solicitors and junior staff adding their ingredients to the toxic mixture. Monty was no longer on the end of the telephone had diminished his circle of friends that operated with impunity. Connelly had heard for himself that Monty had someone who had access to the evidence that mysteriously went missing. The reason that this officer was in charge of the evidence that would be presented on behalf of the prosecution was he was under investigation himself; astonishingly he was relocated to carry out clerical duties. He was in no doubt that he would be dismissed from the force, when his case came up, Monty promised his a four figure sum, if certain clothing which contained the suspects DNA disappeared; it did. The

Crown's case became less robust overnight. At the end of the trial after the verdict had been delivered he couldn't help being drawn to the reporters, he complained bitterly that his innocent client had been through hell, the police had been focused on him because he had unusual nocturnal sexual habits; spying on young courting couples , to relieve himself of sexual tension. He would be consulting his client to ascertain if legal proceedings would be taken against the police. No legal action of any description was taking against the police for the simple reason, he would have to go in the witness box and subject himself and his partner to cross examination from the QC representing Tayside Police; he had declined to take the stand at his original trial.

This would be the murder trial mark two. That wasn't going to happen then or in the future. He had got away with literally murder; but his arrogance knew no bounds. Until the paranoia set it in; his guilt made him into a recluse, neighbours were shocked to read in the newspaper about his peeping tom exploit; he moved to Wales; but someone informed the local news media of his background; and he was hounded out again. The last anyone heard of him he was in Croatia. Monty had bought his business from him for a much reduced price; his business was being boycotted by the Dundee public. Though he was wealthy he wanted to leave, Monty purchased his detached home in a hamlet outside Dundee. Monty was unaware of the double life that he had been leading, he had words with his defence solicitor, he told him he wouldn't have helped if he knew the full background of the case, the solicitor just shrugged his shoulders, and he couldn't care less of Monty's moral outrage, though he declined to tell him so. He was now enjoying being engulfed by celebrity status; he was someone, someone that would be recorded in history for his analytical defence skills. There was contact with a Glasgow based writer who wished to

write a book about the case, when they met up to discuss it, the QC was shocked at how much the writer knew about the rumour of missing evidence.
That had accidently being found then accidently lost...again. The book was aborted due to the double jeopardy law being repealed, if the book was published, any future trial could not go ahead because of the information in the book could be prejudicial to the accused.

*** .

They walked out from Police Headquarters in Bell Street, this would be an informal meeting, but it would have formal consequences; she had been briefed listen and learn, don't attempt to join the conversation unless asked by him. McAveety was still hurting from being dropped by her; Welsh had insisted that he take her with him to meet the editor of the Evening Chronicle. He didn't protest too much, he saw how annoyed Welsh was with this shop -a -dealer campaign, McAveety would be his mouth piece, he would try to convince the editor that he was doing an excellent job, but it was impacting on their intelligence; i.e. and their criminal informants were demanding a much higher monetary reward or they would join the ranks of the informers that were being paid more money from the Evening Chronicle.
McAveety didn't have any fear; he expected that that the editor would listen to his persuasive skills. She didn't. They waited outside the editor's office, then after an age the editor came to invite them in.
'Now what can I do for you?'
'McAveety looked at her then turned his attention to him.
'First of all my senior officers ask me to pass on their thanks for the campaign naming the dealers, however, problems are arising.'
'Oh, what are they then?'

233

'Some of our informants are refusing to gather information for us, due to the money on offer from your lot, amongst other things.'

'Well I am so surprised to hear that, my phone has been ringing quite a lot since the campaign to rid the city of dealers, the first minister will be calling into the office next week, it seems he's rather pleased with the results. You mentioned other things, could you be more specific?'

'No problem…the subtext of your campaign suggests that some police officers are turning a blind eye to drug dealing, this is far from helpful, could you see to it that this mistake is never repeated.'

'It wasn't a mistake, that's the impression some important people think that it is factual, I won't be writing articles that need police approval, I don't believe in censorship.'

'Important people believe that rubbish that has been written! They can't be that important, maybe in their own minds. Your safety could be compromised, you know what happened to the dealers, the people who carried out the executions, won't bat an eye lid, if they wanted you to come to some harm, I'm trying to be tactful here, but you come across as you know better more than the police.'

'If that's the impression, I must apologise, but after receiving the answer to our Freedom of Information request about the funding of the drugs squad, I don't think everything is… well.'

'Well..? Our department is doing an excellent job; dealers are being arrested on a regular basis.'

'Small time dealers, selling ten pound bags of smack, they go into the statistics, classed as dealers, that's just window dressing, why aren't major dealers being arrested, for example the four gentlemen who were executed?'

'Proof, you need a great deal of burden of proof, they

hire the best defence teams that money can buy, and it's not as simple as you think.'

'I think it is, this is not the five families of the New York mafia we're talking about, they were violent thugs, are you saying that the drug squad were not aware of their activities…that I find hard to believe.'

'Things are happening behind the scenes, arrests will be made very, very shortly, when we make them I will make sure you're the first to know, but I need assurances.'

'That's all very gratifying, what assurances do you need?'

'Tone down the articles, less innuendo about police corruption, our job is difficult enough with rubbish like that being printed, it makes our job more difficult.'

'I can't agree with you, there will not be any censorship while I'm editor, if there is an element in the police or drug squad that are not honest, I will expose them, it seems to me that the police are reluctant to carry out this procedure, for whatever reason.'

'Okay, I understand, I'm sure someone will have a word with your boss, I'm sorry it had to come to this, thanks for your time.' They stood up and then left his office. Not a word was spoken until they left the building.

'That's how professionals work my dear.'

She laughed. 'I thought that was a master class in stupidity.'

'I don't think so, he's got the message, and I can tell Welsh that he'll tone down the articles about slow clean up rates of drug dealing and corruption.'

'I don't think that's wise.'

'And how is that then?'

'You pissed him off, he extracted information from you without really asking, in return you got nothing from him, and he trussed you up like a turkey.'

'You really have a lot to learn, believe me he'll soon

start writing about missed bin collections and no grit on the roads.'

'I don't think he will, and what was that about arrest soon of dealers?'

'An appetizer, all planned to whet his appetite, as I said Jane, you have a lot to learn.'

***

The bell was being rung in an impatient manner, he stared at the ceiling and thought so much for the long lie-in, wearily he threw on this dressing gown, and then moved down the hall which was being stripped of the flock wallpaper, the bell was being rung accompanied by banging on the door. He moved passed the scaffolding that was blocking the last three metres to the vestibule door, he yanked it open then opened the main door. A friend from the past stared at him square in the face.

'So this is how the idle rich spend their days?'

The bitter wind snapped at his bare legs. He would have kept them at the door but the inclement weather made up his mind for him.

'Come in.' He took them into the warm lounge, they sat down without an invitation. 'So what can I do for you officers?' He was warming his backside at the coal fire.

'I thought you would have been able to tell us?'

'Robbie, tell your chum, anymore smart arse comments and he will be standing outside…now what can I do for you.'

'It's about the murder of Mr Montgomery.'

'Also known as Monty,' his partner butted in.

'He's really smart; did he figure that out all by himself?'

Robbie tried to suppress his laughter, his colleague his anger.

'You had words with him in The Social bar a couple of weeks ago, still bad blood between you two?'

'There was but there's none now, he's away where it's

236

nice and warm, I'll be honest I didn't cry any tears for him and the rest of his motley crew, what comes round goes around….'

'…what goes round comes round, you mean.' Robbie looked at his partner, he seemed embarrassed.

'Same difference, same sentiment, but to cut down on your precious time, I didn't have anything to do with the murder of Monty, you'd be better looking at his competitors.'

'We are just going through people who didn't like him or held a grudge against him, the night they were all found, can you confirm your movements, that would be on the eleventh.'

'I was home with the family, watching television, when you interview the wife do it here not at Ninewells Hospital, you don't want to start tongues wagging.'

'Will tomorrow night be okay to pop by?'

'Fine, I'll see you and your chum to the door.' They stand up.

'Nice house; you've done well since our days in Kirkton.'

'I don't fancy a trip down memory lane, thank you; I'll see you to the door.'

The door slammed with a reassuring thud. ' Do you think he was glad to get rid of us?'

They walked quickly down the driveway to avoid the incessant rain, in the comfort of the car, Robbie gave his reply.

'Your stupid comments didn't help, you hadn't a hope in hell of unsettling him, when I tell you to be quiet, that's not a request, that's an order, don't let me tell you again.'

Feeling chastised, he decided to eat a large helping of humble pie.

'I know; I should have held back, but he looked so smug, I thought I would show him who was in charge.'

'Oh did you? Who looked like a total wanker at the end

of your inane question; Montgomery also known as Monty, he wasn't looking smug he was feeling sorry for me!'

He tried change the subject. 'The rain isn't half battering down; I think we should hang round here for a couple of minutes it might unnerve him about tomorrow when we interview Mrs Smug.'

'Unnerve him…he'll be in his scratcher, not worrying about us, but you're right about his wife she is Mrs Smug, are you going to start the engine at least… it's freezing!'

He started the engine and turned the fan up to clear the misted windscreen.

'He didn't want to talk about the good old days with you, why was that?'

'There are not a lot of young lads from Kirkton who join the police.'

'He doesn't like us; I mean the police in general, any particular reason??'

'Probably suspicious about authoritarian figures I suspect or poacher turned gamekeeper.'

'Was he bit of a tearaway then?'

'We all were, then we all grew up, me to be a detective and him a millionaire, ain't life wonderful?'

'Looking at the car in the driveway, he doesn't try to hide it…a wee bit jealous, are you thinking you could have done better with your life?'

'It has crossed my mind once or a thousand times.'

'There's him in a big 'look at me' house and there's you in a snug two bedroomed flat and the closie that needs painted, I can see why you're depressed, I bet he's got a cracker of a wife with a lovely figure, then there's you divorced, not a chance of meeting a decent woman.'

'Are you taking the piss?'

'No, I'm just calling it as I see it, have you seen or met his wife then, and is she a honey?'

'Yes, yes and yes she is a honey.'

'When did you meet her?' 'Many years ago…I was married to her for seven years.'

***

Tuesday was coming round too fast, nerves were attacking his normally calm demeanour, there was no way out, he had to be ready in his mind to carry out the exercise with the minimum of fuss but with the maximum of precision. He had returned to reading, something that he had gave up when he left school. He would try anything to try to control his fluctuating emotions that always led him to the same stark scenario; GG was dead, his limbs cast into the unforgiving Tay and left to the mercy of the current that flowed into the North Sea. If he didn't adhere strictly with their instructions he was dead, there was nothing ambiguous, if he was successful in the operation there was a good chance he would still end up joining GG. The latter was more persuasive than the former. The waiting was killing him. He had lost seven pounds his colleagues commented on his already lean physique, he just replied in a matter of fact explanation that he was going to the gym more often, which was true, but not for the obvious reason, he wanted to tire himself out; sleep was hard to come by. He felt his mobile vibrate against his thigh, a message had arrived. He took out the mobile, and then scrolled down to the message; Tuesday cancelled, will keep in touch, enjoy your coffee. He quickly looked round the Starbucks, to him everyone looked suspicious; the mother with the toddler struggling to feed her, the elderly gentleman in the corner on his own reading the Financial Times, two workmen talking loudly; he had to stop inventing demons, there was not enough room in his head. He sipped his coffee, and took his eyes away from the myriad of potential assassins, he looked outside, he stopped sipping his coffee; a male was on his mobile talking; he was Chinese, and he was staring into

239

Starbucks, he caught his eyes and turned his back on him. He held the cup with both hands he was starting to shake; calmness returned the Chinese man was joined by an elderly Chinese woman; they hugged one another then went down the escalators.

Lenny was close to tears; his mind was revisiting his childhood of its own accord, was this like the drowning man seeing his life flash before him? He finished the coffee, he couldn't help looking round for the potential assassin or murderer of GG. He left Starbucks totally dejected he wished now in hindsight that Tuesday was still the day, and Wednesday was when his life would begin again, but now he had to go through all the anxiety once more. He had to slow down his racing mind it was making him walk far too quickly, the travel agent loomed ahead, he would enquire about a weekend break in New York, why New York? He didn't even try to understand, he didn't argue with himself. He came out an hour later with enough information to make him a tour guide; some sense of perspective accompanied him when he left the travel agent. He had planned to go to GG's flat not enter the close, but just to look at it from the safety of the pavement.

The text message had eliminated that altogether.

***

Broughty Ferry was teaming with office parties and others on Christmas night's out, the pubs were opened to one am, an added incentive. Eddings against his better judgement had agreed to an impromptu Christmas drink with Morag. He may as well have taken a webcam with him, he told his wife that a businesswoman who he had met in Dubai was having problems, she had asked for him to meet her, would she mind? She barely looked away from the television the X-Factor was on, but nodded her head it would be better for him to go out he was starting to get under her feet. It was cold, the stars were in abundance; he would walk the three miles from his house to the Ship Inn. His weight had stabilized, his diet had improved immeasurably when he went to Dubai, he now walked everywhere within reason.

He had hoped Morag had something tangible to tell him; there were too many ifs and buts coming into his professionally trained mind. Paul Welsh was living an interesting life, his friends seemed to be kept at arm's length, he had seen him talk to many unsavoury characters, but that wasn't enough to condemn him to any criminal act. When he was a detective he had met violent criminals which he had no doubt were murderers, however no evidence to could be found to back up his unscientific assumption. He had just learned to temper his emotions, time would be his ally. The trail to find the killer of Feeney and the social worker had left no clue, no forensic evidence, not tip offs, nothing. The theory gathering credibility was that one of the dealers had acted alone and had shot Feeney and the worshipper, a hastily arranged meeting was to take place in the industrial unit on Old Glamis Road with whom no one knew, then things went awry for some unknown reason, then a bloodbath commenced. Eddings agreed with some part of the theory but stopped short of seriously considering that someone that all the major dealers had trusted convinced them to dispense with their personal security, which they all had apparently done. Why? No new players had arisen to take over their drugs empires, everything seemed to be moving as normal, and there were no shortage of drugs, very strange.

The Evening Chronicle had come out from behind its conservative image and had been proactive in identifying dealers in exchange for money, dealers were being arrested but let go after a few hours of questioning, their solicitors would be answering all the questions, the best the drug squad could do was make the alleged dealers uncomfortable for a few hours.

The solicitors were speaking off the record to the Evening Chronicle the police were rounding up innocent men and woman because the police were not progressing in their quest to find the killer or killers of Feeney, they couldn't care less about the families of the social worker and the four victims executed in the industrial estate. The police strenuously denied these serious if misguided accusations, they were making progress but now was not the time to show their hand. Eddings understood the unmistakable riposte; it meant that they had stalled the investigative engine.

Vigour and enthusiasm which had been absent in the last months as a detective had returned, he would be able to follow and act on his own instinct, he would be able to tread on someone's toes if he needed to but it would be a light touch without the heavy foot of the Law, he was a private citizen now, he could switch seamlessly without any suspicion.

Former colleagues had called unexpectedly at his house when they heard that he had returned from Dubai, they were surreptitiously asking for help.

Computers were more of a hindrance, old school gumshoe detective skills were back in vogue, who better to ask for pointers? Embarrassingly for him, he bowed to their flattery or so it seemed he was able to ask them where they were with any of the cases, not forgetting the hunt for the Polish gunmen who had murdered the Liverpool dealer in the flat. He was told that was on the back burner, with a decreasing gas supply, Feeney's murder was at the top of the list, but nothing of any significance had been uncovered. Eddings turned their flattery back onto them, 'start at the beginning, including Feeney's personal life, check with the neighbours once more, did he come and go at quirky hours, did he have visitors that came during the day and left much later? How were his finances, check with his bank, it's amazing what could come to the surface. If anything troubles you drop by we'll go over it…together. But I'm no longer a serving police officer, you realise that, watch what you say to others.' Now he had the police working for him,

Morag had uncovered more facts than the detectives working on the case with their Blackberry's and laptops, if only they knew, if only they knew. He was on the brow of the hill, the Post Office bar was packed as usual, the phalanx of smokers huddled in the doorway together in vain against the chill of the winter air, being Broughty Ferry the Tay was sending up the cold icy wind for good measure. Turning right he made his way in the direction of the esplanade, Christmas meant more this year to him, he didn't know why, just he was more optimistic about life, he didn't want to admit it to himself, Morag had made life more palatable, he could talk to her freely, they were platonic friends; it would stay like that. He passed the chapel, the red brick building looking out of place in the quiet street of stone built houses. Feeney had met his contact in the chapel who initiated the meeting? He had known Feeney well, he wouldn't have taken any chances, but he did on that fateful occasion. Then he stopped and stared at the chapel, perhaps he was thinking like the rest of the police, but what if Feeney and the social worker had agreed to meet for some unknown reason, and were interrupted by their killer? His walk commenced with more pace, he would concentrate on the social worker, the police were not probing his background. However; he would.

***

McAveety and Jane left the editor's office Jane had giving her acerbic opinion, McAveety dismissed her opinion, she meant well.

'Leave all the talking to me, you might learn something.'

'We'll see, if Welsh asks a question am I allowed to reply? Or will I have to refer to you first?'

'Time of the month love is it?'

'At least I have an excuse…'

'What's the fucking matter with you Jane? After all I've done for you, at least treat me with some respect.'

'Don't patronise me mate, I'm not one of the old boilers from the North End Club, or haven't you noticed?'

'That's out of order! I've heard the nickname the rest of them give me; the gasman because I service mature woman. I'm surprised at you Jane, and I'm hurt, maybe we should stop seeing each other socially, I know you'll be hurt but you'll get over me…eventually.'

They stopped outside the railings at Dundee High School. 'Fucking hell! Are you for real! Me get over you eventually! I might slash my wrists with a plastic teaspoon. Talk about deluded, we were never an item.

'You weren't the only one on the menu, you were an aperitif. I think I'll crack open a bottle of bubbly tonight…' She was uncontrollably laughing. He moved away from her.

'C'mon the kids are looking at you, Welsh will be wondering where we are, as you can see I won't respond to taunts, I'm too mature.'

'I can see that, don't try to call me again, do you understand?'

'I was going to suggest that, I'm going to ask Welsh to place you with someone else, I don't feel comfortable with you, and you're taking this badly.'

'That's two bottles of champagne I'll have tonight…a little bit of advice try to keep your mouth shut, till we reach Bell Street, I can't manage anymore champagne.'

'Fine, fine.'

They walked in silence to the short distance of Bell Street, he was feeling good, she was astonished at his vanity, at least it's over, and she hadn't hurt him. And as a bonus, she would be assigned to another drug squad member; the day had begun well, it couldn't get any better could it? She looked at him, his confidence was exuding from the way he walked, appearances are deceptive, he was a moron dressed in an idiot's skin. But now she was rid of him. She would be at the Club acting as a hostess; the double life she was leading didn't trouble her and the money was a sop if her conscience troubled her, which it hadn't. Her debts were being blitzed in record time. Red ink would soon be replaced by black ink.

***

The car pulled up at the pavement outside Balgay School; a school for teenage girls who were experiencing some difficulties in their young chaotic lives.

'And why have we parked here?'

'Because I told you to park here, remember I am your boss sonny, and you're getting a little bit flabby, sad for someone so young, let's go.' They left the car laughing.

'Do you really think I'm putting on weight?'

'Look in the mirror, without holding your belly in.'

'Okay I take your word for it; I joined a gym, but have not been because of work and other things.'

'Other things? Like trips to the bakers, Indian takeaways... you've certainly a point there. Forget diets just now, when we speak to the glamorous couple don't be afraid to join in the questioning, even though I will look at you as if I'm annoyed, understand?'

'So you didn't think I was an idiot the last time then?'

'Certainly not.'

'Why did we park the car miles from their house, you didn't say?'

'Out of respect, that's all, don't push it.'

'I'm just asking, a curious detective, that's all. What's his wife's name then?'

'Harriet.'

'Harriet…I've not met a lot of Harriet's, so why did you split up who gave who the elbow?'

'She's the only Harriet I've ever met, and that's enough for me, no one gave anyone the elbow.'

'Oh right, you just woke up and thought this is a nice day for a divorce, then.'

'You're nearly right, add the grass is always greener on the other side, and you've cracked the case, a first in your career.'

'You were caught sniffing around other women, then, any regrets?'

'I wasn't sniffing as you put it I was stupid and young about thirty.'

'Thirty! I'm not thirty yet; that definitely is not young Gary. So we've established you were caught admiring someone else's lawn, then your wife gave you the elbow?'

'I wish I was just admiring the lawn, I was mowing it, and then I felt a sharp pain in the ribs.'

'Any regrets?'

'Only when I'm awake.'

'That bad?'

'An aching heart never heals, believe me.'

'Do you want to talk about it Gary?'

He stops and laughs. 'Are you kidding me? I've got older socks than you. That's the therapy over.'

'Fair enough.'

'I have been unable to get any information from the drug squad, no surprise there, they have criminal informants that could at least give us something to work on, but they aren't prepared to divulge anything, in case it compromises future operations. In other words they don't trust us. The Chief Constable for all his bluster doesn't want to force their hand…why did he take the job then, if he doesn't want to make decisions?'

'Gary, I may be talking out of turn now, but this is what

I've heard, Feeney had all the C.I's. on a USB, it has either being mislaid or stolen.'

'That's old news, I heard that, but that's the glamour boys in the drug squad, just making excuses not to hand over the CI's identities, they have a list, and there is no doubt about that. Once we interview people who knew Monty, I'll go and speak to Welsh about. But that can wait; we'll see what Ronnie and Harriet have to say.'

'Why didn't you tell me you had heard about the USB? I'm your partner you know.'

'Ach grow up, I didn't tell my wife everything, so don't feel hard done by, do you tell mummy everything?'

'What's my mum got to do with it?'

'Still staying with your mum and you're nearly thirty, what do you do for a wild night out, go to the McDonalds drive thru?'

'That's personal…and for your information, I'm seeing someone.'

'Well done, who is he?'

'That's not funny, not funny at all, you're lucky I am not gay, you'd be reported…again.'

'I'm in my fifties, the gold watch is coming into view, I'm untouchable…who is she then, one of your mum's pals?'

'You'll be shocked when you see her, she's one of us.'

'One of us…hmm…very cryptic.

'Her name's Jane and she is a detective in the drug squad.'

'Perfect and well done, she'll come in handy, if we don't get past the brick wall in this case.'

'No she won't be handy, we don't talk shop, and I won't pump her for information. End of.

That'll be them now, do you want to go to the door or will I?'

'You get it Ronnie; I'll make sure the kids don't come down stairs.'

'Fine.' he walked along the hall then pulled open the

door.

'C'mon in gentlemen, a wee bit cold tonight, do you want coffee?'

'No, we won't keep you too long, you've nothing to worry about, Ronnie.'

They move into the lounge. Gary's eyes take on an extra sheen.

'Hi Gary, do you want a coffee, and how are things?'

He sits down. 'Can't complain, you're looking well, and you've done well. No coffee, thanks anyway.' His eyes look around the large lounge.

'Are you sure you don't want a coffee?'

'No we're fine…I'll come straight to the point, Ronnie said he was at home with you and your children, the night the four dealers were found shot, can you verify that?'

'Yes, that's right he was here we all watched television, do you want the children to come down, they'll back up what I've said?'

'There's no need for that. The night you and Ronnie were in The Social bar, Monty was seen going over and talking to Ronnie, do you remember that?'

'Yes, I came over and he walked away, I didn't know him, I think Ronnie said he was someone from school, he was bit of an arse hole.'

'Well he's a dead one now; this is just routine, elimination from our enquiries, that's all. Ronnie do you own a gun or have access to a gun?'

'No,' he laughed.

'That's roughly about it then.'

'What about Doctor Watson, does he have any questions?'

They all look at him.

'How did you manage to buy a house like this?'

'He might look about fourteen but he acts sixteen, you don't have to answer that.'

'That's okay Gary, no secret son, hard work and a big

slice of luck.'

'That's not true, hard work, and more hard work, you make your own luck, he's too modest, I'm surprised you didn't tell him how Ronnie battled his way up the ladder,' she interjected indignantly.

'I'll tell him in the car, I'm proud of you both, we've taking up enough of your time, we'll see ourselves out.'

***

Welsh listened incredulous as McAveety droned on; he glanced at Jane her face was not concurring with his account.

'Was that an accurate description of the conversation with the editor Jane?'

'Well...not exactly.'

'Oh?'

'In my opinion, the editor saw it differently from Jim.'

'Without any interruption from you Jim, give me your interpretation Jane.'

'My view was Jim went Gung Ho with the editor, that put him on the defensive, nothing would be achieved by this method, the editor wouldn't be toning down any stories regarding suspected police corruption, it was a wasted opportunity to get the editor on side.'

'What do you have to say McAveety?'

'I don't agree, I didn't pussyfoot around, I'll admit that, I made my point and if he didn't like that, tough.'

'Jane I want you to give the editor a call, see if you can change his attitude to be more supportive of the police especially the drug squad, we have enough enemies from other departments . Are you happy with that?'

'Sure, I think I can make him see our point of view, I'll do it now if you don't mind?'

'That's what I like to see someone being proactive for a change, call him now...McAveety stay behind.'

His eyes were on fire as she left the office; she had betrayed him as well as humiliated him.

'What did I fucking tell you, eh?'

'I did as you told me, I let him know that we weren't happy with the subtext of the story, he didn't like that, but what else could I have done?'

'You missed out the one word which was crucial, don't you remember?'

He looked at him expressionless.

'Ah for fuck sake you really forgot didn't you?'

His face came back to life. 'I must have forgotten, what was the word?'

'Subtle! Subtle, I can imagine you going in there, trying to impress a female colleague, I have news for you it didn't work, we are battling to get the public on board, you've thrown them overboard, by your crass comments to the editor, how stupid was that!'

'Am I allowed to speak, or are you just going to shout at me?'

He calmed down. 'Go ahead this should be interesting.'

'Have you heard of a woman's wrath?'

The calmness evaporated. 'Just get to the fucking point!'

'Alright, alright no need to shout, I've dumped her, this is her revenge, and you aided and abetted her, so much for solidarity.'

'Wait a fucking moment, I'm not interested in your romantic aspirations, what she told me was correct, because I called the editor myself, he wasn't impressed by the strong arm content of your conversation, and that's the positive side , so don't blame her, and what do you mean about solidarity?'

McAveety had heard enough, he stood up and walked out.

Welsh mockingly praised him for showing initiative. That's all he needed, things were starting to unravel, he had to speak to someone, he knew it had to be Pat Connelly, he couldn't tell him everything, he shouldn't tell him anything. McAveety had added to his burden. Would the editor fall for Jane's less offensive

comments? He himself had blundered , he shouldn't have went to Monty's house, the widow was not mourning for too long, he was perturbed when she had called him, he told her he wouldn't be seeing her ever, this was business, someone would contact her on his behalf. She told him that he had to come over now, she insisted he did. Against all his training and gut instinct he swept them aside and drove to her house near Liff, she said she was alone. She had lied. He had been compromised. Her grief didn't compel her to exchange the marital bed for a single bed. One of Monty's cohorts was now sharing her bed and affections, but one thing she abundantly made clear; she would be sharing Monty's wealth, now her wealth. Her suitor didn't share this selfish attitude, he induced her to take cocaine to heighten her sexual pleasure; it didn't. What her voracious appetite did was make her less business savvy, she started taking risks; her Svengali suitor became more central to her business planning, if he couldn't turn her mind to match his he turned her body into a receptacle for his savage temper. He was boasting about the romance and the money he had at his disposal. She had weaned herself off cocaine, the paranoia was now seldom visiting her, her strong mind returned. Once she had cleansed herself of stupidly getting involved with him, she orchestrated her mental fight back. Paul Welsh was the only one she could really trust, she had no one else she could turn to. The early morning phone call caused him great panic and anxiety, he didn't try to hide his disgust and anger at her; she had no other choice. She was the sole shareholder of the rehab clinic, or her company was.
After the deaths of Feeney, the social worker and Monty, she now owned the shares.
 None of the three deceased could declare their shareholdings. Welsh knew or he assumed this was the context of her call. It wasn't. Her lover was dead in her

bed.

***

He was alone but curiously content. The eerie silence didn't perturb him, Welsh thought this was a punishment that he would rail against, if this was a shot across his bows, he would hope for more. The conversation he kept playing in his head; she had betrayed him there wasn't any argument as far as he was concerned, but it worked out to everyone's satisfaction. Jane was assigned to another fool who would succumb to her feminine cunning, not charm. He was back in the soon to be demolished Alexander multi-storey block. Just him and his warm friend the halogen heater, he just hoped it didn't let him down, the temperature was plummeting. The streets below him were deathly silent, the Delta components factory that worked noisily twenty-four hours a day, had made its last elbow joint two years ago, the area surrounding it had been re-generated, social housing had sprung up, when the multi-storey blocks were demolished houses would rise in their place once again.

There were rumours circulating that a property developer was negotiating   to buy one of the multi-storey blocks, the developer had plans to turn the multi into luxury accommodation, among the facilities would be a swimming pool, cinema and social club. The council were rumoured to be split, some agreed with the developer that the Hilltown would be shorn of it's shameful reputation as an area of drugs, crime and perennial generations of unemployment, the luxury high rise living would attract other developers who would build expensive flats and townhouses, which in turn would bring in businesses. However, some councillors said this would be divisive and cause resentment amongst her constituents; the area should be re-generated by social housing. An opportunity lost. The councilor didn't live on the Hilltown her house was in a leafy lane off the Perth Road. McAveety had sympathy for the developer, the view from the multi-storey was breathtaking during daylight hours or when the darkness fell. The cynical mantra from the Dundee public was always the same; Dundee councillors always took the wrong decision or took stuffed envelopes. McAveety had heard his father talk about when Dundee had a wild-west image, sometimes he missed those days other times he hung his head in shame. But at least he was rid of Jane.

The concierge was glad of some company, he didn't ask why McAveety was here, he just whiled away the hours reading, when he wasn't reading he went into an introspective mode, he should have followed his heart, when he was younger, but like most of the populous , he let his head navigate him to a life of drudgery and greyness. He was a self -taught artist in his spare time, his spare room had hundreds of canvases, sometimes he looked at them with a cruel eye looking for minute imperfections; other times he was proud of how he had captured the light. Fear of failure prevented him from having a professional assessment of his work, he just kept on painting and accumulating work, one day he would have them assessed.

McAveety's page on the note book was empty, he stifled a yawn and rubbed his eyes, the whirring sound of the lift mechanism accentuated his senses. He silently left the upstairs lounge and crept down the stairs to the door, the grinding lift stopped at his floor. He couldn't see the lift from the peep-hole, he pressed his ear against the door; voices could be barely heard above his beating heart. There were two maybe three talking quietly. The faint footsteps became louder they whoever they were, were walking in his direction, he stopped listening and looked through the peephole.

They walked past the door, the poorly lit hallway didn't

give up their identities, they were just shaped shadows, once more he pressed his ear to the door, keys could be heard going into the lock, then being withdraw, the jingle of the keys echoed around the hallway, voices were being raised from hushed tones, agitation from one of them was rising, profanities and insults towards the unsuccessful locksmith. Then silence the door could be heard being opened, the groaning sound of an oil starved hinge confirmed their entrance into the flat. McAveety stepped carefully back from the door, and then climbed the stairs up to the lounge, he grabbed the notepad, and wrote the time that the unexpected visitors arrived and how many he thought were present. He looked out of the window, parked in Alexander Street with lights extinguished was a four x four, he couldn't see if anyone was in the car. This must have been his new neighbour's mode of transport. He quickly assessed the situation, if he returned to the door and listened, what would he achieve? If he remained upstairs he could see for definite how many there were of them, and when the four x four moved away with its human cargo he would be able to photograph the number plate.

He was onto something big, how big he didn't know. The adrenaline stopped navigating through his veins, how was John the concierge, had they tied him up and assaulted him, was he being paid by them to have access to a flat for some unknown reason? But he hadn't betrayed him. That conundrum could wait, he tried to focus his night vision binoculars on the rear of the four x four, the number plate couldn't be seen from the rear, but the exhaust had burst into life, the steady white fumes told him that his neighbours were on their way down, or the four x four was ready to move off, the lights were on. Welsh would not be party to this unexpected font of information; he snapped away with the night vision camera, a cigarette was discarded from the driver's window. The lift could be heard ascending then stopping at his floor, he moved away from the window towards the open lounge door and stuck his head out into the freezing stairway, listening and hoping for voices. He heard them but they were barely audible, they entered the lift and descended. He returned to the window, impatient to see his quarry, they came into his vision; three of them, one of them a woman, she climbed into the front passenger seat.

***

Monty was not as gullible as Welsh had anticipated, he may have warned him by the email to his computer with his credit card details, that proved he had accessed vile child pornography websites, but he was one step ahead of him. Feeney's suspicions about Welsh had been confirmed; he had been manipulated into pervading intelligence that had been gathered on Monty and the other deceased dealers. Feeney had passed this on to Monty, he knew what was coming next, but unfortunately for Monty, Feeney didn't live another twenty four hours, if he did, Welsh would be suspended from duty and would be set for trial at the High Court. Welsh was unaware of the timetable, only Feeney and Monty knew the future. The future didn't include Monty. Welsh had taken the phone call, he hadn't heard of the woman with the Italian sounding name, but he understood the point of her brief conversation. Her deceased husband had spoken warmly of him, when he enquired who her husband was; he felt panic stricken when she cut out the faux Italian accident. He was instructed to meet her tomorrow at a designated place, if he didn't she would go to the crusading editor of the Evening Chronicle with documentation that proved that he was profiting from heroin and other Class A drugs.

He agreed to meet her, but not at her desired location; he asked her to come to his office in Bell Street, if she didn't she could go to the editor of The Times.

She was taken aback at the lack of concern he was

relaying down the phone to her, she paused in her response then he came back, 'I'm sure you would be interested in your late husband's new addition to your family?' She agreed immediately. He never returned the answers to her questions not about the child but about the other woman, the line went dead. She came the next day to his office she wanted to hear with her own ears, if there was any progress in apprehending her husband's murderer. All eyes were on his office, other staff and detectives were anticipating a screeching match from her.

Inside the office things were being discussed at a leisurely pace, no one spoke about corruption, they spoke in a fragmented way, to the uninitiated this was just inoffensive talk, but the two protagonists knew exactly what they were word-fencing about. He wanted tangible proof that she could back up the previous day's conversation which was anything but cryptic. In return he would provide the woman's name. She never brushed upon the name of the child either sex or name.
The woman was the focus for her ire. She requested that she would have a coffee, he picked up the phone to accede to her request, she told him that he should go and get it himself. He did. Gawping faces greeted him when he came out of the office, nervous coughs and shuffling of papers, the silent office had become a vision of human activity. He returned with the coffee, she drunk it then left without saying a word.

He sat puzzled at his desk for fifteen minutes, pondering his next move, confidence draining. He needed an ibuprofen, he opened the drawer and reached in instinctively; he smiled a USB was sitting on the ibuprofen packet. He took it and popped it into his pocket. He would examine it tonight in the privacy of his home in the west end. There would be no point in second guessing the content of the USB. He had been advised against large sums of money going into his two bank accounts. He had not been tempted to splash out on large ticket items, he was openly critical of the builders, he had to watch every penny, he checked the builders' prices for materials against the best prices on the Internet, he had built his persona to be a tight wad. He was advised to take out personal loans to pay for the renovation of his new house in Wormit, he complained bitterly about the rate the bank was charging him, and the decline in the value of his house in the west end, he wished he had sold last year, he would have been twenty thousand better off.

He was not a user of cocaine, he suspected some of his team were recreational users at the weekend, but he had drawn the line in the sand, anyone caught smoking or inhaling illegal drugs would be fired, they would be welcome to take Tayside Police to any Industrial Tribunal, or private legal action. And if anyone took the so-called legal highs, the same applied.

He walked up to his window, rain battered against it; no jogging tonight, he was in two minds whether to go to the house in Wormit; he needed solitude. His mind was made up, he would make up an excuse to his wife why he was going to Wormit, the weather would put her off volunteering her to accompany him. He fumbled for the USB through his trousers; he felt his fate was touching his fingers.

Monty bright as a frog on a dark night, he smiled to himself, if Monty had something on him it would be a first and he wasn't here to gloat. Monty was pure brawn, little brain, his wife on the other hand was intelligent even though she was blonde and dressed like a character from a budget movie about gangsters wives. She had represented him many years ago in a rare court appearance, Monty had an engaging personality and if she liked to hear gory details of him acting on the periphery of the law, his bank balance was more engaging.

She left her husband of ten years, and moved into Monty's council house, she had him looking at detached properties in more affluent areas in no time at all, her name would be on the mortgage, but Monty would be the finance behind it. Catherine didn't accept that he had to be careful with his money; she made him reveal where the money was and who was investing it for him. His blank face at the word investing, made up her mind for her, he had to get rid of his financial advisor, blank stare again. He had approximately a hundred thousand pounds or thereabouts, she placed it with person that would double that sum in a month; they weren't ethical investors

Driving across the Tay Bridge he subconsciously rubbed the USB intermittently, sometimes the feeling of reassurance buoyed him, other times gloom engulfed him, tonight he was in good spirits; Christmas had that effect on him. If Catherine was correct about the contents of the USB he could be in trouble; on the other hand if it was a bluffing exercise, he had nothing to worry about.

The temperature reading in the car displayed it was minus five outside, this cheered him up, potential suicides would refrain from jumping off the Tay Bridge into the icy, dark depths of the all-consuming Tay. Christmas was the season of goodwill for many Dundonians, others it was just another weight that their minds couldn't carry. Debt, marital break-ups or on going mental health issues, burst the dam of hope, dying would be a release from silent black torture. He clicked the button from the car, the gates failed to respond, he felt anger rise again, he moved quickly from the car, and aimed at the sensor, the gates defiantly refused to move. Expletives rang out, he walked towards the gates clicking furiously, no response, he put the remote back into his pocket, and opened the gates manually. He returned to the car and drove into the drive, his seething anger subsided when his eyes caught the twinkling lights that festooned the Christmas tree, a smile emerged through the grimace. He looked back at the opened gates, the grimace returned. The central heating was on; he saw the steam waft from the side of the house.

He was in the mood for a coffee; it could be a long night. The house was warm and inviting, he went into the cupboard and retrieved the laptop from the cupboard in the hall, he placed it on the table in front of the bay window, the Christmas tree obscured some of the view over to Dundee, the kettle came to the boil interrupting the silence of the large house, the click of the kettle seemed to echo throughout the house. He made the coffee and returned to the laptop, he looked at the USB beside the laptop, doubts crashed into his mind, he was looking for excuses not to insert the USB, how would he crack the password, and who could he trust to decipher the jumbled information? He sat down and sipped the coffee, and then waited on the screen to display the section where a password would be needed. The screen burst into life, it was split into a myriad of sections under different headings; he would not need someone from IT. There was no need to crack complicated codes. The first page was headed Expenditure. The next page: Income. The third page: Feeney. The fourth page: Scousers. He was amazed at the stupidity of Monty, he must have done this without any input from Catherine; it was tantamount to a full and frank confession. Was he totally stupid or was he being incredibly clever? The coffee went cold, he was engrossed at the assets Monty had accumulated, bank account numbers were auspicated throughout the pages. Feeney's account and how much was paid in every month. The last page he hoped would be even more informative.

Friends: Paul Welsh; Drug Squad. The rest of the page was blank, no account numbers, only his mobile number. He was devastated; there was nothing to implicate him in corruption or any unsavoury or criminal activity.

This must be Monty's revenge. The Prosecutor Fiscals office could more than fill in the blanks with fantasy and fiction supplied by slighted colleagues and criminals he had sent to jail. Had Catherine deleted any incriminating information from the page? He would just have to be unconcerned, if she did come up with something he was in dangerous territory, he went back to the Feeney page, it was illuminating information, the set-up of the drug and alcohol dependency clinic independent of the NHS, but funded from the government. Millions of pounds were flowing into the company's accounts. He knew where the clinic was, it used to be an old school on the edge of Dundee, it had been refurbished when it was an advisory centre then it started out dispensing methadone and clean needles, the deceased social worker lobbied MSP's that Dundee needed an addiction treatment clinic, it would be easier if it was outside of the financial constraints and bureaucracy of the NHS; it would be less expensive to equip and run he could hand pick medical staff and social workers, this centre would be a haven for people who wanted to be free of drugs and alcohol.

He was successful in his lobbying. Monty was fortunate in becoming the outright owner, after the murders of Feeney and the social worker. Monty had a motive to remove them. Catherine had a motive to remove Monty. The company that owned the addiction treatment clinic had two females as the principal shareholders; they had to be friends of Catherine. She had much to fear from the information stored on the USB; if this information became public through the Evening Chronicle or if it was sent to the Chief Constable she would be questioned and would become a suspect in the murders of Feeney, the social worker, Monty and his chums. The implications were that there is a web of corruption that was deep seated within the drug squad. There was nothing, absolutely nothing which tied him to corruption; Monty was his C.I. hence his mobile number. He was feeling good again. He exhaled long and hard. Monty had left him out when he could have painted him with a horrible brown foul-smelling substance. She would be paying him a large one off payment, after he explained the facts about the drug addiction clinic. He would assist her in keeping the addicts churning through the clinic, he wouldn't demand any monies; he would be satisfied with a one -off payment; he was a man of his word, surely Monty had mentioned that, and notwithstanding she might need him in the future, no one could foretell the future.

He closed down the computer, any fears or apprehensions were disposed of; he had the information, which meant he had the power over Catherine. The unfortunate deaths of the four dealers, made only their immediate families melancholic, the conversations in the pubs in the city centre were along the lines that Dundee had been rid of murderers. Some family member from one of the patrons had been a victim of their deadly trade, it could be argued that they didn't force the heroin to gush through their veins; it was self-inflicted, the same as someone hit themselves on the head with a hammer, it would cause more than a headache.

Michael Jameson heard this verse repeated throughout the bars that he visited to watch live bands. The dealers demise gave him courage to venture into the city centre, always conscious of the person next to him at the urinal, or someone brushing up against him at a crowded bar hoping that he wouldn't feel a sharp pain then a flow of warm blood. He saw former enemies hide their bravado; their connections to the dealers were rarely mentioned. One violent clash he had with one of the dealers' army of henchmen, put it about that the return of Jameson was too much of a coincidence. Jameson had heard this theory, he didn't try to disarm anyone of this incorrect information, and this could repel anyone from causing

261

him unjust harm.1

He was in good spirits, the Guinness was good, and his business was organically growing. He had taken out a short term lease on a vacant shop in the west end; he had watched the amount of advertising on day-time television from companies buying gold from the general public. He followed suit, the shop was fitted out like a high- class jewellers, he had ran advertisements on the local radio stations and full page advertisements in the local morning and evening press. He was staggered at the amount of people who came through the doors, students to grandmothers all seeking a fair valuation on their precious gold objects. Others phoned the office requesting a home visit, a pattern emerged; people who requested this service lived in sumptuous houses. They would be visited by his prized jeweller, who gave them a valuation more generous than the students, he carried the company cheque- book, some didn't want the bank teller to see that the money came from these low -class gold merchants, the jeweller would write a cheque from the investment company that Jameson had acquired with the help of Patrick Connelly.

The Festive season brought more cash hungry people through the doors, the gold was becoming difficult to store due to the amount of trinkets and weddings rings, some barely a couple of years old, the ex-wives desperate to cash in on their brief but unhappy marriages. Some expensive if not rare pieces came amongst the less sought after gold articles which would be melted down; these were kept aside, they would be taken down to London and sold for many times that the value that had been told to the willing seller. Fortune had followed him from Dubai to Dundee. Never in a thousand years had he ever thought that his return to Dundee would result in such a surge of injected cash into his businesses. There had been a literal gold rush in Dundee, and the upsurge in lending would spike in the week before Christmas, the working-poor and others who were on a fixed income would have a good if not expensive Christmas, the New Year would bring the first payment on their Christmas loan; Jameson had them for another year at least. How he loved Christmas.

Paul Welsh had never come near him for an increase in his monthly stipend, he had been good as his word; most unusual for an officer of the Law, he was willing to be surprised sometime; that still lay ahead.

He had been invited to Patrick Connelly's office to discuss options for the proceeds of the sale of apartments from the former The Silvery Tay Hotel, which exceeded all his expectations; his large capital investment was accruing even more money, Pat Connelly had another investment plan that he thought he might be interested in. He was, and he approved what Patrick said. A marina had been planned and approved by Fife Council, the original American investors had been caught in the headlights of the credit-crunch, they were looking for a way out, their bank in America had gone bust, they couldn't secure the finance to turn their ambitious plans into a cash- generating reality, berths and villas had been sold before a sod of earth had been cut. Five figure deposits were sitting in a bank in London. Pat's connections with the Asian community alerted him to the difficulty the real estate company was experiencing securing alternative finance. Their expenditure was in excess of their ballooning gearing, their income had trickled to a stop, potential suppliers palms became sweaty; they wanted guarantees that they would be paid, none could be given. Pat knew the area and had made discreet enquiries, there had been no objections, the local communities and surrounding villages offered no flies to be placed in the ointment.

The company sold the development to an off the shelf company that Pat had set up, they then sold it onto a specialist company that had built marinas in many parts of the world. Michael Jameson had doubled his five million investment in a matter of weeks.

He had done business with Patrick Connelly on just two occasions before, he had laid it on the line for him, you invest x you will make y profit. Why wasn't Dubai like that? He had men in an array of suits and traditional Arab dress try to trick him out of his depleted funds, invest in this complex, invest in this shopping mall, they were asking for a minimum of ten million American dollars, he passed, and didn't live to regret his reluctance. Sometimes when he had drunk too much Guinness he wanted to call the charlatans and tell them that he had made millions in Dundee; in an economic downturn, as opposed to losing potential millions in booming Dubai. But this euphoric thought was discarded, his thoughts returned to Patrick Connelly once again, the monies promised lay snugly and more importantly in his bank in the city of London. He looked forward to his meeting with Patrick tomorrow.

***

'Right do you want to tell what happened here Catherine…and I need the truth, if you want me to help you?' He paced the floor frenetically.

'Look, I'm nervous enough already, could you please sit down, then I'll tell you exactly what happened.'

He reluctantly slowed his pace then sat down, on the chair facing the window which displayed a sheet of blackness, he moved off from the chair and closed the curtains, then returned to the chair.

'Are you happy now?'

'Just get on with it Catherine.'

'I don't know what you're worried about; it's me that has a dead body in my bed.'

'I shouldn't be here, but that's neither here nor there…both of us have to calm down, explain what happened.'

She lit a cigarette and stood at the fireplace, which was down to orange embers.

'John, took cocaine early on in the evening about seven, then took some more when we went to bed, then later I felt him shake, I switched on the light and he was having a fit, he didn't say anything he was just shaking, blood came out of his nose, then he stopped shaking, he was dead.' She discarded the cigarette into the fire.

'Did you take the coke as well?'

'No, I'm off it now; we have to get rid of him.'

'Is there still coke here?'

She nodded, and then left the room and returned from the kitchen with a biscuit tin. 'That's all there is in the house,' she beckoned him to take the tin, he declined, he looked in the tin.

'Did you spike it?'

'No! How can you even suggest that?'

'Keep your voice down, I need honesty, if I don't get it I walk out the door, you can go to anyone you want, I'll ask again, did you spike it?'

'I added some of that Bubbles stuff that's popular with the chavs, and the chav -nots, I didn't want or need to kill him.'

She looked at him, he couldn't hide his disgust.

'It was an experiment that went wrong, is that what you're saying?'

'That could be one way to look at it, but it doesn't matter, he's dead, and we need to get rid of him forever, he can't show up anywhere.'

'Who knew he was here tonight?'

'Going by his nature probably a lot of people, why?'

'Because the police will come looking for him and someone will report him missing, your name will crop up, you have to have an alibi.'

'That won't be a problem, my friend was here up till about six, John didn't arrive till about six- thirty.

'That's good, he never arrived. Your friend can

265

corroborate that, that's good.'

He moved from the chair towards her.

'Get rid of the bed and mattress.'

'You want *me* to get rid of them?'

'No, no, I'm talking out loud, I'll take care of that, getting rid of lover boy is the problem, but I'll think of something, we will put him temporarily in your outbuilding, does anyone need to go there for logs or something else, any bikes or kid's stuff? '

'No, he should be okay there, where will you dispose of him?'

'I don't know, but I'll think of something. He never arrived here tonight, stick to that and you'll be okay, you should pull that off, you're a solicitor you're blessed with acting skills.'

She wanted to respond to him, but didn't want to start a negative slanging match.

'I'll be okay, we can't have him popping up somewhere in the future; it has to be permanent.'

'I know that, but I told you I'll think of the solution, but just now I don't have the solution at hand, you understand that don't you?'

She had managed to agitate him.

'I understand, I'm sorry,' she replied in a contrite manner.

'That's okay…does he have clothes here, his mobile is it still here?'

'He only has the clothes he came in, his mobile is on the dressing table, I used it to call you…I didn't think.'

'You what!'

'God! I didn't realise that.'

'I'm implicated in this, that'll be the first thing the murder squad will do, get his mobile number and check the records , what am I going to say when my number shows up?'

'It's okay, okay, it was one of a number of his phones that are pay -as- you go phones, and they were bought

266

off the shelf.'

'Are you sure…really sure, think?'

'Positive. C'mon upstairs and see for yourself.'

Relief became evident on his face. 'Okay, but we'll move him first into the outbuilding.'

He rummaged in the standalone wardrobe.

'I'll put him into these two suit protectors, it's not ideal, but it's functional. Where are your kids?'

'They're at my mum's, I don't like them knowing I was seeing someone else, so soon after their father's death.' The way she delivered this comment made her sound like a paragon of virtue. Her acting skills came to the fore. Did she want sympathy? First a cesspool of a husband dies then her mourning is interrupted by the concerns of a murderous friend. They carried him into the outbuilding and covered him with logs that had been cut for firewood. He looked around the damp, cold outbuilding. His eyes fixated on the chainsaw; she caught his gaze.

'I'll do it if you want me to?'

'It was only a thought; the forensics would pick up on the blood spots, thanks for the offer. We or rather I will take him as he is; I think it's better that way.'

'Okay, I see you're thinking ahead.' They both looked at the unsuspecting woodpile, hiding a dark secret.

'Did he have any other phones on him, or did he use your mobile or house phone tonight?'

She shivered in the cold dampness.

'No, I was careful, even though he wasn't, he thought he was using me, but he didn't realise it at the time I was using him, and he was an informer for your deceased predecessor.' His face even in the semi-darkness relayed to her, he wasn't aware of this.

'Oh fuck, that's all we need, how long was he a C.I. for?'

'Only a week, unlucky for Feeney, lucky for you I suppose, it's freezing in here, we'd be better going back to the house.'

'Good idea.'

He had been astounded to learn of him being a C.I. In the house they were more relaxed in conversation, they needed each other.

'You'd be surprised at the amount of so-called hard men, who are informants, Feeney must have been very persuasive, and cunning, no one suspects he was involved or taking a cut from every major drug deal.'

He couldn't resist. 'I knew something was amiss.' He stopped himself expanding on the information he had collated, he was more circumspect.

'Oh is that right? That's interesting, what else did you know about him then?'

'That's my insurance policy, if something untoward happens to me or I run into bad luck, others will suffer consequences, much, much, greater than mine.'

'Everybody should have insurance, John, didn't. His wife won't get anything, after all he's not dead is he?'

'That's right, he's just missing.'

***

The cold didn't affect his new found confidence, no adversary had as much as looked in his direction, he wouldn't disabuse them from the gathering credence to the rumour that he had been instrumental in having the four dealers murdered. The dealers expected to take their place on the podium developed vertigo, they had heard anyone who fancied taking their place would suffer the same fate as them, but they wouldn't have their life ended so quickly and humanely by a projectile entering their brains, it would be death over a period of days. The podiums were gathering dust and spider-webs were being spun.

He had walked down Victoria Road many times and through the Wellgate Centre that was resplendent in Christmas lights and decorations, he wondered if he could walk through the Wellgate and out into the

268

Murraygate without hearing Slade's 'Merry Christmas.' This was not the only reason he walked through prominent public places, he wanted anyone who thought to do him harm to let them know he felt safe walking in the city centre. He had just placed a foot outside the automatic door that led onto the Murraygate when *the* song assaulted his musically tuned ears. He glanced at his watch, still twenty - minutes before his appointment with Patrick Connelly. He was in two minds whether to go into Tesco's and pick up The Courier, he decided against this and continued on his way to the Perth Road, who would have thought he would be invited up to the top floor of his office, he could hardly contain his excitement, and this would be the deal of all deals. Paul Welsh was another man of influence, with these two at his side he felt an air of invincibility with every confident step he took.

No more languid pace, he was more vigorous and purposeful as the Perth Road lay ahead, he became more nostalgic about his 'troubled years' the period of his life when he was a semi-recluse, he quickly dispensed with this depression inducing thought.

And there it was on the right hand side; the Deep Sea restaurant. Bittersweet memories, this was where his wife insisted on having tea on Friday's; every Friday. He slowed down his pace, his bottom lip trembled, he proposed to her in there. Since she died, he never had been back; he had even gone off fish for a number of years. He never took his misty eyes off the restaurant; he would go back on Friday, his torturous exile was over, he had to go in and think of the good times. He walked more quickly now, the bitter cold wind made him gulp, but he wouldn't change this for the oppressing heat of Dubai. Walking past the Queen's Hotel, he saw the office of the solicitor who had cultivated and propagated a man of the people image; it was all a sham, he teased certain information from clients, who were involved in various criminal activities, financial and drugs were the crimes he was interested in. Over the years he had become in his peers eyes a Lothario, in private he was a brutish individual when he consumed alcohol, now his face was ravaged with the copious amount of alcohol he was consuming daily.

Michael Jameson was one of the few who knew of his hidden, dark secret life. Ten years previously he had represented him, filing his tax returns, investing some of his undeclared income, both were happy with this arrangement, until Jameson found out the solicitor was slicing twenty-percent of the profits in addition to his ten-percent commission. As the years passed by, his alcohol consumption increased, he was drinking before he went to Court, he was becoming loud in restaurants, he started naming names that were investing in 'black funds,' he became less particular with the paperwork, he had sent an email to Jameson in Dubai, highlighting his misappropriating of his portfolio, he meant to send it to a female financial advisor he was seeing; Jameson looked at the time it was sent, three-thirty am. He kept this information in his head. He couldn't confront him with the wrongly directed email, after all he was still making eye-watering profits; he felt hurt more than being fleeced. After all the scrapes he had put right, sorting out people that needed sorting out, trips to London in The Ritz for him and his collage of women. Some of them married Procurator Fiscals, apparently happily married. He just had to resist firing off an email to him, informing he was aware what was going on. His betrayal still eked away at his brain in the early hours of the morning. That all changed when he asked to speak to Patrick Connelly, he told him all about his assets, which were legal and which assets weren't, he then told him of the solicitor who was skimming some of his profits, without naming the solicitor concerned. Pat Connelly saved his embarrassment by naming him for him. Jameson was taken aback, how he knew, Connelly just smiled and said 'this is a small city with big secrets.' He advised Jameson to liquidate his assets that were illegal, even deeply discounted. Connelly saw the resistance in his eyes; he had seen the look before from many multi-millionaires. Connelly poured him a coffee, and explained why it was beneficial for both of them, the solicitor and Jameson. The solicitor is getting money for nothing; he would pay him from his own funds, and then sell the assets, corporate bonds, blue-chip shares, insurance bonds, making himself a healthy profit. In Connelly's view the solicitor would not try to change Jameson's foolish financial strategy.

'When the money is transferred into his account, contact me, I'll find a nice workhouse for your money.' Connelly saw the well of questions building up in him, he relieved the anguish.

'The Financial Services Authority have been monitoring certain unusual investments , including spread- betting, his office will be raided in four weeks' time, by that time you will be not be on his official client list.' Jameson's apprehension about selling assets at a discount didn't seem so bad; he had one question to ask.

'How are the FSA aware of this?'

'The weekend break that you paid for at Gleneagles? He boasted this to a female companion.'

***

'Would you like more coffee Morag?'

'No thanks Jean, I've really cut down on my caffeine, I drink more water, that's a consequence of living in Dubai for years?'

'Do you think you'll ever go back?'

'Jean, I'm the policeman in the family, you're not,' Eddings interjected.

'That's okay Valentine, no Jean I can't see me ever going back, the bubble has burst in the construction industry, there will be a lot of unhappy people unable to get their deposits back, it's not like the U.K., legal redress over there, is primitive.'

'You were lucky to get out at the right time then?'

'No I saw the storm clouds when others saw blue skies, some of my friends have lost hundreds of thousands, and they're the lucky ones, there will be a lot of people using their balconies rather than the elevators.'

Jean was plainly horrified at this stark, cold-heart delivery.

'It's that bad, really that bad?'

'What you see on the news and in the newspapers, multiply by ten and it will still be understated.'

'You're awfully quiet Val, cat got your tongue?'

'No, I'm just as shocked as you, I didn't realise for a minute it was that bad, I'm glad I'm not there now.

What will the people do, the people who bought the apartments intending to lease them?'

'Simple, they abandon the apartments and fly home to the U.K, what else can they do?' They don't have the money to service their apartments and an investment property. That's the advice I have given to two of my friends, they fly out tomorrow.'

'Things are bad in Dundee, down at the docks where they built those horrible apartments, seemingly that's fell flat on its face, there used to be the Polish workers renting flats down there, but because there's no work, they've left. I heard it being called Whitfield by-the-sea.'

'You're well informed Jean, a lot of investors have lost money down there. But you have a nice house here, have you stayed here long?'

'Coming up for three years, we love living here, don't we Val?'

'Do we?'

'Don't listen to him Morag, he's just in one of his moods, he really likes it here, did I tell you there are a lot of doctors here?'

'I don't think you mentioned that one of them has been struck off, did you darling,' he interjected.

'Now, now Valentine, you always mention to me to wait till a court delivers its verdict before disparaging individuals, or have you changed your mind because he has a different colour of skin from you?'

'You really take the biscuit Jean, a couple of years ago you would have proudly worn a white sheet with two holes cut out…wouldn't you darling?'

Morag was feeling embarrassed, she thought this would be the opportune time to change the subject.

'Do you mind if I go into your garden and admire the view over to Fife?'

Both Jean and Eddings stood up clearly wishing they didn't get into a verbal spat.   'Take Morag out Val, I'll clear the table.

Take your coat Morag it's chilly out there.'

'I'll put my coat on will I?'

'Do what you want, you could wear a white sheet for all I care, there are scissors in the drawer, and do you want me to get them for you?'

He left the table in silence, how he wished he kept his mouth firmly closed.

'I'm sorry, I shouldn't have said that,' he turned to Morag; she's not really a racist….'

She thumped down the teapot. 'Are you clearly going off your head? And for your information the wonderful police have been known to be a tad racist, or have you forgotten?'

He threw his hands up in complete capitulation.

'I think I better not say anything more.'

'Take Morag into the garden will you, you're embarrassing her.'

He opens the utility door then leads her to the rear door that gives way to the garden, when he opens the door; the temperature was as Jean said.

'Well you obviously said the wrong thing there,' she

tried to muffle her laughter.

'She's such a hypocrite at times…don't get me started.'

'Nice view though,' she started to giggle.

'I don't see what's so funny,' he was getting annoyed.

'You, you were like an errant schoolboy, I didn't think you were one to accept criticism, she certainly let you have it.'

'Forget that, what do you think of the view then?'

'It's very nice.'

'Nice? It's fucking gorgeous, nice, that's a joke!'

'Keep your language in check; I don't want you getting sent to bed.'

'I think we've saw enough of the view.' He walked away from her.

***

The old battered blue transit van was delivered as agreed; he had spoken to the trader, who had agreed to have it driven to an address in Douglas. There the money was exchanged and the keys handed over, the transaction took less than two minutes. He felt a fool dressed in a torn boiler suit and oil smeared baseball cap, his face had sprouted four days growth, his ginger genes only reached into his facial hair. The thick glasses totally altered his appearance. The young man in his twenties didn't engage in conversation, he just wanted paid and be on his way. He scrawled his ineligible signature across the document; the seller looked at the block of flats and thanked his God that he didn't have to live there.

Barely a word was spoken between them, each were happy with the bargain they had struck on a cash basis. He watched the low -loader drive away, as soon as it was out of his eye line, he went into the van, he turned the key, and the unmistakable sound of the diesel engine coughed reluctantly into life, he rammed the gear stick into first then moved off to pick up the cargo of death. The drive to her house would test the engine of the van;

the sounds emanating from the engine convinced him it was on its last trip; that would suit him. He drove it up to the door of the outbuilding, and then went to her house, she was dressed as he had ordered, her clothes would be destroyed after she helped load the van. He studied her closely, no frayed nerves were jangling from her face, she didn't hint or enquire where the body would end up, her solicitor's cold calculus, reminded her, the less she knew the less she would be tempted to tell anyone or have her conscience shouting at her. The logs were replaced back in a large neat pile, he stood back and looked at his handiwork, it was too clinical, his eyes liked what he saw but his enquiring mind told him that the symmetry was unnervingly neat, too neat, they could offer up a minute clue. He stepped forward and took a log from the top and placed it on the concrete floor, he repeated this procedure then stepped back and looked at the misshapen pile of logs, he was satisfied now.

Catherine stood puzzled, she didn't share his confidence that an observant detective would automatically think the logs were telling him that something dreadful had happened, she kept this observation to herself. She took off her clothes and placed them into the black bag, he grabbed the bag from her and threw it into the rear of the van, once more he looked round the outbuilding, his eyes were satisfied. He went into the van and took out the blue plastic sheeting that is used to protect roofs when the roofs are stripped of the slates, he covered the body with the sheeting, he glanced at his watch, and told her that he was off, he didn't want any contact from her; he would be in touch. He was a man in a hurry, even in the poorly lit building she was impressed at the planning that had went into the disposal of the body, and the way his appearance had been altered, but she could tell his mind was counting down time.

The drive back to Dundee was uneventful, he had

chartered the course, the annual drink-driving blitz was in its zenith, he had the information where the road blocks would be; he sensibly circumvented them, the last one was at Drumgeith Road. He drove into the Baldovie waste to energy plant, the door of the incinerator was open; it would be closing soon for the Christmas break because of government and the council's efficiency drive due to the omnipresent credit crunch, the plant would be operating on a part-time basis on the run up to Christmas, this suited the employees, as in the previous years the council wanted the incinerator plant to run twenty-four hours over the Christmas period. There would be no treble time that had been paid previously if the plant needed to be operated in the Christmas period. For the last dump and burn, only two men would be needed, it was custom and practice that one of the men would go home as usual, as the last load of refuse was Spartan.

The employee came out to meet him and spoke to him through the jammed window. After he had went over every minute detail, he finally left the van, he went to the rear of the van and opened the doors wide, the employee looked in momentarily, then went back into the plant, he returned with a cage on wheels, which contained empty cardboard boxes, he then threw them into the rear of the van; he didn't think there was any need for this elaborate subterfuge, why didn't they just carry him in and dump him on the conveyer belt with the rest of the rubbish that was going to be burnt to a cinder? All the cameras had been turned off at the precise moment Welsh had insisted and had left nothing to chance; he didn't want anyone to see two men carry in the unmistakable shape of a body. The cameras even though they were not on, couldn't pick up the rear of the van; this was a blind spot, after all this was an incinerator plant not a bullion depot.

Welsh manoeuvred the large boxes over the stricken

body in the suit-covers, satisfied he invited the employee to help move the body into the cage, once they had effortlessly done that, he placed more boxes into the cage. Then and only then did they move the cage into the plant. Keeping his head deliberately down with the cap pulled down to near his eyebrows he placed the body carefully on the static, silent conveyer belt, the employee moved into the office at Welsh's insistence and checked the cameras were still switched off, he returned with the news that they were, he pressed the button on the adjacent control panel on the wall, and the conveyer belt moved with the unexpected addition to the refuse. They stood silently watching it incrementally, and then it disappeared into the furnace. When he turned round Welsh was gone, he heard the engine being gunned.

He stood there an array of thoughts all competing to be opened and analyzed , his vow to kill his daughter's killer was not met in full, but he had at least saw him enter into the gates of hell. Welsh was a man of his word.

The hot water gushing down on him calmed and calibrated his thoughts, he turned around in the wet room, the warm water hitting his back, it eased all the tension, now that the adrenaline had abated. No sooner than one massive problem had been overcome, potentially Catherine could turn the solution back into a problem; he wasn't prepared to accept this. He felt more relaxed, and pleased with the outcome, Catherine should be grateful, no blackmail would work now if she was stupid enough to even think that. Money would be coming in from her without any opposition, she needed him. Monty was out of the picture, she knew all his contacts, and his finances seamlessly became hers she was the sole beneficiary. Any chancer who turned up at her house implying that Monty was due them money, would be told put it in writing and her solicitor would contact them, if they tried to imply violence, they would be dealt with the following day.

The Christmas spirit came in the form of Welsh; the avenging angel. Henry would have a more peaceful Christmas now, some of the anguish about his daughter's death, would be quelled by her killer's timely death. She had been struck by a car driven by him on the Kingsway as she was returning home from a night -club in the early hours of Christmas morning, the whole of Dundee woke up to this shocking news, a young girl had been the victim of a hit and run incident. There was speculation that if the motorist had stopped and called an ambulance she may have survived. Snow helped trace the type of car by the tyre marks and the skid that the car went into, they calculated the speed, the motorist was driving at a minimum of ninety- miles an hour. The car had struck a tree that lined the Kingsway, paintwork had been embedded in the bark of the tree; the crash had awoken residents, and they had given the colour and some of the personalised number plate. The police thought they had him bang-to- rights; they turned up at his house where he was enjoying his Christmas dinner with his wife and infant daughter; he was unmarked. He told the police down at Bell Street in the presence of his solicitor; and that he had left his car at his friend's house at the City Quay, because he had been at the Christmas party there, he and his wife left about one in the morning by taxi. There were other guests there who could vouch for him. They all did, including the taxi-driver. None of them showed any sign of nervousness when they were being interviewed all had a solicitor beside them. The police had to let him go. The case remains open. This didn't help Henry, he turned up at John Roger's house with a golf club; he was arrested, the police tried to convince John to drop the charges; he smiled and said he wanted him charged; he feared for his wife and young daughter's life. Outrage was kept in check by the police but not by the Dundee public.

Welsh knew Henry was a keen gardener; he met him
accidentally, in Dobbie's Garden Centre, and told him to
be patient. Roger's enjoyed the notoriety, no remorse no
regrets. He was known as the Jolly Roger after that
incident. The comments he passed in pubs didn't endear
him to the clientele, such as 'what's all the fuss about,
she wasn't his real daughter she was adopted and pissed,
the autopsy proved it, it was more like suicide.'
There wasn't a chance of him being barred from that
particular bar, owners rarely are.

Henry lost interest in his job as a chartered surveyor,
he declined into himself, cared less about his appearance
and became a recluse who drank every waking hour;
time meant nothing to him, he wanted death to take him.
Welsh went to his house when his wife left him
temporarily, he told him he would have his revenge but
didn't elaborate or expand what he really meant; Henry
looked into his eyes and knew, not hoped, what he
meant. His eyes began to show a glimmer of a shine. He
stood up and thanked him. Welsh had another surprise
for him he had a friend who could get him a job at
Baldovie on a temporary basis.

'If you get yourself together it could lead to a
permanent job.'

He was overwhelmed at this kindness from a total
stranger he unexpectedly met at Dobbies. He took up
the offer, and insisted he wouldn't contact Roger's
again. He was worried about the Court appearance,
Welsh told him not to worry. Welsh left his house, he
phoned his estranged wife at her sister's and told her that
he had found him a job, and he had given up drinking.

He went up to the bathroom and looked into the mirror
for the first meaningful time in months; he was disgusted
at his appearance, the straggly beard and unkempt hair
would have to go. The following week he received a
letter from the Procurator Fiscals office; he opened it

wondering when he would have to appear. It informed him that the appellant had dropped the charges, the fiscal warned him about his future conduct. It must be Welsh who had convinced Roger's to drop the charges. He was bursting to tell his wife the good news; it was just a pity that he couldn't tell her about Welsh. But he, too, was a man of his word.

All these thoughts danced around Welsh's head, Henry thought when he told him that justice would catch up with Roger's, he must have thought he would personally murder him. And when he turned up at the incinerator and told him that Roger's was dead, and he needed to get rid of his body, he let Henry think it was Henry's idea to incinerate him. Christmas was a poignant time for Henry, seeing his daughter's murderer disappear into the furnace along with all the rest of rubbish near the anniversary of the time of his daughter's death was spiritually uplifting for him; Christmas day would be a cause for remembering and celebrating. Welsh turned off the power-shower he was mentally exhilarated... His wife would be returning from London tomorrow, his appearance was back to normal. He dressed, and then went to the bay window, he looked towards Broughty Ferry; the white-smoke from Baldovie was billowing into the night air.

***

The receptionist looked at him warily, but she was still smiling when she invited him to use the lift, and see Mr Connelly. Upstairs in the warm office he was studying the figures; everything was in good order, projected operating profits, EBITDA, etc. Planning for houses overlooking the area was estimated to be priced from seven hundred and fifty thousand upwards. Although the site for these houses was in a designated green field site with special scientific interest, this didn't cause any furrowing of his brow; the fix was in. As soon as the sale of the marina was completed the lobbying would begin

280

in earnest. When the proposal for the marina was put before the planning committee, it was universally but cautiously welcomed. The committee had been assured that the funds were in place, for the ambitious project. No one had predicted that the financial tsunami would break on the shores of Fife; rumours and malicious whispers about financial shortfalls; however temporary elevated into a deafening siren. The CEO of the company was unavailable to meet the planning committee on a number of occasions. The committee didn't wish to look foolish as a number of them had addressed several queries in the Press regarding funding; they repeated ad nauseum. When the CEO eventually made contact by email from Dubai, he made it clear that the company was teetering on the brink of being declared bankrupt; they were in talks with a number of interested parties, one was particularly keen they had more than enough liquidity, however, they wished to tweak the original plans put before the planning committee, in his view it would enhance the marina, but that was for the CEO of the company and the committee to discuss. At this point in time he was of the understanding that the original plan would go through, but sometime in the near future, he hoped the new company plans would be approved. But that was up to the committee. The future plan would be for executive accommodation. The planning committee discussed this with council and government departments, the council were keen as the business rates and council taxes raised would be significant. The Scottish Government had no choice; they had set a precedent; they had welcomed Donald Trump's controversial plans.

The CEO from the company was invited to an informal meeting at the proposed site; he was met at Dundee Airport as his jet from Dubai landed. The council were impressed by the array of experts that accompanied the CEO, after the site visit, the council officials were invited to dinner that evening at the St Andrews Hotel to discuss anything that concerned the council; the CEO insisted that he was not like the vulgar New Yorker, he wanted approval by consensus, and he would not be seeking any sweetheart deals, he didn't want any public money from the Scottish Government or Fife councils. He believed in the free flow of capital. The council officials kept the Scottish government informed of the meeting they acquiesced that the planning committee should accept the dinner invitation from Mr Madni.

Everyone seemed to benefit, there were no losers. However, the people who benefited more financially were the CEO and shadowy peripheral investors of the financial stricken company. The company that was deemed on the verge of collapse didn't intend to cut the first sod of earth, yes, they had spent hundreds of thousands on consultants reports, opened an office in St Andrews in which any sceptical member of the public could view the company's vision. They knew that if they tried to include the green-field site for expensive housing they would have had every protest group mobilised against them, and Internet searches looking for something to impede the development of the marina. They had enticed the planning committee up the marina's path, and then at the most inconvenient time; were prepared to walk away. They had bought the land from another company that was controlled by the company that would build the marina.

Six months previously a representative had visited Mr Madni, he forecast the whirlwind of financial whirlwinds that had swept across the Atlantic from America to the United Kingdom and Europe. Mr Madni smiled at the plights of various blue -chip banks, his smile disappeared when he was told the storm would visit Dubai.

He showed the figures he had obtained from a friend

who worked for an inter-government department; British banks had billions invested in Dubai; mainly in construction. He advised Mr Madni to sell his newly constructed apartment blocks to sellers that had been asking him to name his price, and then when he has done this cancel his future construction projects or better sell them by piecemeal to avoid raising eyebrows.

To say Mr. Madni was worried by this forecast was an understatement, he countered this could be a ploy to buy his assets from him cheaply, and where would he invest the millions that he had realised from the sales? The marina in Fife, in Scotland near, St Andrews, he talked him through the marina and showed him the plans that had been approved. Now he was impressed. When he was shown the Greenfield site with the luxurious houses; he was impressed more. Before he had time to ask if it was such a cash- generating business, why would the company think to sell. Tax evasion was the reason. He thought correctly 'dirty money.' It came with a cast iron guarantee that the planning committee would approve the supplementary plans on the Greenfield site. What better guarantee than to see the planning committee and hear for yourself? Arrangements were made and Mr Madni flew from Dubai into Dundee with his entourage, he was enthralled by the snow on the Sidlaw Hills, but his sightseeing could wait; business always came first. The man from Dundee had been correct about the financial implosion that erupted in Dubai; he had sold all his newly-constructed apartments, and seventy-five percent of his land. His competitors weren't so lucky; they thought they were undervaluing his assets. Mr. Madni was crying all the way to the bank.

***

'Come in!' Jameson walked in as instructed; he was still tanned, which was enhanced by the white T-shirt.

'How are you Mr Connelly?'

'Fine, not as in robust as your health…and your

283

finances,' he passed him the cheque.

'Fucking hell! It was that easy? I...I just can't believe it.'

'I told you that it's a good investment company, it's an off-shoot of the company that you invested in The Silvery Tay Hotel. They had an offer from a billionaire from Dubai; he came over saw the plans for the marina and liked what he saw. Nice profits for everyone; are you finished looking at the cheque, which is a duplicate of the cheque which was sent to your overseas account.'

'You better take his Pat,' he handed it to him then he put it through the shredder on the other side of the room.

'How is your gold rush shop doing?'

His eyebrows nearly hit the ceiling.

'Beyond expectations, vast profits for a little outlay, I never knew there was so much gold in Dundee, and to think I went to Dubai to make money and get away from problems, I like being the prodigal son.'

'Have you heard anything untoward?'

'What do you mean?'

'About our mutual friend from Fife?'

'No... Should I be worried?'

'No, I heard that with those dealers being murdered something was going to kick -off near Christmas, it's probably idle gossip, but I heard it at a Christmas party from another solicitor, he didn't go into specifics, he has acted for some of the deceased, maybe he was feeling me out.' 'Why did you mention Welsh?'

'I didn't, you just did, be careful what you say and where you say it. I just heard that he's been to see one of the widows, maybe nothing in it but he's in the drug squad not the murder squad.'

'You might be looking too far into that Pat, if he was at one of the widows she might have been the main player in the drug deals.'

'If you hear anything, tell me, don't mention anything to him if he contacts you.'

'I've never seen him since we met in his house.'
'That's good to hear…that's business concluded for
today, do you not feel the cold?'

***

Strolling down the Hilltown after midnight was not for
the fainthearted; even if he was accompanied by a
colleague, who shouldn't have joined the police. Lenny
was assigned to him to instill confidence and make him
forget being attacked by five youths. This was make or
break for the young constable, he thought because he
had been in the Royal Marines he would have a certain
aura about him. He was fit, able and willing to go in
where other constables feared. Another lamb dancing
towards the butchers' knife. He had become bored on
his assigned beats; he went to the sergeant and expressed
his unhappiness. The sergeant went out on his rostered
beat with him near the Hawkhill, he tried to be
diplomatic with the young idealist, but the sergeant
became concerned when he heard the exploits that he
allegedly became embroiled in hen he was in the Royal
Marines. He came to the conclusion that he was a
fantasist or a psychopath. The police were under enough
pressure from the editor of the Evening Chronicle either
'being too soft on the criminals who are undoubtedly
have no fear of the Law', or 'some individuals are being
harassed on a regular basis.' The sergeant was not of the
opinion that this gung -ho recruit would be an asset to
Tayside Police; he sat at the canteen table and invited
Lenny to join him. Lenny gulped when he asked him to
sit down at the same table that meant an itch needed to
scratched, Lenny was in no mood to be a scratcher. After
the preliminaries were taken care off, he told Lenny that
'GI Joe' would be joining him on his night-shift beat that
covered the Hilltown; he should be shown some action.
Lenny enquired if that was a wise course of action, he
was told in the affirmative.

Lenny countered that since the dealers were no longer in the game anymore the Hilltown was like the Wild West just now, as there was a vacuum, and heads were being opened as certain individuals were trying to exercise control, he didn't think it was a good idea. There was no debate, he was babysitting GI Joe, he shouldn't worry as according to him he had fought everybody in the world, and he would be able to look after Lenny. Lenny groaned at this endorsement.

He had been involved in a difference of opinion with some neds at the Chinese carry-out shop on the Hilltown, banter turned into verbal abuse, which ended in violence, Lenny and his colleague were the victors, he was taken off the Hilltown beat till feelings subsided, the victims had threatened revenge. Now he was being thrown back to the bear-pit, if GI Joe wanted hand- to - hand fighting he would be guaranteed it. The thought filled him with absolute dread, it was worrying enough the Triads were watching him, now he was fighting on the Hilltown. GI Joe would be joining him on Friday and Saturday night. The sergeant thanked him for his cooperation, he wouldn't forget it; he left Lenny staring forlornly into his soup.

Friday came round too quickly for Lenny's liking; he had a bad feeling about tonight never mind Saturday.

It was double-money weekend, the Hilltown would be awash with the residents spending their benefit money in a weekend, these people were not fans of macro-economics, money would be pooled together to buy drugs and drink, by Monday they would be strung-out craving drugs or alcohol, by the time Friday came round they would have no money, they desperately needed money to buy drugs, house-breaking and shoplifting would be in vogue, old-scores would be settled, violent assaults would be occurring not just under the cloak of darkness.

He met GI Joe in the locker room and explained the

fallout of the benefit money being paid out in one weekend, GI Joe said he understood as he danced around the locker room throwing punches at imaginary predators, he couldn't wait till his feet were pounding the Hilltown and some criminal felt his boot on his or her neck. He declined to take the stab vest, Lenny insisted he wore it or he wouldn't be going near the Hilltown. GI Joe told Lenny that it was a visible sign of weakness, when he was in Iraq. Lenny stopped him in full-flow.

'Iraq would be like a picnic, remember you had weapons over there, here you have a baton which is like a matchstick but less useful.' Ten o clock and they started to walk from Kings Cross towards the Alexander multi storey blocks, he had been instructed to tell GI Joe, about the incidents that happened in these flats, the grisly violent assaults, and the despair of some residents who chose to exit via the balconies rather than the time-consuming lifts, and the aftermath of the limp bloodied bodies that lay broken and misshapen on the pavement. At the Coldside roundabout they came across the first incident of the evening a woman was hanging over the barriers at the butchers. Lenny called an ambulance, it was there in less than five minutes; the paramedics took charge.

GI Joe couldn't hide his disappointment as they made their way past the Three Barrels, even though it had changed its name years ago to John Barleycorns, the public still referred to it as the Three Barrels, it had earned a good reputation for live bands, and boxing contests after football matches when a team that played in Blue visited from Glasgow; the indigenous boxers were often the victors. GI wanted to go into the bar to make the patrons aware that they weren't afraid, Lenny invited him to see the consequences of this harassment, on his own. He demurred from his original assessment. Cat-calling came from a number of youths as they walked past the traffic lights at Cookies Bar, they were baiting them, patrons smoking outside the bar told the youths to go home and OD for everyone's sake. They turned into Alexander Street; the youths turned round and followed them. GI Joe showed the first sign of nerves; he said Lenny should call for back up. Lenny ignored the comment; they had more concern in front of them.

Their friends were emerging in droves from the multi-storey with plastic bags tucked under their arms; he suspected they weren't going to be presented with flowers. GI Joe's head was in danger of spinning off, as he looked back and forward, Lenny instructed him to pull out his baton and pat it against the palm of his hand, he didn't want to do this as this might make them feel aggrieved. Lenny told him if he didn't he was going to take his baton across his head. He took out the baton and copied Lenny; Lenny quickened his step towards the aggressors who were running towards them.

'Don't run or your dead, keep the same pace as me, forget them at the rear of us, they'll slow down, it's this mob in front , when I run at them, you stop and invite them behind us to join in swear at the top of your voice and remove your cap, got it!'

'I think so…what about back up!'

'No back up, this is personal, just stay on your feet and swing that baton, they're all junkies they'd run from a cheeseburger, just clunk some heads.' He took his optional extra from his trouser pocket, the knuckle duster had served him well in the past, he hoped it would sustain him again, he would soon find out he counted eight of them as they ran towards him, the one with a black-eye he recognised as the one from the Chinese carry-out, he would concentrate his ire on him, if he made him take flight the rest would follow.

'I'll take the big one with the shiner you hit anyone to the right or left of him, have you got that?'

'How hard will I hit them I might kill them, I might be better to use the pepper spray.'

'Use the fucking baton, if they get you down they'll kick you to death; fucking hit them with the baton forget the fucking pepper spray!'

The group at the back had done their job, they had moved the policemen as planned, and there was no need to hang around. They were about twenty metres from the group they had kept a steady pace slapping their batons manically against their palms, the group saw that they would not turn on their heels and run, doubts invaded them, the police officers were high on adrenalin, the youths were slowing down the insults were more sporadic; there was no going back. The youths halted, Lenny shrank the space between them with his lopping stride, his baton crashed across his face, he felt his teeth wobble, his second blow landed on his head, blood poured out on cue, he was on his knees now screaming obscenities at his violent oppressor, Lenny varied his shots on his body, the joints.

GI Joe was being pummeled by three of them his baton tucked under his stomach, as his arms protected his head. Lenny left his vanquished would-be assailant begging for an end to the torrent of violence. His request was granted, he moved towards the group who were kicking GI Joe, his baton striking the target, they all ran away. Lenny surveyed the scene, Blood on the pavement, on his baton and on GI Joe. His baton was hanging limply from his wrist; cars were slowing down, the drivers' craning their inquisitive necks. He couldn't wait to hear the comments in the canteen about the battle of Alexander Street, an appropriate and apt name; He felt like Alexander after he had neutralised his enemy.

The high was being replaced with the thought of his mentor GG, he had taught him everything, how he wished he was here to have witnessed this social cohesion, that's what he called trouble ahead; 'time for some social cohesion.' GI Joe was sobbing, I bet he wished he was back fighting the Taliban, no police college could teach this type of social interaction. He helped him to his feet, he felt sorry for this hero of his weird and wonderful imagination, the sergeant wanted him to see the real Dundee not PR exercises on the Hilltown at four in the afternoon with politicians staging stunts, and when the cameras were gone, the politicians would slunk back to their safe havens in the west-end; they didn't feel the residents pain.

GI Joe had some hard thinking to do, he would resign or recalibrate his policing methods, Lenny was not too concerned which decision he arrived at as long as he wasn't babysitting him again. The sergeant would be pleased with his official report and his more truthful report and how GI Joe coped. He wouldn't hold back, he was a danger to himself and his colleague, the only person he felt safe would be the criminal element which were increasing in numbers judging by the number of Liverpool accents that were heard. GI Joe could be targeted by criminals and compromised; knowing his reputation as a man that made ladies swoon.

With the inferring from the editor of the Evening Chronicle, he was convinced that some police officers were venal. GI Joe could firm up that assumption. At the station Lenny painted a more heroic picture of what went on, GI Joe had rushed to assist him as he was attacked by a large group of Neds, intent on violent action against him and his fellow officer. Minimum restraint was used in retaliation; the officers had feared for their lives.

Unfortunately, the CCTV cameras positioned on the soon-to be demolished multis had been disconnected by the council due to some residents complaining that police officers were coercing the CCTV operators into using them for potential criminal surveillance. The sergeant had made it crystal clear that if any of the alleged assaulted youths came forward and alleged a criminal act against either of the officers a plague of drug raids would descend upon them, and some significant drug finds would be guaranteed. This was told to a businessman who was alleged to have operated some illegal import and export business that emanated from Columbia.

The sergeant was told no complaint would be coming from anyone from the Hilltown area. When Lenny was told this he was not surprised, GG had told him of the 'special relationship' the sergeant had had with the businessman.

***

He had watched in hypnotic horror from safety of the Alexander multi-storey, he was settling in for the long, uncomfortable reconnaissance shift. The two constables had acquitted themselves admirably, one more than the other. When he was on the beat, he would not dream of walking about at this time and in this area; soiled nappies, bottles and even a tumble dryer was aimed at the police from malcontents who lived in the multi-storey blocks. Even when they were in their patrol car they were not guaranteed safety, one unfortunate crew parked outside the multi-storey, they had been called by a resident who was being attacked, the call was just a ruse to get the police to come to the block, they parked their car, before they had got out the roof of the car sustained a long and continuous attack from various objects and projectiles; a baby's buggy, a plant plot from an uninterested gardener, and a tumble dryer.

From then on in, the cars were parked across the street. No one was more pleased to see the plans for the new housing, than the decent residents who were surrounded by junkies and alcoholics, who had a penchant for loud rock music in the early hours of the morning. The officers who were based in the Hilltown, were ecstatic that the monuments of violence would be razed; in or around the multi-stories some heinous murders had been committed; drugs and alcohol were invariably involved either being taken by the victim or the perpetrator. McAveety was not sad to lose those days; it could have been him if he had not moved to the drug squad that was being attacked. As he watched the youths run then stumble towards the officers he feared for the worst, he couldn't call the ambush into police headquarters as that would have compromised his position in the multi-storey. There was no guilt or angst as he watched the mob set about the officers, one officer was struck on the head and was being kicked like there was not going to be another tomorrow, the other officer stayed on his feet and rained his baton on one of them and at the same time he was lashing out with his feet.

One youth was lying motionless on the frost covered pavement, the officer then went to the assistance of the office cowering in the foetal position, the baton and punches made them leave the officer and run in the directions of the Hilltown. His conscience was eased. The street returned back to a malevolent silence. Tonight he was hoping the four by four would return to the multi-storey block; this time with packages of some description; the flat that they were using must be a store for drugs or money that was what he was hoping for. He moved away from the window and sat on the small seat with the backrest broken off; he opened the flask and poured out the steaming hot coffee. He held the china mug with both hands, he leaned forward to capture some heat from the halogen heater, it was definitely colder tonight, and the early hours of the morning would see the temperature plummet farther.

This was his weekend off, if he called the police about the attack, suspicions about his lair would be asked, why was he there on his day off? He placed the cup on the floor and took out his wallet, he rubbed his chin; he opened the wallet and took out the credit card statement, how could he have been so stupid? He had the expenditure of a Prince and the income of a pauper. He had five credit cards in his wallet, he could only use one, and that was because he knew the manager from the bank, this was only a temporary two month state of grace, if his finances had not improved the bank would be calling in a debt recovery agency. If his father had known the state he had got himself into he would have disowned him. Things had been different in his day there had been certain perks that would be looked on as theft today. He had got himself into this whirlpool of debt, he would throw himself a life belt; or the four by four people would. Wining and dining Jane, that had been a horrendous judgement; she had used him and abused him. That was a lesson he had to acknowledge, she would be passing him on the ladder of promotion, she had sidled up to Welsh, and she had left him swinging in the wind, he wouldn't forget that. Ever.

The fearful sound of the lift ascending made him move from the seat to the window instinctively, he stood at the side of the window peering down at the dark deserted street except for a four by four its lights on, he crept down to the front door, hoping for some conversation between the visitors, instead of the sterile sound of footsteps and the key in the lock. The lift came to a shuddering halt, the grinding sound of the lift door opening, caused a comment from one of them alighting from the lift.

'That doesn't sound healthy, what if it the lift sticks going down?'

'Just be quiet.'

They walked towards the flat, the key was heard being inserted and then the door closing, he looked at his watch watching the second hand, they were in and on their way out, forty-five seconds, they must be picking up something or dropping off something, there was no

293

doubt. The sound of the lift not descending suggested to him, that someone had their finger on the open button or their foot on the lift door, there must be three of them. The same sounds of the door of the flat being opened, closed and locked, then the short walk to the lift, and the immediate descent of the lift proved his lateral thinking correct. He moved silently upstairs to the elevated lounge, taking up the same position at the window, snapping away with his camera, he changed the camera to video and filmed the two men and woman walk towards the four by four, the two men were carrying holdalls, they looked empty, the excitement grew in his stomach, it was now or never, he had the flat number and the spare key; this was not to his advantage, the lock had been changed, this was not an insurmountable problem; he had the thin tool to adjust the lever in the Yale lock, he had spoken to a locksmith about the Yale lock. He had been most obliging.

'There's no need for you to be here, Catherine, it's not worth the risk.'
She stopped less than a metre from the four by four.
'And when did you become concerned for poor little me?'
'I didn't mean that, I was only…'
'Only what…go on.'
'This is not the time or the place, it's freezing just get into the car, I know why you're pissed-off at me, you'll never except my explanation will you?'
'You got that right, get in the car this conversation will be taken further.'
He pulled her arm.
'And what do you mean by that?' he replied angrily.
'Don't you fucking touch me! Get in the car.'
She climbed into the rear seat, her focus of anger climbed into the front passenger seat. The person beside

Catherine hadn't said a word, or changed facial expression.

The driver engaged gear, ready to move off; he felt his hand on his.

'Before we move off Catherine, we have to talk, this can't go on.'

'You should put a lottery ticket on, that's twice you've been right.'

'Woman or not I wouldn't hesitate too…we'll talk later,' he removed his hand from the gear stick.

'Hold on a minute, this is to let the others know what has been exactly going on, turn off the engine please. You were caught removing money and drugs from the lock-up, John caught you, he had been suspicious of you, he warned me when someone start's using they get careless and …greedy. You thought John wouldn't tell me did you? How wrong you are, and I've not heard from John, have you seen him?'

He didn't turn around; he saw her mouth move in the mirror.

'That was me taking something without your permission, I was trying to set up another supplier, you wanted to do that after the death of your loving husband,' now he was openly mocking her.

'And I paid the money back with interest; maybe you had forgotten that, as you had other things on your mind.'

'That's was your explanation, it might have worked with Monty, or you thought it worked for him you were so wrong, oh so wrong. Where's John?'

'You should know he's being seeing a lot of you lately, have you checked your big bed,' he couldn't suppress his throaty laughter. She was encouraged by that, he only laughed like that when he was nervous.

'You should know about listening to rumours, is that not what you told me?'

'Everybody knows that you are seeing John, it's no big

secret.'

'You've still not told where John is, you seem to be close to John, when was the last time you saw him?'

'You're not a lawyer now, I don't know where he is, probably with another woman; can we get going now?'

'Why the big hurry, do you want to be somewhere else, do you want me to guess where?'

'If we don't move off now, I'm leaving, what's it going to be?'

'You seem quite agitated, is there a reason for this,' she opened her purse took out a cigarette, lit it then blew the smoke over his head. He turned round angrily.

'You know I've got asthma, put the fag out,' he was coughing. She sucked in the cigarette and blew a plume of smoke directly at his face. He coughed and spluttered and fumbled for the door. She left the car and walked round and opened the door to allow him to suck in the cold air. He was breathing in short gulps; the discomfort he was showing was obvious to all. He took out his puffer and inhaled greedily. He moved towards the old Jute mill whose façade was still standing defiantly, progress had failed to move it, and paradoxically, the modern multi-storey block would be razed to the ground before it. She told the occupants of the car to wait, she was going to see he was alright, she took her large purse with her, they thought the same thought; she was going to light another cigarette. He watched her come towards him, his lungs were full of cold but fresh air; he could not let her control the conversation about John disturbing him at the converted gardeners outhouse in the grounds of the mansion.

'So, now that you've recovered from your allergy to smoke, what have you done with the smack?'

'I may as well tell you, but you won't like it, Monty told me to come and see him at the big hoose, he showed me were the money was kept before it was moved, he wanted me to see if I could get a better price, I did manage to get a much better price, he apparently didn't want to tell you, I can't guess the reason.'

He placed one foot against the wall and his hands behind his back.

'Good story, pity it isn't true.'

'That's not the end of the story, he told me that if anything happened to him, this was where the goods and money were stored before they were moved, then he gets killed along with his friends, funny that, eh?'

'I don't like where you're going with this.'

'You inherit everything, then Johnny come early, comes round to comfort you, how good of him, he's got a big mouth, he'll get you into trouble Catherine, you're not the only woman, you do realise that?'

'Fine if that's true, you can see the indifference I'm showing, where's the smack that you moved?'

'I didn't move anything, and do you really think moving smack and money into a stinking flat is secure? I can just about understand leaving the smack; but thousands of pounds?'

'Only three of us know what flat it's in, the one person I don't trust is you and you'll never get the chance of removing any of the goods.'

She pulled out a gun from her purse and shot him in the head, he slid down the wall in a comedic way, his lifeless eyes staring straight ahead, his head fell to the right, she moved closer and finished him off with another head shot. She placed the gun back into the purse, the two occupants never showed any surprise, she walked towards the car, the door was flung open for her, she closed the door and the car moved off slowly; no screeching tyres, just a smooth change up in gears. Her emotions were held in check, the car gathered speed driving to the traffic lights, the indicators blinking; snow started to fall; the automatic wipers came on sweeping the large flakes away. The car made its way up Dens Road, she looked up at the tenement jutting out into

Dens Road, a Christmas tree sat proudly in the bay window, she had spent many happy years there, she was in constant penury when she was studying Law at Dundee University, but they managed financially they always did. Now at this juncture in her lifespan, she was richer than Croesus but happiness eluded her when she started accumulating money in vast quantities. She looked back at the top floor of the tenement, smiling, life was less complicated then. Her hands held the purse tightly, she placed it at her feet; she focused on the present, no regrets. It was either him or me she kept saying silently to herself. Monty had marked his card for her years previously, bit of a wide boy, handy with his fists, and had sticky -fingers. She had doubts about the first two characteristics, but wouldn't argue about his third, he had proven that beyond doubt. The course she had chartered for his death was not as spontaneous as it seemed, someone, more likely feral youths; would find him, and rifle through his pockets relieving him of his burgeoning wallet and credit cards, forensics would pick up their DNA undoubtedly, dirtying the already muddied waters. The police had already pulled him in for the murders of his acquaintances; his solicitor was present when he was being questioned about his movements on a particular night. He said he was busy entertaining a married woman, she must remain nameless as she was married to a policeman, he wasn't prepared to say whether he was a detective or uniformed officer. He was goading the young detective, his senior colleague took over the questioning, his answers became familiar; no comment was the favoured response. He was becoming too confident, too antagonistic, his solicitor smiled through gritted teeth. The detectives thanked him for his time, when the solicitor was out of ear shot, the senior detective sidled up to him and said.

'Goodbye… it was nice knowing you.'

***

He was getting frustrated, he couldn't understand it he followed the locksmith's instructions implicitly. He removed the two thin metal picks, he held the bottom one tightly, and the top one firmly but moved it gradually, he felt the click; but the door wouldn't open. He stared at the lock, it wouldn't defeat him, the two picks were horizontal in the lock, he rubbed his hands down the side of his trousers, he imagined they were sweaty, he slowly took hold of the picks again, same result; he repeated the methodical approach, but turned the top pick another quarter turn, the click was more audible, he pushed down the handle, the door opened silently. Triumph entered the room with him, searched the bottom half of the flat, the flat was empty, he searched through the cupboards, nothing. Creeping up the bare staircase, he went straight to the bedroom facing him, then he stopped, his eyes adjusting to the cold darkness, he went to the built in wardrobe, he opened it quickly, two old television sets were on the floor of the wardrobe, he looked up onto the upper shelf, nothing there. He repeated the same meticulous search, nothing was found, the only objects in the flat were the old televisions, he leaned with his back against the wall, pondering how quick they went into the flat and how quickly they exited, there must be a hatch on the floor for electricians examining wires. Room by room he searched in vain, he looked at his watch; he had been in the flat coming up for ten minutes. He was stumped; he looked at the ceilings nothing there. He went to the room where the televisions were, they must be covering a hatch. He struggled to lift the old style televisions out of the way, the floor showed no sign of an inspection hatch.

The drugs must be in this room, in that built in wardrobe, but where? He stepped back, he lost his balance over one of the televisions, and he crashed to the floor. Annoyance and anger how stupid he had been, falling over the relic of a bygone age that was fashionable for someone to buy a large monstrosity of a television. His ankle was sore, he saw sat on the television, rubbing his throbbing ankle. He could be sitting on a Trojan horse, he moved quickly and turned the television screen to the floor, the back cover was intact, four screws holding it tight, he took out the small pouch and took the small Philips screwdriver and removed them, the back fell away effortlessly, he took the pen torch from his mouth and shone it into the cavernous cave of wires and valves, he pulled away the mass of wires and it gave up its treasure.

A plastic envelope of high denomination notes, he pulled them out, and attached the back cover to the television and then returned it to its original position to the wardrobe floor.

The second television gave up its more deathly stowaway; five kilos of heroin; uncut. His unofficial reconnaissance came to an unexpected but welcome end. He left the flat, the lock closed true; he returned to his lair, took the halogen heater, flask and china cup. He looked round and decided to open the window slightly; cold air rushed in displacing the warmth in the room. His eyes were naturally drawn to the desolate scene below; all quiet apart from a drunk who was comatose lying next to the old Jute Mill wall. As it was Christmas, he would call an ambulance because he was concerned for the drunk's welfare in this snowing, bitter cold environment. He had parked his car on Cotton Road; he would be in his house reassessing his new disposable income. There were two phone boxes or was there just one adjacent to Cotton Road? He couldn't honestly remember if they were still there, he would call for an ambulance for the inebriated fool sleeping against the Jute mill wall.

He tucked the two packages into his heavy dark overcoat; the snow was becoming thicker, his eyes battling to stay open against the unforgiving swirling snow. Collar turned up, he left the multi-storey, the concierge nose was burrowed in a book; see no evil hear no evil. A wise man. Swirling snow was running across the street and hitting the pavements, deserted pavements, no cars were moving, no eerie voices or violent youths cat-calling unsuspecting pedestrians, he looked back his footsteps immediately being covered by the snow, he wanted to jog, but cautioned against this, someone could be looking out of a tenement window admiring the snow, they wouldn't remember a walking pedestrian but they would a running one. His collar of his overcoat was flapping up and down because of the increasing wind, Cotton Road was a minute away, he had replaced his worn out car battery, he was going to do it at the weekend, he was glad he had replaced it after seeing the special offer at the NTS garage in the 'Ferry. He took out his car keys, he was about fifty metres from his car, the lights blinked reassuringly at him, in the car he turned the key, the engine burst into life, he moved away down the snow covered road which was now indistinguishable from the pavement, Dens Road looked more passable, he saw the phone box, and decided against calling an ambulance, no guilt entered his conscience. An ambulance raced past him in the direction of the drunk, he congratulated himself not taking the time and telling the emergency operator that he was a taxi-driver and had saw someone drunk across from the Alexander multi-storey lying in the snow. The car was warming up nicely, the money would take care of itself however the heroin was a different matter. He didn't know who to fence it to, but he would not be taxed to find someone; the heroin shortage was causing a spike in the price of the heroin, his theory was that the dealers were executed to allow the demand to outstrip supply, therefore causing a rise in price. The murder squad was being painstaking in their enquiries; a euphemism for they were in a river choked with effluent without a steering implement. They looked upon him as a figure of fun, he would have the last laugh, if he didn't he would be disappointed, he was fortunate in finding money and drugs; he regarded this as benefits in kind.

***

The sergeant thanked Lenny for looking after GI Joe, his fantasy policing had come to a painful end, he was now considering other careers; it looked as though the police was not his natural forte. The sergeant drank his coffee then left the table. On the other table someone had left a copy of the Evening Chronicle.

He could make out part of the headline …'another gangster shot dead.' He reached over and read the story, the dead man was a known associate of the executed drug dealers, he had been questioned about his movements on the night the dealers were executed, he had been shot twice in the head, and there was no attempt to dispose of the body. The police were following a line of enquiry, but they weren't prepared to say anything at this early stage. I bet they aren't they're clueless. He was positive who was behind the executions of known drug dealers; the Triads, since their cannabis farms in flats and houses had been ripped off, and a nursery in Fife, they had come wreaking for vengeance and they were letting everyone know they meant business; police and dealers.

He immediately thought of the torture that they had inflicted on GG, he felt sick thinking about it. No malice was aimed at his dead friend because he had given up his name to his torturers and ultimately his killers. The recurring thought he had as he battled in vain to succumb to sleep, was had they used the chainsaw on him when he was still alive? He tried to extinguish this horrific picture from his tortured mind by thinking about the story he had heard in the canteen previously.

The murder squad detectives were doing nothing to solve the case, what they were trying to achieve was

302

gruesomely simple, the last standing gangster or dealer was behind the murders, then and only then, would they go to town on him. Lenny laughed that off at first, but knowing the calibre of some of the detectives he soon stopped laughing. He pulled back his thoughts to concentrate on his own predicament, no one had contacted him yet about his penance, they were watching him or so he thought, every oriental person that walked in his direction was viewed as a potential assassin, even old ladies. He would rather put a bullet in his own head than be tortured and dissected in a brutal and systematic fashion. He turned over the page to avert thinking about GG and his potential premature death, the readers' letters page was full of the usual trivial nonsense, he quickly turned the page, the headline affected him more than the front page banner headline. He read the story quickly then the second time in a slow methodical manner; his mind was still whirring; he had absolutely no chance of sleeping tonight, he had to make an appointment with the doctor and persuade her to give him sleeping tablets. Then suddenly he thought better against this, what would happen if he went low in spirits, could he trust himself not to take more than prescribed? He didn't try to answer his own question, he stared at the headline: "Limb washed up on Fife beach."

***

The pub was bustling with everyone in high spirits, or nearly everyone, some had given up on enjoying themselves, they looked comical as they sat sleeping with their party hats askew. Jameson was pleased to be back in Dundee, Christmas was indeed magical. He had another reason to celebrate, another enemy had been eliminated, again rumours were circulating that he was behind the cull of dealers; he had the money and the means. The rumour was taken seriously by the police, they had visited him at his new house, and they knew he was not involved in drugs, but he was known to have had problems with some of the deceased, that was the reason by his sudden departure to Dubai wasn't it? He told them that was the rumour he had heard, but that's all it is a rumour.

The reason he had left Dundee to move to Dubai was two-fold, the death of his wife and his accountant's advice; move to Dubai for tax reasons, zero percent on income, great weather, investment opportunities, stay there for a short period of time then come home to Dundee a trimmer, healthier and wealthier individual.

He took the accountant's advice. He was fortunate to sell his portfolio of assets before the credit crunch hit Dubai. The detectives couldn't argue with his reasons, they were in awe of him, but they wouldn't admit it to one another. One of them asked his opinion on investments, he told him to buy one or two apartments in the old Silvery Tay Hotel; which he had. They departed with this piece of generous advice. Jameson had been very amiable to them, they would now be his unpaid salesmen for the apartments, and they would be evangelical in their sales pitch. He didn't expect them to hint at who or what the reasons were behind the deaths , he never asked, he was just so glad that they all had been removed, he was free to wander about Dundee at his leisure, and go about his daily business. He never tried to dissuade anyone who sidled up to him at the bar or urinal and mentioned that he was involved, he just smiled and winked. When he walked into the previously no -go bars people would step aside to let him through without him asking; he was getting used to this preferential treatment and he was developing a taste for this deference.

The young band struck up a Lynyrd Skynyrd song, they were lucky if they were nineteen, he had older bottles of champagne and whisky in his house. Oh to be young again but not so shy this time, his dad always said that was an asset, he wasn't so sure. If only he had bought this bar, the Waterfront, it was a haven for young talented bands that would have completed his life. However, he couldn't dwell on the missed opportunity, life had been good since his return, he had good contacts now with Welsh and Patrick Connelly, life had taken him in an upward trajectory and his star was burning brightly over Dundee and Fife, turning fifty wasn't so bad after all. Patrick Connelly had told him economic slowdown brings numerous opportunities, he discounted him, he knew different now.

***

He counted the money again, this was the third time, each count matched the previous two, he stood back from the bed staring at his unexpected Christmas gift. Forty five thousand pounds. He pulled the small chair away from the desk at the window, he turned it round and straddled it cowboy style, his financial worries were over; his first purchase with his windfall would be a new combi-boiler, not paid in cash but purchased with his Tesco credit card, he would get the equivalent in points for each pound he spent, it wouldn't raise any eyebrows. The only foreseeable risk was keeping the money in his flat; he wouldn't be stupid enough to open bank accounts in various guises. However, the smack was a completely different matter he had to get rid of as quickly and quietly as possible, but that could wait until he came to a safe and quick way to exchange it for money. He hadn't long to find out who the drugs and money belonged to, he had heard on the radio that another of Dundee's colourful characters had been killed in Alexander Street, he quickly surmised that he had been one of the three persons that had stored the money and drugs in the flat on the same floor as his unofficial observation post. There had been no raised voices when he heard them walk along and go into the flat, something must had went seriously wrong on the descent in the lift, and the person who had killed him must have used a silencer.

The concierge would be visited by someone from the dealers they wouldn't take it lightly that their money and heroin were missing, he was the only one who knew of their nocturnal visits in the empty multi-storey, he wouldn't mention the detective who had made himself at home in one of the flats, if he did he may as well take the lift up to the top of the multi-storey and hurl himself off. He was not too concerned, he wouldn't visit him again.

All that could wait, he had decided to keep all the money together, he had to place it somewhere it would be hidden but easily accessible, he gathered the money together, he counted a thousand pounds, and put this in his bedside cabinet, for now, that money would do for now, he would go to Asda at Milton of Craigie and buy more than enough groceries and bottles of spirits, this was the start of cleaning the soiled money, he would now have more legitimate disposable income his normal grocery bill would not be on his monthly credit card bill, he would reduce the outstanding amount by two hundred pounds, a small start in a long journey. He would fill up his car at the pump and pay with cash, now he was feeling better; this was one Christmas that he could face with optimism instead of dread.

He hadn't been to the North End Club for a while, he had met a nurse in her fifties who had invited him to meet her discreetly there, she was married, her husband worked in a factory on the night-shift, he was invited to her house when he had left for work, his charm was still potent. She had said to her husband that she was working on Christmas Day, he was not totally overcome with disappointment, he would be cuckolding a friend's wife while he was in the North Sea; his sense of derring -do would have been dimmed if he had known what his wife's bedside manner actually consisted of. But he thought he was the only one breaking his vows, he would take no comfort in finding out his wife's shameless and unbounded sexual adventures; McAveety was not her only 'patient' she had numerous lovers female as well as male. She already knew what her present would be for McAveety for their clandestine Christmas dinner, he had thought she would be overcome at the length and expense that he had went to, to make her happy, the most expensive Champagne; but he omitted to tell her that it was a two for one offer at Sainsbury's; it was the thought that counts. During their Christmas lunch there would be a knock on the door, her friend he had known from the North End Club, had just been passing by, she would be invited to share the festive fare, then Fifi as he had affectionately nick-named her because of her blonde luxuriant locks, she would ask him to play some music, slow romantic music, she knew he wasn't much of a dancer, her friend would invite her to dance, then near the end of the song they would go into a romantic clinch; McAveety would be surprised at this but be more surprised at the invitation to join in, the two of them then would lead him into the bedroom. He was not the only male who had fell for this spontaneous gesture, they had orchestrated this on a number of occasions, why they did this they never explained or sought to account for this unorthodox behaviour, the nurse's husband had never encountered this. Jane did not cross his mind anymore, she had used him, to her advantage to weasel her way into the drug squad, and had caught Welsh's eye; Feeney would have saw that she was trouble from the first minute, no flattering of eyelashes or a revealing smile would have made him drop his misogynist guard.

He liked the more mature women, they had seen it all before, they were impressed at his overview of the world, he was well travelled and seemingly intelligent, but most off all he was unfailing in his manners and never swore. He didn't think it was relevant to tell them that that he was up to his bushy eyebrows in debt and his flat was usually freezing due to his archaic boiler, which he couldn't afford to maintain on a service breakdown contract. However, the year had ended in positive fission, the boiler would be replaced, he saw in the local newspapers that a company was giving a trade-in allowance if the hi-spec boiler was purchased which came with a five years parts and labour guarantee. The beige walls were screaming out for decoration, the white cracked ceiling the same; the whole flat could do with a lick of paint. There were some painters who drank in the North End Club, he was sure they would oblige him; cash in hand of course

*** .

Christmas Eve was looming, the house sale had been completed without a hitch, he felt more secure in Wormit; perhaps it was because the Tay separated him from the difficulties and problems in Dundee. At night when he sat in the comfortable chair his eyes were inevitably drawn to the constant white steam that was being pumped high into the cold air from Baldovie. A certain satisfaction grew in his conscience, he had helped a damsel in distress and a grieving parent had seen the cause of his mental breakdown disappear into the furnace. Concerns about another dealer being shot and left on Alexander Street were being voiced in the Evening Chronicle, the Chief Constable was relaying his disapproval to the editor; he was adding to his concerns, things were taking place behind the scenes if he pulled back from inflammatory headlines, he would be the first in the press to know the name of the suspect when he would be arrested. The reply was brief; the editor would not be influenced by anyone from an incompetent police force. Welsh agreed with the editor, there was no leadership or plausible leads; privately he had been told who the prime suspects were, then they would be murdered.

Forensic science was being overtaken by mob expedience, more notably junkies asking to speak to a certain detective, they would give their opinion who was behind the slaughter, but only if the detective gave him or her some smack as an act of good faith. The shortage of heroin was causing an upsurge in street robberies, the ten pound bag of smack had been hit by inflationary pressures, the cheapest bag was now selling for twenty pounds, it had been cut with every available additive, it was of so poor quality that the junkies were becoming more inventive, they were adding crushed sleeping tablets to the heroin, sores were becoming more evident; some suffered strokes that caused paralysis permanently.

There were calls from drug charities for the NHS to dispense safe heroin, until supplies normalised again. Junkies were victims. Welsh studied the statements from various CEO's of charities, he hadn't realised that there were so many charities in Dundee; this seemed to be a growth industry, his eyes caught the statement from the charity CEO that was now a private organisation, they were being overwhelmed by requests for treatment. This was Catherine's clinic in all but name, she was receiving millions annually, he read the statement again, it said it was a charity, was this deliberate. Some parent had wrote to the Evening Chronicle informing the editor that she had been told that the clinic had raised fees for the treatment of drug abusers by thirty- percent, she was openly accusing them of profiteering from the heroin shortage. The CEO had said in their defence that 'their treatment was specialised and life changing, not only for the client but for the family and society.' Welsh had noted that he skillfully avoided mentioning exorbitant costs.

***

He had completed his daily walk to Broughty Ferry Castle, he walked past it and leant over the barrier and stared pleadingly into the meandering Tay, he removed his gloves and rubbed his freezing face. Progress had been sporadic, and then it became static. Was this a sign of him ageing rapidly? The Chicago style murders had convinced him that it was someone from outside of Dundee that had planned and executed the demise of the dealers.

The so called hard men, who lived in Dundee, didn't have the intelligence or patience to initiate such a pogrom.

There was no doubt in his mind that one of the cartel had betrayed the others, the difficulty was separating who was more likely to do this. His ex-colleagues were unanimous in their prime suspect; they had even opened a book on who it was, the book was extended when the favourite was found slumped with half his face on the bloodied snow covered pavement.

Feeney had been loose cannon when he had worked alongside him, he was singled out because he was the head of the drug squad and someone wanted to make a point, a bloody point at that. Internal jealousies came to the surface when Feeney had been first mentioned as a possible Head of Operations, when he got the job, that's when he reorganised the drug squad, his first move was to promote others and move his detractors, two females, who had mistakenly thought they were bombproof; they weren't. He pre-empted the threat of sexual-discrimination by keeping them from being involved in real time operations; he had been tipped off that they were leaking information ahead of raids. He laid a series of traps for them, he treated them with the utmost respect for the first month, he wrote the name of the dealer and the address and time of the raid, and they tipped off the dealer who moved the stash to another address. Feeney kept targeting this one dealer, eventually one of them met the dealer who was becoming paranoid; he wanted to know who was tipping the police off. She was photographed by Feeney himself, unofficially. The dealer was running out of options, he gave her an ultimatum, which she had to accept; 'keep the drugs in your flat, who would suspect that you were hoarding heroin?'

The paranoid dealer was convinced that she was screwing him for more money for this information; he suspected she had some friend calling the drugs -line in the Evening Chronicle about the drugs, the friend would pick up the reward, and she herself was picking up a thousand pounds a time for every warning of a raid. That was the reason how he came to suggesting that she kept the stash in her flat; he would give her ten grand, to keep the stash in her flat for four days. Feeney had photographic and video evidence showing her taking a holdall from one of the dealer's safe houses to her own flat; he even gave her a kiss. Feeney sent the evidence to the crusading editor of the Evening Chronicle. They were both arrested.

***

Catherine sat in her lounge, going over the pulling of the trigger again, his fearful face was burned onto her memory he had hoped it was a joke, but he didn't say anything, it was either him or her; he would eventually have removed her, Monty was no longer around to protect her. One dead in her house, another died due to a work related incident, no regrets for their demise, it had been an eventful week. Her calculations had underestimated how much he had taken, in cash and drugs, he had set up his own small army of dealers, putting heroin onto the streets then removing the supply. A week later the price had went up again. He couldn't help blabbing about his new enterprise when he was drunk to trusted friends; one of them spoke to Catherine about him setting up dealers and his supply of heroin. Everything moved smoothly into place now, she wouldn't confront him; she would kill him, herself.

A message had to be sent out, and it had to be understood. The trusted friend of his was in the four by four as he leaned against the stone Jute mill wall in

Alexander Street, when she pulled the gun out on him, his eyes went to the friend, the friend didn't meet his gaze, he looked straight ahead. She didn't know where his supply was kept or where the money was ending up. The first place was his house, which was being searched, if it wasn't there, it had to be somewhere in Dundee, she wasn't prepared to write the heroin and money off, she was due what she was due. But tonight had been a start of paying the debt, once the police departed Alexander Street the money and heroin would be retrieved from the flat, the outbuilding at the mansion had been stripped of its deadly wares and cash, she couldn't have taken the risk that he went back or had informed the drug squad of the location. Things were different now. The drug money had been laundered before into pubs and property, too many people were gossiping where the money was coming from, certain solicitors who had developed an unhealthy eating disorder for life's fine things, had seen their income dramatically plummet due to the collapse in the property and rental market, and notwithstanding the income of tainted money. Property would be purchased at the high end of the market, what she owned and leased out she would retain. No pubs were bought by her, she had revaluated Monty's chaotic portfolio, she hadn't the heart to tell him that the solicitor he had used had conned him out of thousands of pounds, she suspected that the solicitor had enticed Monty to buy a flat in a certain area for well over the asking price, which he did. However, the seller of the flat had just owned it for six months, it was of no coincidence that she was his niece , who had made forty-thousand pounds in six months; a remarkable return. Catherine had found out this was not an isolated incident, eight other flats had a similar pattern.

  She had made an appointment with the solicitor and told him that she would be moving all rental properties to another company, she didn't say it but he knew he had been rumbled. Her business study degree was of no consequence, the new business strategy was formulated on the Law that frosty December night. No other car was parked up there, no sensible person would be out on a night like tonight, the cutting wind would surely bring another blanket of snow in the early morning. Her mind elevated to more pleasant thoughts, Monty was a lovable character, but he was not for her. The flats in the west end would be difficult to sell, but in the meantime they were returning a decent yield, and she was no longer paying seventeen percent commission to the solicitor, she had negotiated a more favourable deal with a new company, the company had responded to her email, instead of conducting the business computer to computer, the woman invited her down to her office to discuss all her property needs including boiler maintenance. This appealed to her, as she had been let down by various heating engineers, she had a gold standard maintenance plan, which turned out to be fool's gold, nothing would give her greater pleasure as to tell the company where they could secure their exchange heater. She liked the woman called Diane, she had empathy for her, she listened attentively as she told her about the endemic boiler problems that occurred in winter time, the company invoiced her for call-out charges at fifty -pound plus vat, this was in the small print. After a cup of coffee Diane showed her the company's catch -all boiler maintenance contract she was willing to reduce the yearly fee by twenty-five percent if she transferred her portfolio of flats to her company.

Catherine being a trained solicitor was naturally cautious; however she ignored her training and signed. The cold night in her car on the Law made her think clearly, money had to be removed and invested in mundane but cash generating businesses. She sat with the car facing the Tay rail bridge, he pencil drumming against her empty notepad, she wrote the first business down; car wash. There was one up for sale, it needed a complete overhaul, and there was room at the rear of the fore court to install two washing plants. She placed the pencil in her mouth and slowly chewed it, selling cars, buy cars at auction down south and have them brought up. That was two, she needed to diversify more. Her mobile on the passenger seat rang, she answered, the message was blunt; the goods were missing from the tall building.

She hung up without reply, she thrust the notepad and pencil into the glove compartment. The car began to navigate the deep descent, no one else apart from the concierge knew who entered the multi-storey, he didn't know her, she had only entered the multi-storey with her betrayer, and even then she had a long dark coat on complete with hood, and she had a scarf concealing her face with dark glasses on. They couldn't go back, it wasn't worth the risk, she was prepared to write off this expense, she was more sanguine, it had all been a set up, but now the person who had organised the rip-off was dead.

***

The long arduous walk from his house to Broughty Ferry castle was fraught; the visitor to his home had not been invited. He explained that he needed to see him, he was running out of options; he was the editor of the Evening Chronicle. Jean was out shopping, the house was theirs to talk about matters that concerned them both. The editor said he had had been giving his name as someone who knew how the machinations of police politics was conducted. Eddings made it clear that he was talking off the record, the editor agreed to this. He went on to explain that he had been left the video and photographs of the female detectives over a period of time enjoying the company of known drug dealers in

Dundee and abroad at exclusive resorts. He believed that the bearer of the gifts had been Joe Feeney; they had been delivered to his house not the office. It was of his opinion that some police officers more likely detectives, had somehow found out that Feeney had sent the damming evidence. Feeney trusted someone close to him and had confided in him, that person passed on the information to the drug dealers, Feeney was told to go to the chapel in Broughty Ferry for some reason or other and met his death there, the unfortunate early morning worshipper was at the chapel at the wrong time.

His conclusion was that there was still a rogue element of detectives working to obfuscate the murder enquiries. Eddings reaction was not an overwhelming endorsement; 'where's the evidence?'

'I don't have any, it's just my theory; do you have a different theory then?'

Eddings changed tact and spoke warmly of Feeney. 'Could he have been set up?

'Definitely, but without actual evidence there was nothing you could do.'

The editor was expecting a more receptive response, he thought he could have used his time better, this Eddings was no help, he looked and talked with no interest, the only verve in his voice was when he asked who told him to come to his house. That was the only pleasure he took from the unproductive visit, he told him that he couldn't disclose that, and he had been completely wrong, it was plain to see he couldn't help or he didn't want to help, he left the full mug of coffee untouched and apologised for disturbing him.

When he left Eddings was embarrassed he had a better handle on the murder of Feeney than himself, and it all fitted quite well. The rogue element was Paul Welsh, Morag had heard him say in Dubai that he was going to be taken care of or words to that effect, he had the perfect alibi he was thousands of miles away. He was

315

also using a credit card under an alias, it was a pity that the editor didn't know that piece of the jigsaw existed. But the road block was that Welsh wasn't shown any ostentatious signs of living beyond his means. The bank teller he had been using for years said nothing in his account showed any large signs of money going in and going out, the only substantial money that was in his account was the proceeds from the sale of his house.

Next week he would give him the alias he had been using in Dubai, he would do this under the pretence of it was another individual; he might get lucky. Someone, maybe Welsh could have used the editor to find out how much he really knew, that could have been the bold visit to his home. However, he now knew that the editor was digging behind the scenes, this could impair his health. If the editor's theory was correct, Welsh was working for or with drug dealers, he couldn't summon up any argument to weaken the theory, and if it was true, where was the money? He sat down more invigorated, his heart was beating at a higher rate, he recognised that quickening, it was an occurrence when he was near to solving a case. He took the mug of coffee and moved towards the French doors, he glanced beyond the rig at the old boatyard; its lights blinking periodically, beyond that Broughty Ferry castle was obscured by a grey whiteness; snow was on its way to Dundee. He would wrap up more than normal, the temperature and snow would make his daily walk longer and enduring.

Leaving the house he could sense the snow coming his woolly hat was pulled tightly over his ears, his short padded jacket and jeans would not looked out of place in the Austrian ski slopes; he didn't mind he was a fashion aficionado, it usually took forty minutes to reach Broughty Castle, he would endeavour to come close to this as possible. He reached the bottom of Greendykes; the snow met him full on. Trudging along Broughty Ferry Road he moved quickly across to the other side, the trees were bare he could see down into the old boatyard, the rig had been there for months, he didn't see anyone working on it. Morag hadn't been in touch over the last few days, he thought that was a blessing, she had immersed herself in the murder of Feeney and the social worker, he had to reign her in, he wasn't privy to information or leads, she found that hard to accept.

This editor could be useful or he could be a hinder, if he had been recorded he had played it with a straight bat; the two female detectives would end up in jail, if there were more of their ilk, they could make the editor's life uncomfortable, if he had been unscrupulous in affairs of the heart they would bring his misdemeanours into the sterilizing light. He could have mentioned that but that would have made him more reticent, he would use him in some capacity, at this moment he didn't know in what capacity. The cold but refreshing walk had stimulated his appetite when he reached the castle he looked at his watch, only ten minutes longer than normal, he leaned over the railing and watched the thick snow hit the Tay and vanish, the smell of soup being made in the Ship Inn was still in his nostrils, his mind was made up, he would have a plate of soup and a roll before returning home. He imagined the Ship Inn would be cheerful with the Christmas lights that were glowing inside, at a table, in the corner were the editor and Morag enjoying lunch.

***

The elevator came to a silent halt, when the door opened she smelt the fragrance, she breathed in deeply, the sweet smell she failed to recognise, if she remembered where she originally inhaled the pleasant odour, she would stop smiling, he was waiting at the door, smiling.

'Think it will be a white Christmas Catherine?'

'It's looking more likely, hope you have the coffee ready Pat,' she walked past him into his warm office, the fragrance more pungent. The tray was sitting on the

317

coffee table, he followed her in invited her to sit on the
sofa, he sat opposite her then poured the coffee, he
noticed that she had drawn from her briefcase a schedule
for a commercial property, he had seen the name of the
solicitors adorning the schedule.

'How has things been since the funeral?'
'As expected, the police seem disinterested, I'm not
losing any sleep over it, the financial side of the will
have being held up, the police went to court to freeze the
assets, they think Monty had been involved in some
criminal acts, I have challenged this in court, this is just
a tactic from the Crown, I have a funny feeling that the
Crown will withdraw their motion before my appeal
reaches the Court.'
'Oh, why is that?'
'My information is that one of the other deceased's will
and assets has not been frozen or challenged, I want to
find out why? It strikes me as very odd that the others
assets have being frozen and the Crown wish to prove
that they are the proceeds of crime, apart from one.'
'And who was the fortunate fellow?'
'I can't say.'
'I understand,' she saw him looking at the property
schedule.
'I have a strong interest in this property Pat,' she hands
it over to him, his face is unimpressed, he hands it back
to her.
'If you're thinking of buying and this demolishing the
building then erect a couple of blocks of flats, you're
wasting your time, I'm sorry.'
She pulled her knees together and gathered up the cup
in her hands, she sipped the steaming hot coffee, her
eyes betraying her inner excitement, she placed the cup
down.
'The property bubble has truly burst, well, at least with
the new- build flats. No I propose to run the garage as a

garage, car sales, repairs and MOTs.'

'In this economic climate, is that wise?'

'I think so, people will be under severe financial pressure, they will be more likely to hold onto their car for another year or two, or trade up to a younger car, if that's the right term.'

He sat looking at her, she had a point, the banks were reticent to lend even for car loans or funds for refurbishing kitchens. He took the schedule again and read the details of the size of the going concern garage and the space in front, he placed it on the table.

'Have you sourced the cars, and what age of car do you propose to sell?

'Three years, I have spoken to someone down south, he deals with car hire companies, there are a glut of companies trying to make room for new cars, the governments scrappage scheme has made it more difficult to sell these cars, I propose to have forty of them within a month of the garage opening, the garage, office and forecourt could do with a paint, I'll do that first.'

'That sounds as though you have researched this project well, but it's still a gamble in these austere times, Catherine I don't want to see you lose money.'

'I understand your caution Pat, but I will make a good profit on each car, if all goes well now, it can only get better in the future.'

'I understand that, but the police will be interested in how you are financing this, you do see what I'm driving at?'

'That's why I'm here, Pat, for your *expert* legal advice.'

'Do you have capital, legitimate capital that can withstand severe financial scrutiny?'

'Of course, what do you have in mind?'

'I know of an offshore finance house; but perfectly legal, who can help you, but you must have twenty -five per cent of the costs, for example, the cost of the building and the cars.' 'That's not a problem, the money is at hand, but I wouldn't like anyone to know that I was the sole owner, I don't want the police to come in heavy-handed and scare customers away, you know what they do Pat.'

'An off the shelf company, or a shell company, both serve the same purpose.'

'How soon can you have the property tied in a bow for me?'

'Probably middle of January, maybe the end of Jan, I assume you want to shave the price?'

'I'm looking for the best deal Pat, that's why I came to you Pat, if you can get a good deal fair enough but I don't want you still negotiating in March, over a couple of thousand. The reason I came to you Pat is that I trust you, unlike other solicitors.'

'Others? What do you mean,' he was trying to disarm her with his congenial smile.

'Your friend George, the one with the big belly and the big mouth, is that not the reason that the FSA, raided his office last Friday, when he was at the Sheriff Court?' 'You're well informed Catherine, it was only a matter of time, that's the least of his worries.'

'Care to expand on that Pat?'

'Probably not, but if you run with the hounds...'

'..I understand. This finance house abroad it has all the accreditation that it requires to bona-fide trade?'

'The rates are as good as the High Street banks, but it is safer, the finance house is a subsidiary of the bank, hold on a minute, I'm sure I have some literature in my desk, you can study its website at your leisure.' He rumbled in the drawers knowing that the folder was in the bottom drawer.

'Ah, here it is, they are very careful who they take on as clients, but I will be able to vouch for you, I can't see any difficulty.'

She took the folder and placed it in her case.
'That's all I need Pat, thanks for seeing me, here's my card, send any letters or documents to this name and address, don't be concerned about the name, I'll get moving now, oh when will you require the money, the twenty-five per cent?'

'Definitely before Christmas, if you want to bring it here, cash or cheque, I can deposit in the company's account; that will speed up the process.'

'Tomorrow you place the bid, is tomorrow okay?'

'I wasn't thinking that soon, I have to contact the solicitor about your bid, I'll be in touch, it would be best to keep the paper work to a minimum, if it's alright with you can I call you?'

'I understand,' she placed down her case, and took out another business card and gave it to him.
He studied her card, and then placed it in his wallet.

'I'll be in touch I'll get onto the solicitor right away I'll see you to the elevator.'

They walked the short distance he pressed the button he heard the elevator start the short journey, he left her and returned to his office. Through the closed door he heard the elevator stop and the door open, then he heard the smooth descent, he took out the business card and studied it, turning it over and over in his hand, his mind was doing the same. His legal fee from the commercial work would not be challenged by her, he would have a hefty commission from the bank in Northern Cyprus, he was more intrigued where she was getting the twenty-five per cent deposit for the garage and the fleet of cars; fifty- thousand for the garage and a hefty forty- thousand for the total cost of the cars. If the courts had frozen Monty's assets, where was she getting her hands on this ready cash, and where was it coming from.

Who was the dealer that the police were leaving his assets alone, and why? Welsh would know, he would skillfully, steer the conversation around, an innocent enquiry to ascertain how the murder investigation was progressing. Christmas would be more white this year…and more interesting.

As soon as he set foot in the Ship Inn and saw them both at the table, he wanted to do an about turn, however if they had seen him, they would be suspicious if he left. He went to the bar and ordered a plate of home-made soup, he made his way to the window seat, they hadn't noticed him; could it be because he still had his woollen winter hat on. He immediately took it off, it would only be a matter of seconds before one of them noticed him, the editor rose and went to the toilet, he still had his overcoat on, she stood up and wrapped her oversized scarf a number of times around her neck, she picked her up her clutch bag, then squeezed her way out from the table, she followed the same path as the editor, either they were oblivious to him, or they were leaving in an orderly exit on becoming aware of him.

He would bet it would be the former than the latter. The barman came over with the soup, when he had left, he went to the toilet which shared the same hall as the exit, he walked passed the toilet door, and looked out, the editor was nowhere to be seen, Morag was entering her car, he pulled out his mobile and pressed speed dial, her name came up, he didn't place the phone to his mouth, he heard her personal ring tone, she let it ring, she opened the door and sat down, he was bitterly disappointed, he lifted the phone to his ear, it went to voicemail, she drove off, he didn't leave a message. His appetite became restrained; he trudged back into the warmth of the bar. He lifted the spoon, his mobile rang, he took it out from his trouser pocket; it was Morag.

'Hello, I tried to call you about a couple of minutes ago, but your phone went to voicemail, is everything okay?'

'Yes, yes,' she said impatiently, where are you, we

need to talk.'

'I'm walking in the 'Ferry, where are you?'

'I've just left…where do you want to meet?' Her voice had changed from excited to impatience.

'I can be at the Ship Inn in about ten minutes…'

'…Out of the question, I'll see you in Eduardo's (Art Gallery) in fifteen minutes,' she then ended the call.

His appetite returned, his spoon was dipping in more speedily, would she mention the editor, had the editor mentioned to her that he had been at his house, was she his source, had it all been guff about a detective mentioning his name to the editor? He looked at his watch, the soup would be finished in a couple of minutes, he would be at the art gallery in five minutes if he had a limp, he could take more pleasure from the soup, letting it heat his bones. More beachcombers were coming in from both entrances, they were eyeing his nearly empty bowl, hoping they could claim the window seat, he acceded to their wishes. He placed his hat on went to the bar and paid his bill, he checked his change; prices must rise when the temperature plummets. He stared at the receipt; it must be very cold.

He left the bar by the main entrance, the sheer coldness of the wind off the Tay, nearly took his breath away, thank God the gallery was only a short distance away. He thrust his hands deep into his coat, he looked up and saw her enter the gallery; she must have parked her car nearby. When he entered the gallery he saw her flicking through the large size prints.

'Anything nice there?' She grabbed him by the arm and guided him upstairs. 'Sorry about that, I'm just not used to this, I've got some news,' she walked away over to the far side of the gallery, he stood where he was, she walked back and pulled him in her direction.

'And take that ridiculous hat off, it makes you look…'

'…Ridiculous?' He looked hurt.

'Well, comical,' she snatched it from his head.

323

'Over the last week I've been in contact with someone who has access to someone in the drug squad, the information matches up with what we've got.'

'Wait a minute, you're going too fast slow down, talk while we admire the prints and paintings, take a deep breath, try to regulate your breathing.'
They walked in unison, and stopped at the first painting of a winter scene.

'Who is this person and what did he have to say?'

'How do you know it's a male?'
'Is it? His teeth gritted.

'Yes it is, he's the editor from the Evening Chronicle, he's been the cornerstone of the shop -a -dealer campaign, the source of his enquiry has been spot on with information, I think you should meet him.'

'Why?'

'He knows a lot of things, but I think he'll be more open with you, rather than with me.'

'How did you meet him?'

'I knew him from Dubai, he worked as a journalist over there, he's had his eyes opened in Dundee, he doesn't trust anyone, and he has a lot in common with you.'
'Where did you meet him in Dundee?'

'We bumped into each other at a fund raising event for the Conservative Party.'

'How strange, the editor of a left-wing paper raising money for the poor, hungry and disaffected, strange times indeed.'

'Sarcasm, suits you, especially from an ex- detective from a corrupt institution.'

'Oh dear, have I hurt your feelings?'

'You asked where I met him, I told you, you became sarcastic, do you want to really know what he has told me or not?'

'Go ahead, and I'm sorry.'

'Apology accepted. He said that the source had told him that, some people are getting nervous, apparently another thug or gangster has went missing, he had a seemingly big mouth, he was alleged to have been present when a drug raid took place at his sisters; nothing was found, that was about eight months ago, when his sister called him, he came over with a car full of thugs, he asked who was in charge, got his name then left. Ten minutes later, the officer in charge of the raid, took a call on his mobile, he went outside, and then came back fizzing, the raid was terminated the house had not been fully-searched. The thug was still in his car parked outside.'

'Who called it off?'

'Feeney, but that's never been confirmed. The source told the editor that he was in the car when the officer was seething, he was convinced that heroin was in the loft as he had been told, but they had to search that last, to make it look like they hadn't been told; either the thug who is now missing was a top level informant or someone had set him up or his sister up, that was his known address.'

'So he contacted someone high up and they suddenly called it off?'

'That's the way the editor was told how it happened, then Feeney gets shot in a church, it makes sense, doesn't it?' 'You certainly have been busy, how did my name come into it?'

'The source, said that you were incorruptible, you might be worth talking too.'

'I can't understand that part, I was never in the drugs squad, therefore I couldn't confirm the aborted raid, I had left the force by then.'

'But you knew Feeney, you were his partner, if anyone knew Feeney, you would be the best person to ask.'

'I can understand that, maybe someone made the raid up to convince the editor Feeney was corrupt, to deflect the editor away, Joe Feeney can't answer back can he?'

They moved a few feet to the next picture.

'That's true, how will we know that the raid actually took place?'

'I can find out, but who is the missing dealer?'

***

She finally tracked him down to a civil engineers office in the city centre, he was out but she left a number with his secretary. He called back just before five, she explained that she found it difficult to talk over the phone would he be kind enough to drop by on his way home? There were no signs of resistance or nervousness in his voice, he would call in but might be late due to the heavy snowfall that had engulfed Dundee; the roads were more treacherous in the country areas. He knocked at her door, it was near to six, she turned the television off, and opened the kitchen door so that the smell of warm enticing food would make him feel more relaxed.

Bobby had not changed much over the years, he had changed university courses after a year, the Law bored him to tears, he couldn't muster up any thirst for the knowledge that his lecturers were pontificating, he enjoyed anecdotal events from his lecturers about former students who went onto greater things, much to their surprise. Catherine on the other hand, knew where her life would end up, she wanted to know the Law whether she was practicing it or countering it. Bobby took the civil engineering lectures on board, he studied more than he should have, he was a man totally in the need of knowledge of all the great civil engineers, he wanted to be a civil engineer that the public would remember but he also was concerned on how he would be financially rewarded.

Catherine hadn't called his office to make up for the lack of social interaction between them, his company had been awarded a multi- million contract for the new Dundee by-pass, the arterial routes had come to be obsolete, seventy per cent of the traffic coming from the A 90 was heading beyond Dundee, the city was becoming clogged up, the Kingsway was becoming a slow moving car park, its original purpose was to move traffic that was going beyond Dundee quickly and efficiently. A new by-pass had been in the thoughts of planners for years, money had now become available. It could be five to ten years hence before it was started. Catherine had spotted a possible business opportunity on the proposed route, by her measurements one part of the route just needed to be altered by fifty metres, and she would have a gold mine on her hands; a car wash could be built as well as one large enough for articulated lorries, Bobby would be able to advise her, if her proposed site was not acceptable where would it be acceptable? After his soup and casserole he was not offended by her direct question, she didn't want any solicitor or planner to know about her friend's business proposal, she had not offered him any money or inducements; she was asking a friend for advice. He told her that he would look over the plans in his house that evening; he would get back to her after he had made discreet enquiries. Aware of her dead partner's background, he didn't ask the identity of her 'friend.'

CHAPTER FIVE

Baldovan Terrace was quiet, the comings and goings from the top floor flat had come to a sudden halt; either the heroin had been sold and there were no more supplies or the constant heavy snow flurries had put paid to visitors to the flat. That was the opinion of the more senior drug squad officers. McAveety knew they were wrong on both accounts. The dealer was selling tainted heroin, the heroin had been moved from Glasgow simply because anthrax had been used as an additive. A dealer had tried to convince junkies to come to him, he had a better product, the junkies had a regular supplier, she had not let them down, she had invoked good business practice, if the junkies introduced a friend, the junkie would get a free bag, enough for two hits. They had nothing to concern them; she had always treated them like customers, what was the point of changing dealers? They soon found out; the heroin was switched, they injected death into their veins, panic was running through the North End of Glasgow and beyond, affirmative action was needed.

She was removed from her plush stone built detached house by detectives at three am on a Sunday morning, she was alone in the house, and her family were at their villa on Majorca, she was meant to join them later that day. She was well-versed with police procedures, she had nothing to incriminate her in the house, she would be taken to the police station there she would request her solicitor be present, she would not answer any questions until he had arrived and was sitting at her side, after questions were fired at her she would reply 'no comment' with monotony, after a couple of hours she would be released without charge, her solicitor would fire off another missive to the Chief Constable about his client being periodically harassed. The Chief Constable would reply that he understood why she thought she was being harassed, but the officers were acting on confidential information, etc. This was a game; a game of attrition, the Chief Constable would not blink.

That early Sunday morning would be different, she never arrived at the police station or Palma airport. A vacuum needed to be filled, fortunately someone was able to bring order to the chaos that was rampaging through Glasgow, prices went up; and the 'introduce a friend' scheme was ended abruptly; normality returned. The tainted heroin was transported to Dundee; to the car park at Tesco's on Riverside Drive, one boot of a car was left open, the Tesco bag was deposited, another Tesco bag containing perishables was handed over, the heroin was dropped off at an address in the Coldside area of Dundee, it was weighed various powders were added to the heroin, the supplies were then dispatched to various dealers under the guise of an Indian meals delivery service, the dealer would order a curry, the heroin was delivered at the same time, not a sophisticated method but adequate, to date it still worked well.

McAveety had earned the sobriquet 'Supermac' he had uncovered the delivery service.

The four of them sat in the Vauxhall Vectra in view of the flat, impatience and lack of activity from Baldovan Terrace was taking its toll. Expletives and bad- mouthing of absent colleagues were in vogue, except for one; Jim McAveety sat in the back with the wise words from one of his senior colleagues still loudly ringing in his ears accompanied by mocking laughter, 'watch, listen and learn.' He was, he had, and learned an awful lot, he had been right in his assumption of them; they were all phallic symbols, limp ones at that. No one was stupid enough to ask his opinion, the senior officer picked up the phone, 'Abort! Abort!'

That was two nights ago, he reflected on their

incompetence, they really knew nothing, without a CI, they were whistling in the dark, he was sitting in the dark in his favourite chair in his excessively warm flat, information is power, and he was the quietest in the squad but he was the more powerful, he couldn't help smiling triumphantly, the snow was falling heavily, his beating heart was steady. He had never believed in luck, now he was worshipping it, a good deed is never left undone.

He had been paid back ten-fold and that was a builders' estimate seriously wrong.

When he was at a charity function at the North End Club , he was joined at the urinals by an old school friend, he had never seen him in well over a decade, when the lavatory was empty, the friend told him he was in trouble, at first he thought it was financial, he knew that he was a successful builder, was it the recession, no he was told, it was his son, he had gone off the rails, he thought he was dealing, no, he *was* dealing. He didn't want to shop him, he would go to Perth Prison and his mother wouldn't forgive him, could he have a word with him? He can be found at this address, before he could answer, he popped the card into his hand and left. Stunned was not the word McAveety could describe this close encounter; he had not uttered a word in reply. Two well- oiled members came barging through the door, he let them past, and they made it very clear that their conversation ended because he was present. He returned to the table where the mature nurse was sitting, eye contact had been made the previous weekend, she would be coming home to his house, her husband was on nightshift; the opportunity had to be grasped with both hands. He sat next down to his friend, his friend offered sage advice, 'don't touch her with rubber gloves.'

McAveety took his advice and threw it overboard, the friend told him he was going to the bar, 'don't make a move on her; some of her husband's friends are present.'

McAveety didn't reply, he took out the builder's business card and looked at the name and address scrawled on the rear of it. The name didn't cause an intake of breath it was the address; one of the most affluent streets in Broughty Ferry, it was rumoured that the window cleaners used Perrier water to clean the windows. It was perfect camouflage for drug dealing, he would put the errant son under surveillance; unofficially.

McAveety didn't like Broughty Ferry, overpriced in every way imaginable, from housing to beer. The Post Office bar was his usual haunt, he had been in an hour and the son hadn't turned up, most unusual. Spanish football was on the large television screen, it seemed he was intently watching with total concentration, this was a ruse, his seat could see both entrances to the bar. It was filling up and his view was being overshadowed by the group of youths, he knew the son had been out all day, however, he saw him enter the divided mansion, he waited till the lights came on in the lounge, and then he parked his car a hundred metres to the left of the property. That was two hours ago, he had been patient, overly patient, he decided to call it a day, he stood up slowly, consuming the last droplets of his pint glass, quickly scanning the two entrances, the son came waltzing in with two females, he could now imagine what detained him, the two young women went straight to the bar, the son diverted and went in the direction of the gents; now was the opportune time. He placed down the glass on the table and followed him, through the torturous path which was blocked by groups of young people. He felt himself get impatient, he took deep breaths, his mind telling him to calm down; the son wasn't going anywhere.

When he reached the toilet he was nowhere to be seen, the urinals were not being used, one cubicle had the door firmly shut, he went to the urinal.
Listening intently, he heard the sound of someone,

hopefully, the son, sniffing, he pulled in his appendage and zipped up, diplomacy was out; he kicked in the door, the son looked at him with fear matching his eyes, the bank note still in his hand. He showed him his warrant card.

'Don't worry, I'm your best friend, dump the coke down the pan and follow me out.'

He followed without arguing, McAveety took the exit that led into the beer garden which was populated with smokers, even though it was sub-zero, he went up to the bridge and waited, he was been followed like a lapdog; he wouldn't waste this opportunity.

'What's happening here?'

'Just follow me,' was the terse reply.

'No, no, I want to know, I'm not moving.'

'Fine,' he took out his mobile, 'Your dealing has come to an end, you have been under surveillance for the last year, I'm your last hope, I don't give a fuck what happens to you, I'm giving you a chance, make your mind up, I'm freezing.'

He stood in only a short sleeved shirt, he was starting to shiver.

'You win, what is it you want?'

'Just follow me,' he then stopped, 'call your female friends, tell them you had to go back to your house, you'll be back in half an hour.' He nodded and turned his back on McAveety, the conversation was hurried and incoherent. Ten minutes later they were at the boot of McAveety's car, the boot sprang open, he invited the son to take out the holdall, he did without any question, and he closed the boot. He motioned with his head that they were going back the way, the son was right after all, they were going back to his house. In the house McAveety took off his overcoat and threw it on the couch, he stood there with the holdall at his feet.

'Open the holdall and take out what's in there, c'mon I'm in a hurry.'

He knelt down and took out the heroin.

'It's nothing to do with me,' he stood back from it like it was a bomb. McAveety sat on the chair looking relaxed.

'I know that, you know that, and Monty knew that, past tense; its Monty's, but he's not here to claim it, imagine if you were arrested with this, do you think you would be linked with his murder and the murders of the other dealers?'

He started to pace the room.

'No way, I had nothing to do with any of their deaths, your setting me up!'

'Well done, I've always believed university enhances the mind. I could set you up or I can refrain from setting you up. Here's the choice, you give me the money for the heroin, I walk out of here happy, and I give you as a bonus, a warning if you are under surveillance.' He looks at his watch, then at the son.

'Do you really have to think about it?'

'What's to stop you, from setting me up in the future? I need a guarantee.'

'Here's your guarantee, your prints are on the holdall and the heroin, I had a call from you, you wanted to hand yourself in, you murdered Monty and his chums, and took his heroin, does that guarantee you anything but prison?'

'How much do you want?'

'It's worth about half a million, I'll accept a quarter of a million, and then I'm on my way.'

'I don't have that money here.'

'You do, you usually take the money to a friend's house on the Monday evening, I've been watching you, remember, and it's all in high-definition.'

'I meant, I don't have all the money, I have about two hundred k.'

'That'll do.' He left the room, McAveety hoped his well thought out plan would work, he had factored in him returning with a gun; he wasn't the type. He returned with the money, in a small sports bag, which he showed him, then closed the bag.

'Do you want to count it?'

'No,' he grabbed the bag and was walking out.

'What do you think I should do with the smack, I can't go to my regulars they'll be suspicious.'

'Flush it down the toilet.'

He let out a nervous laugh. 'That's madness, money down the drain.'

'The heroin is laced with anthrax; dump it, before it dumps you.'

He closed the door behind him.

***

The laptop was showing reams of information, but it was all mundane, nothing illegal or duplicitous. The USB that he took from Feeney's office was not shielding any lucrative secrets, his notebook replicated some of the information displayed on the white screen Criminal Informants names were just initials, he knew most of them, some he didn't know, but it didn't trouble him, he rubbed his eyes and yawned, it had been a long day, he closed the laptop down and removed the USB, he was still convinced that it would yield some seismic pernicious information. He grabbed the beer off the table, the laptop's white light dulled then disappeared, the only light in the lounge were the lights from the Christmas tree, he moved towards the bay window and his head turned to the right, Baldovie was still pumping the white steam into the dark sky, he lifted the bottle to his lips, still gazing at the plumes of steam; at least he had made someone really happy this Christmas.

From the shadow and safety of the bay window he saw a car stop directly across from his house, he sipped the beer and watched the car closely, the driver's window came down, then returned to the closed position, he got out of the car; a chill came over him, he recognised the driver it was a detective from the murder squad; Feeney's nemesis and a vocal one at that; Gary Spencer. He looked at the laptop, changed his mind then switched on the two lamps, the slow light from the low-energy bulbs increased as he took the lap top back to its home in the hall cupboard, he closed the cupboard door, the bell rang out, he looked at himself in the hall mirror, he looked tired. The bell rang out again just as he opened the door, his smile disarmed the detective.

'Gary! How are you, come in, come in.' He led him into the lounge.

'Nice lounge, Paul... I'm here on semi-official business; I'm hoping you can help me.'

'Take your coat off, I'd offer you a beer but I assume you didn't walk from Dundee, tea or coffee?'

'No I won't bother thanks. The reason I'm here is about the dealers deaths in the industrial unit, I feel the top brass are being swayed by ill-informed gossip, they think it was someone from Liverpool or Ulster, but I just don't buy it Paul.'

He went to the table and lifted the half full beer.

'I have heard that about a hit man from Liverpool, but not anything about Ulster, you mean an ex -IRA man?'

'That's the one gathering credence, it'll take the heat off the top brass as well, we get downgraded, Special Branch takes over, and it steps into terrorism, it's their forte.'

'You think, you think this is a smokescreen?'

'Definitely...without question.'

He sipped the beer. 'Who do you think was behind the killings then?'

'Feeney.'

The beer spluttered out his mouth, he wiped his mouth with his hand.

'Now you've entered the twilight zone...Feeney!'

'That's why I'm here, I couldn't go to anyone else, if I

335

went to anyone else, I would be removed from the investigation, then stood down from duty, till I retired, I know how the system works.'

'Gary, I'm going to hurt your feelings, keep that to yourself, you'll be made a laughing stock, trust me on that one. Feeney had the best clean up rate in the drug squad's tattered history, he came in and razed it, he brought in men he could trust, the money he confiscated from the dealers as well ran into millions, you've definitely called this one wrong, I'm sorry Gary. First of all Feeney was killed before the dealers…did you forget that?'

'I know how it looks, don't you think I've questioned my sanity over this, I've been digging, unofficially, someone, in a senior capacity was involved with the dealers, it had to be Feeney, I can't go into how I actually came to this conclusion, but I will keep you informed…later.'

'Surely, you can tell me something,' he drained the beer and placed the bottle on the table.

'I was coming to that; did you know Feeney's house was turned over?'

'Burgled?'

'No, no, turned over, a search warrant was issued the day he died, sorry the day he was murdered.'

'I didn't know that, why has it been kept quiet?'

Because his house was searched by persons impersonating detectives, the warrant was a fake, his widow said the officers were like real detectives, they said this was all routine, they had to have a warrant if anything was removed from the house, they said that if they got the person who killed him, a defence lawyer could make any information on his laptop inadmissible, they then took his laptop away, and they asked if he had a USB, she said he did, but always left it in his office. His secretary backed up the widow's claim. The USB was removed from his office.'

'How do you know all this? I haven't heard that.'

'His widow told me this when I was leaving, she asked when his laptop would be returned, I told her I didn't understand, she brought me back into her lounge and told me the whole story. I told her to keep this quiet, something was unsettling here, and I knew it wasn't the police or Special Branch, the spiel about the search warrant and inadmissible evidence made me refute it was real detectives.'

'Is anyone in senior management aware of the men impersonating detectives?'

He paused, looked at Welsh, clearly looking uncomfortable.

'Could you give me a beer; this is not going to be comforting...for you.'

He returned a hurtful angst look. He left the lounge and returned with the beer opened. Spencer took a long, long drink; the bottle was three quarters empty.

'They knew about it before me, no-one had mentioned to me before I went to interview her, I only found out when I spoke to one of the drug squad, he knew, did you know?' 'This is all news to me! Why haven't I been told?'

'Why haven't we both been told, someone has kept us out deliberately, now why would that happen?'

He moved from the seat, he went to the kitchen and returned with two beers, he thrust one into Spencer's willing hand.

'If you know something Gary, I'd appreciate any heads up; I'm starting to get a bad feeling about this.'

'And so you should be, you've had someone monitoring your movements, did you have any inkling?'

'No,' he said quietly, he tried to bring order to his chaotic mind.

'It's not the internal boys, it's from someone who worked in the murder squad, but left under a cloud, mental health issues, Feeney's ex- colleague Eddings,

337

Valentine Eddings.'

A sense of relief was slowly bringing colour back to his face; he was almost relieved and dismissive about this news.

'What is the reason that no-one has told you about the visit to Feeney's house, and why is Eddings keeping an eye on me, I thought he was in Dubai?'

'We are not the only ones who have not been told, it seems that there is a police force within a police force, this I do know as fact, that idiot of an editor of the Evening Chronicle, has gleaned more information than we have, he is of the opinion that there is a whiff of corruption either in the detective/murder squad or the drugs squad, and you can't blame him from coming to that, not since the two women were jailed for keeping drugs in their own homes.'

'But why are we under suspicion? I can't understand that?

'Someone from the either the murder squad or your department is spreading lies, you'd be better to find out who in your squad knew about the fake raid, if you do, then it's him or them, I will do the same. They must have a new team some from the murder squad some from the drug squad.'

'I'll have to think deep about what you've said, it seems fanciful…why am I being watched, is Eddings acting as an unofficial officer then reporting back to the renegade officers?'

'That's what I have thought, I can't dismiss it, great minds think alike.'
'Fucking hell! I'm starting to believe you, but I'm hoping you're wide of the mark.'

'It's my understanding that this editor is behind Eddings monitoring your movements, its part of his war on drug dealers and compliant police officers.'

'Senior management has not been too complimentary about cash for dealer's campaign, why would they change their stance?'

'Politics, Westminster MP's are raising questions in Sunday newspapers, they're asking why the local MSPs are not concerned...they're implying that their silence is being paid for. So the MSPs are becoming more visible to the public, did you really think their presence during a low-level drug raid, was not to their benefit as it was being aired on the BBC news?'

'But why would the senior management, be taken in by this, I can't believe that.'

'Well... listen to this, this is manufactured in my own head, they are saving money on any investigation into corruption, the editor is financing Eddings, if Eddings comes up with something concrete, they drift into the spotlight basking in their glory, if it goes tits up, they blame the editor and Eddings who left because of mental health problems; paranoia.'

His beer lay untouched at his feet, worry was taking root. 'I wish I could disagree with you, I watched the news, I said to my wife, I don't think there's an election in the offing, I just dismissed it, but now, I can see what you mean. Who told you that Eddings is watching me?'

'No one...I found out with a little bit of skullduggery. One of the detectives has been saying that me interviewing Monty's school friends is a waste of police resources, catty comments, like that, I was working late, unpaid overtime, trying without success to move away from a rival drug dealer, that could be behind the hit, this detective who was in the far end of the office, answers the desk phone then tells the caller to call him on his mobile, I glance at my papers, giving the impression I didn't hear him say that, his face was guilty, of what I don't know. I had written down the date and time of his call. He left to take the call on his mobile I nip up to his desk , no number had been written down, the phones in the office don't have the one -four one facility, after the fuss from one of the jailed women about human rights

339

privacy. Two weeks later, I see him in the toilet, he has just went into the cubicle, I go to the office and search his jacket and his mobile is there, I scroll down to received calls and at the time and date he took the call at his desk. The number is there. With a little help from an Asian businessman who has a shop selling mobiles and an unblocking service; he comes up with the number.'

'Whose number is it then?' he asks almost pleading.

***

At the pre-raid meeting McAveety was feeling so relaxed, he was thinking who was the idiot who had said money doesn't bring happiness? He was still the 'message laddie' in the eyes of the more educated, younger colleagues. He was a slow learner, but he was learning the vagaries of the drug squad, the inadequacies of the department as a whole were glaring, but now the gaps in theory to practice would work to his advantage. He had been amazed at the way drug money was washed, and how hard it was to prove. It was two o'clock in the afternoon, no one in the room was told where the raid would take place. Two weeks ago stories were circulating that someone was leaking information; the leak was thought to be plugged when the two women officers were removed from their duties and charged.

Raids would not be printed on A4 paper with the times and dates, usually four days in advance, now, raids would be announced just two hours before they happened. Usually questions would come from the assembled detectives, this time the address, photographs and the time of the raids would be displayed on the projector, all mobiles were to be given up when the detectives came into the briefing room, the shocked detectives were told this was in response to the innuendo that was being splashed across the Evening Chronicle The grumbles and expletives built from a whisper into a crescendo, this was halted when the desk was banged by the senior officer; this was an order not a request. When dignity was restored the clearly angry senior officer outlined the intelligence on the suspect; male, age and vague location. Guessing who it was, took place in silence. They were put out of their misery, it was a new face, it wasn't a dealer, it was an accountant who had worked from home for many years, he was a particular favourite with the legal profession

Puzzled faces were the standard; McAveety certainly had not recognised him nor heard of him. He looked like an accountant that enjoyed the trappings of life's larder. Then the grand finale, the dealers' photographs came from a slow fade to sharp focus, one by one; they were all the dealers that had been executed. The officer droned on without giving too much away; this seemed to McAveety like a media sponsored event; they were going to arrest the accountant and remove files in large boxes; to give the docile public the impression that this was a well-coordinated raid. Then the talk became more interesting to McAveety, the new methods how the money was being cleansed then put to work in Dundee, and how the profits from the money became legitimate.

He casually looked around the room the rest were showing signs of indifference, they didn't want to raid an accountant's office and house in the west end; they wanted to hit the dealers hard and frequently. McAveety soaked in every iota of the ingenious methods that the money was being washed. The money in his flat had outstayed its welcome and was not earning its keep. Now it would.

The information came from an unlikely source; a solicitor who was presently under investigation from the FSA; he felt no loyalty to his close confidante; the accountant. Self-preservation was the order of the day. He may have been sloppy and boastful of his 'grey' dealings but he knew that the information he had would persuade the FSA and HMR&C to go gently on him, and would make their obdurate eyes water. He couldn't have a solicitor or even his good friend a QC present, this information he would only offer up once he had a signed letter granting him immunity from the present investigation.

HMR&C coerced the FSA to put down the financial irregularities as an unforced error, due to personal difficulties the solicitor was suffering from. The solicitor had given HMR&C a taster; they now had developed a voracious appetite. There was not a chance that the information regarding tax evasion and money laundering was exaggerated; he was the solicitor who had put the dealers' solicitors in touch with the accountant. His information was solid gold. The raid was in progress, the accountant was in his office sitting in his chair poring over papers with a sandwich in one hand. He was asked his name and date of birth, then he was charged, detectives came in and removed the files from the filing cabinet then placed them in the large white boxes.

The four other persons in the office were open mouthed, they were told to stay at their desks and don't answer any phones or attempt to use any mobiles. The accountant refused to answer any questions; he would answer any amount of questions only in the presence of his solicitor. He didn't query the charges, his financial dealings were all above board; he had nothing to fear. He was frog marched out of his office in front of his horrified staff, two of them burst into tears, when he was forced through the door onto the street he was met by a film crew. He kept the same expression on his face and was led to the car and put in the car with a detective on each side, and then the car sped away with the sound of screeching tyres, this was not a low profile raid.

Small talk was started by the detectives, to no avail, the accountant just stared straight ahead, they were on the Perth Road heading towards Bell Street, his thoughts were in complete order he had nothing to fear he kept repeating to himself. The detectives changed tact, 'you would be going to prison for a long time, unless you cooperated, you're in your sixties, do you really want to die in prison, think of the shame on your family, you'll be dead but the shame will still be with them, are you that selfish?' For the first time his impenetrable defences showed signs of crumbling, he felt the beads of sweat on his furrowed brow, he wanted to take his handkerchief and sate the sweat, he composed himself, by ignoring the doubts and what ifs, that they would be spouting...he had nothing to worry about. The car came to a silent halt at Bell Street, no screeching tyres this time. Nothing to worry about.

He was singing lustily in the shower, it was good that he could take a shower without fear of the hot comforting water turning ice-cold. The thud of the Evening Chronicle hitting the carpet added to his joy, the chicken curry was in the oven, he would devour it and wash it down with a beer while reading the newspaper, he was enjoying the simple pleasures of life; mainly because his money problems were no more. He came out the shower invigorated, he had arrived home at four pm, tired and listless, to fend off the temptation to cat-nap, he made the curry then took the shower, he was sleeping a lot easier now, no more waking up bolt upright with the feeling of impending doom. He towelled himself dry and took the white bathroom robe hanging on the pine door, the Hilton logo was emblazoned on the breast pocket. When he opened the door, he felt the heat coming from the hall, he bent down and picked up the newspaper and took it into the lounge, he went to the kitchen took out the bottle of Becks and placed it on the tray, he retrieved the curry from the oven, burning himself because he used the dishtowel instead of the oven gloves which were on the back of the wooden chair, not even this unfortunate accident could alter his mood, he poured half the curry from the casserole dish onto the plate, picked up a fork from the drawer and placed it beside the plate on the tray.

In the lounge the radio was on in the background, it was nearing five pm the news would be coming on soon. The tray was placed carefully on his knees, he took the beer, annoyed he had forgotten to take the top off it, not to worry, he scooped the large pieces of chicken in his mouth, he was surprised how succulent it tasted, in his left hand he had the folded newspaper, letting it fall naturally, he looked at the headline; his appetite receded: Four critical in Ninewells; heroin contaminated with anthrax. He dropped the newspaper onto the floor, he was tempted to throw the tray and its contents against the newly decorated wall, and went to the window and stared into the swirling snow, the big issue seller was still in his doorway, seemingly oblivious to the snow; he would have swapped lives with him at this exact moment.

The swirling snow was moving from one direction to another matched his erratic thoughts. When he spoke to Clive about the heroin being mixed with anthrax, which he didn't know, he thought he was being smart, he would take his advice and flush it down the toilet, that way, the heroin was gone, he had the money and nothing could connect him to Clive, the smart apartment building had security cameras, if Clive went to the police and said that he had extorted money from him, he would laugh and say he had met Clive's dad at the North End Club, he had asked him to have a word with him, his dad was concerned he was taking drugs. When his story was checked out, the dad would corroborate his. He didn't expect Clive to put the heroin on the street; never in a million years.

He moved away from the window back to his chair, he read the story again, some sense of order came to him, he didn't know for sure that Clive hadn't put the heroin down the toilet, and if he did, so what? The hunger pangs returned, he lifted the fork and tasted the curry, he was chewing it, then a smile replaced worry and despondency, he filled the fork, his mouth was moving in tandem with his mind. If, and it was a big if, say for arguments sake that Clive did put the heroin on the street and it was laced with anthrax, he had unwittingly invited death to his door. The dealers, who hid the heroin and money in the Alexander multi-storey, would know that the person who placed the anthrax strewn heroin on the streets was the person who had ripped them off. The curry tasted sweeter than ever. If Clive said that a detective came to his apartment and sold him the heroin, he would not say that that the detective told him to flush it down the toilet because it was contaminated with anthrax, would he?

They wouldn't fall for that, they would think that Clive was just hitching his wagon to the Evening Chronicle crusade against the evil drug trade and the cosy relationship between the dealers and some elements of the drug squad. The dealers who had been ripped off would exact their ultimate sanction on Clive, and they would be removing a rogue dealer, he was independent not part of the cartel. In a free market economy some regulations would have to be strictly adhered to. Clive was a free spirit that needed to be exorcised.

The money in shoe boxes and in the drawers would have to be removed, if Clive went to the police, nothing could be shown to give credence to his outlandish claims. He went to his bedroom wardrobe and reached into the jacket and withdrew his wallet, he returned to the lounge, his eyes catching the falling, heavier snow, this was not the moment to wonder at the white wonderland. His handwritten notes were nearly indecipherable, Jane commented that he should have been a doctor; he thought because he was so pleasant and intelligent, he was subdued when she told him it was because of his terrible, child-like handwriting. He had

345

written in capitals MLWM; this stood for money laundering ways and means. He looked at the comprehensive list, he didn't want to be too clever for his own good, and he didn't want to be elaborate, simple but effective. He put an x at most of them; he wasn't hiding millions of pounds, no need to travel overseas. Then he stopped and pondered and finally thought the most simple but effective way to hide the money; he would go to one of the many amateur landlords that were suffering because of their empty properties, this would avoid going through credit checks with a management company. He just needed the property for preferably six months, but if the landlord wanted a year-long lease, he would be looking for a discount. It was Thursday so The Courier would have pages of vacant properties. His cover story for the landlord would be simple; relocating.

The Courier was on the kitchen table, he opened it expectantly, he was not disappointed, there were many flats available in nice, quiet and affluent areas, and the price range varied from six to eight hundred. He didn't circle any of them, his name he wrote down alongside that he wrote Financial Advisor, he was looking to rent then buy, his house was up for sale in South Queensferry, he had clients in Dundee, Forfar and Arbroath. He finished the curry; the beer could wait till he called the three landlords and made appointments. The calls took ten minutes, one he dismissed the woman sound too posh and inquisitive, she wanted him to have a credit check which could take a week, he demurred from this as he didn't like to provide personal details and bank account numbers, he was sure she could understand that; she ended the call without saying goodbye; charming. The next one was the most promising, she was a doctor going to work over in New Zealand for two years, but she wanted a year's lease with six-months rent upfront with a deposit, he was able to convince her that a discount was in order, she agreed to reduce the rent from

346

six hundred to five. She had been intoxicated by the housing boom that gripped Dundee, she had bought off-plan as she had done previously, in London, Manchester and Leeds, and the apartments were built off the Perth Road convenient for Ninewells Hospital. Like so many, when the apartments were finished the value had plummeted, the rent she was expecting at the time she signed the paperwork was nine hundred to a thousand. She was in negative equity. Her plan to stay in it then sell it at a vast profit when she moved to New Zealand became untenable; the rest of the block was rented out to people who worked in the bio-science sector. Perfect.

When he had signed the lease he would register the bona-fide address with his alter ego, when the documents were returned he would apply for a credit-card, then when he had used it and had a statement he would open a bank account, a driving licence or passport didn't cause him any problems. When he was in the apartment he could hide the money there then drip feed the money into his alter ego's bank account. Lying awake thinking things through, had been the right thing to do, he was told in no uncertain terms that he would not progress in the drug squad, his mind was not agile or supple enough, he heard that from three of his cohorts, at first he was offended then he answered back, with 'I couldn't see them turning in zebras anytime soon,' he put them out their collective misery; 'I was laterally thinking out loud, they hadn't any stripes, i.e. they were the same rank as him, maybe their minds weren't agile or supple.' He didn't wait on their replies he walked away. The drug squad wasn't smart as hc had thought, duplicitous and deceitful were the current traits that his esteemed colleagues had in abundance, he didn't want anything to do with them anymore. He enjoyed the dark side of the job, the money would compensate for his misery.

***

Driving over the Tay Bridge, his mind was in a state of flux, he sounded agitated on the phone, he wanted an hour of his time, his wife was at a creative writing class at Dundee University; the house was empty. The short drive to Wormit wouldn't allow him to come up with exaggerated situations that may have arisen, the only fact for certain, was that he had been at Monty's house after Monty was buried, why was he there, was he part of the finance that purchased the garage as a going concern? Or was there another more sinister reason? His mind skipped back to the money behind the garage; surely, he would have sounded out the proposal when he was last over at the house when they were discussing the conversation of the Silvery Tay Hotel into luxury apartments? He could also have other illegal income streams that were going through Catherine, he thought that may have possibilities, after all she was a trained solicitor, and she knew how to shape rules and circumvent laws to her or her clients' advantage. The car turned into the street, the gates were wide open, he nosed onto the drive, he looked up at the window he saw a shape at the window, he was impressed by the lights that covered the Christmas tree, he hoped the atmosphere in the house was equal to the brightness of the myriad colours of bulbs.

A path had been made through the thick snow from the drive to the stairs that led to the front door. At the bottom of the stairs he took a look behind him, an old habit that he couldn't shake off, Welsh was dressed in jeans and a white tee shirt, he had a cup in his hand, the steam rushing from it. He was encouraged to move into the house quickly, the door was closed and locked behind him; he waited in the lounge for him.

'Thanks for coming Pat, I maybe over reacting, I'll let you be the counsel on this, take your coat off and have a seat.' He went and told him about the visit from Gary

Spence a detective from the murder squad, he had told
him that an ex detective was watching him, for what
reason he didn't know or understand. Then he told him
the theory about Joe Feeney. He waited on the reaction
from Connelly; he hoped his face didn't match his
impending opinion. His first reaction, didn't calm any
fears, it was a simple, 'Oh.' then silence, which was
causing him panic, just before he asked for a more
expansive response, he loosened his tie.

'This is not good, he knows a lot more, you have to be
honest with me Paul, is there anything that could connect
you to the murdered dealers?'

'Nothing, only I came down hard on the people who
distributed their drugs…if your hinting that I had
something to do with their deaths, I can put your mind at
rest Pat, nothing, nada.'

'No, I wasn't suggesting that, what I am suggesting is
this, the Evening Chronicle have had a tremendous
impact on the publics' psyche, the high profile arrest of
dealers being led from their houses is encouraging
people to phone the hotline, it's more successful than the
police.'

Welsh leapt from his seat.

'That's just not true, I have the stats in my office, and
Joe Feeney had done more than any other senior officer
to be more proactive than anyone in the history of the
drug squad.'

'I am not saying you're wrong, it's just the perception
of the public. I do agree that the editor has some mole in
the drug squad, the information he has been able to print,
doesn't come from some junkie, it's too precise, and too
valuable, not to print then act on, the mole must be
getting paid very well. That is illegal as well, so you
have an editor who says there is corruption in the drug
squad, but he himself is corrupting someone in the drug
squad by paying them, now comes the semantics of that
suggestion, is the money going to the detective via a tip

from the shop a dealer campaign, via a third party?'

Pat was studying his face and hand for his reaction.

'Wait a minute Pat, have I got this right, are you saying that the editor is in a grey area, by paying a detective money for information that could lead to a drugs bust and arrest?'

'Yes, think about it... the state pays the detective to catch drug dealers, why doesn't the detective go to the most senior officer, you, and tell you the information, that's what he's paid to do, don't you agree?'

'Totally, that's not right, are you getting at something else?'

'Off the top of my head, the same detective knows if he's found out doing this, he'll be charged, from corruption to tax evasion, so say he has a close relationship, with a dealer or a wife or partner of a dealer, she is besotted with him, pillow talk ensues, she passes to him information about a rival dealer, the detective induces someone they can trust to call the hotline, the dealer is arrested and the caller picks up the money, and they split the money fifty-fifty.'

Welsh's reaction was of wonderment; Pat could see there was no guilt emanating from any of his pores.

'I'm truly amazed at the suggestions you have come up, they certainly are plausible, but do you really think someone is smart enough to do that?' I'm thinking if some detective was stupid enough to get involved with a dealer, but get involved with a dealer's wife...that's suicide.'

'I am glad you said that, what I'm going to ask you next concerns you, this Eddings I have known him for years, I thought he went to Dubai, is he just home for the Christmas break?'

'I don't have any idea.'

'If he has you under surveillance, have you met anyone to connect you to the murdered dealers, in case he has photographed you and the person, you would have to come up with a plausible answer, for example do you meet any informants face-to-face at unearthly hours?' Welsh aged in front of him, he could almost hear his hair turning grey.

The apartment was furnished to a very high standard, signing the lease and handing over the deposit were without complications, she had told him the numbers on the back of the lease were for any potential problems with any of the domestic units; washing machine, television or problems with the central heating. On Monday he would register with the council tax office, and his new identity would be complete.

The suitcase was on the bed; he opened it and took out the various shirts, jackets and a couple of suits. He tried to space them out, but they still looked they could do with more company, when he was in town he would buy a dozen shirts from Primark, that would take the bare look from the walk-in wardrobe, he took out the three pairs of black shoes and placed hem neatly in a line. He hadn't intended to spend any time in the apartment but it was inviting him to stay, at least a couple of nights a week. Going home to his flat would be a leveler, no large screen television with cable, and no power shower.

The view from the lounge overwhelmed him, this is how the high rollers live, and then he compared his lifestyle, and became angry and embarrassed, he felt justified in his unlawful actions, if the state didn't reward him his independent streak did. The apartment's internal buzzer made him jump, he went to the hall and was horrified, he took a step back and stared at the laughing image.

'Hi, Mr McAveety...come on, I know you are in, I watched you enter the building.'
He didn't reply, he just slowly pressed the button, he entered the building. It was too good to last, his plan had failed at the first hurdle; he just had to play it cool. He opened the door and moved into the lounge, then

changed his mind and went to the kitchen and switched on the kettle, he heard the door close.

'Tea or coffee?

'No thanks, I bet you're surprised to see me, eh?'

'Not, really, you've been watching and following me for days, but you'll have to brush up on your surveillance technique, have you thought about glasses and a beard?'

He moved into the lounge and sat in the ergonomically designed chair, he was relaxed, the fear was gone.

'I've been expecting you, you've saved me a lot of time, now I can return the favour to you, and I can save you a lot of money.'

He was taken aback at this reply.

'You've been following me?'

'Nearly right…some of my friends, my violent friends have been following you, but that's another story, what can I do for you Clive.'

'I came here to…' he lost the thread.

'…I hope you didn't come to attempt to blackmail me, that wouldn't be clever, would it?'

'No, no, I came to see if you can get me more smack, I've got the money waiting.'

'Why? Have you fallen out with your regular supplier?'

'You could say that, he's being too greedy, my profit margins are being cut.'

'Change suppliers?'

'I can't they're all dead, don't you read the papers?'

'Don't be cheeky, I know they're all dead, and how do I know that, because I was there, some of them were trying to cut my margins, so I let them know how unhappy I was.'

'You killed them?' he asked slowly, his face was losing that youthful look.

He didn't respond, he just sipped his tea and stared.

The brooding silence needed to be broken. 'The smack I gave you, was it contaminated? 'He was smirking, openly mocking him.

'No, of course it wasn't, everybody knows who sold that stuff; I'm surprised he hasn't been arrested.'

'Maybe because he's an informer, has that not crossed your mind?'

'Informer? Who cares? Can you get me more smack?'

'Of course, maybe you should stick with your present supplier, in saying that, I like the way you operate. If I supply you, it's only you who buys and picks up the gear. But the price is double.'

'Double! I don't think so, you wouldn't pay it!'

'I can supply you with enough as you can take, but we don't want to flood the market, the price will come down. I mentioned I can save you money, who launders your money, and what is the percentage... his commission?'

'I can't tell you that, and I'm happy with the percentage he takes.'

'I can understand that, what is his percentage?'

'Twenty per cent.'

'I can do it for fifteen, plus I can invest it for you, my friends are professional.' He watched his feet move unconsciously.

'I'll have to think about that, things could get difficult, I would need a good explanation.'

'Here's one, say you're out of the game, tell them things are getting too risky, the Evening Chronicle is full each night of dealers being arrested, no one is going to argue with you, getting out while you have your money and your freedom.'

'I can transfer money, say a hundred grand, to one of your accounts, how much do you expect to give me a return on that?'

Bring the cash here, no transferring money to my account. Twenty per cent per annum, and that's a minimum, look around you, where do you think the money came from to buy this apartment.'

He was rubbing his chin; he had lost over a quarter of a million in stocks and shares due to the credit crunch.

'I'm not comfortable bringing that amount of cash here; and property is risky; the value of this property must have gone down, over the last year.'

'Well you'll just have to get comfy then will you, I deal in strictly cash. You only lose money if you sell in a falling market, when the property market picks up, this block will increase in value, and you are getting rent, each month, plus where did the money come from in the first place, you've got to be realistic.'

His mobile rings, he picks it up from the circular glass table, and walks towards the panoramic window, and waves.

'Sorry about that Clive, it's just my friends making sure I'm alright, where was I?'

'It doesn't matter; you were talking about the ups and downs of the property market.'

'Of course, but never mind that when will you drop off the cash?'

'I'm confused, how will my returns go into my account? , I can't wander about with a holdall of cash,'

'The money will be put into your account from a holding company, we'll have all the necessary paperwork to back it up, and where is your account?'

'Jersey, under another name, I'll drop it off or text you the number of my account in St Hellier.'

'Just pop it into my letter box, flat G, and leave your mobile number, I'll keep you up to date.'

'I'm fine with that, what about the smack, can you get a hold of it, soon, I mean next week?'

'Contact your regular supplier and place an order; and who usually brings it and what car and registration they use and are they armed?'

'Whoa! I'm not getting involved in ripping them off; they'll know I'm somehow involved, no, no way, sorry.'

'It's too late, you're involved and you know too much, you're living now, but you'll be dead within twenty-minutes of leaving here. To put your mind at rest, we'll stop them before they get to your flat, or better still do you know where else they drop the heroin off, and I'm talking about kilos not grams.'

'I don't have a choice do I?'

'You came to me…nothing will be traced back to you, pay up front as normal, we'll take care of the rest,' he took out his notepad and handed it to him, 'the route and car and registration.'

He took a deep breath, and wrote on the note pad then handed it back to him.

He looked at the name in disbelief.

'Are you a hundred percent that this is the car registration?'

'Yes, I thought you would be surprised at who the dealer is, your face is a picture.'

'He's been lucky, up to now, someone is protecting him, he's not exactly low-profile is he, don't you worry, you'll benefit, as long as you keep your trap shut…don't have any drugs or large amounts of money in your flat, it'll just be a matter of time before you get caught, keep the money and drugs somewhere else.'

'I've not had any problems up to now, why change, I have you to protect me, don't I?'

'Do you? I never said anything about protecting you, I'm giving you good advice that's all, my friends wouldn't be so friendly, I think you should be somewhere else now, my friends will be up soon, you don't really want to meet them, stay in touch.'

'I'll get going then, I'll drop the details about the account into your letter box, later today.'

'Fine, be smart and you'll be safe, you know how to get out.'

He left the flat in a state of bewilderment, when he was on the pavement, he looked up and down the street, looking for thugs in a car, he couldn't help walking more quickly than normal, he wanted to turn round and see if he was being watched from the flat, but his car was near, he wanted to seek the safety that it would bring. This was not part of the plan, he thought he would be in control, the lie that he told about the heroin not being laced with anthrax, could have just saved his life.

McAveety sat in the chair pleased that he had reacted better than he thought, Clive putting him under surveillance was an embarrassment, he would have to be more careful, if Clive can hide in the shadows anyone can. He needed to think, he took out the page that Clive had written the name of the dealer, there must be fear amongst the dealers in the city, he was decidedly small compared to the dealers that had been executed, he was even using his own car, unless he was the delivery boy, and he was just talking himself up to Clive, that was a more realistic explanation, Clive had written solo beside the car, this signified no one accompanied him, he wasn't normally armed. He just had to formulate a plan, this would be for him and him only, to see if he varied the route, then pounce on him and take the money. Knowing where he lived he thought that Clive's flat in Broughty Ferry would be the last drop.

The dealer would come in through the small street that joined Strathern Road, he would ambush the car there, the dealer wouldn't offer any resistance. He wasn't concerned what fate awaited the dealer when he explained what had happened; it was an occupational hazard. Clive didn't realise it at the time, but he was now out of the drug trade, McAveety had kept his promise to his father.

***

Three days before Christmas, Historic Scotland had agreed in principle to release the grant money for the Silvery Tay Hotel, the workmanship was of an exacting standard. The email to Patrick Connelly was succinct; the money was pouring in from overseas investors, could he visit the building that they had spoken of earlier, and would Historic Scotland be minded to work with the company again, if the company was successful in securing the dilapidated building? Christmas had come early again; there was no reason why Historic Building could not be encouraged to acquiesce to the company's plans.

Also Catherine had called she had been impatient with the planning department, there were some problems with the additional car-wash plant, but it was not insurmountable, everything would be crossed and dotted by the middle of January, he had put her mind at rest. Then she segued into another pressing matter, one of Monty's friend's had gone missing, she had a brief friendship with him, the detectives had not mentioned this, but they were strongly hinting that he may have been involved in the murders of Monty and the others, they said they weren't sure if he had pulled the trigger, but they were sure that he was involved, they had heard that he was in Spain, had she heard this? She told them that she was not aware of this but she had heard through the grapevine that he had left in a hurry, according to his wife; he didn't come home and take any clothes or more importantly his passport. She asked the senior detective to come out into the garden, she was now speaking off-the-record and everything she was about to say was completely untrue and without foundation, she told him that he had serious money troubles he was in serious debt to people in Liverpool, that's all she knew, they were coming up to give him an ultimatum, that's all she had heard. The detective was pleased and disappointed at the same time; that was what he had precisely heard, then they returned to the house. Pat's luxuriant voice put her mind at ease that was the story he was hearing in the legal fraternity, he didn't think he would ever return to

Dundee. He told her to enjoy her Christmas, if he heard anything he would keep her informed.

Now she would enjoy Christmas, the detectives were just going round everyone who knew him, it was just routine. No guilt, no concern, Patrick Connelly knew what was going on in Dundee, he was not showing any signs of pressure, in fact he was dismissive, that was the all-clear for her...and Welsh. Money needed to be invested quickly and the returns re-invested, Patrick Connelly would advise or guide her along the complicated path. Thinking back to what Welsh had said she didn't understand it at the time, but it was less opaque now, was it him that disseminated the story that 'lover boy' was behind the hit on Monty and his cohorts? A crime of passion, Monty had to be removed, then 'lover boy' could ensconce himself in her life, and be party to Monty's riches?

***

That was his last shift, he threw his jacket onto the bed, his next start would the eighth of January, he was going out tonight with four other police officers, they could all be trusted, he wouldn't be sharing his thoughts with them on his personal dilemma. Notwithstanding, the violent death and mutilation of his friend. He had to keep the conversation light and cheery, no one was aware that he was friendly with GG even when GG was still a detective, GG insisted it would be best for both of them; that way they could share information.

He was dog tired, he would skip the shower and have it once he had woken from his afternoon slumber, it near three pm, a bit of toast then he would set the alarm for six, shower and be out for six-thirty meeting at the Social bar for seven, for something to eat then have a few drinks. Spreading the butter on his toast, he was feeling euphoric since no one had contacted him; maybe it was all off, it could have been if he had refused to carry out their orders he would have been shot there and then, he was taking reason out of an unreasonable situation. The more he thought about it the better he felt, much better and less doom laden. Normal service had been resumed; he was going with that theory, they had their pound of flesh, poor, poor GG.

He had learned his salutary lesson, crime was not for him, he had been given a second chance, and he knew that the Chinese were a merciful race, they were showing him, a westerner that they could be ruthless, but they were showing him mercy; yes that was it! Why would they dispose of an asset inside the police? It didn't make an iota of sense, they had made their position very clear, mess with us, and we can kill you. GG was the sad statistic; he didn't want to add to their total. Things were looking up, they would pay him a good price for inside information, it was suspected that there was an illegal gambling joint in Dundee, the Chinese community were suspected of operating it, the police were not looking too hard, the Chinese community were law-abiding, any malcontents were dealt with internally by elders; no one wanted to guide them to political correct modern methods. Let sleeping dogs lie. GG gave him that information, he had seen Feeney coming out of a house owned by a Chinese businessman, dressed in casual clothes, he gave the impression that they had met many times before but didn't expand, he never thought to ask. The new casino in the Westport was a roaring success, gamblers were coming from other parts of Scotland, but for all its good points, gamblers who had ill-gotten gains from untaxed and illegal businesses, being seen at a plush bone-fide casino caused them deep unrest. The phantom illegal gambling house or den would still have customers who were legitimate but camera shy, they would not be unperturbed standing at the roulette table with thugs and thieves, and the odds were better at the illegal casino. The illegal gambling den could still stand proudly cheek by jowl with the new and shiny casino

He struggled to finish the toast, a sure sign that he was becoming weary, GG was never in the distance from his thoughts. He had been nurtured and educated by him, he drove him around the hotspots of Dundee and shown where the dealers stayed where they stashed the drugs and the youths who acted as runners. The Butterburn multis were seeing new tenants arriving from the Baltic states they would be picked up at the pub; John Barleycorns at six am, they worked hard and sent money home, some enjoyed the construction industry, others didn't, the naked racism shown and shouted at them on a daily basis, were hurtful and diminished their views of the citizens of Dundee. Lenny was horrified to see who was behind the building sites, men who traded in anything as long as it sang to their tune; money. GG told him of the plan to rip-off the dealers, it was dangerous but the rewards would easily outstrip the danger, GG would not entertain the 'what if' that Lenny voiced.

There was nothing to worry about. But that was then, today he had plenty to worry about, he hoped the alcohol would dull the feeling of malevolence that he saw in strangers faces.

The orange juice was nice and cold, he couldn't force himself to finish the toast, his weight was dropping, nearly a stone, his colleagues had mentioned this he said that he was going to the gym and running more, even in the snow. The worry was taking its toll on his physical and mental health; and he didn't have any peace of mind. His mind fluctuated between abject depression and instant euphoric thoughts.

If only they made contact and gave him the deadly instructions, he could live with the consequences, he just wanted the uncertainty and angst to disappear, and he could kill someone, if his own life could be retained. The yawn came unannounced, he tried to stifle it, but it was impossible, his jaw ached. Time for bed, he took the toast and dumped it in the bin which was overflowing and needing emptied, he would do this chore when he woke up. He became annoyed with himself for not switching on the electric blanket, this helped him soothe into a sleep of some sorts. He moved into the bedroom and switched it on, it wouldn't take long to heat up, in the meantime he went to the wardrobe and took out the clothes that he would be wearing, he felt so tense, he didn't want to climb into bed with anxiety still in his stomach, he would go for a long hot shower, he hoped this would aid his sleep and empty his mind of dark thoughts. The shower he took was longer than he planned, the steaming hot water was more comforting than his warm bed, if only he could sleep standing up, refreshed but also dead on his feet, he turned the shower off, the steam filled the bathroom, but he could still make out the dark circles surrounding his eyes. Once dried he was ready for sleep, he crept into bed, the heat welcoming him, he pulled the pillow down, his eyes came awake, he pulled the object from the sanctuary of the pillow; it was a gun with silencer attached.

***

The car he would be intercepting was parked in the Sainsbury car park, this was not part of the plan, he waited on him coming out. After ten minutes he returned to the car. The car park was busy, he inched forward through the snow, his prey unaware he was being stalked, out onto the dual -carriageway, he was certainly not taking any anti-surveillance techniques, but instead of turning left towards Broughty Ferry and to Clive's flat, he moved into the left hand lane and was driving towards Whitfield, he followed him into a cul-de-sac and he parked, he was expecting him to go to one of the houses, he didn't, he waited at the side of the road, and pulled out his mobile.

A pizza delivery van came into the cul-de-sac, the van

stopped, the delivery driver came out with a large pizza box and handed it to him, he opened the lid of the box and smiled, the driver handed him the keys of the van, he went to the van and placed the pizza box on the passenger seat, he didn't lock the door. He returned to his car, where he pulled out a plastic shopping bag and returned to the van. The pizza delivery man went into a house. The van did a u turn and drove towards Broughty Ferry, after five minutes he was convinced it was going deliver something more potent than a pizza to Clive, he took a right turn then waited on him coming down the hill towards Clive's flat, he parked the car in the adjoining street, the van would stop at the give-way sign. No nerves were being shredded, he had in his mind what he would do, simple is best. He waited under the moonlit shadow of the overhanging tree, the headlights of the van came over the brow of the hill, he stepped back into the comforting blackness, he heard the car slowing down, it was almost at a stop now, he stepped forward and yanked open the passenger door, the driver instinctively drew back in fear, he lifted the plastic bag and the pizza box, the car sped forward with the door still wide open, fear of being shot convinced the driver not to argue. Slowly he crossed the road his large footprints in the snow, he wasn't showing any signs of concern.

  He placed the pizza box in the boot, he kept hold of the plastic bag, inside the bag was heroin wrapped in cling film, he took the four packets out and sprinkled the contents on the pavement, it mixed in with the grit without too much effort. The plastic bag he placed in the yellow grit bin, and then he drove home to enjoy the pizza.

  At home he placed the pizza box on the kitchen table, he opened the lid slowly; no pizza, he wasn't moved to tears; he took out the contents all neatly packed together; 20 thousand pounds. He took the money and placed it in the wardrobe, the pizza box would need to go to the communal bin where it would feel at home with the students' pizza boxes. He crushed the box and took it down to the rear of the building; his night's work was complete. At the table enjoying his moment of triumph, he sipped the beer; delivering heroin from a pizza delivery van was ingenious.

***

Staring at the ceiling didn't sate the fear that gripped him; all the optimistic scenarios that settled in his head seemed ludicrous. The moment he dreaded was dawning, the gun, silencer and bullets had been delivered, no signs of forced entry, this lot could probably enter Fort Knox with aplomb. The anvil in his stomach was not ready to be moved, he recognised the taste in his mouth; helplessness, he was his own judge and juror, now he had to take the next step; an executioner.

The mobile on the dressing table rang out with the ominous ring tone, he moved at speed from the comfort and warmth of his bed. The voice didn't ease his whirring, tortured mind.

'Has the tooth fairy been?'

'You could say that,' he felt the chill of his body match his fear stricken voice.

'That's good…how are you feeling…nervous?'

'I'll be glad when it's over, when does it happen?'

'Soon, son, soon, it'll soon be over, then you can get your life back together, you're doing us and yourself a favour.'

'How did you manage to deliver the goods, with me being at work?'

'That's part of the service, just leave it in the same place and we'll retrieve it, don't worry about that, just leave it in exactly the same place, that's important.'

'Will it be before Christmas or after Christmas?'

'I'll call you soon, 'bye.'

The fear had gone, no longer was his mind congested,

after the hit, he would return the gun under the pillow, they would return to his flat and take the gun away. They could just call the police and give them the information, where would that leave him in Perth prison for the next twenty years? He was insistent, 'the same place.' He just didn't care anymore, his mind was emptied, he returned to the sanctuary of his warm bed, the gun under his pillow didn't cause a ripple of anxiety, he fell into a deep sleep, pointless worrying. Four hours later the alarm awoke him, he felt refreshed and ravenous, he instantly recalled the phone call, he just accepted that was the price they were extracting from him, for stealing and disrupting their business, how would he have reacted?, he knew how GG would have reacted, he sprung out of bed determined to have something substantial to eat, but not too heavy as he had been unable to keep it in his stomach; a frozen pizza would do, it would not put him off his meal later. He went to the fridge freezer, took one out and opened the microwave door, in the oven was an envelope, he took it out and opened it, it was a photograph of a man in obvious distress, he was tied to a chair his clothes had been removed, his chest was blood strewn, his face the same; it was GG.

CHAPTER SIX

He looked through the spy hole, he opened the door instantly, he breezed past him, he closed the door and followed him into the kitchen.

'What's up?'

'I don't know but something's definitely up, I had a visit from Pat Connelly, someone is watching my movements an ex-detective, who happened to be an ex-partner of Feeney.'

'Why is he watching you?'

'I don't know, here's his photograph, do you recognise him,' he handed the black and white photo graph to him. Jameson shook his head and handed it back quickly

'Can't recall him from anyplace.'

'Are you sure...think!' his voice had a sharp edge.

'Positive, I've got a good memory.'

'He was in Dubai the same time as you, any boozers or parties there you might have got into a conversation?'

'Definitely...I don't recognise him, what was he doing in Dubai?'

'A security consultant...it doesn't matter, as long as you're sure you haven't met him that puts my mind at rest. Has Pat been in touch with you recently?'

'Just about the Silvery Tay Hotel and other business, he never mentioned this detective; did you say what his name is?'

'Eddings, Valentine Eddings.'

'That's an unusual name for a detective. He must have retired from the police if he was working in Dubai.'

'Not only is that an unusual name, he had an unusual character flaw for a detective...'

'...Bit of a boozer?' He laughed.

'No...he was honest, no fiddling overtime sheets or expenses.'

'Sounds like he should be in Parliament.'

'You are still a bit of a comedian...I'll get going, don't

mention any of this to Pat, okay?'

'Sure…you didn't say why he was watching you?'

'That's right,' he stood up and walked out of the kitchen closing the door behind him.

Jameson was not perturbed; he had the best protection he could imagine. From a senior officer tipped to be a future Chief Constable of Tayside. It was always said in jest by other officers out with of Dundee that Dundee had the best policemen that money could buy. This was not an accountant's appraisal, this was from experience; he had paid Welsh a large dowry himself, but he wasn't complaining.

Welsh drove back from Jameson's house, questions had been answered but not emphatically, Jameson, didn't know anything, that just left Pat Connelly, his visit to his house had been an exploratory fishing expedition, unsuccessful on Connelly's part, but illuminating for him. Catherine, had she said something about his visit to her house, when she wanted her unwanted bed mate removed? Maybe that was why Connelly had asked if there was anything to connect him to any of the executed dealers, he had to become more careful with his dealings with Connelly and to some extent with Jameson. This editor was becoming an immovable object in not only his brain but in the publics' assertion. He eased his tightened fingers from the steering wheel; as long as Catherine kept quiet he had nothing to worry about.

Gary Spence he trusted, he had done him a favour, there was obviously a whispering campaign gathering pace, no doubt it started from the higher echelons in the murder squad, they had made no arrests, and nothing seemed to indicate that any arrests were imminent, tell some journalist that there were suspicions that there was a whiff of corruption emanating from the drug squad, the spotlight would change to the drug squad, he knew how the game was being played. The Chief Constable was still annoyed that his house which had been fully double

-glazed at the taxpayers' expense because of a 'security issue that could only benefit certain terrorists, if his double glazing was discussed in public.' Feeney was widely acknowledged to be the source behind the tip-off to the journalist from Edinburgh; he didn't trust cub reporters that worked for the local press. Now he had two enemies, the Chief Constable and the local press. He was in Feeney's shoes, but the antipathy still continued against the drugs squad, that encouraged a siege mentality, Welsh kept stoking the fire. In his favour as head of the drug squad he had his biggest ally beside him, a montage of dealers that were behind bars, the murder squad were anemic; they had leads, but no arrests. He had to come up with a big fish that needed to be landed accompanied by a major drugs cache. He had someone in mind, someone who was semi-retired but was still generating funds from the drug trade; he was a CI near the top of his list, he only came to Welsh when he needed another dealer to go on holiday for a couple of years, he would now return the favour he would mention that information had come to him that he was to be targeted, arrested and jailed. Someone had information that had been extremely accurate, he would try to delay the arrest, in return he would have to help him, if the information was undisputable, he could convince his superiors to switch to a juicier target. That would be the story; he would drive over to St Andrews tomorrow and speak to him. His daughter was soon to graduate, she had to concentrate fully on her forthcoming exams, and she had just become engaged to the only son of a Lord; it could be a short engagement.

The phone rang on his desk, the senior detective needed to speak to him, outwith office hours, could he make it? Normally, he would have said to him no, and be sarcastic by offering the lame excuse, he had dealers to arrest, haven't you murderers to arrest as well? These weren't normal times, he had to see what was on his mind, for his sake as well, they agreed to meet up, he suggested a café or somewhere else, he told him the Discovery ship, then they would go for a walk, long or short it depended on the content of the conversation.

At ten pm, he waited in his car at the Olympia car park, a smattering of snow was blowing through, a car drew up behind him in the deserted car park, he didn't recognise him, he put his hat and gloves on, and left the car, the other driver followed suit. Welsh started walking towards the car, he opened the conversation.

'I won't ask how you are; you look like shit, feeling the pressure?

'My wife said that to me when I was leaving the house, I wish I could say the same to you, but you're looking well.' They were both facing the Silvery Tay Hotel.

'They're doing a fine job, a pity no local builder had the balls to buy the place.'

'Do you mind if we walk Paul, rather than talk about a building?'

'Sure…follow me,' he led the way towards the Hilton hotel, so what's on your mind?'

'The execution of the dealers, has hit a wall, pressure is being applied to us daily, and things are getting desperate. What have you heard?'

'The same as you, detectives becoming marginalized, cliques forming, Chinese whispers, drug dealers were behind the murders, they were from Liverpool.

'Or Glasgow, detectives from the murder squad are being paid by dealers to look the other way, detectives from the drug squad were involved in luring them to their deaths, delete as appropriate, and that's the more plausible theories,' he was laughing.

'I've heard all of them and more, but that's not why I asked to meet you, this is going to be difficult…I believe I'm being investigated from other detectives, and I have proof.'

He stopped walking.

'Have you done anything wrong?'

'I could go to jail.'

'Keep walking, what have you done, that you think could go to jail?'

'Monty, had my mobile number stored in his phone, I told him to delete it, he didn't, I took money from him a couple of months ago, I gave him information about another detective, personal information.'

'Who was the detective? And had he been blackmailed?

'I don't know if he did blackmail the detective, it was Gary Spence.'

'What information did you give Monty?'

***

The commercial agent was beginning to believe that Dundee was coming out of the economic slump, the long wide shed at the periphery of the docks had been modernised at great expense, tenants had been enquiring about bespoke commercial units, the ones they had for lease were not large or suffice for their needs. The small family run company went into debt for the first time, the father resigned and hand handed the profitable company over to the oldest son, he had been telling his father for three years that the company should have at least thirty-percent leverage, his father was quiet and introspective the opposite from his son, who had a MBA from Harvard, his son was impatient to take over the reins from the father, he was being railroaded into early retirement. The logistics and storage company never carried any leverage, he quietly pointed out to his son that leverage was another name for debt, and debt is an uncompromising mistress; she is loathed and feared. The son ignored these injudicious comments, he always put his arm around his father's small stature, 'things were different now dad, we have to borrow and expand, we need to purchase or construct large multi-purpose storage units, the building industry can't throw up houses as quickly as buyers want them, people are selling their houses and moving into rental accommodation sometimes up to a year, they need a clean, secure environment to store their furniture, build them and they will come.'

The father's argument that the construction industry was a bubble, what if it burst? They would have units, purpose built units standing empty gathering interest payments with no income coming in, what other use would the hangar type units be used for?' The son went into a monologue, using every business cliché ever thought of, it only caused more tensions, the father told the son, he thought that his business plan was flawed and speculative, if he saw that the bank would as well, and the bank would reject his plea for leverage. The son replied he had a meeting earlier in the week, the business manager thought his business plan was sound and viable, it needed the father's application and monies would be released. Instead of being angry about the son going behind his back, he would be charitable he had been out manoeuvred, maybe it his business ethic were consigned to another era, his reputation had taken decades to form, it might be tarnished and torn to shreds if his portentous view came to pass.

He handed over the company to his son, for a knockdown price of five million, it was worth fifteen million, he thought this was an inflated value; he valued it at nine million. The papers were signed and sealed, his son offered to keep him on as a consultant, he refused to take up the position and eye-watering salary, his garden was more tempting. Then the buying spree began in earnest, land was bought and units were erected, the almost invisible company was becoming more prominent in the business and public view, antithesis in his father's judgement.

Two years later, the cold, bitter and unforgiving wind

of recession blew up the Tay, knocking business plans for six, a year later the banks were in trouble, they had not done due diligence on business loans, leverage dried up. The business had put too much faith and hope into the storage units, the son thought he was getting ahead of other competitors by buying out established removal firms at well above the market rate. The fleet of old and new removal Vans and Lorries were stored in one of the units near the docks, a testament to his hubris and ignorance; his father's garden by contrast was blooming. He was now in a buyer's market, some units were sold off at less than half what he had paid for them, he needed the cash to finance the interest payments, he couldn't acknowledge the siren whisper of his father's words late at night and early morning, 'a bubble market always bursts, leaving behind broken companies and promises.'

The muesli lay undisturbed, he was unshaven, even though noon was approaching, he didn't want to venture into Broughty Ferry, the unforgiving looks of failure he felt on his neck made him uncomfortable; he couldn't see a way to stop falling into the financial abyss. The assets of the company were diminishing, the income was drying up, leases were coming up for renewal, and businesses would be looking for more favourable terms and more flexible leases. The superstructure at the docks was the jewel in the crown; it was the largest unit which could potentially ease the company's financial woes. Some of the potential tenants were asking him for more and more discounts, it was tempting even though it would make the company more solvent in the eyes of the bank, but anyone can sell a tenner for a fiver. He just had to hold his nerve, and hope the company becalmed instead of sinking in the choppy financial ocean. All he needed was one company to lease the structure, that's all he needed. Plenty of interest was being shown for the unit, some offered to buy but again wanted deep discounted, he didn't bite, another call came as he was passing , aimless time staring out of the window, playing business solutions in his head, he would be meeting someone at two o clock at the unit. No enthusiasm could be mustered, but he had to shower and shave he was looking desperate, he had to conjure up a different persona, he didn't need the figures at hand they were all stored in his head, the papers were to make him accentuate business acumen. Driving along Broughty Ferry he pulled into the car wash, his BMW was splashed with the salt off the streets, it was money he grudged but they did a good job of his car.

  At the unit he saw the prospective tenant standing patiently outside her 4x4, he didn't recognise her, he smiled as he walked towards her, and apologised for being late. Her icy stare melted he was very handsome and slim; he couldn't surely be from Dundee. The two massive doors opened obediently when he activated the small hand held device.   When the doors were fully opened the lights came on incrementally. It reminded her of a baddies lair in a Bond film. The assortment of Lorries and vans standing in line like a regiment of soldiers added to her commercial plan. He went on to show her how the unit could be sub-divided into four sections, either by remote control or easily movable partitions.

  She insisted on seeing the partitions been moved into place then returned to their original section. They were now nearing the end of their conversation laden walk, he opened the rear doors, a ramp ran from the wide doors to the docks, the icy wind entered the unit; it didn't seem to unnerve her, or halt her asking every conceivable question from the business rates to the electricity supplier. He pressed the remote to close the doors, she told him to wait just now, she took out her mobile and filmed the docks, and then stepped out onto the ramp keeping her mobile as steady as she could; she spun round and filmed the massive structure, and asked the doors be closed then opened again. Her blonde hair was whipped into her face by the whistling freezing wind; she stopped filming and returned to the protection of the structure. He was taking nothing for granted, but she seemed as if she was genuinely interested, however, he had seen that look before on prospective tenants, they all wanted the lease for a peppercorn rent, desperate he was but he wasn't stupid he had to hold his nerve, this structure would save the business or be an anchor round his neck, which he wouldn't be able to cast off. Then she asked the question he never anticipated.

'Would you like to go for a coffee to discuss the terms of the lease, I'm very interested, and I'm sure you will be as well after I put a business proposal to you.'

'Sure,' he replied hesitantly and he was blushing, 'where do you want to go, I'll pay.'

'A gentleman as well; things as looking up, if we don't move soon we'll freeze to death.'

'Sorry…okay, go to your car, I'll lock up here, I won't be long.'

'I'll wait, the Carlton Hotel is nice, is that okay?'

'That'll be fine, anywhere would be fine.' They both watched the doors close then walked to the front of the structure, all lights were switched off and the massive doors closed with near silence.

'You lead and I'll follow,' he said.

'Fine, you won't get lost now,' she teased.

'I hope not, but it wouldn't be the first time,' he replied as he climbed into his car, trying to subdue his excitement.

At the Carlton they agreed the terms of the lease and signed the relevant documents, subject to a final analysis of their respective solicitors. They spoke for another hour about themselves, nothing controversial, just polite conversation. He couldn't wait to speak to his father. She was content on business and on a personal level, when the lease was signed he let out a sigh of relief, he confessed that his business judgement was misjudged or naïve, he had been overtly over ambitious, according to his father, now, looking back he was correct, the company was producing profits as much as he had forecast, but when the recession was over the company would be in good shape, he had all his units ready and his fleet of lorries were also in place. He hadn't asked her the purpose of her business, it didn't concern him, and he didn't want to come across as intrusive.

It was Catherine who brought up her business as he hadn't asked; this would be beneficial to his company as well as her own. She was bringing in pre-owned cars from England, it was in her interest to buy as many as possible as this business practice achieved a big discount, her plan was two -pronged, she would transport the cars up by ship into Dundee, minutes later the cars could be in the unit ready for sale either in the unit or up at her garage. If he was to lease or buy car transporters; that would be a cash generating business, other garages would hire his company to ferry cars down south.

She was a woman that didn't possess a Harvard MBA, but her business plan was without a flaw, maybe his father was right, 'to know the business world you had to work in business, to see what was what, sitting in a classroom only made people arrogant.' His father was the most humble human being he knew in business. His father would have warmed to Catherine, she spoke and thought like him. Plans were made to meet at her solicitor's office Patrick Connelly, he agreed, but tonight he would be on the auction websites' checking out the rate for cars being transported, and then see if he could pick up a car- transporter that could bring them up and down from Dundee to England. The compulsory single payment in advance for six months of the lease would be able to bring his payments up to date, the bank were applying pressure. The main dealers of cars would be worth emailing, they may be looking for a regular and local logistic company.

Everything was fitting into place, the bitter wind of economic change had to change soon, he aimed to be there when the wind dropped and had some warmth. He noticed she didn't wear any rings, but she was no one's fool, even though it could take as long as four months to organise the shipping, she wanted the unit from Monday, he just hoped the solicitor wouldn't try to achieve more favourable terms before he handed over the cheque, which he wanted to hand over personally to his business manager at the bank. He couldn't afford to deviate from the verbally agreed and signed documents even though there was a seven day cooling off period, which didn't incur any cost to either party. He left her enjoying the coffee, she didn't want to venture out now that the snow was coming down, she would leave later when it subsided. He wanted to reply, 'but that's what a 4x4 is meant for these conditions,' but couldn't risk it.

The roll-on roll-off ferry was planned to be operational in February, she would use her wily feminine charm, and regular shipment of cars from England, maybe even Europe to bring to Dundee, to seek preferential rates. Her next meeting with Patrick Connelly would be interesting and lucrative, would she be allowed to sell and valet cars in the cavernous unit at the docks? Patrick Connelly had sent her a text pointing out that a former garage near the Kingsway was up for sale it had permission to convert to a car-wash, it was on an arterial route, he knew a company from Glasgow who specialised in constructing and installing the car wash plant, she planned to visit the site and envision if she could make it a viable concern. The site was being used as an unofficial car park; this gave her a guide to see how many cars could queue to enter the car wash. Traffic lights were positioned twenty metres from the entrance of the garage, this could encourage passing trade, if they were stopped at the lights; she was definitely interested if the price was not too prohibitive, she would be slowly withdrawing from the drug trade, slowly but not completely.

Jonathon Capeworth would help her maintain the distribution of heroin from England to Dundee; unwittingly. Quality cars would be sourced and brought up by ship and lorry, the cars on the ship would be clean due to the strict and thorough customs procedures. However, the cars on the transporter would have heroin secreted within the bodywork. She was injecting much needed cash into Jonathon's leveraged logistic company; he was returning an unattended favour. Parallel and in tandem with this invisible business she would have her car sales, car valet and car wash businesses, all cleaning the tainted money from the invisible business that she didn't record on her tax forms to her accountant. That were her tasks for today taking care of, she wanted to clear herself from her former beau, the dense but lovable Monty, who had the beautiful scent of money excreting from every pore, but had no business sense.

It was the perfect opportunity to move on, her house would be placed on the market, discreetly at first, she was hoping Patrick Connelly could arrange a quick and quiet sale.

The past had to be removed from her memory bank, it was time to move on, the universal advice from her divorced and drink addled friends. She would indeed be moving on, and expanding her businesses, she had seen a plot of land in Broughty Ferry near her friends, she planned to build a modern but expensive house on the plot, which had magnificent views over the Tay and the hills of Fife. In Monifieth she had purchased a site that had at one time had a thriving garage on it, but it struggled from the recession of eighty-one, it had never recovered, the owner failed to secure permission to raze the garage and office and erect luxury apartments, it was placed on the market with no planning permission; she snapped it up.

The site was purchased blind, she had went against her better judgement, Patrick Connelly dismissed her concerns about the previous owner failing to be granted planning permission, he told her that the owner was myopic, there was absolutely no chance of permission being granted for building apartments, and just as well, the flats if built would not be as valuable as he envisaged due to the economic downturn, the council had did him a massive favour but he didn't appreciate this. However, his information was that the council couldn't see any problem if it was turned into a car-wash. She would have the market sewn up, north, south, east and west, and with the volume of traffic crisscrossing the city, her cash flow would be formidable. No one not even her closest confidante needed to know her business assets. Patrick Connelly would not be party of her invisible import and distribution business, in which the profit dwarfed all her legitimate businesses.

Patrick Connelly had offered to supply the builder to erect her new house, when Patrick offered no-one turned him down, that meant he had guaranteed you a good deal and at a fair price, the builder he had in mind built bespoke homes for his affluent clientele, Catherine had joined the exclusive if secretive cabal, no one knew each other but they were aware of each other, sometimes one would see someone leaving or entering Patrick's practice, no words would be spoken, just a slight smile or acknowledgment of the eyes. It was not too dissimilar to the drug trade.

Building her house would start in the first week of March, the house and landscaped grounds would be completed by the end of July; guaranteed. Dealing with Patrick for the business of installing the car wash equipment and the builder of her house was to the benefit of all parties, monies would be released at certain stages of the erection of her house, on the other hand, all monies for plant, equipment and labour had to be paid in advance and in full, Connelly saw the alarm running behind her wide-eyes, as ever, he used his Irish charm to sedate her fears, 'by paying up front, she would be getting the ultimate discount, and thus was the reason, the company would be experiencing cash flow difficulties and would be going into administration, the monies from her would allow the owner to start up another business that could benefit her and himself, but that was in the future, did that put her intelligent mind at ease?'

She was still showing slight uneasiness, Connelly went into overdrive, he went into the drawer of dreams as he called it, and took out literature showing the true costs minus vat, and the cost the contractor was offering; there was no comparison. It was buy two get one free, literally, she sought no other incentive, Connelly knew people who operated within the law, but had no moral compass or compassion for creditors. However, even though she was sourcing and distributing heroin, and had taken a human life, she still felt she was more moral than the contractor.

The Evening Chronicle was taking a less belligerent view of the drug squad, positive stories were climbing through the cracks, the drug squad had a tougher job than the Evening Chronicle had realised. Government sources had been in touch; the executions of the dealers were planned and executed by persons who lived outside Dundee, and it could not be ruled out from another country. The source had spoken to the editor for an hour; the paper couldn't elaborate any further as it could compromise operational procedures. Eddings was puzzled, he reluctantly accepted that there could be corrupt detectives, he had no other choice when the two females were arrested and convicted ; it seemed very strange that the editor was taking a softer, more sober

378

view of the drug squad and the police in general. He was totally mystified, had the editor been persuaded to take this surprising stance or something from his past may make the public change their views of him? He smelled a rodent. Welsh had been under his watchful eye, nothing seemed to be out of kilter in his life, he was married and didn't live beyond his means, he had sold his house in the west end when he had been promoted to head of the drug squad, he purchased a house in Wormit not beyond his salary, the only thing that tingled his spine was that Patrick Connelly had visited his house in Wormit, he didn't know if he was a regular visitor, it could have been innocent, however, it could have more sinister connotations.

Morag had invited him to lunch at the DCA he would ask her why her friend had been changing tact on the corrupt police officers to how they were doing a fine job in difficult circumstances, without the sarcasm that would be difficult. All and all, he had time to look over his notes from Dubai and in Dundee, he believed Morag was half right, Welsh was up to something illegal, why else would he use another name on a credit card and purchase property in Dubai, he couldn't have financed that from his salary, and his wife wouldn't know about his alter ego. But, he was behind the murder of his senior officer? He couldn't accept that. Tomorrow before lunch, he was going into the bank where he hoped Welsh's alter ego would have a bank account, if he didn't he was at a dead end, if he had an account this could be his yellow brick road.

When Morag had phoned and arranged the luncheon date she was in an excitable mood, she had told him that the person behind the marina in Fife was his old boss Mr Madni, she didn't know if the Daves were with him. He was surprised to hear this, no one had contacted him; he thought Dundee didn't hanker after them, they would be in South Africa for Christmas, or at least he hoped that was the case. She had other news for him, but he had to be patient, she would tell him tomorrow. It would be an interesting lunch tomorrow, they had plenty of topics to discuss, he hoped Welsh had an account at the bank, that would be a start and it could lead him to the reason behind the death of Feeney.

The following morning Eddings went into the bank, his contact was looking fit to burst, Eddings felt the heat of excitement run up to his collar; he must have information on the mysterious Trevor Perkins. He waited silently in the queue, he expected the bank to be quiet at eleven, but it was busy with customers withdrawing large sums from their account to celebrate Christmas even though many were atheists, strange, very strange. His eyes never left the teller, he was next in line, the customer was talking excitedly about her Christmas break in Majorca, how she was looking forward to some sunshine, she couldn't stand the snow it got her down. Eddings was tempted to butt in and tell her that Palma airport was closed due to a snow storm; the reporter said more snow was expected over the next few days, but he couldn't, though he wanted to. Now it was his turn, he asked to withdraw a hundred pounds, the teller smiled counted out the money and handed over a sheaf of paper it was a statement.

He turned the statement round so Eddings could see it, he could see an array of figures printed, the teller was tapping his finger on the top of the statement on the name; Trevor Perkins, this would be worth a healthy payment from Eddings. He took the money and the statement, the teller wished him a happy Christmas, Eddings winked at him, that's all he needed; he would see him in the Ship Inn where the senior tellers went for their Christmas evening meal; Eddings would be there tonight.

It was still too early to go to the DCA, he would go for a coffee, he went to the Pancake Place, and sat at the rear of the café, he would sit and read The Courier, but his eyes would be on the bank statement of Trevor Perkins, it would make interesting reading.

The waitress came over and took his order, he opened the newspaper and folded it in half and lay it on the table, when the waitress returned with the coffee and left, he brought out the statement and placed it on the newspaper, it was indeed interesting reading. First of all Trevor Perkins stayed in London in Notting Hill, his account was from the Private Client section of the subsidiary bank, small and exclusive, large sums of money were being managed in a portfolio of funds; stocks, shares and currency exchange. Trevor was indeed a clever Trevor. Payments to his credit card company ranged from fifteen thousand to eighty thousand. Welsh must be doing a lot of overtime; he thought sarcastically, the balance of his account was showing three hundred thousand and twenty pounds. Where was the money coming from and where was it going and what was he buying? It certainly wasn't items from EBay.

The executed dealers, was he paid to help set them up from a rival consortium or individual? The monthly payments going into his account were large and excessive for a Chief Constable never mind a middle ranking officer, were the payments pay-offs from dealers? He couldn't think of anything else. Perhaps it was money from his properties in Dubai, did he still own them and rent them out?

Four cups of coffee and his strategy was now very different from this morning, Morag couldn't tell him anything more, it could be time to cut contact, he would be in a clearer frame of mind once he met her in the DCA, Trevor Perkins would not be raised, he might guide her away from Welsh, he didn't know how but he would try to bring in some other person. The place was staring to fill up, or maybe it was because the snow was falling heavily and more frequent, he smiled seeing the early morning shoppers come in with snow on their heads and coats. It was time to make the short journey to the DCA, Morag might be able to explain the editor's less belligerent stance towards the drug squad of late; if it came to it he would bring it up himself.

On Reform Street the wind was blowing the snow from the direction of the City Square and Caird Hall, he put his head down and made his way to the DCA, the city centre was busy, the weather wasn't keeping the shoppers at home, he heard a couple chatting at Boots, he had heard that the buses would be going off for a couple of hours. Eddings shook his head, a wee bit of snow and Dundee grinds to a halt, it was different in his day.

There had been a car accident at the Perth Road, a lorry spreading grit had pranged a car in front, it was gridlock now, cars were slithering trying to manoeuvre around the stricken vehicles, horns were blasting from impatient drivers, he crossed the road, and glanced back at the scene of turmoil, a bus was parked outside the Queen's Hotel, a wedding was taking place; it was a gathering of the clans, the bus was adding to the chaos from the vehicles that were involved in the accident at the bottom of the Perth Road, some of the guests emerging from the bus were taking exception to the vitriol abuse towards the contingent going into the Queen's.

A couple of them were being held back by other guests, from going over to the occupants of the taxi telling them to get the bus moved…now! He passed them refusing to make eye-contact the aggressive behaviour was spreading amongst the guests, woman were starting to get involved, he could hear the distinct west of Scotland accent, he quickened his pace, screams bellowed out he refused to look round, guests were over at the stationary taxi, the door had been yanked open, a female was being dragged out by her hair, another passenger from the taxi came out from the other side to give assistance to his female friend, he pulled the kilted guest to the ground and was kneeling on top of him, hitting him repeatedly, other guests joined in and attacked the passenger from the taxi, the wailing of sirens coming down the Perth Road, he couldn't resist a brief furtive glance. He wasn't disappointed; the melee were shouting and screaming insults, they were fighting amongst themselves, the police cars came down the Perth Road, at a snail's pace, behind them the ambulance was still flashing its lights and the sound of the siren was giving him a headache, now he could understand why Morag refused to venture into Dundee; it was inhabited by morons.

He blamed it on the snow and his reasoning was cogent, if it wasn't snowing the lorry gritting the streets wouldn't be out, thus avoiding crashing into the car, and there wouldn't be a tail back from the Perth Road. The taxi would have been able to pass the bus at the Queen's Hotel without too much difficulty, result no car crash or violent mob from the bus attacking the occupants of the taxi. Yes, it was definitely the fault of the snow. But, unfortunately, he couldn't bring this up at the lunch with Morag, she would be shocked then she would rail against Dundee, again. If only he had left the Pancake Place five or ten minutes later he wouldn't have to walk past the DCA and the Queen's, to waste time, it was definitely the fault of the snow. He crossed the road onto the other side and watched the police herd the guests into the hotel, insults were being hurled at the police, they would need back up, the kilted guests were goading the police to arrest the taxi passenger who was being treated by the paramedics, he had head wounds the snow was splattered with his blood, it was him and her that started it. Obviously.

He quickly moved passed the bloody mayhem, across the street at the entrance to the DCA he saw Morag view the scene open mouthed and shaking her head. Moving quickly across the road, he heard the bystanders gave their glib interpretation what had happened. In a group of four workmen, he heard one of them say he had heard a bang, the guy being treated had been shot in the head, from a hit man in the taxi, Morag saw him and repeated what the workman had said, he couldn't disguise his disgust at her repeating arrant nonsense, he grabbed her by the arm and moved towards the DCA.

'What's the matter with you?'

'You, you should know better, a gun man shooting someone in the head!'

'Oh, I suppose you know what really happened then…and let go of my arm, you're not a detective now!'

He let go her arm, they walked into the DCA in an awkward silence; she smiled at the staff member who took them to the table. Eddings apologised, and then explained what triggered the incident. She was crestfallen and apologised for raising her voice, they both laughed. Eddings understood why the workman jumped to the conclusion about the hit- man, with the murders of Feeney and the executions of the dealers, coupled with the hysterical headlines in the newspapers; Dundee was gripped with fear and conspiracy theories.

Then he caused her to laugh when he explained his snow caused it all theory. She laughed and praised him for his avant-garde thinking

Then she brought up the inevitable slur on Dundee, 'if this is what took place on a mundane day, at the week-end was it AK 7 happy hour?'
He didn't attempt counter the accusation; he just agreed with her, she ordered lunch for them both and then told him the reason for the lunch date, she had news for him. She was taking up the post of managing director of the new marina and leisure development in Fife; Mr Madni's new project.

'The offer must have come as a shock…Dubai coming to Dundee who would have thought that would happen?'

'You can safely assume I was knocked sideways. He sent a car round and whisked me over to St Andrews, over lunch he offered me the position, talk about making a dull day shine.'

He was pleased for her, the pain of Dubai had been washed away by one of the protagonists that caused financial meltdown, and in a perverse way was bringing her long-lost happiness back, she didn't tell him she was overjoyed, she couldn't disguise it.

'And what's his business model then?'

'Same as usual, to make pots of money, Dubai has made him think more and act less hastily, he had let go all his business advisors except one, the one who has been with him since he started his construction company thirty years ago, it was him that scoured the globe for stable investments, and it was him that suggested that I would be the perfect candidate, I know the area, and I know the clients from Dubai, they will be able to put their trust in me, but that's not the only reason I asked you to lunch, I want to offer you the position as my P.A.'

He raised his eyebrow, and scowled.

'No thanks, personal assistant, I've got that position at home I'm a husband.'

'You won't be fetching me coffee or things like that, you'll be meeting clients at the airport and helping them settle in and feel welcome, the salary is forty k.'

'That's a very tempting offer, what did you say your salary was?'

'Ha bloody ha! I didn't. I won't tell you either, that was very cheeky asking that.'

'So how much are you going to be paid?'

'End of story.'

'Okay, when do you start your new job?'

'After Christmas, you can start in May, it's up to you, I won't cry myself to sleep if you don't accept.'

'Thanks very much, talking about undermining my confidence…'

'…That's business, in the police you did what you practically wanted to do, in business things have to be discussed, and then acted upon.'

'I'm lost, what do you mean?'

'Nothing, forget that, it's just an observation that's all. Paul Welsh…anything?'

'Still keeping tabs on him, nothing unusual in his lifestyle, have you heard anything?'

'Nothing…I think I may have heard an innocent conversation in Dubai and got slightly excited, I have thought long and hard about this, the only thing is why would he use another name when buying properties and making hotel reservations?'

'Don't be too hard on yourself; I have had the same thoughts over the years when I was working on difficult cases. The credit card is the key. Maybe he doesn't want his wife or anyone else to know about buying property in Dubai.

'Or he could be doing something illegal, which is a long way from setting up his boss to be murdered.'

'I feel a lot better now, now that I have got that off my chest, I'm sorry I've sent you on a wild goose chase.'

'Not at all…your friend the editor seems to have scaled back on the dealers and is less critical of the police, he doesn't mention corruption anymore.'

'He's done his job, dealers have been brought before the courts and he removed the two rotten apples from the drug squad, he said there is no more juice to squeeze. However, he was visited at his home by a prominent policeman, he didn't say who it was, but he was impressed at what he had to say.'

There was a silence.

'And…what did he say?'

'That he had given the police a kick up the arse, that they all needed, and that the police had suspects in mind who had killed Feeney, the social worker and the dealers, they were a gang from Liverpool, but they had evidence but not enough to take them to court.'

'That's interesting, and there's certain logic to that, how many of the minor dealers being arrested are from Liverpool, the majority. Did he tell you what evidence that the police had?'

'No, he said the officer told him, but it was circumstantial, no smoking gun, was the term he used, but what he did say was that someone from within the force must have aided them. I think he was referring to the two women, but they're hardly going to come clean now are they?'

Eddings was left with his own thoughts; it was like watching two movies at the same time.

'Are you alright, you've went unusually quiet?'

'I was just thinking, this editor must have some information to have a senior officer visit him, and the same senior officer admits to him that the force had become complacent. I went to my senior officer about five years ago with concerns, the new university educated detectives were glued to their seats watching computer screens, I told them and the senior officer that they should be out in the field, learning the nuances of suspects, the topography of crime scenes, but I was told…shut the door quietly on my way out.'

'He really said that! Really?'

'He certainly did, and that made my mind up to leave if the chance came around.'

***

She stepped out from the wooden entrance on to the icy pavement, the lane was in semi darkness even though the streetlights were valiantly trying to cut a path through the darkness; it wasn't looking idyllic like it did in the daylight, it looked menacing. That was her last stint as a hostess; she had accumulated enough money to clear the lion's share of her ever mounting debt. To continue living a double life would end in tears and in prison, she couldn't take that risk, she had explained it all, her reasons were accepted. It was a good experience, it had expanded her mind, she was able to see how there was a dichotomy in the society she had immersed herself in, her day job arresting drug dealers her night job, handing out class A drugs.

It was only the impoverished society she would arrest; the affluent society would be afforded every worldly pleasure. Gingerly walking up the small narrow lane towards the Perth Road, his parting words kept coming back to scream at her.

'You never know we can maybe work together in the future?' There was no undercurrent the way he delivered it, she just felt unsettled, the more she thought about it, the more she became concerned. She forced herself to think of the challenges ahead, she had been invited to Paul Welsh's office, he had something to discuss with her, she was told by a number of officers, that he was going to shake up the drug squad, the pressure was being brought by the Police Committee, the revelations in the Evening Chronicle about corruption and turning a blind eye, had a cathartic impulse, the drug squad had to be changed and seen to be changed for the publics consumption at least.

Jane was being fast tracked to an inspector. There was resistance to this unexpected move by some of her colleagues, but unbeknown to them, they would be moving to less glamorous but new pastures. Welsh welcomed this suggestion from the 'suits' too many of Feeney's fan club had still not taken to him, this would be an opportunity to serve a cold dish to them, he would force feed them if necessary. With the salary increase she would be able to move from her flat, she still pined for Broughty Ferry, that was her area that she felt able to relax, breathe, and enjoy life.

Welsh had covered everything that he had to make her take the job, if she had any doubts; he had alleviated them he had even had the foresight to request that additional funds be offered to her to allow her to relocate to a more area with less security concerns. This request was rubber stamped. He had pointed out to the 'suits' in light of the dealers and Feeney being murdered it was in everyone's interest that every reasonable security aspect should be looked at, she had to be moved whether she agreed or not, it was better to encourage rather than tell her she had to move. The suits agreed.

The Editor had been kept informed of the new regime that was being constructed; certain elements that had been uncooperative were being moved. The new appointee had new ideas which were consistent with modern police methods. The Editor in return told the suits and Police Committee that less negative and more ebullient articles would be prominent in the newspaper. Jane didn't trust the messengers who told her that she would be offered the inspector's job; they had made it very clear in the past that she was only in the drug squad through positive discrimination, nothing else. She never offered up a defence, she just sat back and took it but never accepted their opinion. If there was any veracity in what they had said, she would take gratuitous pleasure in seeing them squirm, and see the scowl and contempt for her change into a welcoming smile; they weren't fooling anyone. If, and it was a big if, if she was offered the position, the two detractors would be removed, she would ask Welsh if this was viable. If he agreed without a fight, she would ask for more concessions. All this was churning in her mind, she was feeling more relaxed, at the top of the lane the bitter wind chilled her to the marrow; she pulled her scarf more tightly round her neck.

'Feeling the cold Jane?'

'For God's sake! You frightened me, what are you doing here?'

'I like the dress, been at a party?'

'Look I'm freezing, what is that you want?'

'Nothing to worry about, I'll drive you home.'

They move towards his car in silence, she breaks it.

'So what's on your mind sonny?'

He starts the car and moves off.

'When you get the job as inspector…you won't get rid of me because of anything personal, will you?'

' Look, I've heard the rumours as well as you have, I'm not counting my chickens yet, so what you're asking and what I reply to you is all hypothetical, all I am saying to you, is other officers will have something to worry about…but you don't, unless I hear this conversation from anyone else, do you understand?'

'That's good to hear, I was told I'm being moved.'

'Drop me off here; I'm not far from home.'

'Are you sure?'

'Positive, this will do here.'

He brings the car to a halt, she leaves without a word, and he's thinking she's got the job, she's acting like an inspector, at least he's safe, I wonder who the others are that she was talking about? He waves at her as he passed her, she fails to respond, he comforts himself by thinking her head is down she didn't see him. She did see him; did he see her leave the club?

***

Catherine could act on her instinct rather than deferring to Monty, she had had her period of mourning, it was brief but she had created a semblance of heartache, that was then this was now. Her Christmas shopping trip down to London had given her time to catch up with a friend she had known only from brief coded conversations on the telephone. In Harrods at the pizza restaurant she sat at the fifties style counter and struck up a conversation with a harassed women with a toddler. In between conversations about Christmas and the constant snowfalls, she told the woman about the new route that drugs would be coming into Dundee, the quantity would be much larger than previously, the cars would be the perfect and nondescript foil, coming up by a car transporter. The driver wouldn't be showing any display of nerves as he would not be aware of the extras that some of the cars would be carrying. She lifted the cup of coffee to her bright red lips, Harrods was teeming with shoppers from every nationality, different tongues could be heard above the cacophony of excited children, and wailing toddlers, her eyes looked north, south, east and west, she didn't see any familiar face from Dundee, that had any connection to the drug squad, Welsh had told her what to look for innocent shoppers, vis-à-vis members of the public, she studied them near her and some in the distance. The woman had calmed the tired child down, she was sitting there all smiles and exuding serenity, Catherine put the coffee cup down and looked furtively across the parlour, no one was watching them, now was the perfect time to leave and return to her hotel in Knightsbridge, tomorrow she had an appointment with the upmarket estate agent, she had money to burn. The properties in Mayfair always retained their value no matter what any economic storm rained on the proletarian who bought ex-council houses for inflated figures, she had imbued this to Monty, he was of the impression that ex-council houses even in the most crime ridden area were still good value. London had wealthy individuals who wanted to stay in the safest and affluent areas, Mayfair was the answer. The properties she would be viewing were valued from two million to three million, the residents were fashion designers, architects and sculptors, and she would fit in perfectly. Next year she would be out of the vile but lucrative drug trade, she aimed to base herself in London with a new legitimate career.

Dundee was starting to look Lilliputian, the sprawling metropolis of London was drawing her, the garage and car washes would be sold, she would be cash rich, once the house was purchased in Mayfair.

Her next objective would be to secure an office in Mayfair she aimed to return to Law, she would have to study English Law to secure accreditation. The final cut would be selling her sprawling house outside Dundee, Patrick Connelly suggested to her that she should make a clean break from Dundee; the police would always look on her in an unfavourable light, because of Monty. The advice was sound. Her exit strategy was not the product of spontaneity, it was a measured process. Her analytical legal trained mind had incubated and rejected some financial plans. She was in overdrive, her tax planning and financial projections were being nurtured by Patrick Connelly, her undeclared income did not cause him to furrow his brow, tax avoidance and tax evasion were legal and illegal respectively, but they had the same theme to minimise tax. He would give her a name to take her voluminous amount of money, the tax expert would visit her at her convenience, and the result of his professional service was the option of relocating to London. He suggested purchasing property in Mayfair and opening a law practice in Mayfair also, some of the start-up costs could be offset against her tax demand.

Welsh would be told that their financial arrangements would be terminated; but in view of his cooperation in another matter she would give him a golden goodbye payment, if he was not ecstatic about this she would withdraw her generous offer. There would be no dark threats; she knew things about him that would be best kept under wraps. The business partner from Liverpool would be told after the last consignment was sent to Dundee; that there would be plenty of people willing to fill her petite expensive shoes. Gnawing away at her in the small hours was the thought that she wouldn't have been able to do this if Monty was still breathing, his death had created an opportunity to return eventually to the legal world that was alien to him, but to insulate herself from guilt she consoled herself that if it were not for her, Monty would have still been living in his ex-council house and would have ended his days in prison, she had shown him the finer things in life, which sometimes were not apparent to him.

London was her natural home to live and work, the theatre was on her doorstep, Monty for all his big heart took pride in being a philistine, because he had persuaded her to go to the Edinburgh Playhouse to see the mind-numbing Riverdance, he thought he was a culture paragon. Seeing swathes of people stamping their feet was not one of the memories that she would take into her dotage, the only thing that Riverdance gave her was a blinding headache. On the other hand, Monty was in his element. Her refined and classical schooling sat uneasily with Monty's sparse and erratic education, though he was good at woodwork, bird tables was his forte, which he sold to garden centres. For a violent man, he was at heart at home with the simple things in life. It took a while but she had turned round his life, cut down on his drinking and made him look at some of his friends in a more sober and measured view. She had been proved correct, some were skimming money from the deals, and using the money to finance deals for themselves, they weren't circumspect how they did this; he had to take action, violent action. Two friends had their legs inserted into a log-separator; she still remembered occasionally their horrific screams that had echoed from the woods.

***

Walking along the Broughty Ferry road didn't seem like a good idea now, the wind was blowing the thick snowflakes into his face, traffic had thinned out, it had just gone nine pm and the cars that were passing him were doing so infrequently.

Welsh was never far from his mind, he suspected Morag accepting the job from Madni tempted her to forget her fears about Welsh, if her conversation conveniently omitted mentioning Welsh, she would be able to concentrate on her position in charge of developing the marina. He would go along with this, she would not ask if he had any information on Welsh; she made it abundantly clear she didn't want to hear his name uttered again. That would suit him, now he would be able to see how Trevor Perkins was living his life, without Morag chirping in his ear. The days of the long lunches and trips to Edinburgh had come to a natural and mutual close. No sepia memories would haunt him, they had enjoyed each other's company, but that's all they required, a break from their sameness of their one paced lives. The thicker the snow came down the better he felt and the more lopping stride he took on the virgin snow.

Welsh would become under more intense scrutiny, he couldn't go to any of his ex-colleagues, or the cat would be out of the bag as soon as the phone call ended, his font of knowledge was the bank teller, and he would give him a large spade to do the discreet digging. If the teller were able to produce something fruitful, he would arrange to meet a like-minded soul in Gary; he had the same sensitive nostrils as him, they were the only ones who smelt something less fragrant. Morag was out of the way now; he could fully focus on the curious Mr Welsh and his alter ego Trevor Perkins, two identities, one person, who had multiple assets. Then his pace became less forceful, Joe Feeney…was he hiding anything or were his secrets taken to the grave? Feeney could wait; he had to exhume any secret from Paul Welsh, first.

The lights from the Christmas trees in the windows of the houses he was passing gave him reason to be optimistic, at Greendykes Road the traffic lights were covered in snow it didn't matter no vehicles were in sight, he quickly crossed the road, in five minutes he would be in his house, he hoped Jean would be in bed watching television, he needed to go on the web, something he needed to clear up to satisfy himself, it was probably insignificant, it was just what Morag had said about the marina development. When he got into the house he would ask Jean if she wanted hot chocolate, then make it if required and then stay in the darkness of the kitchen gleaning information from the various websites; including the marina development.

He had read in The Courier that the original company had ran into financial difficulties, he wanted to find out whether any other company had been interested in buying it before Mr Madni came to the rescue, knowing how these middle-eastern businessmen worked, ethics were foreign to them. He was not the white knight portrayed in The Courier.

***

Welsh was woken from his Christmas Eve lie in, he opened one eye, 4.10 am, his wife just turned on her side, his mobile was still ringing on the chair in the corner of the bedroom. He leapt out of bed and grabbed the mobile and clothes from the seat, he saw the name, anxiety replaced his annoyance. 'Get over here, I'll put the kettle on, do you want breakfast?'

'What is it all about Pat?'

'Breakfast or not, you've two seconds …'

'…Okay, a bacon sandwich,' he was cut off. He balanced the phone on the balustrade and pulled on his trousers, he went into the bathroom and washed his face in darkness, he didn't want to see how he looked in the mirror. Pat was careful when he contacted him, if he was doing this at this unearthly hour something was up, he patted his face dry and pulled on his shirt, his socks and shoes were still in the room.

He opened the bedroom door and crept in retrieving them, once he was shod he crept down the creaking stairs, his car keys were still in his pocket, the smell of alcohol met him at the bottom of the stairs, his wife had consumed half the bottle as they talked in the kitchen, he was glad he didn't have more than a couple of glasses, his top coat was in the lounge on the chair near the bay window. The bad feeling returned he knew what awaited him was bad news, how bad, he didn't want to put under scrutiny, but it would be bad. He looked at the landscape of the lounge an idyllic scene to lift the spirit of a Victorian patriarch before he retired to bed, ready for the excitement of Christmas morning. He closed the door and stopped for a moment with his hand still on the brass handle, he hoped he was not observing the lounge and this house for the last time, that unnerving sensation returned. In the driveway he started the car and scraped the freshly fallen snow and ice underneath from the windscreens. As he was doing this he couldn't help averting his eyes from Dundee, not to the Baldovie plant but to the serene west end of Dundee. Pat was no doubt watching him; he wasn't in the mood for a playful wave in his direction. His assertion was right on the button, Pat was watching every movement, his biggest fear was that Welsh would be talking on his mobile, this would have made him consider their relationship to be placed on the edge of a precarious abyss, if needed be he was prepared to stand and twist his foot on the hand of Welsh and send him into the dark depths. If he had been that stupid he would have to take the ultimate sanction, not himself but someone who would agree to Pat's solution.

The Jameson's whisky was cooling his fervour, her word was to be trusted; she told him that 'things were moving at an alarming pace, Welsh was under investigation from an unnamed outside force, he had to find out from Welsh what was going on.'

He sat down at the old table his hand affectionately caressing it back and forth, so many deals, problems and solutions had been spoken and shouted out over this table, he was looking for another solution to a problem, that he knew Welsh carried within him, if he wasn't candid he wouldn't be able to help.

Jane respected Pat, he understood the undercurrent in what she had disclosed to him, she was advising; if you have done anything illegal with Welsh; destroy any trail that connects him to you. He didn't press her to elicit her view on Welsh, she was obviously speaking from a ladies room, he heard the laughter and screams high above her conversation; she must have been in a night club, she called him at 2.30am. Her words were not slurred or seemed panicked she was in control. For nearly two hours he had analysed her conversation he wrote the words on the large A4 notepad. Underlining certain words and circling others. Underneath he wrote his connections to Welsh, no paper trail existed, but words could tumble from his poisonous mouth that could result in a raid on his office from every government department. If he could elicit every illegal deed that Welsh had undertaken he would be able to assess the impact it would have on him. He could be worrying about nothing or he could be able to reduce the mountainous problem to a molehill. Until he turned up it was all speculating guesswork, his mind was more flaccid than excitable. The worst case scenario was that he was involved in the murder of his superior officer, or involved in the deaths of the dealers, if that were the case there had to be a reason or plenty of reasons of different denominations. If this was the case and he prayed it wasn't, Welsh was at the apex of financing drug deals.

Over the many decades in Dundee he had seen numerous cover ups; from police officers having perks with prostitutes male and female; to Councillors having friendly chats with officials on planning committees.

Who would convince any recalcitrant colleagues who had clouds of doubt about planning permission for homes. Everyone had secrets. However, police officers had been retired early with full entitlements as long as they went quietly. The sight of known dealers being able to walk about like homogenous law-abiding citizens may have had a malevolent effect on their fragile probity, their salaries in their eyes were pitiful, maybe it was time some of the proceeds of crime should take a diversion into their back pockets, who would know any difference? But conspiracy to murder a senior officer in the drug squad was treading fantasy. Conspiracy to murder dealers might sit well with some members of the public, but in the eyes of the Law, this was eye-popping.

The piercing whistle of the kettle coincided with the dull almost apologetic rap on the door alerted him to return the Jameson's to the drinks cabinet. He looked at himself in the mirror above the mantlepiece, he was looking calm and assured, he turned round and walked to the front door. He strode past him then paused halfway down the hall and pointed to the all-consuming silence of the lounge. Pat nodded and followed him into the lounge which was in semi-darkness, the light being forced into the overpowering darkness by the small lamp at the bay window. He sat at the table where Pat had placed a mug of tea and a bacon sandwich. Welsh began to talk, he was halted by Pat who told him to eat the sandwich and then he can tell him some news which disturbed him. He nibbled the sandwich, his appetite was waning, he forced himself to eat it quickly as possible which was difficult as he became nauseas, Pat just stared at him his face expressionless. He shoved the plate with the crusts in his direction; he took the plate away into the kitchen, and then returned smiling. The nauseas feeling subsided.

'What's on your mind Pat?'

He pulled out the wooden seat and leaned forward on his elbows staring with menacing intent.

'The fragrance from Boots perfume department can't

begin to mask the stench of corruption inhabiting
Tayside Police Headquarters; you're being investigated
by another police force, why?'
He stopped drinking the tea and placed it on the table.

'I've not heard anything...investigating me? Why?'

'You've got to be candid with me Paul, I'm going to
ask you difficult questions, I need honest answers before
I can evaluate how corrosive they will be to your well-
being and liberty.'

'What, well-being and liberty, what the fuck does that
mean, what do you know, what are you holding back
from me!'

'Please keep your voice down,' he points his finger up
at the ceiling.

'Sorry Pat, what do you know and who told you, this
could be just malicious misinformation being bandied
about.'

'I know, and I fully understand your excitable
demeanour, all I can say is that I was told by someone
who is not low-level in the police, but that's by the by,
you are being investigated you don't know why, and my
source doesn't know ...yet.'

'I'm getting worried Pat, why I don't know, but I'm
feeling mired in something.'

'I am going to ask you some questions, I need honest
answers there is no room for any ambiguity , veracity
must run through your answers from beginning to end,
do I make myself clear?'

'Yes.'

'What has happened in Dundee over the last few
months has been unprecedented.

'Feeney and an innocent worshipper were murdered,
along with less law abiding citizens, did you have
anything to do with their murders?'

'You're kidding me...this is bizarre! Me...involved in
the murder of Joe Feeney, come on Pat!'

'I had to ask... what about the dealers, including

Monty?'

'Same answer Pat, absolutely nothing to do with them, nothing.'

'That's that established, now I have to go under the membrane, the dealers that were murdered apart from your normal police duties, did you have any contact with any of them on a social basis?'

'No, I have noised some of them up in the past…'

'…That's normal police duties, I'll give you an example, have you ever tipped any of them off about planned raids, or accepted any unsolicited gifts from them?'

His mouth was drying up, he lifted the mug to his lips, giving the impression that he was thinking deep and hard.

'No…I don't think so.'

'That's not good enough, if you said that in the witness box, you've just condemned yourself, what have you done to help them, any of them, I need to know.'

'I leant on Monty, he was trying to blackmail someone that I'm not prepared to name or give the reason why he was being blackmailed, don't press me Pat, please.'

'That's fine, that's a link with Monty; did you elicit money from him?'

'No, I just warned him, if he continued to blackmail this person, he would be pulled into Bell Street every couple of days, and his house would be raided in the early hours, I could make life difficult for him.'

'What was the outcome?'

'He stopped the blackmail, then we went back to our normal lives, he went back to his criminal life, I went back to my life, trying to put scumbags like him into jail.'

'Have you had any romantic liaisons with any criminal's wife or daughter?'

'No,' he was laughing, no Pat.'

'Have you ever been to any criminal's house while they were elsewhere, I'm talking about any of the deceased dealers, before or after their deaths?'

'No definitely not, the detectives investigating the murders would have but not me I wouldn't have any reason to go to their homes would I? Maybe some detective has being playing away from home, and I have been mentioned, see what I mean about misinformation.' He was feeling much more relaxed now.

'For the avoidance of doubt, you have never been to their homes, for whatever reason, since they were murdered?'

'Absolutely, never, what reason would I have to go?'

He stared at his face in the semi-darkness, no flicker of guilt shone.

'That's what I asked myself, what reason would you go to the home of one of the deceased unless it was an affair of the heart.'

'I can put your mind at rest Pat, nothing dodgy was going on; you do believe me?'

'Implicitly, I just have to ask these awkward questions, I'm not judging you on your moral standards.'

'I understand, Pat.'

'This blackmail business with Monty, to clear this up, did you have to go to his house, to advise him to resile from this course of action?'

'Pat, I'm aware what you're saying…no, I was never at his house, unless it was being raided, when he lived in Douglas, yes, I was there when it was being turned over, but since he moved in the sticks amongst the landed gentry.

'I have had no reason to visit him on police business or otherwise.'

'That's all I needed to know, if I hear anything else, I'll contact you again. You're free to ask me anything that's troubling you.'

'Nothing's troubling me Pat, apart from your phone call, but now you've put my mind at ease, at least now if I am requested for an interview, I'll know what's awaiting me, other detectives will be interviewed as well, so as not to alert me it's only me that they're investigating, forewarned is forearmed.'

'Regarding our business matters, I think it would be best to call a moratorium on any future projects, keeping contact to a minimal, until this all blows over.'

'That's fine with me Pat, there's no paper trail from my bank account to yours, don't worry about that. Just a pity this diversion came up, in this recession we are all doing rather well, but we have got to remain vigilant, not become complacent, and be totally honest with each another.'

'That's a perfect summation…time to catch up on some sleep, thanks for coming over.'

Welsh rose from the table, sleep was the last thing on his mind, he still wasn't clear why he was under investigation; he just had to act in a normal and professional manner. He was itching to reveal who Pat's source was.

'No problem, I feel a lot calmer now, driving over that bridge I was doing eighty- before I realised.'

'Watch the road, in these conditions it would be unwise to take chances, if I don't see you before Christmas, have a merry if not peaceful one.'

'Thanks Pat, the first Christmas in a new house is always special, you have a good and peaceful one as well, and are you going to Midnight Mass?'

'Try to stop me, there is meant to be heavy snow, but we'll be there, remember minimal contact.'

This was the first wedge in their business relationship; he had to create a chasm between Welsh and himself. Both of them lived and operated in the bubble of mutuality, Welsh had helped him over the years and the favours were returned tenfold, other more unscrupulous solicitors had advanced their potential magical powers in making evidence disappear or tainted. However, their whispers fuelled by alcohol became more brazen and high-pitched, older more venal solicitors were horrified by the outlandish claims that were being discussed at lunch in certain hostelries, a counter balance was discussed by the influential cabal. A consensus was formulated over lunch; the two bright but arrogant solicitors would be overlooked when serious cases would be brought before the courts. If they were not diverted the game would be changed and become less lucrative. Decades of latent agreement between prosecutors and defence agents would collapse into chaos. Favours in court could be dispensed on the uttering of an innocent phrase, when it was made the prosecutor would notch down the rhetoric, and then the defence would become more confident and knowledgeable, the jury were being spoon fed, and the prosecution didn't do anything to curtail their appetite. The common denominator was that the two solicitors were employed in the practice that was under investigation for financial mismanagement of an elderly widow's share and investment portfolio.

Patrick Connelly had put the coin in the slot that activated the machine of the FSA into motion, the two boastful solicitors were seconded to a conservative practice where they knew where their place would be in the legal fraternity, they wouldn't be suffering from altitude sickness, they were reintroduced to their desks at the rear of the building, the offices were affectionately known as 'paradise gulag.'

They had played out with the rules of the game; they had to see the errors of their ways. The senior solicitor requested that he meet Pat for lunch, he agreed. Over the two hour lunch, he requested advice from Pat; he was astonished at the hurtful advice. 'Sell the practice to me, and retire, that could diminish the more serious charges of fraud, if you agree to this, after a thorough audit, it would come across as a clerical error and a breakdown in communication, that would leave you with a censure from Law Society, rather than staring at a High Court judge from the dock.'

He wanted to reply, can you pull this off, then sure, but he tried to bow out with some dignity.

'If that's the price I have to pay, I'll pay the bill, what about my staff?'

'All would stay apart from two solicitors, they have brought the profession into disrepute, you don't need me to inform you of their drunken boasts, you took your eye off staff development, they were whoring themselves and trusted confidantes to unscrupulous people; that they must had known would repeat to others that didn't share their contorted view of how the Law works. They will be moved.'

An ill-wind sometimes brings good fortune in its slipstream, the client for the Legal Aid Board would be advised of the new owner of the discredited practice, the legal aid payments would be able to continue after all, but would decline after a respectable chronological period had passed. The rogue practice would be returned to a moral and legitimate practice, all pyramid investment schemes would be scrutinised and monies that had been lost to clients would be reimbursed with a fulsome apology, this would clear any doubts that the previous solicitor and investment manager and their methods had been removed. The disadvantaged clients were in the investment section of the practice; their forefathers had invested in the embryonic stage of the United States of America, and India. Their riches had flourished until seven years ago when the old investment manager was persuaded to put on slippers and smoke a pipe.

They had to get him away from the investments of the clients by any means necessary; he would have never accepted this new leverage upon leverage investments that his clients were persuaded to adopt. He would only have one word to describe this new blue- sky thinking investment strategy; bubble. He was not a Financial Advisor, he was a stockbroker as he insisted on being called; his elderly clients came into his small but paper strewn office that his floor could be easily mistaken for an extension of his desk, some of the younger grandsons with their degrees asked why their grandparents' investments had not been invested in the technology sector, he told them simply it was an investment bubble, that would go pop.'

'Could he be more candid?

The grandparent touched him on the forearm and smiled,

'We understand totally, we won't keep you any longer from your work.' That was in 2001; the stock market had never recovered a decade on, but 'old Gregory' had liquidated the stocks, his clients were bereft of shares but cash rich, he had timed it perfectly. Pat Connelly went round to Gregory's house that was in a conservation area of Broughty Ferry and knocked at his door, he wasn't expected but was welcome going by the elixir in Gregory's eyes, in the lounge he had tea and scones and they both were hesitant to say why the visit. Pat was smooth as silk; he told him that he was now operating the practice due to the ill-health of the solicitor. He wanted him back as the stock-broker not an investment manager; he placed the sparse contract on the desk the only information missing was the level of salary.

'Fill in the salary; I know you're a reasonable man.'

Gregory wrote the figure. Pat looked at it and frowned. 'You're too modest,' he scored out the figure and replaced it and showed it to Gregory, 'that figure reflects your true worth.'

He signed the deal and anticipated Pat's next move.

'On the grapevine I've heard clients have left over a short period of time, I can visit them and explain that time can be turned back.'

He stood up and shook Pat's hand, he walked him to the

door, the stoop was losing its hold over his body. He now had a purpose in life again.

***

The excitement of Christmas Eve eluded him, but the façade of joy fooled his wife and neighbour, this would be the first Christmas that they would be driving over the Tay Bridge to the Dundee for Midnight Mass. He needed to contact someone from the old guard, someone who knew where every scandal was hidden; Gary.

The conversation with Connelly whirled in his chaotic mind. For what he could remember of the conversation, it was an internal matter not any business transaction, no-one else in the police were aware of outside hobbies. He called him on his mobile, it was just after eight am, darkness still had a hold over the city, he convinced him to meet for breakfast at the new restaurant on Riverside Drive, the bacon rolls were on him, Clark was too long in the tooth to ask what the breakfast was all about, but if he had called him this early something was up.

Daylight had finally pushed the darkness away, Welsh was nowhere to be seen, nine- fifteen, he could have still been snuggled up in his bed, this meeting better be worth it.

'Sorry, I'm late, there was a crash on the bridge, we would be better going inside; its freezing, looks like a white Christmas.'

They walked into the diner, it was sparsely populated, Welsh invited him to take a table at the rear of the diner, he returned with two bacon rolls and two mugs of tea on a tray. He took the tray back and sat down.

'Thanks for the bacon roll, now what's troubling you?'

'I was told that I'm being investigated, from another force, any idea why?'

'Oh dear.' He shook his head and took a large bite out of the roll.

'You're not the only one.'

406

'Oh...who else is being investigated then?'

'Feeney's old squad, every one of them, it seems that the two ladies who were jailed for concealing drugs in their homes have tired of their Spartan surroundings courtesy of Her Majesty, their solicitors have been invited through to Edinburgh by another new task force that deals with corrupt police officers and seizing assets of convicted individuals. They are interested in information that the two ladies are willing to trade.'

'And what is the deal, they get out of jail earlier, what is the information they are willing to trade?'

'Nobody has said anything, a lot of smoke and mirrors, the dealer that they were storing drugs for is dead, they can say anything they want, any secret the dealer had was left in Old Glamis Road. Everyone will be interviewed about their time in Feeney's squad, they are after tittle-tattle, once they have collated all the interviews, six month down the line the report will be made public, the allegations will be unsubstantiated. This elite squad are under pressure from the Audit Commission, the squad costs more money to operate than they have brought in from seizing assets.

Self- preservation.'

'Where are you getting this information, and do you believe it?'

'Sources must be protected, come, come, you know that. Why don't they investigate their colleagues in Glasgow, I'll tell you because...never mind.'

'Because of?'

'Doesn't matter. Just expect to be make yourself available for interview, there will be plenty of farmyard manure in their questions, don't be alarmed, you've got to bear in mind the two ladies are being giving a hard time in Cornton Vale prison, there's plenty of Dundee criminals in there courtesy of the two ladies.'

'It still rankles, but I suppose I have to accept it, when will the process begin?'

'Today at three, I'm the first, I'm looking forward to it, and I'll be asking more questions than answering I know that for sure.'

'Why are you getting interviewed you weren't in the drug squad?'

'I was for a month; remember one of Feeney's protégés got himself involved with a member of staff?'

'No… Oh yeh, I remember that now, it was a domestic dispute, he was put on gardening leave for a while I mind of that now.'

'That's what happens when the police actively encourage gays to join the force; I told everyone that would listen that would be a bad move. I was right wasn't I?'

'Fuck's sake Gary, the world has moved on, I suppose some of your forefathers said that about women, that's what held you back you say what other people, think.'

'I'm not going to get into an argument with you Paul; I like you as a friend and a police officer, that's my opinion that's all. Changing the subject, looking forward to Santa coming?'

'As long as he doesn't knock on my door with a chequered hat on…sorry for being sarcastic, yeah, I'm looking forward to it being in a new house and that, what about yourself?'

'It's just another day, but don't let my pessimism dampen your spirits.'

'Where are you spending Christmas then?'

'I'll make it hard for you with a multiple choice; Barbados, Thailand or Constitution Street?'

'Any friends joining you for festivities?'

'I've got two turkey steaks and I'm not sharing them with anyone!'

'Come across to Wormit, what have you got to lose?'

'Thanks for the offer and the bacon rolls, I've got to go.'

Watching him leave the diner he felt pity for him, in his fifties and the loneliest man in Dundee. Christmas

408

tomorrow, and he was indifferent. Marriage maketh the man or it will destroy him, it had destroyed Gary but made Welsh. He was in no hurry, he had time on his hands, everyone would be interviewed Connelly never said that, he could have just heard part of the conversation, when someone might had said 'we'll start from the top and work our way down.'

That was not implausible. He would go with that. If Gary was interviewed on Christmas Eve, they were making a point, would they be leaving the city then return in the New Year, if so where were they staying? They usually operated in a tight group, probably no more than four, where were they staying in the city? Doubtful. There had been no contact with Catherine, his involvement with her was strictly to protect his stipend from Monty, he was gone but she took up the reigns without any problems, there would be no need to do her any favours; he preferred that way of doing business. The two jailed detectives in Cornton Vale would be attempting to lie their way to freedom, the bigger the lie the more chance that someone might take them seriously, he had nothing to fear from them.

Some of their colleagues might have indiscretions that they would prefer to stay motionless, but it still may cause resignations from officers of a lower rank. Sacrificial lambs to justify the squad's lofty opinion of their painstaking work.

The bacon roll had satisfied his hunger and Gary had eased his troublesome mind, it was pointless fearing what he didn't know. Gary and Connelly would not be told of each other's different views on the impending interviews, he would be relaxed when talking to Gary but showing signs of being pensive when or if Connelly called.

Wormit may have just been a few miles away, but it just sank in how glad he was out of the city, he was just minutes away if either of them wanted to talk, but the

Tay separated him from potential headaches. What wouldn't surprise him but he deliberately stopped from telling Gary, if the internal affairs squad wanted a senior officer's head on a pike, they could easily make Feeney's head a perfect exhibit for public consumption, not by evidence by but by supposition and innuendo, the twins of perceived guilt. Feeney's notebook and USB would be better destroyed if his house was searched by invitation or warrant, they could pin anything on him, including Feeney's murder, stranger things had happened. When he first started as a police officer, he was told by his sergeant, in the early hours of the morning about the case of money equals power. A relative of a wealthy family that had several family members in the judiciary were able to influence an open and shut case of rape. The victim's underwear which would have had her assailant's DNA on them, mysteriously got lost in transit, this was the prosecution's trump card. And to make the prosecution's less robust, the prosecution's QC was fortunately promoted and had to go overseas to a meeting of the Heads of Judiciary of the Commonwealth in Bermuda, the meeting was due to commence at the same time as the opening of the High Court trial. The replacement QC was competent, but this was not the trial for him, he was out of his depth. The defendant walked free with the slimmest of a majority verdict, he then left Dundee; he was believed to have relocated overseas. 'Power and money equal influence, never forget that son.'

Welsh never did, he thought maybe the sergeant had embellished the story, but he got his hands on the transcript of the High Court trial, he had underplayed his opinion, there was an unpleasant odour from the transcript. He had seen the nepotism card played by senior officers over the years, a little word in someone's ear would have becoming a barking order by the time it

410

came to the arresting officer's ears. Drop it. He was in a nest of vipers fortunately for him he had an endless supply of anti-dote, he was confident he would never be bitten. Promote bitter and dangerous enemies before friends, he thought this was an oxymoron, but it all made perfect sense to him now.

This quiet time he had to himself had a cathartic effect on his mind, chains of doubt had emasculated him, however; the optimistic opinion of Gary had made him feel liberated. This could be a warning, it might be better to evaluate his relationship with Catherine, it would be better if she paid him a one-off lump sum instead of the monthly gratuity, he had to make it an attractive figure, for her to jump at it. That would be a better strategy, an end to their business relationship would be premature but it would be safer in the long - term. He wouldn't try to second- guess what Catherine was doing with Monty's legacy she was the grey-matter behind the brawn, it would be better to terminate while he was ahead. The less he knew about her business plans the better; it would be beneficial to bow to ignorance in this case. The money that Catherine would give him would be invested for the future, and Patrick Connelly was the perfect advisor.

He would not invest it personally but leave it to one of his shadowy financial advisors. The tea was still warm, he sipped it slowly, Fife was obscured by the sudden heavy snowfall, he was not concerned, he enjoyed the winter scene, he had not seen this amount of snow in decades, by the time he had driven over the bridge the snow may have become less dense. Today would be a lazy day with his feet up, he had DVDs given to him last Christmas, he would be able to watch them without any disturbance or distractions. He ran to his car which was covered in the thick snow, traffic was crawling along Riverside Drive, commuters probably. More fool them he thought.

In the City Square the much ridiculed synthetic
Christmas tree was covered in snow, the wind was
whipping some snow from the branches, the Caird Hall
pillars festooned in bright red ribbons were meant to
represent giant Christmas crackers or so the legend had
grown. He was now on his winter holiday; he had been
complaining that he would be overlooked for the week
between Christmas and New Year as usual, the most
violent period of the calendar. After much lobbying he
was unexpectedly summoned to his line-manager,
someone was looking for his period in February would
he be interested in Christmas Eve till January the third?
Lenny was savvy, however his youthful looks portrayed
him as naive, levers had been pulled in his favour, by
who he didn't care, he now had the chance to earn his
life back, or some semblance of a life. The police would
be stretched to the limit due to the parties that ended in
violence and the numerous street-crime incidents, under
the cover of this madness he might be able to carry out
the foul deed, return home, then go to a party, with
plenty of police officers as his alibis. He prepared to
meet the person he had met in Dudhope Park, looking
over from the entrance of the Overgate Centre he was
hoping the contact would come alone, then he saw him,
he was standing by one of the pillars of the Caird Hall,
he was on his own. It was time to get this meeting over.
He walked over into the City Square, the snow was quite
deep, he couldn't be bothered going round the edge
where the snow had been cleared, he subconsciously was
trying to prove his lack of fear. Half-way across the City
Square the contact moved towards him, he was carrying
a bag of sorts, he tensed up when he saw the bag in his
hand, as he came closer, the fear multiplied, there was
something solid in the bag. He took it from his left hand
and passed it to his right hand, they were just metres
away from each other, 'tonight's the night' he said, and

passed the bag to Lenny, and walked on.

Lenny came to a sudden halt, he wanted to open the plastic bag and see what secret it held, instead he just kept walking climbing up the stairs to the Caird Hall, at the top he turned round, the contact had melted away amongst the Christmas shoppers, even though it was late morning, the town centre was a hive of activity. He opened the bag behind the pillar, a plastic container of screws; he was mystified, what does this mean? The lid was tightly shut, it wouldn't budge, frustrated he took off his gloves and placed them between his knees, his nimble fingers forced off the lid, he moved the gold coloured screws about in the container, the treasure was uncovered; four bullets were in a clip at the bottom. Relief replaced the fear; at least he knew what was required of him, but still no name of his intended victim. He scrambled the screws over the bullets and snapped the lid back on, and returned it to the bag. His mobile rang out into the silence, the shrill ringtone bouncing off the wall of the Caird Hall, he needn't ask who was calling; his rosy cheeks lost their colour.

CHAPTER SEVEN

Browsing in Harrods her phone rang, number withheld, she automatically went on the defensive, the call was short but definitely not sweet. Just as well as she was leaving, this would have spoilt her Christmas. She would not deviate from the arrangement, no golden silence payment, something was amiss or was in motion, as long as she paid him his monthly retainer, she had him wrapped in her arms, he couldn't do anything. However, if he wanted a severance payment to relinquish their agreement, then she was worried, seriously worried. She had told him that she would discuss a pertinent matter after the New Year celebrations; she would not discuss any further investments until then. If he was recording the call, she gave the impression that she was discussing a legal matter; she had obfuscated the meaning of the short-conversation. As she walked from the bustle of Harrods and the warmth into the chill of the street, she decided to walk back to her hotel rather than take a taxi. Maybe he was thinking like her, he wanted out, she was easing herself back into legitimate businesses, she could tell him that she would be giving up her previous career; that would end her insurance policy, and she would no longer be paying him the premiums. That would be her reasonable explanation; he had more to fear from her than she from him. However, something must have happened for him to want to end his money-for-silence scheme. The drug dealers in Dundee it could be argued would have difficulty joining MENSA, the world was changing, the writing was on the wall in six -feet letters, but still they refused to believe their own eyes. No longer would they be dictating terms and conditions to their suppliers in Liverpool. The suppliers had learnt all about the myriad of small dealers in the city, they had established safe houses in leafy suburbs, there was no mass influx of construction workers with smooth hands and rough manners, that had worked for a year, but someone had talked to the police, and they were ran out of town, no charges were intended to be brought against them, they were acting for the indigenous dealers.

In Liverpool information was collated and dissected, they had returned to Liverpool with their heroin between their legs but they would return with more vengeance than the Passover, and they would be staying. Notwithstanding, they would be removing the dealers; and Dundee would be established the hub of distribution. There had been a meeting in Glasgow; from now on Dundee up to Peterhead and its hinterland would be theirs. The Glasgow dealers could distribute drugs in the west up till Perth; beyond that it was all the diocese of Liverpool. They weren't interested in having cops on their pay-roll; that worked fine in the eighties and nineties. Respected civilian workers in the offices of Police Headquarters were worth more than any avaricious drug squad officers.

The slaughter in the industrial unit on Old Glamis Road had shoved theory unceremoniously aside and let practice take centre stage. The bloodletting day in the chapel in Broughty Ferry had been arranged with the social worker, Feeney had previously been negotiating his contract with the scousers who he hated, he wanted to change the terms and conditions. They had wanted him out, and wanted him to arrest the list of dealers that they would hand over when he accepted his 'golden goodbye' severance package. They thought it was generous, Feeney told them he saw 'no merit in their derisory offer; they could shove it, he was going nowhere, and they would be going to jail if they were lucky.' They had no proof of him being involved in any drug cartel which was true. Feeney wouldn't be frightened into any pact with the scousers.

The meeting in the chapel would be Feeney requesting the social worker to lobby the city's MSPs and high-ranking police officers and take their case to the Scottish Government in Edinburgh for more funds and the establishment of a clinic or respite centre. And also warn the social worker about the brothel being under surveillance; it had to be shut down immediately.

The scousers had not replied to Feeney's implied threat, they would send one of their emissaries to deliver personally their short, sharp and bloody reply. And to emphasise that their diplomatic mission was over they convinced all the main dealers to attend the impromptu meeting in the industrial unit, there and then they told the dealers that things would be changing for the better...for them.

The slaughter took place over forty minutes. One by one the dealers saw one of their ilk tortured and eventually mercifully killed, but not before the barely living dealer gave up certain secrets that they had with certain drug squad officers. Their executioner told the others staring in disbelief they had better divulge every bit of information or they would end up like their friend or friends. The humming noise from the small chainsaw kept their concentration from waning. Some of their bodily functions erupted prematurely. Embarrassment and fear unlocked any reticence. They had all been violent in their adult lives, striking hapless victims with baseball bats and golf clubs, but this violent episode being played out on the floor of the industrial unit, and they were the main actors went beyond even their wildest nightmares.. The actors were indeed actors, real-live actors; the event was being recorded on a mobile phone. This was the proof that the dealers were playing their own independent game. Feeney's name was mentioned by every one of the dealers. He was the head of the snake. Not-one of them would be able to warn Feeney or any of his subordinates; they would pick the fight with Feeney at the time and place which suited them.

After the slaughter, houses, flats and lock-ups were forced open and money and drugs were removed and taken to Liverpool. Thus the shortage of heroin caused the drug dependent individuals to go on a crime spree. The scousers stepped in to fill the breach at vastly inflated prices. Legalised heroin was rushed into health centres, the addicts had to be pacified, this was a short-term measure, but if the press knew, the public and politicians would be under tremendous pressure. After a week this temporary measure was swiftly retracted. The scousers stepped in.

Feeney was always one step ahead of his detractors, whether from his critics in the police, politicians or the scousers. He had always a fall-guy ready to heap guilt, suspicion or blame on; their bewildered faces never helped them shake off the guilt. Eddings and GG were just two of the high-profile victims of innuendo or corruption. Feeney had elevated his reputation in the Scottish Parliament, he had giving a well- researched and cost effective paper and then gave oral evidence not to stop but manage the spiraling drug dependency that had engulfed Scotland for over a decade. The policy committee on drug culture and the consequences, where he would recommend the professional private sector would tackle drug and alcohol abuse, and let the NHS get back to its core role and out of treating drug dependency on an ad-hoc basis. The private- clinics would be the ideal laboratory, nothing else to date had worked, and this alternative was more cost-effective than dispensing methadone. He had attended many seminars and always praised local councillors and MSPs for their attention to detail and their courage in tacking the scourge of the evil drug trade.

All political parties invited him to think-tanks and brainstorming meetings sometimes for the weekends at plush hotels such as the Dunblane Hydro and Gleneagles Hotels,

It was better to isolate themselves from the distractions of meeting the public. He came away from these seminars more confident about his financial future, the all-party committee were clamouring for him to set up a think-tank and present the findings in two years' time, he politely refused, citing his never ending battle with the drug barons that blighted Dundee and the villages that surrounded it. Some of the politicians had tears in their eyes as they listened to him give personal battles with certain individuals who seemed more strangely concerned about raids on dealers' houses and the effect it had on their off-spring. When he had won the battle *and* the war would he consider leaving the police and join the politicians on a policy committee? He would think long and hard before he made any decision.

To his admiring audience he gave a slide show of the dealers he had put before the courts, and their millions of pounds of assets that had been confiscated and then had being used against other dealers, so in effect the dealers assets and money were being used against other dealers. The politicians liked that one, they were eating out of his hand, and they liked the way he went about his business, never blaming politicians dissimilar to certain heads of drugs squads in Glasgow and Edinburgh, he wasn't playing the media against the politicians, he was embedded in their memories.

Before he handed in his sniffer dog, he would offer up another fall-guy to the gullible editor, public and politicians; Paul Welsh. He had no evidence forensic or otherwise against Welsh, but he perceived him as a threat, his gut instincts had never let him down, he had to be removed either by legal precedent or his favourite alibi, innuendo. Feeney never got the chance, Welsh had much to thank the dealers and money-men from Merseyside, if it wasn't for their antipathy for Feeney and their timely intervention, he would certainly be removed from the drug squad or ended up in Perth

Prison.

* * *

The Glass Pavilion restaurant shone brightly against
the black starlit sky. She had avoided going there with
Monty, he was insistent that they dine there they had the
money the clothes, why couldn't they enjoy their
money? She told him they had the clothes, the money,
unfortunately for them he had notoriety as well. They
had to live their lives in the shadows away from the
wannabee criminal celebrities. Sometimes the shadow
was more dangerous than the substance.

However, today was different she had been invited to a
late lunch with the owner of her unit at the docks. He
was smitten by her, this lunch was just to go over the
details of their agreement again, she didn't mind. Her
head was slightly ahead of her heart, she would bring up
a joint venture into a new business, he was worried about
more leverage, but she wasn't, she could turn down the
heat on his concerns; all she needed were his approval
and his signature for the loan application with the
London private finance company. Patrick Connelly
would do the rest. She was removing the stench of
Monty's money from her legitimate new businesses, her
dining partner would add to the creditability of her new
ventures. Christmas morning would the re-birth of her
inner self that had been held hostage by the guilt of
Monty's illegal activities, some days she would
flagellate her conscience for organising Monty's money
from drug deals, other day's she would enjoy his
memory and his money over a cold crisp bottle of
champagne. The millions that she had hidden away
would see her into her dotage.

When she finally moved to London she would suggest
that he would take over the running of the company, and
if there was an off-chance that the contraband had been
discovered she would be in London.

She would have no active part in the day to day running of the car sales, and other haulage business. She would be beyond suspicion, but not above it. Monty had given her an excuse to escape her incident free but boring marriage, his death and finances had opened many, many doors. She didn't need a compass to navigate her way to even more riches, but she was portentous to understand that things good and bad must come to an end. The dealers' murders brought everything into a cold, clear sharp focus.

The window of her car was opened slightly to allow the smoke out, she thought better and more clear when she smoked, her hair with the new tints made her look more glamorous, his car drew up behind her, he was wearing a dark suit and a shirt and tie, it reminded her of Monty when he had to appear at court, he walked towards her car he stopped and pulled open the door, he was smiling as if he had difficulty in keeping something secret. She had been with Mr Boring, Mr Rough, now her patience could be paying off, he was definitely Mr Smooth. He took her hand to help her out. As he closed the door of her car, small flakes of snow fell on cue. Christmas would be much, much different this year; business could be mixed hopefully with pleasure.

***

'What did he say?'

'Nothing really, he just wants me to keep him informed what's going on, I think you're barking up the wrong tree, this editor, where is he getting the information?' Eddings pondered, looked over at the diner then looked at Spencer in a mischievous manner.

'I think you're wrong Gary, the information has been spot-on up till now, something is going on, I'm sure Welsh is involved... Turn the heater down I'm boiling here'

'Involved in what?'

'I don't know, but you'll have to grit your teeth and show patience. Do you think it was wise advising him of the interviews coming up?'

'Oh…I wouldn't argue with that, he trusts me and I trust him, even though you don't, if he is up to something he might, and I stress, might sound off to me.'

'Things have changed since I left the force, it seems less congenial.'

'When was it congenial? I can't remember anytime it wasn't a clique -ridden organization, you've only been away a couple of years at most, get a grip!'

'Is everything alright? You seem out-of-sorts; it's not normally your style.'

'Ach, I'm sorry, its just things, things like Christmas and what-might-have- been, just ignore my rants, it's not you it's me, I'm sorry.'

'You've nothing to be sorry about, I've been down there, and it's not pleasant, and for the record I hope Welsh is clean; or at worst not too many stains on his shirt, if you know what I mean.'

'I hope so as well, and everyone from the top to the bottom carries around some stains, it's just the times we live in now, serial criminals making complaints against police officers, human rights! They're not even human!' Eddings and Spencer burst out laughing. Things are so different now, I mean really different, you can't kid people on anymore; that could be deemed as harassment.'

'You're getting old, just like me, I'd hate to see the state of the police in ten years' time, probably won't be wearing uniforms because it curtails their freedom to be free spirits or something.'

'I don't know about that, but when it comes we'll be shocked for a minute then carry-on as normal, another right-on political stunt.'

'Probably…you can come to my house for Christmas dinner there's plenty to eat and drink.'
'Naw, thanks for the offer, but I've got other plans.'

***

In the office, the small lamp failed to fill the room with enough light, he wasn't complaining, he was going over his paperwork, he was pleased how careful he had been, if Welsh or anyone else alluded that he had advised or had openly participated in any fraudulent or criminal scheme, there was no paper-trail leading to him from anyone else, or pungent aromas. His emails smelt wonderful as well. Every Christmas Eve, he would be pulled to reminisce where he had come from the sleepy hamlet in Ireland to where he was today, it wasn't thoughts of how wealthy he was, but how he had overcome institutional bias against his religion and his country, this was the direction his moral- compass pointed him in the direction of the Asian then the Polish community, he knew what they were suffering. The Polish builders had returned home, but they had fond memories of Patrick Connelly and the city of Dundee. He had set them up in a luxury flat, at a subsidised rent; the builders didn't cause him any concerns. He was the facilitator between the young multi-millionaire property developer and the Polish builders, who had come to Pat with genuine concerns. He listened to them and the next day called the property developer to invite him to lunch, he declined the invitation as he was too busy, he was told that it was urgent and in his best interests.

He was waiting outside the restaurant showing his impatience, Pat was twenty-minutes late, when he did arrive he invited him into his car and drove off without any explanation, some protests were aired in the car, he was told in a gruff voice to shut up, they stepped out the car at the summit of Dundee Law (Hill), Pat handed him a pair of binoculars and told him to concentrate on the west-end then gave a running commentary on his late father's life story, he told to him to focus on the university and lectured him why he should think himself lucky and it was his father's money and Pat's contacts that eased him into the university, his academic qualifications were not suffice to make him a student of much promise, Pat arranged for a tutor, he entered the university by the skin of his teeth, but left with enough brains to satisfy someone with two- heads. Pat told him to aim the binoculars on Broughty Ferry, and versed him in the chronological time frame, of the battles for converting mansions into flats with the planning department and building control. Did you really think it was your charmless attitude that made the planning and building control departments overcome their myriad of objections? He knew the answer.

And so it went on for nearly an hour, the hubris eventually fell from his shoulders, what was it he wanted? Less hours and an increase in wages for the Polish workers, each would be given a rise of a hundred pounds, and you're still getting a bargain, and the hundred pounds would be cash in hand, you were frequently using this paperless method. The money should be lodged at his office every Friday, in case you forget. He understood.

The Polish workers were grateful to Patrick Connelly, they had a collection for the homeless and disaffected at Christmas time in Dundee, Patrick Connelly topped up their generous donation and it made front page news.

He said it was the Polish construction workers way of saying thanks to the people of Dundee who had treated them so well. Then they went home to their families in various towns in Poland. That was the heart-warming thoughts of the past, but the future was less fulfilling, he couldn't get Welsh's clandestine meeting with Catherine in the early hours out of his head. He had given Welsh the opportunity to unburden himself, but he was not forthcoming.

Catherine had played the same card. Were they working in tandem? Was she behind the deaths of Monty's fellow dealers, she and Welsh pick up their business and their profits? It had to be something like that; Catherine funnelling Monty's stained money into a legitimate business, could the profits for the deceased dealers be mixed in with Monty's? If they were he was totally against cleaning their money. Looking on the debit side if they were implacably involved they would have brought someone or other persons from outwith Scotland, that he was absolutely sure. On this occasion the less he knew; the better for all concerned. It would interesting if Welsh would be at the Christmas Carol service at the Christmas tree on the Perth Road, before they went to Midnight Mass. Tonight would be a quixotic and worry-free occasion if he can overthrow the various pernicious scenarios he was playing in his mind before he left the office. When he had these disturbing thoughts this was the time to ease himself from potential problematic individuals, if he stuck with them he would be well-rewarded but his demeanour would be there for all to see. He wasn't prepared to take the risk.

He had been successful in approaching the business advisors of Mr Madni and showing them potential business opportunities in Dundee and in Perthshire. Catherine was a smart lady but she may have secrets that could be exhumed one day, Welsh was clever also, never indiscreet, never showy, but that meeting with Catherine, that was never far away, if only he knew the reason he would be able to accept it but not agree with it. It was the not knowing, that affected him deeply. He looked round the office and looked at the old sofa, memories of many influential people who had sat their forthcoming with business, criminal and personal concerns.

Rich and powerful they maybe, however, they had

worries similar to people on State benefits, children who were errant, spouses who were violent away from the glare of the public and friends, but who were upstanding individuals that were upstanding attendees' of the church and members of the Rotary Club. It was time to end this nostalgic movie, he switched off the light, his mind was now free, only the sound of his feet on the wooden floor were louder than his thoughts.

He was the only person in the building, the echoing sound of him walking to the lift made him feel uneasy. He was troubled how his ebullient mood was quickly waning; foreboding and a fear of the future enveloped him as he entered the lift. He kept his finger on the open button and stepped back into the hall and looked left and right.

Outside in the battered car an individual observed the office return to darkness, hopefully Connelly would emerge soon.

***

The conversation played over and over in his mind, his strong Chinese accent made it difficult to understand, but he repeated the message back to him slowly.

'This would be the only task that we ask of you. You stole from us, when the task is completed, you're free. We are honourable people.'

The pint he had been nursing in Mennies Bar on the Perth Road had rising in temperature, he was mentally prepared, kill or be killed.

The choice was stark; GG didn't have a choice, tortured, killed then butchered then his limbs cast into the unforgiving Tay, the thought of it sent an unpleasant felling from his stomach to his brain. If the task was completed and they were honorable, he could look forward to the New Year like no other. Promises of riches; ended up like dust in the desert, they had got too ambitious, ripping off the Triads, once was brave, ripping them off repeatedly was downright foolhardy, he couldn't blame GG, his confidence couldn't be challenged, he never uttered any other possible outcome, they walk away, they wouldn't need to run. No blame was attached to GG for naming him to the Triads; the thought of GG holding out as long as he could, until a knife sliced him and ended his life made him wince.

The bar was in a state of human merriment, he was the scowl in the corner, he had to lift his mood, he looked at the lager, picked it up then consumed it quickly, one more drink then he would go home, have a meal, shower, and then prepare for the life-changing event. If he was successful; life could return back to some kind of normality, he would keep his head down and work in a diligent manner. Seven pm and still morose, he had to eject this mood, he hoped the fresh, cold lager would lift his spirits, all about him, people of all ages were in high spirits, studying their drunken faces, he was envious of them, they didn't know how lucky they were, if only they knew what he was about to do, their expansive smiles would crumple. He returned to his seat he was glad that no one had sat at the table next to him and trying to strike up a conversation, the call would come and he would be on his way, it would be later as the Chinese caller had told him to eat and sleep for a couple of hours, he'll feel better. All he could reply throughout the brief conversation was a limp okay
. The jukebox was playing all the usual Christmas songs, a group of young women came in replete with party hats; one went over to the jukebox then joined her friends at the bar. For the first time that evening he was smiling, he envied their effervescence and vitality, they may have massive hangovers on Christmas morning, but they would all remember this Christmas Eve. Last Christmas by Wham! drifted to a close, then a Killers song came und they erupted into squeals of delight, they started dancing with not a care in the world. He felt his

feet tapping, the song had the hook; 'Can you read my mind? If only they could read his. Doubts that he carried with him were disappearing, 'aim and shoot' was his mantra. ' Simple.

***

Staring into the mirror, he knew he was a hypocrite but he didn't feel like one, midnight mass was excellent theatre and he always came out of the church feeling better than when he went in, but he still didn't believe in God, he was doing this for his wife's sake. She told him many times before, he was kidding himself on, she knew he believed, she had heard his anguished cry for help from God during the night as he was suffering from some unknown terror, she didn't bring it up in the morning.

His tie was straight and he looked good, he flicked his fingers through his greying black hair, his wife had shouted upstairs that his drink had been poured; he said he was on his way. He looked like the cat that had got the cream, it had been a fulfilling year, he was thinking about the money, he was thinking about Catherine and her bedroom accident, disposing of his body had been challenging, but the look of delight as they watched him disappear into the furnace was exhilarating, if there was a God surely he would have smiled at that?

Gary Spence had been interviewed; it was all routine stuff; 'is there someone who is acting in a peculiar manner that you know of?' He had nothing to worry about.

He pulled himself away from the mirror, he switched the bedroom light off, he couldn't take his eyes off the view from the window, Dundee's lights were twinkling, he moved towards the window, his hands were on his hips, he could see the Christmas tree on the Perth Road, a crowd was gathering, he looked up at the sky, maybe the Met would be correct tonight snow was on its way.

He turned religiously to Broughty Ferry, Baldovie was pumping the papal smoke high into the sky, his smile grew as wide as the Tay, no feeling of impending doom, feelings of pride, and ridding Dundee of an odious character, sadly there would be queue as long as the Tay trying the deceased shoes on. He pulled the curtains tightly shut, a queasy, nauseous sensation washed over him, he pulled the curtains apart and let the moonlight rush into the room, instantly he felt better. He made his way downstairs convinced the feeling was because he had closed the curtains too quickly. His wife commented he looked awful; he looked as though he had seen a ghost of Christmas past.

He brushed aside her concerns, he took the beer and took a long, long drink, his wife looked at him with genuine concerns, was this the best time to tell him about his pleas to the Almighty during the night? His colour came back, he was shaken, but he didn't know what was the primary cause; something was embedded deep in his unconscious. She sipped her orange juice. He assured her everything was alright; he changed the subject from his health to the Christmas carols at the Perth Road. This subject lightened her mood; she was tempted to say that she enjoyed the carol service as much as the service in the church, but didn't want to offer the chance for him to ridicule her. He went on to say a lot of the Polish community had returned home, due to the recession, the locals had to carry the standard.

***

He had stayed longer than he had anticipated; the joy of Christmas had penetrated his impervious mind -set. Glancing at his watch had become a nervous tic; he removed the watch in the gents. He had estimated the time in his head, a couple of minutes either side of his unscientific calculations didn't cause him any undue worry. His fate and his quarry were in the hands of kismet. It was time to heed the advice of his Chinese master, eat and sleep. Reluctantly, he left the bar and hailed a taxi, an alibi if things didn't go according to his plan. As the taxi drove down the Perth Road he looked at some of the iconic buildings as if he was a wide-eyed tourist, smokers were huddled together shivering in the bitter cold; when nicotine called they all obeyed. He felt the chill of fear, failure and a future in a prison cell engulf him, he tried to stop a tear emerging, if things went wrong, he was going away to prison for a long, long time, if he was successful he would have his life back, was it a life that he cherished? Away from the joyous scene of the bar, he felt lonely and vulnerable, he felt the mobile vibrating against his thigh; but it just moved as the taxi negotiated a corner. The taxi pulled up he pulled out a ten pound note and wished the driver a peaceful and merry Christmas. Up the stairs he walked, a man resigned to his fate, unwilling to turn the key in the lock, his mind cranking up devils that await his presence. In the flat his subdued feelings lifted slowly, he had to force himself to think positive thoughts, he threw the keys onto the kitchen table, he knew he shouldn't have another beer, but he need something to aid him to sleep. He took a pizza out of the freezer and put it into the microwave, while it was cooking he opened the bottle of beer and went into the darkness of his lounge, contemplating when the call would come, looking out of the window, he watched a couple the worse for wear try to navigate their way on the snow covered pavement.

They were vainly trying to help one another. Lucky devils, they don't know they're living. The ping of the microwave called him to the feast that was ready for his consumption, whether he was hungry or not he was going to finish all of the pizza; it would be the first. Once the pizza had cooled, he ripped it into four pieces, to his amazement he enjoyed it, it was the same pizza with the same toppings, the loud ticking of the clock drew his attention, ten- minutes- to- nine, he hoped to be in bed by nine. He put the last slice down on the table, and then went into the cold bedroom; he switched on the electric blanket and pulled the curtains tightly shut. In the kitchen he consumed the last slice, it had taken him over ten minutes, but he had managed it, for the first time. That was what he had to do when the call came, be determined and return home, shower and change then go to the party, he wouldn't need to act he was happy, he would be exhilarated. He stifled a yawn, he was happy and he was tired; all frenetic nerves had exited his mind and body. He retired to bed and left the mobile on the bedside cabinet. Maybe it won't ring?

***

Behind closed doors and sparkling Christmas trees, Christmas was not universally welcomed. Memories were being stirred, loved ones remembered and revered. Marriages that were on the surface secure and happy last Christmas had either ended or were in the unstoppable course to be dissolved. Some of the recent divorcees had plunged head first into second marriages only to rue ending their first marriages. Picking over the bones of the failed marriage things didn't look so bad. Now they were smiling to the observant world and telling everyone that life was much better now. When the alcohol was flowing the tears would also flow to a childhood confidante, they had made a monumental mistake, they were living a lie, beyond the façade of the big house, and expensive car, their life was empty, of the most important facet; contentment.

Gary Spence could have written the above, but he couldn't tell anyone how he felt, not just at Christmas but every waking hour. Even the copious amount of alcohol and women that he enjoyed couldn't dull the pain of his failed marriage. He didn't blame his revered ex-wife; mea culpa. He stayed away from colleagues parties, he didn't exactly enjoy his own company but he was safer on his own. No amount of cajoling from well-meaning younger colleagues could persuade him to give up his beer and DVD box sets of American cop shows, he was an admirer of The Shield and The Wire, that was the police force he would like to have joined, where the criminals were treated with baseball bats and clenched fists. He was on his third bottle of beer, the last time he felt the spontaneity of happiness rush through his body was when he was told of the blood bath at Old Glamis Road, when the victims' identities were released he was ecstatic. If he had thought about killing the scumbags in Dundee they were on the list; if he was avaricious he would add one more name to the death list

In the pub the following weekend, much speculating was being discussed, as usual he listened and smiled inwardly as outlandish theories came forth, when he was asked his take on it, he replied.

'I don't know who did it, but I admire their handiwork,' he wouldn't expound anymore when goaded. Then he went back to a self-imposed purdah and listened with a mixture of awe and stupidity as the self- appointed top detective gave his theory then supposedly backed it up with 'facts'. Everyone stared in unity at him he was basking in his own self-importance, he returned Spence's smirk.

'Anything to say Gary, you seem to find something amusing?

'You're right; I do find it amusing, very amusing...I think you're an affront to stupidity.'

Then he made his second mistake, he lunged at Spence, he was punched back to where he was previously sitting, pontificating to all and sundry. That was the reason he didn't attend any get-togethers, he couldn't listen to anyone, including his ex-wife, though in the silence of the room he wished he had. He would never marry again, nor live with another woman, he couldn't restrain himself, nor would he, he was his own man; there was never any doubt about that.

***

Patrick Connelly and his wife walked down from their house towards the Perth Road, his wife insisted they walk from Magdalene Green then take the long narrow lane than ran from Magdalene Green to Perth Road; the lane was dark and steep. Their voices in the silence of the lane gathered an extra octave, their laughter as they spoke about their early courtship and how they sat for hours in all seasons on the bench, staring over to Fife, and wondering where fate would take them. As his wife remembered things he had forgotten, he looked at the snow covered roof of the imposing mansion that acted as the gambling club, he smiled at the names of the elite and discreet membership; she had mistaken his smile as an endorsement of her memory. Near the summit of the lane, he sensed potential trouble, voices of aggression were tumbling down towards them; she became mute. He reassured her that everything would be alright; he held her hand more tightly and forced her to increase her pace.

Twenty metres and the aggressors came into view, they stopped arguing amongst themselves and became silent, they stepped aside to let the elderly couple past, Pat had whispered avoid eye-contact with them. They were into the bright lights of the Perth Road, and were relieved to see party goers walking in both directions, he looked back at the three men in their thirties, they locked eyes, he felt uncomfortable, that tingle was moving up his spine, his wife noticed him shake, he said he had a feeling someone had walked over his grave. She pulled him closer, his face matched the snow, she stole a look at the cause of his discomfort; she didn't recognise any of them. Across the street a group of young people were in high-spirits, their minds emptied the malevolent experience from the three men, his colour and smile returned.

'Oh to be young again!'

'That's alright for you to say Patrick; I wouldn't go back again if the Lord Almighty invited me, I'm happy where I am, aren't you?'

'I would change some things, but when I look back, we did not bad.'

'You forget all the struggles, living in a cold damp flat with outside toilet, and the derogatory remarks from the bigots, no thanks, we've came through all that, they were not all champagne and roses, you don't forget horrible experiences like that Patrick.'

'You're right, we don't have to sit at the back of the bus anymore; we take it all our good fortune for granted don't we?'

'No, you do, I thank God every night, without him I don't know where we'd be.'

'We are lucky…Christmas is magical, how many people do you think will be at the tree tonight then? She looked at him horrified. He felt a sharp tap on his shoulder.

***

The noise from the motor-bike woke him from a deep peaceful sleep.

He was surprised at the ease he fell asleep, he cocked one eye at the clock he had only been asleep for just over an hour; he smiled then closed his eye. He reached over for his mobile, he had no missed calls, he placed it on the pillow and then pulled the quilt over his head, his mind never questioned the morality of his task, if he had a conscience it was out partying; nothing was troubling him.

The powerful motor-bike had been expertly parked between the cars, he looked up towards Lenny's flat, it was in darkness, good boy he thought, taking the advice of a wise but violent Chinaman, he pulled up the sleeve of the tight fitting biker's leather jacket to check the time; plenty of time, Lenny had drunk more than was advisable, but if it eased his nerves and made the job easier, he was not too concerned.

Mennies Bar had been an implosion of merriment, he had discreetly observed Lenny his face had shorn itself of worry, the group of well-oiled females had made his job easier, when they put The Killers songs on the jukebox; he thought that the name might have caused him to think twice what lay before him; it had the opposite effect, he had consumed four pints, two pints of lager and two pints of shandy. Sandwiches were on the table and at both ends of the bar, Lenny was certainly not on a diet, that was a good sign, he had seen a few men crumble just before they had to complete their side of the bargain, which left Lenny no choice; there were no second chances with this organization.

The car drew up parallel to the motor bike, the door sprung open; he went into the rear of the car.

'All set then?'

'Everything's going to plan, I've got faith in our boy, how about you, some regrets or doubts?'
The car moved off without any reply. The male on the passenger side turned round and smiled at him.

'Don't worry, its Christmas, we'll be on the M6 when it all kicks off, this time tomorrow we'll be flying from John Lennon airport to Tenerife, thousands of miles away from this snow.'

'Our car is parked just round the corner, I filled it full of juice, we won't have to stop till we're in Liverpool; the roads should be quiet tonight.'

'So it's up to you Mr Quiet, it all depends on your good self, it's been fun and profitable , I'll give you the text message when he leaves his flat, just make sure he follows through.'

'Nothing to worry about,' said the male in the

passenger seat.

'I know that, I'm just making sure this will be a success, for all our sakes.'

The car came to a halt at the Queens Hotel, the front and back seat passengers went into the bar of the busy hotel, the driver lost all tension when they left. He switched on the radio; he liked the classical Christmas carols. If destiny was kind, life would return to a sense of normality.

***

At the end of the watch night service, smiles and the shaking of hands outside the church were being fondly exchanged, family members saying goodbye and making their merry way to their cars and homes. Connelly saw Welsh with his wife hurriedly walk up the Perth Road, strange? He surmised they would have their car parked in the car park of the bank which was in the opposite direction. The snow flurries came down, people looked up to the heavens; it was a white Christmas after all, the Met Office had been proved correct.

Welsh and his wife crossed the road and made their way into the university grounds, he felt more at ease, knowing Welsh, he had pulled strings somewhere or it could have been his wife who had wangled a parking space.

In ten minutes he would be exchanging presents with his wife beside the mantlepiece as they had done for forty-years.

The swirling, blinding snow had in his mind over stayed its early Christmas morning welcome, they valiantly battled their way through the church goers and groups of boisterous young people who were making their way to the night clubs in the city centre, the vision of him warming himself and drinking an Irish whiskey increased his desire to reach home in record time, much to the annoyance of his wife who told him to savour the snow and the excitement of Christmas. He slowed down then encouraged her with a description of her present that was waiting to be unwrapped. Across the road sitting in his car, the occupant smiled, he was warm, the two of them were in obvious discomfort, he took out his mobile it was picked up on the second ring. The message was brief, he gave him the name of his quarry, there was no reply; he was told there was a motor bike between two cars about twenty- metres from the entrance to his close. In the car to his left the boot was unlocked inside the boot was the crash helmet, a biker's leather jacket and keys. There was also a mobile phone. After the task was completed he would be called and told where to park the bike, and leave the gun, helmet and jacket. He then gave him the address.

Lenny had been awake and showered from eleven pm. He had been killing time, now was the time to do the killing. He shot out his arms and spread his fingers, they were steady, mentally he had been prepared, the victim's death would be a shock, but once the fake obituaries were withdrawn from the publics' gaze, the sympathy would descend into a vitriol epithet. One life hopefully would disappear before his eyes; then his life would be brought out of deep storage. In a strange way he felt he was honouring his mentor; GG. He had mentioned the victim when he spoke about what was wrong with the justice system, 'those lawyers and do-gooders nowadays, could exonerate Pontius Pilot, because he had a difficult and stressful childhood, they didn't mean to kill Jesus it was a prank that went horribly wrong.'

He recalled how bitter he was. He checked the bullets in the gun, which was quite heavy; aim and shoot, aim and shoot. Convinced he covered every eventuality, he zipped up the dark tight- fitting jacket complete with hood he fitted the snug woollen beanie hat and pulled on the tight black gloves, he moved along the hall and stared through the spy-hole into the semi-darkness of the close, all was still; he gulped then opened the door as quiet as he could.

The cold still air met him full in the face, he locked the door then tiptoed down the stone stairs, listening in case someone came in from the street, all was quiet, he moved with purpose and his eyes searched hurriedly for the motorbike, he saw it, it looked powerful, someone was across the street relieving themselves and enjoying a kebab at the same time, he guessed that was an infraction against hygiene. He felt light-hearted, he opened the boot the black leather jacket would fit over his jacket without much difficulty, the bike roared into life, he had the-planned route in his head, avoiding the areas covered by CCTV, he purred the machine down the Perth Road, he took a left then eased the throttle back to an aggressive hum and let the bike follow the tyre marks in the snow, he had to nurse the bike when he felt the wheels hit patches of snow covered ice, he questioned the wisdom of coming this way. His visor was attracting the snow flakes, he wiped them, his vision was much clearer now, he used his feet like stabilisers, and felt more confident mentally and physically.

When he was out of this dark slippery lane, he would be back on more stable terra firma. Patrick Connelly turned instinctively around, his hearing had always been acute, his eyes sighed at the sight of the motorcyclist inching his way down the dark and semi-dark areas of the winding lane. It was apparent to him that his wife had not seen or heard the motorcyclist, he wanted to run but couldn't leave her; she would have stood her ground and demanded an explanation. His throat became dry; he developed an irritable cough, which he tried unsuccessfully to suppress

His visor was pushed up now; his eyes were more observant, at this slow speed it was safer to see the landscape in panoramic vogue rather than peering through the visor. On the right hand side a wooden door had been left off the hatch, it was banging intermittently , it made him feel nervous, he moved his chest he could feel the gun impacting against his chest, he coyly looked at the wooden door, this helmet impaired his hearing, he never heard the old man or his dog, they both came out of the door, the dog was excited and tried to launch itself at the bike, the old man yanked it back with a series of tugs, and shouted at the dog, or that's what it looked like, his shouts were muffled. He could lip read the old man apoligising; he raised his black leathered arm in acknowledgement, while staring straight ahead. Patrick Connelly and his wife simultaneously turned round to see the frenetic antics of the dog and its irritable owner, she wanted to check if the motorcyclist was hurt, she was positive she had seen the dog snap at his leg, Patrick told her not to get involved. The motorcyclist was increasing his speed.

***

'I told you, you can't live without your mobile, I knew you would take it, you just can't help yourself, just a couple of hours that's all I asked?'

'I'm on holiday, but you never know when I might be needed, just a force of habit that's all, we're not going to fall out are we?'

'You're pushing it, even though you promised me that you wouldn't take it, I left mine, what is the problem? Do you want someone to tell you they need you in Dundee, you've got to learn to relax… it's easy you know.'

'Watch your speed…'

'Oh dear, I'm ten mile over the speed limit on the Tay Bridge going to Wormit…I expect your mobile to ring, then you'll be instructed to arrest me. Relax Paul; I've killed my speed, happy now?'

To break the tension, he turned the radio on.

'It's good to hear the cheesy songs at Christmas, do you

438

think we'll have our ears assaulted by Slade or Wham!, before we reach Wormit, and are you willing to wager a tenner. I say we won't.'

'You're on… It's lovely seeing the snow fall, even in the rear-view mirror Dundee looks lovely.'

'Is that because we're driving away from it, guilty conscience?'

'Hardly,' she laughed, it's not as if we've emigrated is it…that's a lovely start to Christmas morning, I saw you turn down the radio, turn it up and hand over the ten pound note please.'

'You don't miss a trick don't you, I'll give you the tenner when we reach the house; you trust me don't you?'

On the opposite carriageway a police car is travelling at a high speed with its lights flashing, he couldn't help turning his head round. 'Maybe there's a freebie going on at Rough & Fraser's…'

'…Ooh, you can be so cruel, can't be anything that serious, I can always find out if you really want to know.'

'Don't you dare!'

'I'll check to see if someone has tried to call me, is that alright?'

'We're nearly home, check and put it away, in the house it goes back on, I only asked for you to leave it at home for a couple of hours while we were at midnight mass, nothing life-changing, and you couldn't even do that, could you?'

'I'm sorry, it's a force of habit, I know that's no excuse, it won't happen next year, I promise.'

The car stopped outside the gates of their house, she pressed the remote, the gates wouldn't respond.

'These gates will be the death of me,' she pressed the button repeatedly. 'Fuck!'

'Language!' he couldn't control his enjoyment at seeing her in a state of anger.

'How much did we pay for these fucking time-saving gates?'

'I'll call the engineer out when the Christmas holidays are over, I think it's the cold weather that stops the signal from the remote.'

'That's comforting to know, so we wait here till July, and they still don't work, he'll tell you that it's too hot, I'll speak to the engineer we want replacement gates, there's obviously a major fault, cold weather my foot, I didn't know there wasn't any electric gates or garage doors in Alaska, strange that, don't you think?'

'Close the window, you've made your point, I'll tell him that the gates have failed to open on other occasions, I'll tell him that we want new gates or our money back, how does that sound?'

She had calmed down.

'That's a very good idea; are you going to be a gentleman and get out the car and open the gates?'

'You can really be bitchy at times, do you think you can manage to drive into the drive without any problem or will I go into the house and get a torch?'

'I'm sorry Paul...please just go and open the gates, I need the loo now.'

He left the car and walked across the slippery pavement, cursing Fife council for not gritting the pavements. He pulled one half of the heavy gate into the driveway.

Out of nowhere the motorcyclist ran past his car carrying a gun, Welsh was pulling the second half of the gate open, he stopped automatically when he saw him come to a halt crouch and aim the gun at him, he tried to see inside the dark visor. The shots broke the serene silence. He fell onto the snow covered pavement, he lay there motionless, she watched from the car unable to believe what she had just witnessed. Welsh was like a frozen statue with his hand on the gate, he began to shiver, and it wasn't from the cold, fear had invaded his body, he felt the warm urine run down the inside of his leg.

Neighbours came to their doors and windows.

'You're a lucky man...hold on while I call the chief and an ambulance, not for Evel Knevel here.' While he turned his back, he looked at the sprawled body, seeping blood, motionless, dead. Welsh still stood at the gate unable or scared to move, his wife sobbing with her head in her hands. Spence ended the call and walked over to Welsh.

'Someone from your past preserved the future for you,' he signaled for him to come from the gate. Welsh's wife was left sobbing in the car; there was silent agreement that was the best place for her. They both stared into the other's eyes; there were no signs of atonement.

An awkward silence filled the void, Spence sensed stones had been flung in the past; the sobbing in the car filled the air. Welsh walked away from them and went to comfort his wife.

'What was the all about,' asked a mystified Spence.

'You'd be better to ask him...'

'...No, I'm asking you, something is not right here, you save his life, and he just stares at you in a cold manner, what happened GG.?'

His mobile rings he walks away from GG who is left on his own, he walks over and goes on his haunches; he thinks that he'll be overcome by grief and guilt, after all he was the architect of Lenny's brutal death, it was just a pity that he couldn't have fired shots at Welsh, two birds that would no longer be able to sing. He knew that Spence was a member of the armed response unit and was armed every minute he was on duty. He was just as shocked as Welsh's wife at the speed of the event unfolding, when he pulled out the gun and told Lenny to stop, he didn't wait for a reply; he just popped the bullets into him when he didn't turn round. He expected Lenny to fire bullets into Welsh then Spence to shoot Lenny

dead. Spence would have been the credible witness at
the enquiry that followed. Spence ended the call and
walked over to GG and tapped him on the back, GG
looked at him, Spence didn't say anything; he just
indicated with a slight movement of the head that he
should follow him.

Welsh had spoken to his wife she wasn't sobbing
anymore, he indicated to her that she would be best to
stay put, till the police and ambulance arrived, then he
walked towards the gate and stooped down and peered
at the electronic sensor, he waved his arm for them to
come over. Spence looked at GG in a most apologetic
fashion.

'You'd be better to stay here.'

He walked over and looked at what Welsh was
pointing at, he was animated , he pointed to the car and
the direction where Lenny ran from towards him, Spence
nodded his head, and then took him by the arm and
walked away from the gate in the opposite direction
from GG. After about ten metres he stopped, they both
looked at GG.

'There's obviously been a problem with you two in the
past, I would advise you not to look so coldly or be
limited in your praise of GG, when you are giving a
statement, because if you do you're handing them spades
to start digging, if you want certain things not to see the
light of day, be more thankful, be glad you'll see
Christmas morning daylight, do you understand me?'
Welsh had been thinking along the same line.

'I understand, it was just, just that I felt guilty, I
advised Feeney to remove him from the drug squad,
Feeney had told me he suspected that he was cooperating
with a dealer, he asked my advice, he didn't name GG, I
just told him if he had reason and proof, get rid of him.'

'Don't mention any of this to the detectives, they'll
eventually find out that he left under a cloud, I'll tell GG
that I know the full story, you had nothing to do with

him being removed, that was to do with the drugs in his car, you had nothing to do with that. If anybody is the bad guy it's Feeney. Got it?'

'I'm happy with that; I can understand the hatred he has for me. I knew tonight that something would happen, but nothing as dramatic as this, I was thinking the lights on the Christmas tree, or the oven would pack in. I was having a wee difference of opinion with my wife when we were driving home from midnight mass, something daft, I promised not to carry my mobile to midnight mass. But I did take it.'

'That makes sense, I tried to call you but you must have had it switched off, I wanted to tell you not to answer your door and stay away from your windows.'

'I checked my mobile when we were on the Tay Bridge; I had no missed calls; that was when I saw a police car speeding from the Fife direction going towards Dundee.'

'That was a litany of miscommunications, I called a senior officer, as I didn't want any misunderstandings, but he fucked up, he thought I said that I wanted the Fife police to go to your house and warn you, he did, but you didn't update your contact details, they were going to your old house in the west end, he couldn't understand why I wanted the Fife police, but didn't want to argue or query my instructions. That was the reason you saw the police car bombing along the Tay Bridge.'

'Right,' he said slowly, 'and I've figured out why I didn't get your call, there's a black spot about the Newport area, where you can't get a signal.'

'God, that's right all I heard was 'can't connect you please try later.' 'Do you want to know how GG comes into the equation?'

'Of course!'

Better to hear from the horse's mouth.'

He calls him over. Taking deep breaths, he walks slowly over, similar to an actor on opening night hoping he remembers his lines, and he is convincing when the lines are delivered.

'GG you know Paul Welsh, he succeeded Joe Feeney, tell him what you told me.'

'I know him alright,' there was a hardness in the way the words came out; he had to keep his hatred in check. 'He was just doing his job, Feeney told me, it was you that said I was corrupt, you had been told this by a C.I. he just went by your judgement. Was it you that placed the drugs in the boot of my car, things can't be changed, I just need to know that's all.'

'No, definitely not, and it was Feeney that told me that you had an unhealthy relationship with a dealer; he never named you, I said that the officer had to go, it meant storing up trouble if he stayed.'

'I believe you, but I hope you understand my bitterness, I was the fall-guy for what I never understood, but from what you've told me, Feeney was using you against me, he must have been up to something that wasn't right, I can only speculate.'

'This is all news to me, this sounds like a police force within a police force, we can talk about this later, but GG tell Paul why you contacted me, and make it quick, the detectives will be here soon, and they'll separate all of us then take statements.'

'Well, Lenny is or was a young police constable, he came to me saying he wanted to be a detective and asked for guidance, I told him to come to his work, don't take sickies and build a cordial relationship with the young neds, and housewives on his beat, when you eventually get to be a detective you'll know every dealer, every housebreaker that used to be on your beat as a police constable, they'll be able to help you when serious crime happens, likes of murder, serious assault or rape. When Lenny heard I was suspended then charged and taken to court, he swore he would get revenge. After I appeared in court and the verdict came back as not proven, I walked free but I knew that was the end of my career, I resigned to keep my pension.

'Lenny came round to my flat with booze; beer, whisky and vodka. When I was drunk I must have told him that you and Feeney had set me up, I didn't realise what I had said, the next morning I forgot all about it, Lenny didn't mention it. I had never seen him from that morning maybe ten months ago, or it might be longer. I thought he didn't want anything to do with me because I had been taken to court and had resigned.

'I heard all the stories, there was a deal done with my solicitor if I resigned I would get a not-proven verdict, total rubbish. Tonight I got a text from Lenny after midnight saying he was going to sort Welsh out like he sorted the others out. I called him back immediately; he told me what I had said when I was drunk then hung up on me, I called Gary and told him the story, he came to my flat to pick me up, the intention was if Lenny turned up I could persuade him to go home, I never thought he meant he was going to shoot you, but Gary didn't discount this.'

'He must have planned this, he put Vaseline over the sensor on the gate, knowing that I would get out and open the gates manually, or if I didn't my wife would, and he would run over to the car and shoot me, with my seatbelt on I would be a sitting target. And when he mentioned the others does he mean Feeney and the social worker?'

'I don't know, the forensics will examine the gun and bullets,' said Spence. The sound of sirens coming towards them, made them look at one another.

'I'm due you an apology, GG, I'm sorry.'

'Apology accepted, but I'm due you an apology...' Spence interjected.

'You're due Paul an apology? You've just saved his

life!'

'And I'm due Lenny an apology, if I didn't tell him about Feeney and Welsh, sorry Paul, we wouldn't be standing here in the freezing cold on Christmas morning, and Lenny would be enjoying himself at some nightclub, but because of my drunken rant, he's dead, and you could've have been dead as well.'

The fleet of cars and ambulances came to a halt in different directions outside his house. Detectives walked quickly from their cars, they looked at Lenny being examined by the paramedics; then walked over to the three of them.

'GG don't mention the drunken conversation with Lenny.'

'What!'

'Paul's right, it'll just open more wounds from your past, say nothing, you've suffered enough, and don't look nervous, they're coming over.'

'Okay, I'm just shocked, that's all.'

Spence walked over to the two detectives and took them to the gate, they all examined the gate, one of the detectives called over the forensic team; they took photographs of the gate and told the detectives to stay away. Spence and the detectives moved towards Spence's car he pointed out the direction the motorcyclist ran from. They moved from the car and retraced the path the motorcyclist had run

Approximately one hundred metres from Spence's car on the opposite side of the road the motor-bike was purring leant against a tree pointing in the opposite direction. He was looking to depart as quickly as possible, he wasn't taken a chance that the powerful motor -bike would fail to start. They walked over to the tree and called the forensic team over. They walked away before they were told to remove themselves from the crime scene. Welsh and GG observed the men walking back towards them.

'Is it a really good idea for me not to mention what I told Lenny?'

'Listen to us, if we were in your shoes and you in one of ours, you would do the same, and you don't know what Lenny was up to do you? You have never seen him for months, people change, he might have been working for someone who paid him money to kill me, and who killed Feeney? Have you thought it might have been Lenny? And if it was he must have killed that innocent social worker, leave it with the detectives GG, you don't want them deviating from this, and into your past. They'll know soon enough about you resigning.

'But don't give them an excuse to connect you to Lenny in all this, you saved my life, Lenny wanted to end my life, that's the way we play it; you're the hero here, not a suspect.'

They stopped short of them.

'Can we have a word with you Gordon, or would you prefer to be called GG?' He looked at Welsh, and then slowly moved towards them, one of the detectives mouthed to Welsh if he was okay, he nodded his head. Camera flashes were appearing everywhere, the motorcyclist was like a prized exhibit, as would be expected. His wife was still in the car in the passenger seat a female detective was talking to her, she seemed to have stemmed the flow of tears. Uniformed officers went to neighbours houses and were interviewing them when it was established that none of them had witnessed anything significant they were thanked and invited to go back into their homes and close the doors.

No one had come near him, he would be interviewed last, that would give him time to examine the chaotic landscape that lay before him, and to thank lady luck for smiling on him once again, but his luck must be ebbing away somehow he thought, he couldn't be that lucky. When he was in Dubai , he knew that Feeney was going to be taken care of, Monty had told him so, Liverpool dealers had come to the end of their tethers with Feeney's avaricious demands, he didn't know the exact day when Feeney would be murdered but he would be taking advantage of his demise,

Michael Jameson was in exile, Feeney's death would create a vacuum, the Liverpool dealers didn't know about Feeney having a slice of his former loan-sharking empire, if he could convince Jameson that he was instrumental in having Feeney removed, this would allow Jameson to return to Dundee with the violent threat removed, of course there would be a price to pay. He had worked this out to his pecuniary advantage in Dubai. When the call came that Feeney was dead, Monty told him that there was a problem, someone had got to Feeney before the Liverpool dealers, they weren't worried, but Monty was, who had killed Feeney and the church goer? Welsh was perplexed, what church goer? Monty explained that this church goer was going into the church as he met the assassin coming out; it was a professional hit. The brief call ended, Welsh sought out Jameson, and told him the good news, he was free to return to Dundee but wait a couple of weeks while his business which had been transferred to another criminal would be offered back to him.

Welsh gave him the name and bank account number of his consultant's fee which would be paid in every month to the account. Jameson was delighted with the terms and conditions, he was bored in Dubai and he had never felt safe, give him the raw naked violence of the Hilltown any day. The rush of adrenalin of his good fortune was repeated when his life was saved by Spence and GG. He was saved from being implicated in Feeney's murder and he was saved from certain death on Christmas morning. That was some Christmas gift from lady luck. The white marquee tent was being erected over the motorcyclist's body. The detectives left Spence; they were coming over to him.

Welsh his wife, Spence and GG were taken to Police headquarters in Dundee, they were interviewed in a relaxed manner, only GG had knew Lenny personally, Spence had not knowingly come across him, he was just another uniformed officer. Welsh said the same. The history of GG going to court inevitably came up, Welsh straight-batted all the questions, he wasn't aware that Feeney had a grudge against GG, or GG against Feeney, however, since he was taken to court, he resigned, he could see why he wasn't seeing eye-to-eye with Feeney.

But Feeney had mentioned to him that at least he was removed from the force, so it was not a bad second prize, or words to that effect. It seemed to all concerned that Lenny felt in a perverse way that he had to take revenge on behalf of GG, and he blamed Feeney. The forensics would show whether the bullets removed from Feeney and the social worker were the same match as the bullets in the gun he had held in his dying hand. That would have to wait till after Christmas.

The detectives interviewing GG grilled him more intently as he had calculated, of his arrest and subsequent appearance in court. He couldn't explain why he would be set up, but he was convinced Feeney was instrumental in the set-up, but he didn't have the proof. He wanted to say something off-the-record. The DVD recorder was paused; the detectives were more relaxed; they knew something would come out of his mouth that would cause them a monumental headache. GG told them that he had thought long and hard, he had acres of time now that he was no longer employed, he had made a massive dent in the drug distribution network in Dundee, everyone congratulated him, from the Chief Constable to ordinary civilian workers in Bell Street, it seemed everyone had a friend or family member affected by drugs and he was making a massive difference, he had the crime statistics to back him up, not the phoney ones which stated crime in Dundee was going down, which coincidently, an elite committee would receive large bonuses, you can see where I'm going here. Crime goes up no bonus, crime comes down... The only person never to come near me and acknowledge I was doing a good job was Joe Feeney. Now why would that be?

'You tell us,' one of the intrigued detectives replied.

'I believe Feeney was involved in the drug trade, I was a threat to his income, he and a dealer or dealers set me up. Does it make sense to both of you?'

They looked at one another.

'We would have to look into what you have said GG, you understand that don't you? Can you give us a minute?'

The other detective opined spontaneously. 'It makes sense to me...if what you said was accurate, we'll talk to you shortly?'

'Sure, I won't be here much longer will I?'

They closed the door behind them and walked along the corridor. The older detective grabbed his younger colleague by the lapels.

'What the fuck are you playing at...makes sense to me. Well I've got news for you; it doesn't make sense, end of. Do you get it?'

He forces his hands from his lapels.

'It does make sense, what are you afraid of...do you know something that you don't want to share?'

'You better explain that.'

'Why don't you want to check out what he said is true, and what if it is true, what are you afraid of?'

'If we go and dig and find nothing, what do you think Welsh will do? Thank us for trying to taint his boss, his dead boss. I'm on a short list for promotion; I'm not going to fuck it all up, for the ramblings of a disgraced detective.'

'He was found not guilty, wasn't he?'

'No, no he wasn't, he was found not proven, meaning if

further evidence came up he could be tried again, that's why he was forced to resign, Feeney couldn't take the chance of him being put on trial again and found guilty.

'All the convictions of dealers his evidence contributed could be called into question; you don't need me to explain why, do you?'

'But if he is telling the truth, we just ignore it?'

'We have got all we required from him, everything he said is straight-forward, even his tan, he's been over in Tenerife in a three star hotel, that's easy checked out. His young friend Lenny thought he was doing him a favour; he blamed Feeney and Welsh for his resignation. Mad, but that makes sense.'

'Okay, do we just ignore his off-the-record statement then?'

'That makes sense also, when we go back leave the talking to me.'

They open the door, GG is smiling. The younger detective activates the DVD, his detective hands GG a coffee, theirs are on the table untouched.

'That's everything, enjoy your coffee and we'll drive you home, are you looking forward to Christmas lunch then?'

GG feels as though his conversation had been ignored. He's is truly delighted but masks it well.

'Just another day I'm sad to say, when I get home I'm going straight to my bed, hopefully I'll be able to sleep, but I doubt it, how stupid was Lenny, I just can't believe he was even capable of doing that.'

He sipped his coffee looking for a reaction in their eyes. The younger one had believed him, the older one probably as well, but he had a reputation for not kicking over stones.

'The mind is a complex instrument, a wee push and it can go awry,' the younger detective replied.

***

In the comfort and quiet sanctuary of his flat, he cracked open the bottle of champagne that Lenny had brought. It would be a fitting tribute to his young but naïve colleague, he wasn't a friend. But he had had his uses. Welsh is still alive, he rued the speed and professionalism of Gary Spence. But two out of three was still a result. Monty had helped him when he had been under investigation for an alleged assault on a dealer who had committed the mortal sin of using his own product, the sharpness of mind became blunt, inner thoughts that usually remained in his head, came out of his mouth, he wanted more areas in Dundee, and in a drug induced stupor, he bad- mouthed Monty who was his supplier. Word got back to Monty; he told Catherine over dinner that he had to be taught a lesson. Catherine told him violence would attract attention, did the dealer have an Achilles heel? Monty could only think that he was using the product, he would get lazy and be picked up by the police, he would cough up his name, but there was nothing to connect him to the dealer. His solicitor had written to the Chief Constable about the constant and pernicious harassment of his client, all because of junkies were mentioning his clients name. This was a witch hunt, he was willing to have this information tested in open court and after the inevitable not guilty, and the Chief Constable would be sued in the Court of Session for harassment.

From thereon Monty was treated like royalty. The dealer was eventually caught red-handed with heroin, GG was the arresting officer, the mask of professional conduct slipped; he took him into a room in the drug den and punched him square in the mouth, two teeth ejected from his mouth went he came to in the ambulance, GG stuck to his story, he acted in self-defence. Word had reached him from the Procurators Fiscals office that charges would be imminent. Monty knew where he went for a pint on Tuesdays.

He told him about Welsh setting him up with child-
porn on his laptop, was there anything he could do about
it, and if so was there anything that he could return in his
favour? As it happened he could, he mentioned about the
scurrilous charges that were being prepared to be served
upon him.
Monty was outraged; imagine these idiots in the PFs'
office even believing a junkie rather than upstanding
officer of the Law. They parted on the best of terms, this
was the unholy alliance of gamekeeper and poacher, and
their roles would interchange over time. Even excrement
is useful thought GG. The following week he received
through the post that the allegations had been withdrawn,
this was not news, he had been told that verbally from a
solicitor at the Sheriff Court. The solicitor was Patrick
Connelly. Monty had kept his side of the barbed
bargain; he had to come out with something that
convinced him that they were mutually good for one
another. Monty could not have been convinced any
more. The evening he met GG up at the industrial unit
on Old Glamis Road, he was amazed at the amount of
incriminating photographs of him.
The favour had been returned many times over. GG
dismissed his thoughts and his thanks about the
surveillance photographs. He didn't know they had been
taken by GG himself, he had told Monty that there was
an elite secret squad that had an unlimited budget, he
would be the first dealer to be brought down, the jury
was handpicked no matter how flimsy the evidence was
against him, he was going to be found guilty, and the
judge was going to sentence him to fifteen years, and no
parole would to be considered for at least twelve years,
all his assets of his partner's would be confiscated, he
and Catherine would have to employ expensive QC's,
the court ruling would be strung out for years, due to

more evidence being uncovered, the legal fees alone would bankrupt them both. Monty was wild-eyed he believed every harmful word, what can I do? The first thing he had to do was trust GG implicitly and act on his advice. GG explained that certain dealers in the cartel were informants of the highest degrees, they had been compromised. They passed on information about the other dealers in the cartel, including Monty. He would be the first to be arrested, the informants had insisted on this requirement. He must not mention this to Catherine or his solicitor, if anything leaked out; he would be arrested on GGs' say so. Monty stared at the photographs his mind whirling, flitting between life behind bars and the betrayal of others; he was impatient to know who the vipers of Judas were.

GG told him it was time to make a decision, he either cut his ties with the cartel or they cut him to pieces, and he meant that, they were prepared to kill him, and the police would give his murder a cursory investigation, it was pre-ordained. Or he could act with GG, get all dealers in this unit and extract information so he could hear it with his own ears. As Monty was unofficial head of the cartel they wouldn't question a meeting, for example say that the dealers from Liverpool had a new cheaper product but they wanted to ascertain that everyone was in agreement in the quantities that they would be buying, someone from Liverpool would be there to answer any questions, and he would be masked to hide his identity. Monty acknowledged that they would be curious to attend the meeting; anything that enriched them always brought a favourable response. GG gave him the date when to arrange it. Dundee United and Dundee were playing each other in a Scottish Cup Tie, supporters of both teams parked in the industrial estate, there would be police officers in the vicinity, best to get the dealers dropped off near the industrial estate then they could walk to the industrial unit, nothing suspicious.

The police would think that they were supporters
returning to their cars, tell them to wear football scarves.
Sub-consciously they would have no fears, the police
were all around Old Glamis Road, and it's not as if they
would be shot would they?

Monty clicked. He warmed to what he was saying;
shooting was too good for them. Monty was guided
through the script, when he introduced the friend from
Liverpool with the mask, he would go over the fictitious
sales and distribution strategy. He would say that they
had a mole in the Intelligence Drug Unit, that there was
an informant in the cartel, then he would pull out a gun
and order Monty to tie the dealers to the chairs, if there
was any sign of resistance he would shoot the resistor,
that would impede any acts of heroism. All the while
Monty would look petrified, he would get a few punches
in the face to emphasise the seriousness of the situation,
Monty would become impassive and offer no retaliation,
the others seeing Monty reduced to a feeble hulk, would
think many times before attacking the Liverpool dealers'
mouthpiece. Monty played his part with Shakespearian
attributes, the cartel seeing the tears and the smashes in
the face he was taking without an angry insult in
response, made them look at one another. They all
walked to the chairs and offered Monty their hands to be
tied behind their chairs, almost apologetically. GG stood
in front of them he wanted information, who was telling
the bizzies information, he went up to the first one, he
remained silent, he told Monty to punch him, while this
was going on, he went for the small humming machine
that was used to cut logs. Urine came onto the concrete
floor.

One of the cartel shouted out, he was an informant,
Monty looked at him through synthetic tears, he couldn't
believe what he was hearing. They all listened to the

tearful confession, he looked at Monty, uttering his sorrowful apologies, interspersed with 'he couldn't face jail again, he would rather die, he had no option.' GG granted his wish he wouldn't go to prison, he ordered Monty to come over to him, he gave him a gun, he walked over to the quivering wreck of human misery, he stuffed an oil rag in his mouth and shot him in the back of the head. This exercise was repeated, Monty carried out the grisly instructions, disgusted with the confessions of the cartel, no last words of defiance, just simpering pleadings with the instructions of their executioner. There was now only one left, the others had had a hand or a foot sliced off. Monty had to play this section of the charade without a blemish on his otherwise flawless performance. GG would order him to sit down and try to extract information from him, telling the other dealer that if he doesn't tell where the money was and who was holding the cash, Monty would get a bullet in the head, Monty through anguished cries told him to tell who was holding the money, he did, he said the money was in a unit on the Blackness Road. Monty tearfully thanked him, he felt the gun pressing against his head, no concern was occupying his mind this was the time when GG would move the gun to the dealers head and let rip. That was the last thought of Monty. GG let off two shots into his head. The other dealer didn't have time to think, he was dispatched to the same place where Monty was released to.

All this death and destruction came by the vindictive mouth of one Joseph Feeney, if he hadn't arranged for drugs to be planted in the boot of his car, he would have been enjoying Christmas thinking of how many dealers would be cursing the name of Gordon. It was his finger on the trigger that shot Feeney, the innocent person in the church and Monty, not forgetting the useful idiot in the flat with Lenny. But if the insidious Feeney hadn't hatched the plan to incriminate him they would all have

456

been enjoying Christmas. Welsh had his Christmas fairy to thank in the guise of Gary Spence, who wasn't universally popular.

Monty had contacted the dealers in Liverpool at the behest of GG, he had told them that he believed some of the cartel had killed the dealer in the flat and stole the heroin and money, he believed that one maybe two were criminal informants of the highest degree. Now was the time to expunge them and start afresh, with Monty as the de facto distributor in Dundee and the north-east.

It would be beneficial to both parties. Monty would take care of the dealers; arrange someone from Liverpool to meet someone in Dudhope Park and tell that person that they were working with the Triads; they knew that person was involved in raiding their cannabis farms. He would be given an opportunity to amend for his foolish behaviour; he would be told that his friend had given his name up after systematic torture and finally death. As expected Lenny seized the moment and agreed to eliminate the person whose name would be revealed at the appropriate time.

Lenny's mobile would be found in his flat with GG's number dialled at the time he said it was dialled. Everything he had said stacked up. The enquiry would clear and suffice with the starting premise Lenny was a troubled individual and acted alone out of misplaced loyalty. Lenny wanted to make a name for himself as a policeman in Dundee; he certainly achieved that and more. Once the forensics had examined the bullets they would see that they were fired from Lenny's gun, they matched the bullets in the dealers' heads, Feeney and the church goer.

He was financially solvent if he lived to a hundred years of age, the scousers were free to control the drugs in Dundee now, he was ambivalent thinking of this, he had helped them and they had helped him, he was not involved anymore. However, what troubled him were not the deaths of the innocent and some of whom were not innocent but, that he had not a scintilla of a troubled conscience. He sipped the champagne Lenny had given him for a special occasion it never tasted so sweet.

The End

30977389R00257

Printed in Poland
by Amazon Fulfillment
Poland Sp. z o.o., Wrocław